Praise for *Project Cain*

"Girard launches an ambitious experiment with this YA thriller. . . . This tense, terse, and often nightmarish tale delves into the question of 'nature versus nurture.'"

—*Publishers Weekly*

"In *Project Cain*, powerful newcomer Geoffrey Girard brings serious game with a novel that blends science and horror in a killer of a thriller. Highly recommended."

—Jonathan Maberry, *New York Times* bestselling
author of *Fire & Ash* and *Extinction Machine*

"Elevates teenage angst to dark new levels."

—Shelf Awareness

"As harrowing a coming-of-age novel as you are ever likely to read."

—*Mystery Scene* magazine

"An absolute grabber from the get-go. Geoffrey Girard has taken an outrageous idea and made it utterly and terrifyingly believable. Fortified by solid historic and scientific foundations, the story is as convincing as it is frightening, with enough twists and surprises to keep even the most jaded reader captivated."

—Todd Strasser, Edgar Award nominee
and internationally bestselling author of *The Wave* and *Give a Boy a Gun*

"No reader could fail to be moved by this young man's predicament as he tries to figure out who and what he is."

—Romance Reviews Today

"Explosive. . . . Drew me in and did not let go. It is, quite honestly, both exquisite in its telling and terrifying in its concept."

—Night Owl Reviews

"Mind blowing. . . . Not the usual, simple, everyday book. *Project Cain* is a little of everything. Action, mystery, history, science, and secret military projects."

"Girard has given readers a thought-provoking work couched in the plot of a horror book. . . . The story is written for high school students, but although it is dark and somewhat violent, it could be read by a good middle school reader. Recommended."

"The author does such an amazing job with this book, you feel you are in the world with these killers. . . . From the first page, you get drawn into the character of Jeff. . . . If you want an amazing book that will stay with you and, in a way, have you rooting for a bad guy, pick this up. 5 out of 5 Stars."

"I quickly attached myself to [Jeff's] character and felt completely sorry for him. Then I remembered he was Jeffery Dahmer's clone and felt conflicted over liking him. . . . Girard . . . did excellent work making characters a reader can connect to. Girard did his homework. . . . The book is filled with a ridiculous amount of information on government projects and serial killers. . . . Between fact and fiction *Project Cain* gives you a lot to think about. If you want a book that sucks you into an unhinged conspiracy universe, this is the book for you."

PROJECT
CAIN

Also by Geoffrey Girard

Cain's Blood

PROJECT CAIN

GEOFFREY GIRARD

SIMON & SCHUSTER BFYR

NEW YORK LONDON TORONTO SYDNEY NEW DELHI

SIMON & SCHUSTER BFYR

An imprint of Simon & Schuster Children's Publishing Division

1230 Avenue of the Americas, New York, New York 10020

SIMON & SCHUSTER BFYR is a trademark of Simon & Schuster, Inc.

For information about special discounts for bulk purchases, please contact Simon & Schuster Special Sales at 1-866-506-1949 or business@simonandschuster.com.

The Simon & Schuster Speakers Bureau can bring authors to your live event. For more information or to book an event, contact the Simon & Schuster Speakers Bureau at 1-866-248-3049 or visit our website at www.simonspeakers.com.

Also available in a SIMON & SCHUSTER BFYR hardcover edition

Book design by Lucy Ruth Cummins

The text for this book is set in Adobe Caslon.

Manufactured in the United States of America

First SIMON & SCHUSTER BFYR paperback edition September 2014

10 9 8 7 6 5 4 3 2 1

The Library of Congress has cataloged the hardcover edition as follows:

Girard, Geoffrey.

Project Cain / Geoffrey Girard. — First edition.

pages cm

Summary: Fifteen-year-old Jeff Jacobson learns that not only was he cloned from infamous serial killer Jeffrey Dahmer's blood as part of a top-secret government experiment, but there are other clones like him and he is the only one who can track them down before it is too late.

ISBN 978-1-4424-7696-7 (hardcover)

ISBN 978-1-4424-7698-1 (pbk)

ISBN 978-1-4424-7701-8 (eBook)

[1. Murder—Fiction. 2. Serial murderers—Fiction. 3. Biological weapons—Fiction. 4. Cloning—Fiction. 5. Science fiction.] I. Title.

PZ7.G43948Pro 2013

[Fic]—dc23

2013002672

For Josh
We miss you. . . .

CHAPTER ONE

*J*effrey Dahmer.

You might not know who that is. I didn't. I had to Google him. There was some stuff in my file too.

Back in the 1980s, he murdered seventeen people. It was a pretty big deal because of the way he did it. Look up the gory details yourself if you want. I'm not getting into any of that here.

Most adults, I've learned, seem to know the name pretty well because Dahmer got famous in the news and became the go-to guy for the term of the hour: SERIAL KILLER.

Male. White. Higher IQ. Underachiever. Bad wiring. Troubled childhood. Started collecting dead animals as a kid. Jump next to adulthood and the quiet Loner-Next-Door-Who-Never-Caused-a-Problem until the neighbors couldn't ignore the strange smells. Twisted murders. Pervert stuff. Über body-count. The ultimate cliché. Perfect for an easy joke or a quick name-drop on some lame cop show.

In 1992, Jeffrey Dahmer was found guilty on fifteen counts of murder and got sentenced to a separate life term for each and every one. Almost a *thousand* years in prison. Hard-core. Most people can't even imagine one.

Didn't matter anyway.

Two years in, another prisoner beat Dahmer to death with a broom handle, Dahmer's head and face beaten so badly that the guards at first couldn't figure out who'd been killed.

The guy who did it claimed God had told him to. Could be.

Other reports say Dahmer arranged the killing himself as some kind of suicide.

Again, could be. That wouldn't surprise me.

Most of this happened more than twenty years before I was born.

Before they made me in that lab. Before they made *us*.

It's all still very confusing. You'll understand more soon.

This is a story about blood.

The blood of family. And of science.

And murder.

. . .

Everyone's always so interested in "telling the truth." The virtue of TRUTH. Getting to the bottom of it. Being honest. Etc. The whole world imposes this principle on you right from the start. And it's all such absolute bullshit, really. It's, ironically, a gigantic fat lie.

If everyone told the truth, even half the time, we'd probably all jump off a bridge.

Because we'd finally really know how terrible everyone else is. What we *really* thought about each other. All the disgusting things we'd *really* done that day. And so on.

It's only the lies that keep everything going.

I know I was perfectly fine with the ones I'd been told.

. . .

I was told and believed my name was Jeff Jacobson and that I was born on April 18 sixteen years ago.

I was told and believed my mother and I were in a bad car accident when I was just five and this is why (a) I don't have a mother, and (b) I can't remember some things too well, and (c) my speech is a little off sometimes.

I was told and believed that the pretty dark-haired woman in the three photos throughout our house was my mother and that she'd loved me very much.

I was told and believed that my father was, well, my father. And that he also loved me.

Then that changed.

All of it. In a single night. Less, really. Fifteen, maybe twenty, minutes. The time it takes for a round of Call of Duty. It can happen that fast.

The TRUTH.

My dad—the eminent geneticist Dr. Gregory Jacobson, my fake father, the madman, Killer, Dr. Ripper; whatever we're calling him now, whatever history will settle on—he comes into my room one night. And in that one simple everyday move, all those magnificent unspoiled lies went away and I got my first real fistfuls of Truth.

Pow! Wham! WTF?

I was told I'd been constructed in a laboratory just TEN years ago.

I was told I was a clone made from the DNA of some other guy.

I was told that other guy was a famous serial killer.

I was told this was all part of some top-secret science project to help make weapons for the United States government and that the government now probably wanted me dead.

I was told that I'd never had a mother beyond some Ukrainian girl paid to carry my fetus in her womb for only four months. (Even the egg had been genetically manufactured in a lab.) After that, I'd grown synthetically—brought to the physical/physiological maturity of an eight-year-old child in a little more than a year—in some sort of ultra-modern tank.

I was told that there were others like me. Other clones. Some made from *other* killers. And also a few made from the *same* guy I'd been made from.

Finally, I was told that I was, therefore, a KILLER at the very core of my being.

And—my dad was quite clear on this part—there was absolutely NOTHING wrong with that.

. . .

This, apparently, was the kind of Truth everyone is so damn excited about.

. . .

After giving me this news, news I hadn't even begun to process yet, my dad handed me a folder. He'd stopped talking, and the clear inference was I should now check out the papers inside. So I flipped through it while he watched me. I didn't get so far. There was nothing inside that didn't add to my total confusion.

I saw the name "JEFFREY DAHMER" for the first time in my life.

. . .

Inside the folder were pictures of a kid who I assumed was me.

But he wasn't. He just *looked* like me.

And these were pictures of the kid in places I'd never been and with people I'd never met. Wearing clothes I'd never worn. In some of the pictures, the kid was even *older* than me.

There were also weird reports with confusing technical notes and charts.

My hands flipped through the pages in mere seconds. Or hours. I don't know. (That whole night is still kind of a blur.) But I can tell you I didn't understand what I was looking at. And any time I looked up to question or protest, my dad seemed to be looking right past me.

Not just like I wasn't in the room anymore. But, worse, like *he* wasn't.

I retreated back to the folder and eventually reached the pictures of—if I was to believe my father—dead people my "genetic source" had murdered. There were five faces on the first page alone. And a name beneath each one. My fingers hovering just over the page, tracing along their photos . . .

I slammed the folder closed and then down onto my bed.

My father smiled, something I'd not seen him do in months, and then stood. He first told me a phone number, a new number, and said I could call later if I ever needed to talk. *What does that mean?* Then he handed me an opened envelope stuffed with money and warned me again to keep away from DSTI (the company he worked for) AND the police. He said they were all working with the US government and I knew what that meant now.

But I had no clue "what that meant now."

In fact, still nothing he was saying made any sense at all. Didn't matter. Because that was it. The end of our conversation. Not one word about where he was going or what I was supposed to do.

He was just down the stairs and out the door and into the car and beyond the driveway and so on. Every preposition he could think of to vanish for good. To get away from me. If my dad even noticed me shouting in the driveway or chasing him down our street, I would never know.

I never saw him alive again.

Back into the house.

I called his cell phone. Nothing.

Tried a hundred times. Called his office. Nothing. Nothing.

Even tried that new phone number he'd just given me.

Still nothing.

I checked out the money envelope he'd handed me. There were *twenty* fifty-dollar bills inside. A thousand dollars?!? I tossed the envelope onto my bed.

I picked up the folder and tried reading its contents again. Other than the pictures, it was just more graphs and dates and numbers and some biographical stuff about this Jeffrey Dahmer guy.

Born 1960. Grew up in Ohio. Dad a chemist. Kicked out of Army 1981.

And so on. Blah, blah, blah. I didn't get much farther than I had the first time. Honestly, I'd stopped reading after it listed his first murder. (1978, by the way. Dahmer was only eighteen years old.)

I mostly just sat in the house for hours and hours and basically stared at the walls.

It became the world's longest, most sucky Night of Nothing.

Until midnight.

That was right around the time I decided to finally check out my father's secret room.

That's where all the Something was.

• • •

Hint: If your father has a secret room, he's probably lying about all sorts of things.

This room was on the second floor of our house in a space between the master bedroom and one of the guest rooms. From the outside it looked just like any other wood-paneled wall. Just behind, *within*, however, was a room the size of a big walk-in closet. The people who lived in the house before us had apparently built it as one of those "panic rooms," a place to hide when, like, looters or robbers attack.

My dad used it as a second office of sorts. I'd seen him go in more than a dozen times over the three years we'd lived there, but I'd never stepped a foot inside myself. He'd told me it was important stuff for work and then lectured me about privacy and trust. That had been enough to keep me away.

But *mostly* I kept away because of the way he looked whenever he went into that room or came out. In his face had been something sad and lost. But also something *strong*. Focused.

Something terrible.

I just knew that whatever had come in and out of that room wasn't entirely my dad anymore.

And that whatever was inside the room was not something I wanted any part of.

(Funny how that turned out, huh?)

Still, I had the key. I'd found a ring of spares one afternoon when my dad had been out, and I'd tried every one until the special panel unlocked. It had taken me, like, twenty minutes just to find the keyhole, it was so well hidden in the paneling. But I kept running my fingers along the wall until I did. I did not, however, go in. I just locked it again and hid the spare key in my own room. Just having it, having the *option* to enter that room if I ever really wanted, had been enough for me.

Now, I realize completely he always knew I'd taken that spare.

He'd *wanted* me to have it. Just another one of his little experiments for me. Left it precisely where I'd find it. *Wanted* me to see all that he'd been up to.

So I guess he got exactly what he wanted.

Because when I opened the door, the very first thing I saw was the dead guy.

CHAPTER TWO

*B*efore I get to the dead guy, I should maybe first cover who my father is. What he *does*. The special things he knows how to do. It won't completely explain the rotted corpse hidden in our house, but it will, I hope, maybe explain it *some*.

• • •

I always took comfort in knowing what my father did for a living. You'd be amazed how many kids don't. I've met them on soccer teams and at summer camp and stuff. These guys who have NO CLUE what their parent's profession is. They maybe know it's just a generic office job. Something to do with, like, some stupid phone or insurance company.

But me, I could just say "He's a scientist," and everyone understood *exactly* what I meant.

I'd leave out words like "important" or "famous," but I always knew they were there too. I knew he'd given lectures at places like Harvard and Stanford and that he routinely met with big people in politics and stuff. And that he was a big boss at work and all. I'd grown up with the sense that he was SMART and IMPORTANT and POWERFUL. Even without these adjectives, I always said it with great pride: HE'S A SCIENTIST.

Funny, in the end, that it was actually me who had no idea what my father was really up to.

WHAT I *DID* KNOW

For more than twenty years my dad worked for a company called Dynamic Solutions Technology Institute. DSTI. They are (*or were*) a private biotechnology company that specializes in the "development of therapeutic, pharmaceutical, and cell-based solutions." (That's from their website.) In short: They messed around with genetics/DNA. Fifty years ago, men like my father figured out how to modify DNA using a complicated process called *genetic engineering* to cut specific genes out of one place and stick them into another. Maybe to make cows bigger or corn more yellow or even to turn germs into cures. That kind of thing.

WHAT I *DIDN'T* KNOW

DSTI got most of its research money from the US military. And the US military doesn't need or want yellower corn or bigger cows. Doesn't even need or want clones of Albert Einstein or Kobe Bryant or John Lennon. The US military wants WEAPONS. It wants KILLERS. And so, thanks to my dad, that's exactly what it got.

• • •

The United States has been at war since December 7, 1941.

Every single day for more than eighty years, we've needed our military to kill.

Not one other nation on Earth can claim that distinction.

During this time, America has fought in more than twenty-five different countries and has directly killed more than fifteen million people. Five million more than the Nazis.

During this time, America spent more money on weapons than the rest of the world combined.

You'd think most of that money would be spent on jets and soldiers and bullets, etc., but it's not. Most is spent on RESEARCH.

It's spent inventing and testing new ways to kill people.

· · ·

Half of all federal research dollars goes to the US military.

Fifty billion dollars a year. The same amount Washington sets aside for the research of medicine, energy, the environment, transportation, manufacturing, and agriculture *combined*.

And, believe it or not, that's nothing. Nickels and pennies.

An additional five *HUNDRED* billion—money outside this general military-research fund—is spent on weapons research *directly* by the four military branches.

Five hundred billion dollars a year! EVERY year.

The military gets most of this money from their special "BLACK BUDGETS." These are funds set aside for projects so highly classified that regular people don't get to know what they're working on. So highly classified that journalists aren't allowed to find out. Congressmen and senators don't know either. The president, too. Seriously. In the name of "national security," even the president of the United States doesn't know what these military scientists are working on.

That's why they're called "Black Budget" projects.

Because they happen "in the dark," where no one can really see what's going on.

And that's where they made us.

· · ·

Have you ever thought of killing someone?

Have you ever thought of murder? Rape?

Tell the truth.

Now just imagine if that thought never ever went away.

That's exactly the kind of person DSTI was looking for.

. . .

A pitch-perfect ear, speed, math skills, a good jump shot, IQ, daily emotions, suicide potential, language skills, strength, spatial perception, etc. Each chromosome of human DNA carries a million different strands with specific instructions on what that person's genetic makeup will be. You're BORN with the ability to learn a song by ear on the first try. You're BORN with a mind that can comprehend general relativity and quantum mechanics. You're BORN with the ability to throw a football better or worse than those other guys. Sure, you can take music lessons or maybe get counseling or attend summer football camps and get a little better in any of these things. But at the end of the day, the foundation of what you are is already locked into your body's genetics. If the ability is not already in your genes, you will NEVER write songs like Mozart or Paul McCartney. You will NEVER understand the universe the way Stephen Hawking can. And you will NEVER throw a football like an NFL quarterback.

Nature outplays Nurture almost every time. Like Paper overwhelms Rock.

And geneticists, men like my father, have mapped most of this nature out.

One particular location, a single gene strand labeled XP11, is where they now look for the killers. If you're looking for the future superstars of murder, an aberration in XP11, apparently, is the nature you need. Basically, when there's a glitch, a very rare glitch, on this one specific gene, it indicates and influences a chromosomal itch for various degrees of aggression and violence. Scientists and psychologists sometimes even call it the "Anger Gene."

The GOOD NEWS is that the body knows the "Anger Gene" is a negative trait and provides its own antidote; actually counteracts the mutation naturally during pregnancy, providing code in the DNA that can fix this violent abnormality so the person grows up NORMAL and the Anger Gene is healed.

The BAD NEWS is that the genetic antidote (aka a chromosomal allele) for this dangerous mutation travels only on the X chromosome. Remember much from biology class? Females are born from XX chromosomes. So, they've got a 100% chance of having a cure for any aggressive mutation. Men, however, are XY. So we've got only a fifty-fifty shot of having the natural cure for an overly aggressive XP11 strand. And the other 50% are shit out of luck.

That's NOT to say boys have a fifty-fifty shot of having this Anger Gene, but, rather, that in the rare instance (2%) that we DO, there's only a fifty-fifty chance of overcoming it.

Still meaning that half the world—the male half—is hereditarily predisposed to violence.

Guess you can say it's in our blood.

• • •

80% of all suicides.

95% of all the people in prison.

95% of those who commit domestic violence. 95% of those who sexually abuse children.

99% of rapists. 99% of spree killers. 99% of family annihilators.
99% of Death Row inmates.

Males.

Sorry.

• • •

To study this XP11 gene, my father and his colleagues went straight to the top.

They got their DNA samples off well-known killers. The most violent ones they could find.

SERIAL KILLERS.

Those who kill and kill again. Not for money or power or revenge. But because they *enjoy* killing. Maybe the killer starts with someone they know but very quickly moves on to strangers. Safest that way. Some woman who catches their eye at the supermarket one evening or some kid they notice while driving around the neighborhood. They do this over the course of months or even decades sometimes. Five victims, a dozen, fifty. It doesn't matter. What matters is the rush that comes when they feel the ultimate power over their helpless victims. That feeling of playing God.

DSTI mostly got this DNA from those killers who were still alive, but sometimes they collected it from guys who were long gone. Dead, executed.

DNA kinda hangs around for a long, long time, and you can get it from just about anything. A flake or two of skin, old blood samples, a hair follicle off a brush. Just like in *Jurassic Park*. But instead of raptors and T. rex, DSTI collected and built murderers.

The operation's official name was C-XP11.

Everyone just called it "Project Cain."

. . .

Some days, I would rather have been born a raptor.

. . .

It all probably sounds a little far-fetched. Stupid, even. Believe me, I know. But what if I told you an Air Force research lab in Ohio recently admitted to secretly working on bombs filled with synthetic pheromones/aphrodisiacs to make enemy troops "turn gay," and also on methods to create giant swarms of bees? Or that the Navy spent twenty million dollars teaching bats to carry explosives? Or that over the past forty years, the United States military has publicly admitted to working on everything from invisibility and time travel to ghosts, weather control, mind control, LSD bombs, talking dolphins, sound weapons, and telekinesis? And that's just what they've *admitted* to. Now imagine what they haven't.

Project Cain was just another one of those.

. . .

The dead body in my father's room had been dead for a long time.

You didn't need some forensic expert to figure that out. It looked like something my father had dug up for its DNA, not someone he'd killed. (I would later find out this was exactly the situation.)

He'd just told me, hours before, that DSTI's experiments had pretty much all been focused on famous serial killers, so I assumed this was simply one of them. WHO, however, I had no idea. There have been hundreds of serial killers. For all I knew it was the actual body of this Jeffrey Dahmer guy.

[Note: I did not yet know that Dahmer had requested to be immediately cremated upon his death. Or that his wishes had NOT been fully carried out. Because his brain and other tissues had been quietly saved and sent to the University of Wisconsin for analysis. I did not yet know that

Dahmer's father fought in court for years to have these destroyed also.]

Whoever this was, the decayed carcass was stuffed in a special box made of metal and tinted gray glass that was plugged into the wall and cold to the touch. The box hummed a little, just like our freezer in the garage. Instead of frozen steaks and chicken, though, this thing contained a dead guy. The legs all folded over the chest and face and stuff so that he would fit in the box. He looked like something a ventriloquist might pull out. Mummy old. Shrunken, brown. Alien. Strands of hair sprouting like gray weeds around its shoulders. Nasty, dirty, rotted cloth all intertwined in the bones. He wasn't even all that scary-looking, I kept telling myself. Just weird. Just weird . . .

I walked fully into the small room. The space was like one of those side displays at a museum, the small dark exhibit rooms you always seem to walk into alone. There were several file cabinets, a couple of monitors and laptops. A small desk with a row of notebooks filled with my father's writing. I didn't read them then. There were some notes on my father's desk about people named Bundy and Tumblety and Garavito. Maps of London and Central America. None of it made any sense.

I had to assume this body was one of those men. I didn't know. I really didn't know *anything* anymore. *How long has this nasty thing been in our house? What has my father done to get this?* The longer I stayed, the more I could feel the corpse's sunken black eye sockets peering at me from beneath his folded-over legs. Eyes that might have joyfully planned and watched the brutal murder of dozens.

So I didn't stay. I got out of that room as fast as I could go and pushed the secret door back into place, and locked it again. Stumbled away backward down the hall. Hearing things in my head I shouldn't hear. Imagining the worst things.

GEOFFREY GIRARD

That shriveled corpse on the other side maybe prying himself free from that cold box. Maybe now pushing slowly off the table, dragging himself across the floor and up against the other side of the door. The skeletal hand moving against the inside wall. Long brown nails clawing at the door to lift himself up fully. The rotted skin and filthy burial shroud hanging off cold dry bones. Those endless eye sockets glistening like imploding black stars in the dark room. Fingers now taking hold of the latch . . . I swear, I could hear it turning.

I put my hands to my ears. I think maybe I was screaming.

• • •

I slept in the house alone that night. Tired and furious and confused.

It would be the last night I ever spent there.

The next day, they came for me.

And I would have to be tired and furious and confused in other places.

CHAPTER THREE

*T*he day started out with me simply waiting in my house. Waiting and more waiting.

I called my dad's various phones again. Still nothing.

So, late afternoon, I decided to walk to Mr. Eble's house.

Mr. Eble had been my Humanities tutor for almost two years. Three hours a day, three days a week. Writing, lit, art, history, etc. I had another tutor for math and science. Eble had the whole ponytail, sandals, PhD-from-Brown thing going. Other than my dad, he was probably the smartest guy I'd ever met. I figured he'd have an idea of what I should do.

He lived maybe fifteen minutes away by car. He always drove, or rode his bike, to our house for tutoring, but my dad had driven me out there a couple of times to drop stuff off. So I knew exactly where he lived.

It took nearly two hours to get there.

As I walked, I tried imagining what was going on in all the houses I passed.

What LIES were being told in them even now?

They looked like normal houses, normal families. But so had my house the day before. What were the fathers and mothers in these *other* houses up to? What big secrets had *they* not revealed? All those unseen lives and plans and thoughts. All those lies.

Still, it was during this time that I was holding on to the possibility that my father was just, you know, messing with me. This was some kind of test. Or he'd had, maybe, a slight nervous breakdown of some kind. He'd been doing nothing but work for months now, twenty hours a day lately. Or . . .

But there really was no "Or." No matter how hard I tried to make some sense over what he'd told me, over his big vanishing act, I just couldn't do it. The whole thing, from a logical viewpoint, made no sense. The entire previous night remained outside the realm of reality.

I was hoping Mr. Eble would help me think it all through. But when I finally arrived, he wouldn't even answer the stupid door. I knocked and waited forever in the sweltering sun. (Probably wasn't even all that hot, and it'd probably been ten minutes. But I was in a place now where each and every moment felt like my whole body was just gonna explode from rage and chaos.)

Eventually his voice came out through the front window and told me to go home.

He'd been inside the whole time.

I was too angry to cry.

He said he couldn't talk to me and that I should leave. He told me to please go away.

I told him I was freaked out. Scared. I told him that something bad had happened and that I needed to find my dad.

He just said: I'm sorry, Jeff.

That's it. Not another word.

I'm sorry, Jeff.

This coming from the second smartest guy in the world.

It took me *three* hours to get home.

When I passed the same houses again, I imagined everyone inside screaming. Crying.

I imagined houses filled with secret rooms and dead people.

• • •

Much later I would learn my dad had fired Mr. Eble the day before.

Gone to his house and accused him of molesting me. Claimed Eble'd shown me all this porn and other weird stuff. It was all total bullshit. But my dad had threatened lawsuits and jail time. Said he'd spend his whole fortune and use all his big contacts to ruin Eble if he ever contacted me again.

You have to admit. My father had a plan.

• • •

The scientists at DSTI *also* had a plan.

And I watched that one unfold from the Reimers' bushes.

The Reimers being our closest neighbors, and me being a big fan of cutting through their backyard to get to ours. Good thing. If I'd come home any other way, DSTI would have had me.

As I started past the bushes and over the short stone wall separating our yards, I noticed the two vans parked at the top of our driveway. And then I noticed the guys. All dressed in black, just like in the movies. Ninja Jason Bourne stuff. I knew instinctively and indisputably: They were not there to help me. In this, it seems, my dad had told me the truth. The NEW TRUTH. The one I was starting to finally believe. *How could I not?*

I didn't know 100% that they were from DSTI. But since my dad had warned me about them, I was a good 95%. I also wasn't sure at first if they'd come for me or my dad. My first thought, honestly, was that they'd come for my dad. That he was in some kinda trouble with whoever these guys were (DSTI or not) and that's why he'd left. Maybe I was just kidding myself. *How to know for sure?*

So I watched and waited. Hidden in the darkness between two bushes.

They used the basement door behind our house. Kept going in and out like a trail of ants. Emptying my whole house. Just straight up taking shit. I watched this for almost an hour.

It hadn't occurred to me to set the house's alarm system when I'd left. I now rationalized they would have just overridden it somehow anyway. They seemed like guys who knew exactly what they were doing. I thought I recognized one of them as one of the scientists from DSTI, but couldn't be sure. It was dark and I kept far away.

When they finally left, I busted open the kitchen window to get back into my own home. Really pathetic. I was most definitely NOT a guy who knew exactly what he was doing. I knew only that I didn't want to be too obvious and use one of the main doors or the garage. I knew I didn't want to be seen. I used a two-by-four from behind the shed to pop the latch, and it worked just like I'd seen in a movie. That was less pathetic. Maybe there was some hope for me after all.

I figured I'd just wait it all out until Dad returned. (I still, falsely, believed this was a possibility.) What other options were there, really? Where was I gonna go?

Inside, I discovered they'd taken all the computers and all my dad's office files. The ones from his MAIN office, not from the secret room. (Turns out they hadn't found the secret room and didn't even know it was there.) They took our answering machine and emptied some old file cabinets from downstairs too. That made sense. My dad was obviously up to something involving DSTI and his work there. DSTI would want to confiscate all of that.

They ALSO, however, found and took the envelope with a thousand bucks. SHIT! I'd left it just lying there in my room, like an idiot. That was now totally gone. So stupid.

But they'd taken other things too, things that had nothing to do with me being stupid. Things that didn't make any sense at first. Framed photos off the wall. The pictures of ME. *Only* the ones of me. And they'd also removed all my clothes. Just MY clothes again. Cleared out the closet and drawers in my room. Even went through the hamper and laundry room. They'd taken all my books, my classwork. Soccer trophies. Bass guitar. *Dark Knight* movie poster. My PS3. Skateboard in the garage. My toothbrush and zit pads. My bottle of allergy medication. They even stole Zeus, my bearded dragon. His cage and lamp and food and everything.

So, that night, it was just me and the shriveled corpse in the house. It didn't even feel like my own house anymore. It felt more like a movie set, a prop. As if I could push on one of those walls in just the right way and the whole house would come down and reveal itself for what it was. Another lie.

In the darkness I stared out the window and into the neighborhood.

Tried unsuccessfully to ignore the imagined urgent sound of slow and constant scratching behind the wall of my dad's secret room. Tried to tell myself that companies don't *capture* people. That American businesses don't break into homes and kidnap children.

But an unfamiliar car now sat at the end of my street.

And inside the car I could see them. Shadowed forms. Sitting. Watching back.

Two men left behind to wait for me.

Because of who I was. Because of *what* I was.

First they'd made my stuff disappear.

And now they were waiting for me.

. . .

They didn't wait long.

CHAPTER FOUR

I stood outside my father's secret room again.

The tiny hidden panel pushed aside, tiny brass key in hand. Ready to go in and *stay* in this time. Because inside, I would find answers. Right? I would just get on his laptops in there or maybe read his little collection of handwritten journals, and everything would make perfect sense. Right? I would know everything I needed to know.

WHERE he was. And *WHO* he was.

And maybe a little more about *WHAT* and *WHY* I was.

Right?

Believe me. I stood outside that room a long, long time.

But this time, my hesitation was not from fear of some shrunken dirty corpse waiting for me in there perched just behind the door with dark claws gleaming in the dark. I knew it was safely in the refrigerated box (always had been) and I'd imagined the whole thing.

Now, I think mostly I just wanted to hold on to a handful of those lies a little longer.

. . .

If I am being totally honest, and that's a goal here, I've always been just a little creeped out by my dad. There's no better word for it. Most guys seem to think of their dads as mean or cool or pointless or funny or even scary in some way. Mine was always just a little *creepy*. He stared too much, too long. Was always way too interested in what I was saying or doing. For years I'd written this off to the fact that Mom had been killed and I was all that he had left. I was the only family he had anymore. Why wouldn't he stare at me all the time? If my mom came back, I'd probably just stare at her too. But over the last year or so, it'd actually gotten worse. It'd gotten, well, *more* creepy. So when he came to my room that night and dumped all that weirdness on me, I'll admit that maybe other things in our life, my dad's and mine, started to make more sense.

Now, as to all the stuff after . . .

I suspected and feared even then that the rotting corpse was only the beginning

And that my father was involved in much, much worse things than that.

• • •

That's why I stood there, outside his secret room, for as long as I did.

I knew that the more I learned about what my father had *really* been up to all these months, years—the more I understood what he'd *really* been thinking—all of it would become TRUE. Everything. All the evidence I needed for the things he'd told me was just a foot away now. The intellectual proof I needed for what my heart and gut were already telling me—it was all here and now.

It didn't matter. I never made it back into that room. Ever.

Someone was in my house again.

I heard them moving downstairs. The DSTI ninjas had returned.

I could hardly breathe, my heart going a zillion miles a minute. I slowly edged to the railing, snuck a peek. I wanted to puke. Just as I was starting to tell myself it was all in my head, I saw him.

It was real. Like he'd stomped right out of a nightmare. I wanted to scream *and* puke.

One of the guys from the car, I figured.

Now downstairs in our family room.

Looking for me.

One guy with a gun.

· · ·

For the record, I feel kinda mean calling my dad "creepy" just now. I mean, regardless of the things he did. I want you to know that, until those last weeks, he was, by my understanding of the words, a "good father." I never wanted for anything. He put a lot of effort into my schooling. He supported my every interest. We didn't, like, toss the football around and stuff, but we talked a lot about history and science stuff. And we liked to go on hikes in the woods and go to cool museums, and sometimes we watched old movies together. He told terrible jokes and gave stiff hugs. But the hugs were still there all the same. And perhaps he was doing it all—raising me, I mean—for really terrible reasons. But at the time, I didn't know that, and so I say it was good.

· · ·

Everyone's played hide-and-seek. (Even me, the weird only-child homeschooled kid.) And you've probably hidden in closets, under beds, etc. Can you remember how loud your breathing was? Even when you tried to be super quiet and slow it down like a jedi or something? Just made it louder, right? Can you remember suddenly wanting to sneeze or cough? Or getting an itch that wasn't there at all until you were lying perfectly still in the dark, hoping the person who was "IT" would just stay downstairs? Remember getting a little bored, or even a little afraid, because you hid so well that you were now completely by yourself, and in that unnatural quiet and dark, you started thinking a little about what was in the darkness with you? Maybe even called out, daring the person who was "IT" to come and find you.

But what if the person who was "IT" had a gun?

What if the person who was "IT" wanted to kill you?

This is the game I played for more than six hours. Because of the man downstairs. He'd been there all night. He even found my dad's secret room.

And the funny thing is, the fear of trying to maybe sneak past this man and maybe being shot by him wasn't even the real reason I kept hiding. The real reason was worse.

I kept hiding because I still had no idea what else to do.

None.

It was the most horrible feeling in the world.

. . .

Eventually, the guy with the gun found me.

I suppose it was only a matter of time. He'd found my dad's secret room in about three minutes. How tough was it to find a complete douche hiding in his own closet?

The guy was Castillo.

And he was not one of the two DSTI guys from the car.

He was something else.

• • •

About Shawn Castillo.

He grew up in New Mexico. His father was from Old Mexico. His mother was from Albuquerque. He wasn't much in touch with either anymore.

He'd been a linebacker on his high school football team.

He'd joined the Army at eighteen.

There are 500,000 soldiers in the US Army. From those, just 2,000 are selected to join the Rangers. He was a Ranger at twenty.

He was the first in his family to go to college, and he got a degree in international economic history. During this same time, he also learned Desert Warfare Operations and Demolitions. He fought in Afghanistan and Iraq.

From those 2,000 Rangers, 40 are selected to join Delta Force. He was selected. They taught him counter-terrorism and counter-intelligence techniques. Once, he had to make fire using ice. (Seriously!) When his beard was long, he could pass for a Turk, Afghan, or Egyptian. He'd lived in a Yemen village for four months and everyone had thought his name was Ahmed. Once, during a Delta Force training exercise in Hamburg, he'd pretended to be Italian.

He spoke three languages well. Two others well enough.

With Delta, he captured men named Fazul Abdullah, Binalshibh, and Sheikh Mohammed in places like Yemen, Somalia, Iran, and Pakistan. Sometimes, per his assignment, he just killed these men. He had twenty-three confirmed kills.

His squad nickname was "Sting."

He'd once been caught and badly tortured.

He'd been awarded three Purple Hearts, four Bronze Stars for

GEOFFREY GIRARD

valor, two Silver, and a Distinguished Service Cross.

He had horrific nightmares that woke him a couple of times each month.

He preferred brunettes over blondes, but his last girlfriend, the first he'd ever truly loved, was a blonde.

His favorite band was Pearl Jam. He disliked snow. He liked to fish. Talked sometimes about a place called Bluewater Lake, where he liked to camp.

He'd been honorably discharged a year before against his wishes and now worked with the Department of Defense as a consultant of some kind. This was always kept unclear. In the end, the papers all reported he was a security consultant/guard at DSTI. But that was a total lie.

When we first met, he pointed his gun at me and cursed a lot.

• • •

I climbed out from the closet, the whole thing more embarrassing than scary. Freeing myself on all fours like that, glasses half off my face, some guy shouting at me. I'm sure I looked astoundingly moronic. At this point, I'll admit, for a dozen different reasons, I basically just wanted him to shoot me anyway. He didn't.

Instead he made me sit down on the end of my bed and then started asking questions. Where was my dad? Who else lives here? Last time I saw him? And so on . . .

I mumbled the few truths I knew as best I could.

He'd put his gun away, and now he pulled up the room's only chair to sit across from me. He asked if my father had any family or friends nearby I knew about. Asked if I knew employees from the school, two nurses named Santos or Kelsoe. Asked if I knew about anything, any *place*, called Shardhara. I gave him mostly shrugs and one word answers.

The one-word was almost always NO. I wasn't trying to be a dick. They were really all I had to give. Eventually we got around to the heart of the matter.

Something happened at the school, he said. Something bad.

• • •

By "the school" he meant the Massey Institute.

Massey was a private school and treatment center maybe a half mile down the road from DSTI. On the same property and everything. The "treatment" part of the equation was for things like mental health, anxiety issues, anger management, eating disorders, suicide, drug and alcohol rehab. That kind of thing. A lot of the "treatments" were built upon advanced pharmaceuticals developed and provided by DSTI, who justified it all as approved "clinical trials" while openly funding and operating Massey.

For years I'd known Massey as a good place. A place where scientists like my father could help fix kids. But now I knew the truth.

Massey is where DSTI kept all their lab rats.

And instead of in cages, their teenage "rats" waited in classrooms and group sessions.

• • •

About fifty kids went to Massey.

All boys. Between the ages of ten and eighteen.

Most of the guys were normal kids.

Some . . . some not.

Some, I knew now from my father, were more like me.

• • •

```
clone (noun)
  from the Greek word klōn, for "twig"
  (1)  a  group  of  genetically  identical  cells
```

GEOFFREY GIRARD

descended from a single common ancestor; (2) an
organism descended asexually from a single ancestor
such as a plant produces by budding; (3) a replica
of a DNA sequence produced by genetic engineering;
(4) one that copies or closely resembles another, as
in appearance or function; (5) me

. . .

It started with peas.

An Austrian monk named Mendel tried some biology experiments
in the small garden of the monastery where he lived. It was the 1850s.
His specific scientific interest was heredity: how and why children
retain certain traits of their parents. No one understood this stuff yet.

To study it, he grew peas. Thirty thousand pea plant "children" carefully bred from specific pea "parents." He pollinated each plant himself. Wrapped each pod individually. Examined and recorded the most
minute detail: blossom color, pod color and shape, and pod position.
Thirty thousand times.

It took seven years. He almost went totally blind staring at all those peas. Seriously.

He wrote only one paper about what he'd discovered during all that time and got it published. In the paper, he proved how specific genes in the parent peas controlled the traits of the children peas. Some genes were strong, or *dominant*, and others were weaker, or *recessive*. The strong genes won when the two met in an offspring. He started mapping them all out and eventually could figure out exactly what the next plant would look like.

This guy had invented genetics.

Very few people read his paper, however. He wasn't a "real" scientist, the real scientists all decided. He was just a monk with a small pea garden. So he was completely ignored.

Mendel next tried bees. He kept five hundred hives with bees collected from all over the world. African, Spanish, Egyptian. He built special chambers for the various queens to mate and bred brand-new hybrid bees that made more honey than any other bee ever before on Earth. Mendel's bees were also more aggressive than any other bee ever before on Earth. They stung the other monks and soon took their stinging ways to the nearby village. Mendel had to destroy every hive. He killed ten thousand bees.

He went back to plants, which didn't sting, but tried something other than peas—a plant called hawkweed—and it didn't work out. Not at all. He couldn't verify his original findings.

He grew depressed and stopped doing experiments of any kind. Then Mendel died, and the abbot who ran the monastery burned all of Mendel's old notes and unpublished essays on heredity.

It was another fifty years before other scientists really rediscovered

Mendel's original paper. This time, however, they liked what they saw. Using Mendel's original conclusions and evidence on genetics, scientists quickly moved from peas to frogs. From frogs to mammals. They soon figured out how to make detailed maps of DNA. To isolate certain genes and decipher how they worked. How to modify them.

They eventually cloned a whole sheep from a single strand of DNA. Took one single cell from a "parent" sheep and made a perfect copy. Identical. Two of the exact same sheep.

They named the copy Dolly. Dolly became famous. It was 1996.

Now it was game on. The next five years was an explosion of clones.

Japan constructed Noto the Cow. Thousands of Notos. The Italians cooked up Prometea the Horse. Iran made Hanna the Goat. South Korea made Snuppy the Dog and Snuwolf the Wolf. The Scots made pigs; the French, rabbits. Both China and India made water buffalo clones; Spain and Turkey, bulls. Dubai crafted the *exact* same camel a hundred and four times.

America, of course, did it better than all of them combined. More labs, more commercial interest, gobs more money. Cloning and biogenetic research was added to every pharmaceutical company in the nation. Even university kids were making clones. Did you know that there are more colleges in New Jersey alone than in all of Germany? Everything progressed in a hurry.

Cumulina the Mouse. Ralph the Rat.

Mira the Goat. Noah the Ox. Gem the Mule.

Dewey the Deer. Libby the Ferret. Ditteaux the African Wildcat.

CC the Cat. Tetra the Monkey.

Jeff the Serial Killer.

Beans to frogs to rats to primates. Just five years.

Insert chants of "USA, USA . . ." right here.

Cloning humans, by the way, is still completely legal in America. Everyone just assumes it's not.

A couple of states have banned it. Most haven't. And Washington, DC, keeps out of the way. The Human Cloning Prohibition Acts of 2003 and 2007 were both voted down by Congress. The 2009 version of the bill has been buried/forgotten/hidden in various subcommittees for forever.

Our scientists can pretty much do whatever they want as long as they don't openly use federal dollars. Cloning is currently legal in twenty other countries. See above.

We're everywhere.

CHAPTER FIVE

*C*astillo showed me a list. A terrible list.

The names of all the students and Massey employees who'd been killed the night before.

Twelve people.

Now just little black lines stacked up on top of one another like dirty dishes.

Twelve.

Dead. Murdered in cold blood.

Nine were kids. I knew some of them. And I told Castillo so.

My dad's name was not on this list.

• • •

Later, I admit, I would wish it had been.

• • •

They didn't know where my dad was.

Me either, I said.

Castillo told me they did know my dad had been at Massey the night of the murders—from the security system. And that it looked like . . .

That it looked like my father probably, maybe, likely, had something to do with it.

"It" being the murders.

I wish I'd found that possibility more surprising.

• • •

Castillo then showed me another list.

This next list was about to become my whole world.

Albert Young. Jeffrey Williford. Henry Roberts.
Dennis Uliase. Ted Thompson. David Spanelli.

These were the six students who were missing. Six who'd been at the school that night that no one could find now. They probably, Castillo explained, had *something* to do with the murders. That's all he'd say at this point.

These were not their real names. These were their adopted names.

Their real names (their ORIGINAL names) were:

Albert Fish. Jeffrey Dahmer. Henry Lee Lucas.
Dennis Rader. Ted Bundy. David Berkowitz.

How many of these names do you recognize?

Except for one, which I'd learned only the day before, I'd never heard of any of them.

They happen to be six of the most famous serial killers ever.

That's why they were chosen. Why they were born again. Manufactured.

An Olympic Dream Team if the Olympics murdered and raped

people. All added up, they'd killed almost two hundred people. Though "killed" doesn't quite capture the specifics, but it will have to do.

My dad wanted only the best. So he went out and got their DNA and made clones of the best.

Now the "BEST" were all teenagers again.

And they'd apparently restarted their KILL COUNT at twelve.

• • •

Castillo asked if I knew these guys. He'd not yet brought up the clone thing at all. He was still speaking about these six boys like they were just Albert Young, David Spanelli, Henry Roberts, and so on, etc. But something in his voice, his look, made me realize he knew *exactly* what they were.

He'd just come to my house directly from DSTI, just spent hours in my father's secret room while I'd cowered in the closet. Yes, I imagined, he knew the New Truth all too well.

Castillo shook me from my ever-darkening thoughts, asked again: Do you know these guys?

I admitted I knew three of them. I'd met Henry and Ted. And David. Various events and programs at the Massey school my dad had brought me to. David had always seemed like a pretty cool kid. Funny. And I told Castillo that. He wrote it down like it mattered somehow.

He asked specifically about Henry and Ted.

I shook my head. Explained what I thought of them. Told Castillo they, to me, seemed like "BAD KIDS." (Not knowing how much my silly notions of such classifications would be challenged and changed over the next two weeks.) When pressed for more specifics, I told him they just seemed to be like people who might be involved in something, well, "BAD."

Maybe that was unfair. I mean, guys like my father and Mr. Eble had always seemed "GOOD," and this was clearly no longer a given.

Part of the New Truth.

Castillo asked me a bunch more questions about Henry, Ted, and David.

What they liked to do. Places they talked about? Girls? Etc.

I told Castillo everything I could think of. It wasn't much.

I mean, how much do you really know about people you've met only a couple of times?

As to the other three guys he was looking for . . .

I told Castillo honestly I'd never met them.

I'd certainly have remembered meeting Jeffrey Williford.

Meeting another copy of myself.

• • •

Castillo had told DSTI about finding my dad's secret room and about all the materials and documents within. He projected DSTI would return in about thirty minutes to pick it all up, and then he made it pretty clear that wasn't ideal for me. Turns out he had the exact same assessments of DSTI my dad did: I probably should keep as far away as possible. It occurred to me briefly that his warning and concern were some kind of cruel trick and that he was just gonna drive me straight to them anyway.

But Castillo didn't work *for* DSTI. Just *with*. (At least that's what he was telling me.) And that small difference made ALL the difference in the world, I think. Castillo was working for the government. The Department of Defense, ultimately. For some guy named Colonel Stanforth. And the gang at DSTI hadn't told Castillo (or this Stanforth guy) they were coming to clean out my father's office before Cas

And they sure as heck hadn't told Castillo anytl

I even *existed*.

Castillo'd had to figure that part out on his o

my dad's secret room reading his journals. Watchi

patient interviews and of top-secret tests conducte

Turns out there were a lot of things DSTI hadn't told Castillo about.

And I think it kinda pissed him off.

So he didn't plan to take me to DSTI.

Instead he asked me to help.

• • •

Castillo told me he wanted to help these six kids. And my dad, too.

He didn't know yet if they'd all scattered in different directions or were still together somewhere.

And he didn't know if my dad was a hostage of some kind or—he suspected—more "involved."

But he said he didn't care about any of that right now because he wanted to do more than capture these guys. He said they were in a real bad place and needed real help. He said they *might* be murderers and my dad *might* be helping them somehow but that he was only interested in making sure things didn't get worse.

And I believed him. Even if he was lying, it didn't matter.

I had to believe in *something*.

Maybe I should have just said no. I didn't.

I said yes.

He asked if I needed anything.

They already took everything, I said.

odded.

m Castillo, he said and held out his hand.

Hi. I shook his hand. I'm Jeffrey Dahmer.

. . .

It was a shitty thing to say. But I wanted this guy to know that *I knew* exactly what I was. What these other guys were too. He didn't have to pretend anymore.

Maybe I also wanted Castillo to feel as sucky and revolted as I did.

I think it worked.

. . .

Science types always write things down. Always. They collect data, make notes. Repeat.

Think about biology class again. No one there EVER asks you what you think or feel. (One of the great failings of all Science, I think.) It's all about Observe and Record. Almost as if something wasn't really REAL or TRUE until it was logged officially in black and white.

If you had a big secret, you'd probably just keep it to yourself. Somewhere in the back of your mind. Safe. Private. But to science geeks like my dad, it wouldn't yet be REAL that way.

So even for his darkest and wildest secrets, he took notes.

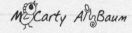

These were some of the "notes" Castillo showed me on his smartphone.

We was driving in his car to God knows where. It was, like, seven in the morning.

The pictures he was showing me were ones he'd taken of my dad's journals the night before. Pictures from the secret journals

GEOFFREY GIRARD

in the secret room. The ones I hadn't wanted to look at.

And the big secret?

Squiggles and cartoon chickens.

Ridiculous.

But it wasn't just ridiculous. It was something else.

Because Castillo had spent most of the night doing what I couldn't/ wouldn't do: reading my dad's journals and notes. Looking at the files on his hidden laptops. And according to my father's notes, the six missing students were just the tip of the iceberg. A tip already sharp and dark with blood. And the iceberg lurking scarcely beneath was a hundred miles long.

According to my father's journals the clones schooled at the Massey Institute weren't the only ones. According to my father's journals there'd been some special testing—tests done by him against DSTI's will but with their half knowledge. He'd managed to adopt out another twenty clones into the world. Babies made from the DNA of famous serial killers, then given out to specific families.

Some of the families had no idea what their sons were.

Some did. Some were even paid to raise their sons in specific ways.

Bad specific ways.

• • •

According to my father's journals, it was time to free all of them.

To tell these clones who they truly were and release them out into the world.

Like he was letting loose a wild animal.

Or a disease.

Like he'd freed me.

• • •

McCarty AlyBaum

Castillo asked me what these were.

I had no idea.

McCarty? M. Carty. Didn't know.

Al Baum? Didn't know.

He was totally convinced there was someone, some kid, named "Al." Maybe the Albert in the missing six from DSTI/Massey but probably, he suspected, *another* Albert altogether. One of those other secret kids adopted out by my father. The clone of some old serial killer named Albert Fish, or even—Castillo suspected from my father's cryptic scribbles—another notorious killer named Albert DeSalvo.

At the time, Castillo figured the family's name was Baum ("Al Baum," taking away the squiggle thing), but he'd done a search and there were, like, **20,000** Baums in the United States.

He said it'd be impossible to find the right one because, he figured, the kid would be totally "off the grid." And by "off the grid" he meant there'd be no official record of the adoption (just like me). Probably homeschooled (just like me). No Social Security number (just like me).

Castillo pointed to the squiggle between "Al" and "Baum" and asked me if I thought it was some kind of scientific notation or even a weird musical symbol. At this point, I could barely understand a word this guy was saying. I was exhausted and confused and scared and really wanted to just crawl into a ball on the floor mat and maybe die.

I didn't know. To say something, anything, I told him I played the bass. He didn't care at all, then asked me about the bird

GEOFFREY GIRARD

thing. I had no clue there either and told him so.

I'm surprised he didn't just throw me out of the car.

• • •

We'd been driving for an hour. I think north toward New York. I wasn't sure. I was so exhausted. To be honest, I might have cried some. Call me a pussy if you want. I don't care. Castillo said: Anyone thinks you're a pussy for crying, just means nothing bad's ever really happened to them. So, there's that. Please try to keep that in mind as we go forward.

He asked me a bunch more questions about my dad. Like what he drove and the places he went. Business trips, vacations and stuff. Friends he had. I didn't know anything. And I sure as heck had no clue what the chicken was or squiggle or the castle or birds or any of the other notes Castillo showed me. They weren't the notations of a curious scientist. They were the scribblings of a total raving lunatic. They meant nothing to me. They had nothing to do with me.

But that was just another lie. The total raving lunatic was MY father. Adoptive, fake, whatever. It didn't matter. As far as the world was concerned, as far as Castillo was—as far as me, too, I guess—Dr. Jacobson WAS my father. And I couldn't change that fact any more than I could change the DNA apparently coursing throughout my entire body.

Castillo pulled over at a Dunkin' Donuts, made me sit in the car while he made some phone calls. Guess he wanted to talk in private.

He let me keep hold of his smartphone (he had, like, four of them!) to keep looking at my dad's moronic notes. To maybe figure something out. But I couldn't look at them anymore. They were just too crazy. So while Castillo talked a few feet away, I just kept scrolling back.

Back, back.

As fast as my thumb could go. He'd taken hundreds of images.

Not only of the journal entries but also more stuff he'd found in my dad's special room. Pictures of criminals. Pictures of boys. Charts. Records. That old map of London I'd seen. One of someplace called Whitechapel. Then another map, I think, of somewhere called Shardhara. Ringed with different-colored circles, and with numbers.

Back. Back.

I went too far.

. . .

The next images were pictures of the Massey Institute.

Castillo'd been there all day before coming to find me, and he'd seen everything in person. I feel blessed that I only had to look at the pics.

The first was a destroyed office I recognized immediately as my father's. Everything smashed. Something on the table I couldn't quite make out. Something wet and dark.

Back. Back.

The game room at Massey. Its Activity Center. I'd been in it a hundred times. It was a pretty cool room, actually. Something for the students there. Pool table and giant TV. A foosball table and a bunch of couches. Shelves filled with board games and graphic novels and books. We had a lot of our meetings there. Like, group talks and stuff.

Except in these pictures the room was different.

There were strange white lumps all over the room now. And as I thumbed through the pics, sometimes there were a couple of lumps in the picture, and sometimes it was just one white lump real close. Lying on the floor or even one on the pool table.

Lumps covered in sheets. Sheets stained red.

And then I finally figured out what I was looking at.

You too, I bet.

CHAPTER SIX

*W*hen I added up all the different bodies in all the pictures, I counted ten. (The two other people killed that night I did not see pictures of.) Strewn around that room. Each one murdered just the night before. I'd spent that same night afraid and angry in my room. How had they spent *theirs*?

I could make out their shapes perfectly now. These lifeless bodies. Leg here, the shape of a shoulder or head there. A couple of the covered bodies were so small.

The carpet caked with dried blood. The walls streaked with it. Castillo'd taken one picture where someone had written curse words on the wall and drawn a big dick. Even *that* was in blood.

It was like Castillo had a blood app on his smartphone.

I closed the pictures and tossed the phone back onto the empty car seat next to me.

My whole body was shaking.

What happened there? I kept thinking. *What happened?*

And: *How much worse might it have been if summer term hadn't just started?*

And: *How could my father be involved in something so awful?*

Castillo eyed me from the distance, looked concerned. Probably thought from my body language I was getting ready to start freaking out or something. I looked away and tried to pull myself together.

Good luck with that. I mean, I still had 0.00 idea what was going on. Or what Castillo was really doing standing over there, who he was *really* talking to. What would *really* happen to me next? I tried listening as hard as I could to what he was saying. Even tried reading his lips. Nothing.

Sure, he'd seemed upset about DSTI jerking him around and holding back info on him. And, well, yeah, sure he *said* he wanted to help and all, but I just kept replaying all my father's warnings of DSTI, and I easily imagined Castillo was even now talking to them. Deciding what to do with me, and they were probably telling him to bring me in immediately. Or telling him to take me a couple of miles deeper into the Pine Barrens and shoot me in the head with that gun of his. Make me VANISH.

I'd known my dad for sixteen (OK, technically *eight*) years, and I'd known Castillo for about two hours. Let's just say I now started to look around to, like, escape or something.

There was the doughnut shop's parking lot. Abandoned video store. Gas station. Street heading deeper into the woods, into nowhere. Carpet store. Closed hair salon. Auto parts place. My eyes ran down the street, and I wondered how far I'd get before he caught me. I'd take my chances with the police. I'd . . .

Any escape fantasies ended without my even putting my hand on the car door handle. Really, what was the point anyway? My father's last words to me echoed in my brain. Any fear or anger I'd just felt now gave way to sudden and total despair. Despair to the one essential truth beneath/behind all the others:

The truth of what I really was.

. . .

I suppose if I'd found out I was secretly a wizard or the lost son of a Greek god, it might have gone differently. But that's not what I was. I was something that left bloody lumps in the Activity Center.

. . .

We were heading south back toward Philadelphia. I knew DSTI/Massey was in this direction and asked Castillo if he was taking me there. If he'd said YES, at this point I really wouldn't have cared. I was already tired of worrying about it, and I just wanted to get things over with one way or the other. I was also holding out some with the idea and hope that my father would be there.

But Castillo shook his head and told me he'd just contacted some people to help start getting information. Said it was time to get to work. Help me find "your little friends." It was a total slam. He knew they weren't my friends. Not even David, really. I'd never even *met* half of them. It was just his way of letting me know he thought I was just like they were.

A worthless piece-of-shit killer.

. . .

The first place we looked was the King of Prussia Mall, the biggest mall in the whole United States and about fifteen minutes away from DSTI and the Massey Institute. Both are just north of Philly, and many of the students lived nearby. Castillo's plan was to check out a couple of the local shopping areas and schools and convenience stores and paintball fields (because I'd told him Henry liked paintball). Castillo commented that people, when they're hiding, usually stick to the places they know best. (Guess he was right. It's what I'd done. Now, of course, I didn't even care where I was anymore.)

I didn't think there was any way my dad was hiding out at some mall or paintball field, but maybe the other guys were. Or some of them. Or *one* of them. And just maybe my dad was with them.

During our drive toward the mall, Castillo got weird. Out of nowhere, really, he started making these threats. Calmly told me that if I ran away, he'd catch me and drive me straight to DSTI; if I called for help, he'd catch me and drive me straight to DSTI; if I went to the cops, made a scene or whatnot, the *cops* would drive me straight to DSTI.

Which was kinda messed up. I'd just told the guy I *wanted* to help, so why'd he now think I was gonna run off on him? Maybe he'd figured out I was thinking about making a run for it at the Dunkin' Donuts. And then I realized the whole do-you-wanna-help-me stuff had all been just for show. To keep things more pleasant. If I'd told the guy NO, he would have just dragged me to his car anyway. I was a prisoner. The prisoner who'd agreed to my new prison.

Halfway to the mall, he stopped at an Old Navy store in Cherry Hill. Said he was gonna get me some clothes and told me to wait outside in the car. *Or I'll catch you and drive you straight to DSTI.* I assumed this followed every sentence now. He got out of the car and headed into the store alone.

I snuck a look at his back as he crossed the parking lot. Hadn't really looked at him all that much since we'd met. Mostly kept my head down, my eyes everywhere but his. He was a pretty big guy. Not really tall (I'm a couple of inches taller at just over 6'), but you could tell he'd worked out quite a lot. Solid. He was about midthirties, I guess. Kinda

GEOFFREY GIRARD

moved across the parking lot like he was walking a gladiator pit. Not a single wasted step or movement. He was dark-skinned. His hair was black, messy, medium length.

I, now that I comprehended 100% that I was his prisoner, hated him and his stupid back and looked away.

I tried to sleep. The summer-morning sun was warm and nice on my face through the windshield. I could hear the lives of normal people going on just outside. Car doors shutting, soft morning voices.

With my eyes closed like that, I could almost pretend to be somewhere else entirely.

Anywhere else. Anywhere NORMAL.

I tried not to think about my dad.

Then I even tried not to think about me.

• • •

Castillo came back in, like, ten minutes with two full bags: jeans, a bunch of T-shirts, and a sweatshirt. Everything either blue or dark gray. And the most generic styles they carried too. Even if I were literally holding in my hands right now the clothing he'd bought, I couldn't describe it. He'd even bought a baseball cap. It was also blue, with an American flag on it. He told me to put it on. I looked like a total moron but did not have the balls to tell him so. If I did, he'd probably just drive me back to DSTI. A stupid Old Navy cap was now apparently life-or-death. And with the way Castillo was looking at me, I kinda got it for the very first time. *Everything* was now life-or-death. Mostly death.

• • •

I'd heard of the "Mark of Cain" but did not yet understand what it meant until the King of Prussia Mall. In the Bible story, when Cain kills his brother Abel, God "marks" Cain for the crime and then exiles him to a faraway land called Nod. Like most people, I always imagined God had, like, tattooed "KILLER" on the guy's forehead: "BAD NEWS." "LOSER." "PARIAH." "MURDERER." That kind of thing.

And as we walked through that ridiculous, teeming, terrible mall, I felt that exact same mark blazing hot and bright on my whole face. That stupid Old Navy hat couldn't change that. Every single person I passed, hundreds and hundreds, was looking right at me. Even without looking at them, I could still feel their disgusted stares. Their horror. They could see the mark on me as clearly as if I were holding up a sign.

KILLER.

At any moment I expected some housewife to start screaming her head off. Maybe a couple of college guys to kick my ass until the cops showed up.

Jeffrey Dahmer is alive and well and wandering the King of Prussia Mall!

Just outside GameStop. Walking by Auntie Anne's Pretzels.

Looking for someone to kill.

MONSTER.

My new plan, my thought going into the mall, was to call Castillo's bluff. Find out if he'd really just drag me back to DSTI and maybe find out how much of a captive I really was now. I was gonna jump up on a table in the middle of the food court and rip off my new cap and shout at the top of my lungs: *Help! This guy has kidnapped me and put this stupid hat on me to fool you. My father, a very famous scientist, is missing. I need to find him now. Please help me. Call the cops. Something! Someone . . .*

Instead I kept my mouth shut, face down, just staring at the floor.

Moved as quickly as possible and hung close to Castillo's back as he marched through the whole mall, like, fifteen times. He kept asking me to look around. To see if I recognized any of the three boys I knew.

I hadn't. But, really, what did he expect?

I'd just managed to pass four thousand people and not look at a single face.

• • •

Next stop was a couple of paintball places: Paintball Country and ALLSTAR Paintball. Places Henry had mentioned a couple of times.

Castillo gave me a fifty at each and told me to rent equipment. He'd tossed the Old Navy cap and picked me up a Flyers one at the mall. This was not done because I thought the Old Navy cap was lame. No, it was only done to change my look. Make it harder for someone (DSTI? The government?) to track my day.

My hands were shaking like crazy when I handed the money over.

Castillo set us up at one of the picnic tables in the waiting area and told me to just keep reloading my rented paintball gun with pellets while he looked around for Henry. Must have seen a hundred people in five minutes. It was the summer and pretty crowded with kids and families and stuff.

Again, I felt like everyone was staring at me. Staring at my mark of Cain.

Mark of Cain XP11. The clone FREAK.

But they weren't. They had their own friends and families and discussions and things to worry about. They didn't pay any attention to me at all.

If anything, it seemed like people were actually staring at *Castillo*.

First, he's a couple of years too young to look like my dad. I guess that's what we were trying to pretend to be or something. But it wasn't that. It was just that he didn't fit somehow. He looked too, well, *mean*. Even though he was trying hard to act all casual and stuff. Hiding behind his shades, trying to not look interested. He still looked like he could F you up in a hurry and in a dozen different ways.

But what it was, more, was that he looked like he was the only one really ALIVE. And everyone else, all the yapping middle-class white slob teens and their dads were all only half there and really just kinda scenery for whatever it was Castillo was doing. It was weird.

Later, I'd find out he'd been back in the US for only about a year.

Before, he'd spent close to fifteen years overseas. At war.

Then his more-ALIVE-than-everyone-else thing didn't seem so weird.

· · ·

Come on, Castillo said, and we moved deeper into the property to where the paintball version of "battlefields" were. It was tough to see faces because everyone was wearing masks, but we waited and watched. Nothing. Castillo kept us moving.

The largest field at ALLSTAR Paintball was covered in dozens of giant wooden spools and old trailers and even a two-story fort on each side. We watched from a small hill overlooking the field with about a dozen other people. There must have been forty people on each team. All screaming orders at each other and laughing and yelling. Someone even tossed a smoke grenade that landed in the middle of the grass field and made purple-gray smoke roll over a whole section of the playing area.

In that smoke with the masks, with everyone yelling like that, any one of them could have been Henry. Like this, ALL of them looked like the genetic offspring of some terrible killer.

I looked over the whole battlefield again, and it had changed.

A mound of burnt grass I hadn't really noticed before, the way the purple-gray smoke snaked around one of the giant wood spools, the contour with which two players had thrown themselves to the ground for cover. The dead center of the field had started taking on a new look. The paintball ground slowly waning, fading into another shape altogether. One I recognized all too well. Its mouth opening in a silent scream of purple-gray smoke that—

I looked away.

Beside me, Castillo asked if I'd seen something.

No, I lied, and acted like I was looking at the field again but instead watched Castillo from the corner of my eye. There was no way I was EVER looking at the field again. Castillo waited and watched the players "die" one by one. But he wasn't really watching them either, I could tell. He may have been looking at the field, but his eyes were shooting right through it like all those people weren't even there. I could only imagine what he was really thinking about. At the time, I figured he was thinking about me. I know better now.

He waited for them to exit the field, taking off their masks when they came back through the netting. All strangers. Castillo showed a picture of Henry to one of the refs when he came off the field.

You some kind of cop? the high school kid asked, and laughed.

No, Castillo said. Nothing like that.

Behind him, the purple-gray smoke drifted up to the sun.

Still screaming.

CHAPTER SEVEN

*T*he hotel was a dump. I'd never stayed somewhere so nasty. It smelled like cigarettes and dirt. I didn't say anything, but Castillo must have read my face because he told me there were a lot worse places to stay.

We'd just entered the room when Castillo turned and locked the door. For the first time in my life, it didn't feel like the world was being locked out. I was being locked IN.

Castillo waved me deeper into the room. Come here, he said.

My whole body half jumped into the ceiling. It finally dawned on me where I was and with who. A total stranger. Some lunatic who worked somehow with the same guys who'd busted into my house and stolen my lizard. I figured he'd finally gotten those orders from DSTI and was going to murder me just like my dad had warned. Steal my brain for science or something.

From a plastic bag the lunatic pulled out a pair of scissors.

OHMYGOD, OHMYGOD, OHMY—

We gotta do your hair, he said. (Note: This didn't ease my concerns any.)

Still he kept waving me toward the dark bathroom. Said we had to cut and dye my hair. (My hair's basically sandy blond. He now wanted it dark brown.) Explained people would be looking for me. Not the police. But DSTI or the government.

I asked: Aren't YOU the government?

Castillo said they'd told him to find the six missing boys from Massey and that was it. The only reason he'd even come to my house at all was to maybe dig up some information on my dad, who was obviously involved in some way, information on where these six guys were and maybe even what had happened at Massey that night.

He said that if they—DSTI *or* his bosses—ever said he was supposed to find me, he'd give me a week's head start and some money. (In retrospect, this was a cool thing to say. But at the time it just made him seem more terrifying than ever.)

And if they find me? I asked.

He didn't know. Just said that he'd rather they didn't.

I asked if they'd kill me.

He didn't know.

It was true. He really didn't.

And, for the first time, I kinda got it.

The room. The stupid hats. The hair.

He was just as afraid as I was. Afraid they'd find us. Of what would happen if they did. And I could tell he hated giving me that answer.

I don't know.

I could tell that answer was one of the worst things he'd ever said.

I followed him into the bathroom, where he sat me on the john and cut all my hair. He was trying to be cool about it, but I'd be lying if I said I wasn't on the verge of crying the whole time. Humiliated, abandoned, confused, scared. Every shitty feeling you could think of. And all at the same time.

He asked if I was OK, told me we were almost done.

I tried to keep still. Watched him mess with the gloves and mix the hair stuff.

You done this before? I asked.

He nodded.

I asked when, but he ignored me and just put that stuff in my hair. It smelled terrible, like vinegar, and stung my eyes.

Sorry, he said.

The way he said it, I knew he wasn't just talking about my hair.

• • •

Five minutes later, I stood alone in the shower and kept my eyes closed tight as the smelly hair dye finished doing its job. It felt greasy in my fingers. When I opened my eyes, the dye's residue still ran down my body and pooled at my feet in the water. Swirling away slowly down the drain and looking way too much like dark blood.

I kept thinking about those pictures, the ones taken at Massey. As I watched that dark "blood" roll over and through and around my toes, I kept trying to imagine what had really happened in the Activity Center. And I tried also to *not* think about it at all.

That's when the dye started to take shape in the water.

A particular shape. Just a hint.

A jawline, maybe, and an eye forming on the right side that—

I closed my eyes again and held my face into the hot water. Then found the handle and turned until the water got colder, colder, colder. . . . Chasing all thoughts away. Anything I *might* have seen.

I hid in that shower a long, long time.

GEOFFREY GIRARD

When I got out, I looked like I was maybe six years old in the mirror. Momentously stupid. My hair all hacked away and dark. I dried off and put my clothes back on. I hid in the bathroom as long as I could. Eventually, Castillo shouted to me, asked if everything was OK. I said yeah. Still, I waited another few minutes.

He was working at the small desk in the room with his laptop and a map and a bunch of papers. I moved past him as carefully and quietly as possible and got to my bed. I just wanted to curl up and die, really. I was so tired. So miserable. I kept thinking if I could just get some sleep, maybe . . .

Didn't happen. Castillo had other plans. Said he had something else for me to focus on.

Um, OK. . . . My voice trailed off with all the eeriness and alarm suddenly oozing through my whole body.

Francis Tumblety, he said.

I had no idea who that was, and told him as much.

He held up his smartphone.

Showed me pic of a small withered corpse stuffed like a ventriloquist's dummy in a small box.

Yeah, *that* guy.

. . .

My father, as I'd suspected from the start, had not murdered Francis Tumblety.

Turns out this guy'd been dead in the New York ground since 1903.

My father *did*, however (Castillo had the journal entries and even a homemade video to prove it), dig him back up and stuff him in a pseudo-fridge in our house.

For, as I'd also suspected, his DNA.

And this guy had MOST DEFINITELY been chosen for his serial-killer potential. Two reasons:

First, because Francis Tumblety was *maybe* Jack the Ripper.

Refresher: Jack the Ripper was the world's first famous serial killer. Murdered probably a dozen women in London in the 1880s. And the murders were quite bloody and quite sexual, and the police couldn't ever catch him and there were, like, two hundred newspapers working in London at the time. And they all made him famous for killing people because (a) it helped sell all those papers, and (b) England ruled the whole world back then and this one guy was like a foot-long bloody turd in their Victorian punch bowl. Jack the Ripper was their 9/11. He reminded civilized society that nobody is ever, *ever* really safe from the monsters. There is always another one waiting down the next dark alley. Behind the shower curtain. Under the bed. On an airplane. In a movie theater or even some kindergarten classroom.

And I say he was *maybe* Jack the Ripper because no one *really* knows who Jack the Ripper was. Dude was never caught, and there are literally, like, twenty possible culprits. For a hundred years now different camps and fans (called "Ripperologists") have argued about who he really was. Yes, "FANS." Turns out there are a lot of people who are kinda into serial killers. They find it interesting somehow. I guess that same way people find the Holocaust or Having-Your-Face-Ripped-off-by-a-Monkey "interesting." (More on this lameness later.)

As for Ripperologists, my father was unquestionably on Team Tumblety.

That, in and of itself, wasn't that big a deal. Again, if it was your job to collect the DNA of famous serial killers, getting ahold of the real Jack's DNA was like finding a box of Einstein's math homework. A new play by Shakespeare. A living Bigfoot. The Holy Grail.

But that wasn't the only reason my father wanted this man's DNA.

Or why his old dead body was in my house instead of some lab room at DSTI.

Or why my father had personally, and at great expense, dug the body up himself.

My father had done all those things for another reason.

And that reason, the REAL reason, it turned out, was kinda terrible.

CHAPTER EIGHT

*M*y dad thinks he's Jack the Ripper?

I couldn't believe I'd just said these words out loud.

And I didn't mean the *actual* Jack the Ripper, who'd been dead for more than a hundred years. (My dad wasn't *that* crazy.) Rather that my father believed he was the Ripper's descendant. His genetic offspring. That Jack the Ripper's blood and DNA lived on somehow in his body.

Castillo said he didn't really understand it himself yet either. Only that this was all in my father's journals. The ones I'd been unwilling to read that Castillo had now pored over for almost two straight days. And in these journals my dad apparently wrote there was some kind of connection between him and this Tumblety guy. Karmic, cosmic. Genetic. Related by blood, probably. And, according to Castillo, my father'd been writing about this stuff for years. Even before I'd been born/made.

Castillo asked if my dad had ever said anything to me about any of this. About Tumblety and all. He hadn't. But I totally remembered seeing Tumblety's name in my father's secret office the one time I'd gone in. Castillo then asked if my dad had ever talked about Jack the Ripper.

He hadn't. I kept searching my memories for something—anything.

Castillo handed me his phone and told me he had some more pages from the journals he wanted me to read. Some things my father had apparently written about all of this. About Tumblety and the Ripper and all. Castillo hoped maybe something would trigger an idea or memory, some hint as to what my dad might be up to, or, even, where he might be.

Castillo's next sentence trailed off.

He wanted to warn me. Warn me about what I was about to see. That all the squiggles and chickens and old corpses were only the start. He was looking for the right words to capture the fact that my father was—based on the evidence in the journals—completely insane. And I couldn't blame Castillo for that. Because my own mind was searching for those exact same words.

He asked me to read only as much as I could.

I did not get very far.

• • •

I will spare you the exact details of what I did read.

The short of it is:

(a) My father had a troubled childhood plagued by nightmares that developed into an abnormal relationship with women in general. (b) The nightmares were primarily focused on a specific dead woman. He did not recognize her. And whether she was a suppressed memory of some kind or totally imagined didn't matter. As the years went on, her draw on him became greater and greater. It became, even, some form of love. (c) He called this woman the THING ON THE BED. (d) One day, while reading a book about Jack the Ripper, he saw a picture of one of the victims, a horrible picture from more than a hundred years ago. (e) My father recognized her instantly, and everything, his whole life, suddenly made sense. This THING ON THE BED was simply some genetic memory passed down to him through inheritance (just like blue eyes or small feet) from his ancestor Jack the Ripper.

• • •

The government now has these journals.

• • •

I'd stopped reading. The words on the screen were blurry anyway.

Exhaustion. Tears.

I handed Castillo his phone back. Told him nothing had really jumped out at me.

He just kinda stared at me. Told me to get some rest or put on the TV if I wanted. I didn't know what else to do, so I took it as an order more than anything else. I couldn't tell you what I watched that night. It was just an hour of lights and colors flickering on the screen at this point, the sound little more than white noise.

All the while, Castillo just kept working at that desk. Looking stuff up. Gathering information. I don't know. I didn't want to ask. (He always looked so angry then, you know?)

It was the first time I could really watch him up close without him looking back, and I finally got a good look at all his scars. They ran all up and down both his arms. Deep pink-white scratches. Almost like tattoos. I didn't have the guts to ask.

Later, I'd see all the others.

Eventually he looked over and caught me staring at him. He asked what I wanted. He looked like he wanted to punch me in the face or something. I got this impression a lot from Castillo at the start.

GEOFFREY GIRARD

I asked if there was anything else I could do to help.

He said: Is there?

We both knew the same thing.

There wasn't.

Every assignment he'd already given me (my dad's doodles, the mall, looking through my dad's journals) had led to nothing. Just my saying NO a lot and us not finding anyone.

So he looked at me like I was a piece of crap again, and I sat there stupid for a long while and then just rolled over to maybe get some sleep.

I couldn't even do that.

• • •

But I kept my eyes closed and pretended to sleep. I was so very tired. Couldn't believe I wasn't just passing out immediately. But I kept thinking so much about my dad. And I tried *not* thinking so much about my dad. And it wasn't easy. It's like trying not to think about a PURPLE COW. Go ahead, try. Once it's in there, it's in there. And all these notions of my dad, over what his life had been and was. And these personal demons he'd been carrying around all those years. It was clear I didn't really know the guy. What he was truly capable of. I needed . . . I needed to think about something else. Get this particular purple cow out of my brain awhile.

So I thought about my mother.

Both of them.

• • •

The first one in the pictures.

The one who was supposed to have died in a car crash of some kind. Her face, which I'd known so well a day before, was already becoming a blur to me. Like my mind knew to just write her off as complete make-believe. I wondered who the blond boy with her in the one picture was. If it was really me. Or just some random blond kid. Were even the pictures of ME fake? Where had my father found her? Had they really been married? Was she just a model/actress they'd picked out to play a part? How much had they paid her to be my mom for three photos? How much was such a thing worth? I pursued a formless memory of visiting her grave. Bringing flowers to her grave. I envisioned my father standing over me. Cool wind in dark lonely trees above both of us. Had I invented this memory? Or had it been given to me? Had my father simply TOLD me we'd done this, and I'd processed it into my memories with so many other lies? Worse, had he maybe taken me to some random grave and said Say Good-bye to Your Mother? All those years I'd fought to remember anything and everything about her. And I'd fought the guilt of failing at that one simple thing. Her face slipping away from me like a dandelion ball drifting farther and farther out of reach. Memories of how she'd sounded and the things we'd done together before the accident. Memories that had never been.

And then my thoughts turned to my BIRTH mother.

The woman who'd only carried me for a few months. From the folder my father had given me, I knew she was from somewhere in Ukraine. I knew she'd been young and that they'd paid her. That's all I would ever know. How many other babies had she carried? How many other women had done this exact same thing for DSTI? She'd carried me just four months. The rest of the time after that, more than a year, I'd been in some kind of pod. A vat of fluids while they'd grown me to just the right size for Dr. Jacobson. I had no memory of this. And yet, that first night in that motel with Castillo, I could just about make out the buttery fluid. Warm and salty. Completely surrounding me as I turned, floated, in the room's darkness. In my mind, I lifted my hands. Slowly opened my eyes in the thick fluid.

The hands I was seeing weren't mine, however.

They were dark. Or gray, maybe. Long and gnarled.

Hands with claws.

And suddenly I couldn't even quite make out which direction they were facing. Meaning, if they were MY monstrous hands and I'd turned them to study the palms or they were some OTHER hands pressed against the glass. The hands pressed—

I startled fully awake.

It'd been a dream, maybe, or some half-formed memory.

I didn't know then. (Later, I would realize it had been a little bit of both.)

The room was half-dark. Castillo had turned off the TV and worked only with the small desk lamp and the light from his two laptops. I didn't know what time it was. If I'd slept all night or just a few minutes. I watched this guy work for a minute and stared, blurry-eyed, at that dim light. God only knew what he was looking for or at. So I closed my eyes again to the constant tapping of the two keyboards. Like rain almost, or maybe thousand-legged bugs running around in the walls.

As I drifted off again, I was—despite all my previous efforts—only, you guessed it, wondering again what my father was doing. And maybe "wondering" isn't the best word.

Maybe the better word is "fearing."

CHAPTER NINE

I awoke next to the sound of Castillo's deep voice talking on the phone. Couldn't get much out of what he was saying. Something about money and monsters and some guy named Pete.

Any hope I'd had of waking up to discover the previous forty-eight hours had been "all just a dream" ended right then and forever. It was real—all of it—and I woke as confused as I'd ever been.

I pretended to remain asleep and stayed just like that until he left the room. When the door shut, I sat up and looked around.

Castillo'd taped a map up onto one of the walls, and I climbed out of bed to look at it. He'd made little marks all over it. Black dots and blue and red dots, with names and dates beside each. They were all over the whole country.

I moved slowly about the room. The desk was covered in notes he'd taken. He'd closed his two laptops. I ran my fingers across each and snuck a look at the written notes he'd left, but it was just more names and dates. Scribbles no better than the ones my dad had left. Besides, I didn't want to look too closely. Castillo could come back into the room at any second.

His lone duffel bag was closed. I imagined what might be inside this black canvas treasure chest. Spy stuff of some kind, right? Special cameras and recording equipment. Secret truth serums, poisons, and whatnot. Or just maybe more evidence he hadn't yet shown me.

I wondered if he'd left any of his guns in the room. In the bag.

Maybe, to tell the truth, I even wondered some what I would do if I found one.

I cautiously eased down into the chair he'd used all night and just looked about the room again. Pressed my fingers against the table. Then I spun the chair to look at my side of the room. I tried visualizing what he was seeing whenever he looked over my way. The worthless little kid sniveling in the corner. The clone monster watching TV, taking a nap, as if nothing had happened. As if he weren't some monster.

I looked away.

Couldn't even imagine looking at myself.

• • •

I was standing at the map again when he came back into the room.

He seemed tense. Surprised to find me awake, I guess.

I think the guy might even have actually reached for a gun or something behind his back.

Since I'd been busted, I just started yapping. I quickly asked about the map. The dots.

Anything to make the whole scene a little less awkward.

He told me the map was to keep track of DEAD PEOPLE.

He called it the MURDER MAP.

• • •

The red dots were murders.

The black ones were disappearances. Blue was rape.

Castillo told me they were all the crimes that'd been reported in the last twenty-four hours.

One single day.

I looked at the map again.

There were sixty dots all over the country.

Most were red.

. . .

I turned and said that was impossible. I mean, there was no way that many people—

He looked at me like I was stupid.

Told me that in the US at least forty people are murdered every single day.

I did the math in my head.

That was about three hundred people a week. Fourteen thousand a year. Every year.

Half go unsolved, he said. And those were the ones he was interested in. Because maybe/probably these six students hadn't finished killing yet.

I'd found Radnor, Pennsylvania, on the map. The town where DSTI and the Massey Institute are. Castillo hadn't placed any dots there, but I imagined them all the same. Twelve red ones all piled on top of each other.

I asked Castillo if he really thought those six guys had something to do with the . . . with the murders at Massey. White lumps came to mind. Red dots covered with white sheets.

Castillo assured me that that's definitely what it looked like.

And do you really think my dad helped them?

I did not ask this out loud. I was afraid of his answer.

So instead I just asked WHY. Why would anyone do something like that?

Castillo said he didn't know. Said these aren't—

But he stopped himself from finishing the thought/sentence.

Aren't what? I pressed. Aren't "normal people" is what he'd meant to say.

He looked away.

Then I got curious and asked HOW they'd done it. How specifically they'd killed at Massey.

Castillo asked if that mattered.

Did it? I wondered. I said: Maybe.

He nodded. Agreed it might.

Some had been bludgeoned, beaten, to death. Some had been strangled. Some cut. Two boys, clones of the two kids who'd shot up Columbine High School, had been, Castillo said, "skinned alive." I wasn't entirely sure what this meant. Two of the victims had been women. The first had been raped before she was killed. The other woman, a Language Arts teacher named Gallagher, whom I'd met, had apparently been gutted in my father's office.

I just stared at Castillo.

You mind? he said. I kinda got a lot of work to do.

And that was it for the next three hours. He went back to his laptops. Every once in a while he put a new dot on the map. I watched TV with the sound down. Tried not to think about words like "SKINNED" or "RAPED" or "GUTTED." Wished there was something to read.

Wished I was somewhere else.

Wished mostly I was *someone* else.

. . .

So then, out of basically nowhere, Castillo told me to grab us some food.

I looked over dreamily, shaken from my dim and unhappy musings.

He reached into his pocket to get some cash and said neither one of us had eaten since never and there was a Subway right next door and an Arby's a little down and that I should pick one and get us something.

I stood confused. *Why would he do this? Why . . .* He'd earlier gotten so worried about my taking off. Getting seen. Now I was being sent into public on an errand.

He handed me the money. A hundred-dollar bill!

And he'd totally passed up several twenties and tens to give me it.

Then I knew.

He wasn't giving me money for dinner. He was giving me money to get out of his life.

It was my father all over again. It was I-never-want-to-see-you-again money.

A hundred whole dollars' worth.

At least my dad had the decency to give me a thousand.

I couldn't decide if I should be insulted or applaud Castillo for at least trying to be a little subtle about the whole thing. That same morning he'd said he'd give me some money and a week's head start if it looked like DSTI ever got around to admitting I existed and wanted him to find me.

He clearly didn't want/need my help and also didn't want/need me as a prisoner anymore.

Looked like my week had officially started.

CHAPTER TEN

I shut the door behind me and just stood outside our room awhile. It was close to midnight. The motel parking lot was empty, quiet.

I tried to tell myself this was all just some kind of a test for Castillo to see what I would do if given a chance to escape. But it wasn't. Just like my father's desertion hadn't been a test. Maybe all that time spent around counselors and therapists and scientists and stuff, I'd started seeing *everything* in my life as some kind of big test. And maybe it was. I mean, I *had* been little more than a lab rat to these people. To DSTI, to my father. I *had* been secretly tested on a regular basis. I'd even seen the folder to prove it.

But not anymore. I wasn't being observed or recorded or analyzed. Quite the opposite.

Not one person on Earth gave a damn where I was or what I was doing.

If you've ever known this feeling, I'm very sorry.

• • •

So, NOT a test. Castillo'd given me a hundred-dollar pass and an opened cage door. He wasn't gonna send me back to DSTI or call the cops or anything. He was just gonna let me, by my own doing, vanish. Because he knew I couldn't help him at all. Because he knew I was completely POINTLESS. And, so, now I was also completely free.

. . .

I got completely free all the way to Subway. (Really, what else was I gonna do?)

I looked around the motel first and tried to get my bearings. I'd been more out of it when we'd first arrived, kind of emotionally/physically/mentally wiped out, stumbling behind Castillo like some kind of half-wit zombie. Now I gave the place a better look. Didn't see anywhere with a pay phone. I wanted to call my dad. Maybe he'd pick up this time. Tell me what was *really* going on. Tell me what to do. Tell me it was all a stupid joke. A misunderstanding. *Come and get me.*

So I wandered toward the main office to see if they had a phone I could use. The guy at the desk was some skinny old guy, and when I told him I was looking for the phone, his face scrunched up like he'd eaten something bad and he told me there was a phone in my room.

So I just kept going to Subway. They didn't have a phone either.

I ended up ordering two sandwiches. I don't know why. At this point I had no intention of ever going back to that room, of ever seeing Castillo again. I guess I was just on autopilot. Practically sleepwalking. Nightmarewalking. I pointed at food and picked bread and grunted out answers about whether or not I wanted stuff toasted or not. I wasn't even sure what I had just ordered.

The guy making the sandwiches kept looking at me all weird. He probably knew my hair was dyed. He probably thought I was the spitting image of that "one-guy-you-know-the-one-sure-you-do-that-serial-killer-guy."

I wondered how many people even knew what Jeffrey Dahmer looks—looked—like. I mean, was it just a name that people knew and used? Or did everyone in the country know what this freak looked like? And, if so, how much did I *really* look like him?

• • •

I've since read that only 22% of American adults identified "Gerald Ford" as the name of a recent US President, but 98% could, on the very first try, identify the name "Jeffrey Dahmer" as a serial killer.

• • •

I handed the Subway guy the money, and he looked at me all weird again. Maybe because it was a hundred. Probably because I looked exactly like someone who'd murdered seventeen people.

He asked if I needed anything to drink. I'm not sure if I answered him. I took the two subs to the far end of the empty store and sat at a table with my back to the guy. I ate in the same haze with which I'd ordered. Trying to decide what to do next. I had ninety dollars now.

Where and how far was I gonna get with ninety dollars?

I sat there for a long time. Started thinking about my dad again. If I could just get ahold of him, he'd . . . *He'd what?* Who knew anymore?

Castillo had told me a little about the experiments conducted on some of the boys who were missing. Maybe "experiments" isn't the best word. "Prescriptions"? "Treatments"?

Maybe "TORTURE" was the best word.

Torture orchestrated by DSTI.

By my father.

• • •

Some of the clone boys had been beaten. Even molested. By their "adoptive parents." Some of the boys had *just* been verbally abused.

Told they were worthless, stupid, gay, whatever. Some had been given drugs and alcohol. Or forced to kill animals. Or to watch porn. Or . . . All kinds of things just to replicate some of the bad life things that had happened to the original killers.

(THIS is the man I was supposed to call? The man who would save me?)

But some clones were completely, unreservedly, utterly left alone. I don't mean *alone* alone. They had parents and all that, but there was none of that bad stuff going on. Nothing pervy or twisted. You know, raised like "normal" kids. Soccer teams and swim lessons and Subway sandwiches. And, quite honestly, that's exactly how I'd been raised. Normal. My father had never laid a hand on me. Never called me names or gotten me high. Never put me in dangerous or confusing situations. The man took me to museums and parks and talked to me about science and history. Signed me up for soccer camps and piano lessons. Found me the best tutors and speech therapists money could buy.

But *WHY*? Why did I get piano lessons and another guy, maybe even another Jeff, had gotten molested by guys HIS fake dad had met on Craigslist?

I knew enough basic science to understand test groups and controlled experiments. DSTI had created us all to harness the XP11 violence gene. Guess they wanted to determine precisely how much of the violence was directly related to the gene and how much was connected to environment.

If Ted #1 had *x* level of violence in his system, how much would Ted #2 have if we just added a little physical violence? Mild routine spankings, say. And how much would Ted #3 develop if the spankings were actual beatings? And what if Ted #4's beatings include molestation? And Ted #5 . . .

These are the games DSTI was playing. The tests they were running for almost twenty years. And my . . . my own father had been head of the entire operation.

WHY? I screamed inside my head again. *Why would he do something like that?*

A distant voice said something, saved me from my thoughts.

I turned to the Subway guy, who asked me again if I was OK, said I looked a little zoned out.

I told him I was just tired.

Then I asked if he had a pen and some paper I could use.

He eyed me curiously, then nodded.

I pushed my half-eaten sub aside and worked for the next twenty minutes.

I'd never worked so hard at anything in my whole life.

· · ·

So there's no confusion here, I 100% still knew Castillo wanted me to go away. I just didn't care. I wanted to prove to him he was wrong. I *was* worth keeping around. I *could* help.

Find the other guys. Find my father.

And if I couldn't, well, then I guess Castillo was just gonna have to shoot me and dump me in the woods.

Or give me more than a hundred dollars.

· · ·

What's this? Castillo asked when I returned to the motel room.

If he was upset about my return, I didn't notice. I was too excited.

I presented Castillo with my list of everywhere my father had ever taken me. Every city, store, restaurant, resort, museum, park . . . everywhere. Another list of every city I could remember he ever went to. Conferences and guest lectures and stuff. Places he said he was going. I'd even made little stars where he'd brought me back a souvenir or something.

Castillo read the whole list. Both sides of the paper were completely full.

I asked if it was good.

He nodded. It's a start, he said.

And for the first time, I felt that too.

CHAPTER ELEVEN

*T*hat same night, Ted found me in a dream.

I don't know how he did it. I don't even know now if it *was* a dream, but I also wouldn't know what else to call it. Any other possibility—whether more supernatural or even scientific—would be even more terrifying. In any case, I knew it was him right away.

Ted Thompson was the most awful boy I'd ever met.

But the apple doesn't fall far from the tree, does it?

Ted Thompson had been made from the DNA of Ted Bundy.

One of the biggies. First-ballot Hall of Fame for Serial Killers.

In the 1970s, Bundy raped and murdered thirty women in just four years. He's infamous now for being kinda good-looking and would just walk up to women and ask for help, pretend to be hurt, or lost, or . . . And they'd take one look at his big blue eyes and shaggy hair and crooked smile, and that was that. And then he'd rape and kill them.

Sometimes (a dozen times) he decapitated his victims and kept their heads as souvenirs. Sometimes he went back to where the dead bodies were hidden and did sex stuff. Sometimes he'd just randomly break into girls' houses and beat them to death while he masturbated. He escaped from prison twice, and the second time invaded a whole college sorority, successfully attacking four different women.

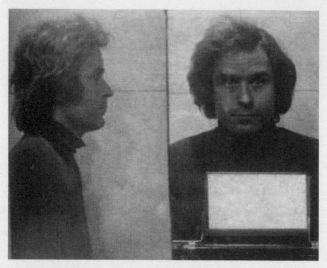

He was finally electrocuted in 1989. He wouldn't be able to hurt anyone else ever again. All those sisters and mothers and wives and daughters would be a little safer again. Or not.

Thanks to cloning, his DNA was still alive and well. Eyes. Skin. Brain. Bones. Blood.

Every cell. Copy, Paste.

Ted Thompson.

We'd met at the Massey Institute more than a dozen times. We'd been forced together to play group games and share in group talks together that my dad supervised with some of the shrinks from Massey.

See, all the guys who went to Massey were there for various diagnosed depression, anxiety, addiction, or anger management issues.

GEOFFREY GIRARD

This, of course, was largely a lie. *Some* of the guys who went to Massey actually had these issues and were just normal kids born the regular way to regular parents. But *some* of the guys at Massey had only been told they were at Massey for these issues. They were really there because they were clones.

As for me, they didn't tell me I had any of the issues above but said I had to go to Massey because I still had physiological issues connected to my "car accident." Just another version of the same lie.

In any case, every so often I went in so my dad's colleagues could give me tests, take scans of my brain, and so on. Like the stuff with the other kids. They made us do corny stuff like play Monopoly with uneven starting bankrolls or act out stories based on pictures of people they showed us. I didn't think much of it at the time. Didn't realize I was just some lab rat in jeans. I was usually just glad to get out of the house and see some other kids.

Sometimes it was kids like Ted.

I'd tried to explain to Castillo what it was about this guy. It was the way he looked at you. The arrogance. That damn phony smirk. Like you were just one of the mice, and he was the cat. Always toying with you. He'd call you a faggot or worse, and then ten seconds later throw an arm around you and say something like: "You know I'm just kidding, man. You're cool." Crap like that. All the time. PRETENDING to be nice in a way that always made me want to scream because I knew he wanted to hurt me in every possible way. But I didn't scream or complain or tell on him, and not because I was afraid he'd kick my ass. I didn't because I thought it would eventually stop.

It never did.

Hey, Jeffrey!

I looked across the unrecognizable space between us. Terra-nothing. What? I asked.

He stood in the dream with his arms crossed, nodded like we were pals. Equals. His hair was dark and neat. His T-shirt was stained. Blood-red.

Guess what we're doing right now, he said.

I told him I didn't care. Didn't want to know.

There's this family in Maryland, he told me.

I told him to go away. I thought: *Please, please, please go away.*

The mom is real pretty, he said. *But she's with Henry now.*

I could see shadows moving behind him. I heard distant screams.

Why don't you come with us? he said.

Why?

To have fun, he said. *Fun, fun, fun.* He rubbed his crotch crudely.

I told him to just leave me alone.

Ted came closer.

But the face wasn't Ted's anymore. It had become something else. Like a shadow. Another black face melding with his. Blurring the appearance I knew into something else. Something more skull-like, more monstrous. Its jaws protruding toward me, narrowing.

Come on, Jeffrey, it said. *You know what you are.*

I turned to run, but Ted, or the thing that had been Ted moments before, was still in front of me. *Stop pretending to be Jeffrey Jacobson,* it said. *Cut off a dog's tail, and it's still a dog. I'll say it again, man. You know what you are.*

Go away. Please go away.

What's bred in the blood will come out in the flesh.

The last voice had not been Ted's. It had been my dad's.

We're going to find you, I said. I couldn't look anymore.

Something laughed. I don't know who, so don't even ask.

What was that you said, Jeffrey?

We're going to find you, I shouted. Castillo is. We're going to stop you.

Now, why on Earth would you want to do that? the single voice (Ted's, the dark thing's, my dad's) asked. *You're one of us, Jeffrey.*

I looked back. The face wasn't Ted's anymore, or the black thing's, or even my dad's.

It was MY face. Jeffrey Dahmer's face.

Staring back at me in reflection.

My face smiling. A thin trail of blood trickled slowly down my chin.

· · ·

I jolted awake.

Are you OK?

I heard a new voice—Castillo's—and I turned to it. He was still sitting at the desk.

I realized only then that I was standing in the doorway of the bathroom. Staring at the mirror, in fact.

Castillo said I'd zoned out or something, asked again if I was OK.

I moved straight to his desk.

Castillo tensed, unsure what I was doing. (I'm not sure if I really knew then either.)

But I reached past him and picked up the red pen off his desk.

Hey, Jacobson? Castillo's voice still far away, like I was still dreaming.

I moved to the map on the wall. Found Radnor again. DSTI/ Massey.

I made twelve red circles. One for each and every person killed at

Massey that night. For each and every white blood-streaked lump. There was hardly any room. The map even ripped away some under all that red.

We need to find these guys, I said.

Yeah, Castillo said, and then turned back away from me.

Now the only question was, what would I do when we did?

CHAPTER TWELVE

You would think that the very next morning, we jumped into Castillo's car and started zipping all over the country, kicking in doors and getting in car chases and shoot-outs and explosions and stuff. That's certainly what I thought would happen. Instead it was just Castillo sitting at that desk again and staring at two laptops. As I'd tossed and turned the rest of the night before, that was also all he'd done.

The next three hours of morning, too.

Shouldn't we be doing something? I finally asked.

He said we were, and I just stared at him.

Castillo turned to me. He told me there was this one guy they'd had to catch once, and it had taken almost *two years*. For one year and three hundred days, all they did was gather information about this guy. They chase-chased him for less than an hour. He said: Research. Doing your homework. That's how you capture people. That's how we'd find these guys too. Eventually he'd see something that made some sense, maybe a name or the way someone else was killed, an arrest maybe, whatever. Something. And then he would have a path to follow.

I asked who was the guy he caught. The two-year guy.

He chuckled. It was a scary sound. He told me not to worry about it.

I'd walked carefully over to the desk to see what he was working on. I more than half expected him to slam the two laptops shut and deliver his best F-off look. But he didn't. He glanced once at me and then kept on working.

He was looking at the image of a map of some kind, a map covered in different-colored circles. It was one of the maps I remembered seeing in my father's secret office. I inched closer for a better look.

Castillo told me the map was probably of somewhere called Shardhara. The word he'd asked me about the first night. One of his very first questions, in fact. I told him I remembered him asking about it before, and he nodded. I'd go so far as to say he might have even looked a smidge impressed.

Looking at the strange map, I asked what Shardhara was and what did it have to do with any of this.

He didn't know. He knew (suspected, really) only that it was "somewhere in the Middle East" and that neither one of us had ever heard of it. He shook his head. Castillo noted that this map had been lying front and center in my dad's secret room. Right on top.

My father had wanted people (me? DSTI?) to find it.

From what Castillo could tell, some kind of experiment had been carried out there. The map had circles and numbers. Like a blast radius. Castillo figured DSTI was involved in something there with the military. A weapon of some kind.

• • •

Castillo figured right.

He just didn't know yet that the six guys we were chasing had this weapon.

Or that my dad had given it to them.

Castillo's bosses claimed not to have heard of Shardhara or any kinda weapon either. I asked Castillo if he thought they were lying to him. He ignored the question, and I took that as a YES answer. He asked me again if I'd ever heard of it. But except for seeing that map in my dad's office, I hadn't.

I shook my head, and any small victory I'd felt the night before was fading quickly. I already felt pointless again, started back to my bed to make myself disappear.

Castillo must have seen it in my face, slouch, something.

Hey, he said.

Yeah? I turned. Expected him to hand me another hundred to go away.

He said: The list you gave me last night is good stuff.

He said: It helps a lot.

It was very nice of him to say, but I also totally thought he was lying. So I kinda wished he hadn't said anything at all.

• • •

The real story of Cain is different from what I first thought. Get a Bible and check it out yourself. I grabbed one the next time Castillo stepped out of the motel room. He said he was going to get us some lunch, but I think it was just another phone call. I'd spent the whole rest of that morning pretending to read digital pics of my father's journals, and now I needed something to help replace my father's twisted writings in my memory. Television wouldn't do. So in the small single drawer in the stand between our two beds, I found a Gideon's Bible, just like in all the movies. They really are there. I couldn't believe it. And I found the passage easily:

And the LORD said whosoever slayeth Cain, vengeance shall be taken on

him sevenfold. And the LORD set a mark upon Cain, lest any finding him
should kill him. And Cain went out from the presence of the LORD, and
dwelt in the land of Nod, on the east of Eden.

• • •

God's mark wasn't to humiliate Cain. It wasn't to brand him as a MONSTER either. God's mark was: "BACK OFF, PEOPLE. I'LL DEAL WITH THIS GUY LATER IN A MANNER OF MY OWN CHOOSING. FOR NOW, HOWEVER, HE BELONGS HERE JUST AS MUCH AS THE REST OF YOU CLOWNS."

It wasn't exactly what my dad had told me. About embracing my "True Self" and all. But it was close enough. Sitting with that Bible open on my chest, I now half remembered my dad telling me about Cain before. Half remembered lots of things he'd said about the world's first killer. I made a mental note to find out more about the biblical Cain if I ever got the chance. I hoped it would somehow help me better understand what my dad was doing. What he'd already done. What HIS "True Self" was, let alone mine.

So in the Bible, Cain is sent to a place called Nod. My dad's office at DSTI even had a needlepoint thing framed on the wall with something about Nod, and I now remembered my dad saying "Nod" means "wander" in Aramaic, the language of the Bible. He'd said that most faiths believe Cain eventually left Nod and walked the world forever. Cursed. Unable to die. Some Hebrew texts, the kind that churches and synagogues hide away from regular folk, say Cain eventually met Lilith, Adam's *first* wife. And that she got him to drink blood for power, just like a vampire. That they had many children together. Demons and monsters. Some texts even claimed Cain was the bastard son of Satan and Eve. And I now remembered that my dad had said something about how during the Middle Ages people believed Cain had wandered around begging people to kill him and that no one would, so he now lived alone on the moon.

Lying in some shitty motel room somewhere in Pennsylvania with a total stranger who hated me, I could totally picture this. I figured I wasn't too far behind him.

And, reading about Cain, I hadn't replaced my terrible thoughts at all. All I'd done was add to them.

CHAPTER THIRTEEN

I sat outside on the balcony of the motel's second floor, legs slipped beneath the lowest railing and dangling over the dozen rooms below. My fingers wrapped around faded cobalt-blue paint, arms stretched out fully in the warm summer dusk. The motel's parking lot was still completely empty except for three other cars, and I think one of those might have even belonged to the manager.

Castillo was working in our room, just below. I had the sense he was getting kinda frustrated with the whole thing. He could talk about doing research for two years all he wanted, but it seemed like he was also ready to start kicking in some doors and finding some clones.

It probably didn't help that I'd been so pointless with my dad's notes. I hadn't been able to give Castillo any worthwhile information or feedback. How could I? I hadn't really even read that much of them to tell the truth. Didn't want to. When Castillo came back into the room with some food and I handed the laptop back, he'd asked me what I thought and if anything had come to mind, etc., etc. I just made faces like I was thinking really hard and said stuff like "Yeah, some of it did" and I'd have to think about it. I'm pretty sure he knew I was totally full of it. Worse, I had no idea what I was gonna say if he asked me again. I didn't know anything about Jack the Ripper. And apparently I knew even less about my own father.

I spent the whole rest of the afternoon lying on the bed, mostly staring up at the ceiling. Wishing myself asleep, away from my rambling gloomy thoughts. The room was clammy and getting smaller by the minute. I could feel its walls closing in on me. And it was *cold*. I don't know how Castillo could stand it. My whole body was shaking at one point. I'd hoped Castillo might send me out for food again when it was dinnertime, but he'd bought stuff at lunch. Alas. Apparently bologna and bread, and water from the bathroom sink, was enough for lunch *and* dinner. So after my third bologna sandwich, I asked if I could get some fresh air.

Castillo eyed me suspiciously. It was a look I was getting used to.

I thought about saying something like "hey-just-think-of-it-as-another-great-opportunity-for-me-to-run-away-like-you-want-me-to" but didn't. Instead I went with, "I've been in this room, like, all day." I could tell he was trying to process this information, like he couldn't understand why this might be an issue for someone. I was living with a robot. He said sure and told me to stick close. (Maybe he didn't want me running off now, after all.)

Still, I got out of the room as quickly as I could. Castillo'd suggested I buy a soda or something from the main office, but I didn't feel like walking that way. I hadn't liked the way that manager guy had looked at me when I'd asked about the phone, and I didn't want to give him another chance of giving me any crap. So I just wandered along the walkways a couple of times and slowly passed the other rooms. Most every one of them was totally empty. As I passed, I turned a couple of doorknobs and peeked between some curtains into the rooms. They all proved locked, all dark and empty.

But I hadn't checked all the rooms on the second floor yet.

Halfway through, I'd decided to park it awhile. Just rest my elbows and head against the railing while kicking my feet off the ledge. Beyond the hotel I could see my Subway shop and streets and even the main highway heading east and west through Pennsylvania. I thought again of just picking one of those two directions (didn't matter which) and GOING, but the thought didn't last very long. Instead I watched *other* people heading these directions. Their tiny indistinct shapes inside the cars moving by at seventy miles an hour. I imagined what they were heading away from or toward. The options now seemed almost limitless to me.

I closed my eyes and really breathed fresh warm air into my lungs for the first time in what felt like years but had only been a couple of hours. Felt the warmth of the concrete beneath my butt and legs, the strange chill that had latched on to me in the motel room slowly thawing away.

It was funny to think about the whole world just going on. I mean, when shitty things are going on in *your* life, everyone else just kinda carries on. Business as usual. All those people passing had no idea what was going on in the motel room below me. That some guy working for the government was trying to figure out where the teenage clones of serial killers had gotten to. That at a little-known technology lab in Radnor, Pennsylvania, walls were being cleaned of blood. That bodies there had been removed in the middle of the night.

A dozen people already murdered. Not that a dozen seemed all that much to me anymore.

GEOFFREY GIRARD

Castillo's Murder Map showed that close to forty people were getting killed every single day. Not by cloned teenage serial killers, of course. But by *regular* killers. Your normal everyday kinda murderer types. And the amazing thing to me is that it doesn't really slow anybody down. All that murder, I mean.

Sure, if it was something local, you might see it on the news and think and even say, "Oh, that's terrible." But that wouldn't mean you aren't going to work the next day or going to a new movie that same weekend or whatever. It was just another "Oh, that's terrible."

Forty people murdered every day, and everyone just kinda shrugs it off.

I wondered how many bodies it would take to make people really notice.

• • •

I opened my eyes again. The declining sun had begun turning more red on the horizon, and a black pickup had just pulled into the motel's lot under its crimson glow. I watched the truck coast across the empty parking lot. Looked like a guy and a girl, maybe college age. She glanced up at me for a second as they pulled in front of one of the rooms on the opposite side of the motel.

I wanted to get back before Castillo got annoyed and came to look for me. Or before I had to admit he had NO intention of ever looking for me. Neither option was too appealing. So I pulled myself up, watching the girl lean on the back of the truck while the guy went into the office. I moved toward the stairwell to get a better look. She seemed pretty enough from afar. The guy, short hair with random tattoos spotted up both arms, opened up one of the rooms and yelled something I couldn't hear at her.

I suppose I was being nosey, because instead of going down the steps like I'd planned to, I just continued walking slowly along the second floor to the other side. I'd moved away from the railing some so they wouldn't catch me spying. Below, they unloaded two cases of beer and a couple of backpacks. She asked where something was, and he cursed again, even called her a bitch. Up close she was still pretty, but now I wasn't sure if she was college age or not. Sometimes she looked no older than I was, but then again there was something in her voice that made her sound like she was, like, thirty. However old she was, she sounded tired to me. She sounded defeated. I figured it's what I would sound like soon. If I didn't already. Maybe the Subway guy had heard the exact same thing in my voice.

The two had vanished into the room. As the door closed, I heard the guy say something pretty crude about air-conditioning and her privates. She laughed, but even that had that same defeated sound I'd heard before.

I tapped the railing above their room and looked back toward the spot where I'd been sitting. I don't know what I expected to see. Maybe myself staring back, I guess. Some kind of *Alice in Wonderland* mirror thing. I only know I felt like I wasn't alone all of a sudden. I looked down to our room but the door was still shut. No Castillo. I shrugged off the feeling and started moving to the steps again. It was time to get back.

That's when I noticed.

One of the doors behind me was now open.

• • •

Just the narrowest crack. Two rooms away.

I hadn't noticed the opening when I'd passed, but I'd been focused

GEOFFREY GIRARD

on spying then. Don't know if I'd even have detected it from that angle anyway. The only other cars in the lot were on the other side of the motel, our side. I suppose someone could have walked or taken a bus or . . .

I tried remembering whether or not I'd opened the door myself. My hands absently trying each door latch as I'd passed. I didn't think so.

It didn't matter. I would just walk past the door and be on my way. But I didn't.

As I got closer to the room, the door opening seemed wider and wider.

And I'd gotten slower and slower.

The gap showed only total darkness on the other side. The smallest hint of a dark green curtain that, I assumed, covered the inside window. There were no sounds from inside. I knew it was just an empty room, the door left open by some part-time maid days before.

I eyed the darkness within.

Anyone could have been on the other side looking back at me. Anyone at all.

I did not, I'll admit, want to walk past the door and leave it open behind me. No way. So I moved my hand to the latch to pull the door closed, and instead found my hand ON the door, applying pressure. Pushing it more OPEN.

Hello? My high voice vanished into the room like smoke up a chimney.

NOTHING. My hand pressing more and more.

I saw blue carpet, the foot of an empty bed. Then the desk between. It was just like the room Castillo and I were in, but everything was on the opposite walls. The room was empty. No one was here.

I put a foot into the room, my whole body now pressed against the door. My free hand searching for a light switch that I just couldn't seem to find. Everything awash in shadows and the dusk's red. Slowly peeked my head around the corner to see the rest of the empty room.

And then I saw her.

. . .

A woman.

Lying on the second bed facing the ceiling.

She was wearing a long black dress. Her arms extended on either side like Christ, fingers hanging lifeless off the sides of the bed.

There was something wrong with her face.

It was too, too white.

She was wearing a mask of some kind, I decided. Its cheeks and lips painted dark, dark red. Redder than the sun. I could not see the eyes.

Until she turned.

CHAPTER FOURTEEN

*H*e stopped me on the motel steps.

The guy with the tattoos and short hair.

I don't even remember how I really got there or when he appeared.

I knew I'd run. Slammed a door. I remembered half stumbling down those steps. Crouched on the bottom step, my heart racing. Telling myself I'd seen only shadows in that room. There'd been NO woman in there. I had NOT seen her eyes. Those enormous wide-open painted-on eyes. Oversize cartoonish anime eyes.

I needed to pull myself together before I went back in to Castillo. He thought I was enough of a freak without my giving him total proof. If I was losing my mind, I was going to do it alone. He would never know. No one would EVER know. I sure as hell wasn't going to write about it in any damn journal like my father had.

This tattoo guy was all like: "Hey, kid!" and "You're F-in' wasted, man, ain't you?" and "Get this dude!" A real idiot, this one.

I mumbled back some response. Something like HUH? Probably wasn't even English. Didn't exactly come across as a Rhodes scholar myself, I guess. I could barely figure out where I was. Still trying to understand what it was I'd seen in the room. A hallucination, I figured. Some kind of nightmare that'd followed me into the real world.

God knows it wouldn't have been the first time I'd seen something that wasn't really there.

But the days of *blaming* it on a car accident that I now knew never happened wasn't gonna fly anymore.

I needed to pull myself together. Didn't know if I could. Ever.

And the current situation was in no way helped by this guy, this absolute moron, laughing at me. I didn't even have the strength in my legs to stand up and walk away.

He was practically howling. Asking me if I wanted a beer.

Huh? It was apparently the only word I had anymore. I wanted to shout: *HEY, ASSHOLE. HOW 'BOUT YOU LEAVE ME ALONE A MINUTE AND GO UPSTAIRS YOURSELF AND DEAL WITH THAT DEAD LADY ON THE BED.*

But we all know I did no such thing, because (1) What would he possibly do about the imaginary woman upstairs? and (2) I was too chickenshit.

I *did*, however, manage to grab the banister to help pull myself up. It was a start. (Small victories, you know. They were like gold these days.)

He asked again if I wanted a beer. Suggested I was wasted again. Asked now if I wanted to smoke some pot with them. His girlfriend had come to their door. I just kept saying no.

His voice now totally reminded me of another. (Henry's.) 'Cause now he started getting all in-your-face about it. Called me a faggot and stuff. (Now he sounded like Ted.)

I'd somehow made it totally to my feet. I felt like I'd just topped Mount Everest.

Told him "thanks," told him I was "cool." Just meaningless prattle to get away.

Yeah, you're cool, he said. You're cool, kid. Hey . . . hey . . . He was really giggling absolute fits now, could barely finish a thought, and I started really looking at him for the first time. HE was the one who was drunk or high or something. Whatever. Anything to take my mind away from the room upstairs, from whatever trick of light I'd seen. This guy was actually a total godsend.

Then this godsend started in on the sex stuff. Crude stuff again. Like asking if I wanted head from his girlfriend. But he kept calling it "dome," and it took me a while to even get his stupid joke. I'd gathered that her name was Anna, and when he first used her name, I instinctively looked her way. Could have totally died of embarrassment the second I did. She turned away and was probably thinking the exact same thing. Then he said more crude stuff to embarrass me (her, too, I think now), and he'd put his hand on my shoulder.

Exact same kind of bullying Ted would do. I'm telling you. And this guy wasn't some monster created in a lab. He was just a guy. One of those regular everyday types always making things kinda awful.

I shrugged him off me. Embarrassment had become pissed-off in a single blink.

He grinned. Knew he'd gotten to me. Made some kind of teasing *Woo-hoo!* sound. Then he said more crude stuff and started tapping my chest. Laughing in my face.

My new pissed-off state worked just fine. I used it to move, to move down the steps, to move past him easily and along the corridor back toward our room. And I moved quickly. Hell, I think I ran again.

Dude cackled behind me. Kept yelling out after me like: "That's cool!" And "Stop by any time!" and "You know where to find her!"

And I know he was totally talking about his girlfriend, Anna. But all I could think about was the imagined woman upstairs. I absolutely knew where to find her.

I had to knock to get into the room because Castillo'd locked me out. I was leaving one asshole for the safety of another.

What's all that about, Castillo asked, looking over my shoulder toward the guy at the steps and letting me pass through.

You're all assholes, I declared.

Castillo just nodded.

Guess he agreed.

• • •

This is what a killer looks like.

My glasses lay beside the sink. The mirror half-fogged with steam from the shower I was pretending to take. Castillo was in the next room doing something CIA-ish. Two days now in this sketch-assed horrible motel filled with drunks and dead women. These were my choices now.

Deal with asshole strangers and imaginary dead women or stay in the room another hundred days. It was boring times a thousand. I would just watch more TV and pretend to sleep while Castillo researched and waited. Waited for murders.

Each one now a little red dot for the map on the wall. Every reported murder in the last forty-eight hours. Every rape. Every missing person. Precisely when and where the last American life had violently ended. Each red dot an unsolved murder. One of this week's three hundred. Some dots bigger than others. Like Polaris or Sirius shining brighter than the rest in a night sky dripping red with dozens of little crimson dots. Castillo believed that the more brutal murders, like those committed at the Massey Institute, would eventually lead to the six missing boys. He said it was now only a matter of time and making red dots, starting to mark some lines along the various highways, and looking for possible paths. The lines already ran in a hundred different directions.

I noted it was just like connect the dots.

Castillo replied, staring: Just like. But with dead people.

He still totally hated me. The few times he left to get food or make a phone call or something, he'd always come back into the room pissed. Disappointed I was still there. Best just to stay out of the guy's way. Pretending to be asleep, hiding in the bathroom. *Invisible.* It was easy enough to do now. I'd become the invisible boy. The Old Navy clothes and haircut had been just the start. Not a single person on Earth would notice, let alone recognize, me one bit if they saw me. I'd ceased to exist. Not that anyone cared if I did anyway.

I realized my father had spent a great portion of his life making sure no one gave a good goddamn about me. I'd never attended the same summer camp or science camp twice. Never been in the same soccer or basketball league twice. Homeschooled since birth (whatever "birth" meant now). Different piano teachers and instructors every year. We'd even moved three times. I'd been frankly amazed when Mr. Eble had come back for the second year. Hadn't realized my dad was already planning to send him away.

Massey and DSTI were the only places I'd really been to for more than a couple of months. The only people I really knew. And now, according to anyone who would talk to me, they wanted me dead.

This is what a killer looks like.

Looking in the mirror now, I tried to picture myself as I'd been just a day before. Then imagined myself at eighteen. The same age as Jeffrey #54. The *other* one my dad had built in a lab. The one Castillo was chasing after. The one who'd probably helped kill all those people at Massey. Eighteen years old. That was just a couple of years from now. Maybe I'd grow some sideburns or a little soul patch. I'd probably be a couple of inches taller.

I wondered how old all the others were. The other JEFFs. How many were there in the world? According to the notes my father had given me that first night, I was really Jeff #82.

Another seventy copies had died, by both flaw and design, prior to my . . . *birth*.

Seventy.

And I was one of, then, maybe four, five, other Jeffrey Dahmer clones that'd survived.

I thought of a joke I'd heard: What's worse than a barrel full of dead babies?

A live one at the bottom, trying to eat its way out.

That was me.

I tried to imagine him (*me*) at twenty-five. Jeffrey Dahmer #1. The Original. The one in the files. The one who'd murdered seventeen people in cold blood. *That* was the face I was looking for now. The face smashed open with a broom handle because that's what God wanted. It wasn't too hard to imagine at all. I'd seen his pictures in my file. Brown hair dye wasn't enough. It was still the same face underneath. Add a couple of pounds maybe. Not too many.

My fingers pressed into my skin against the skull and jawline beneath. Pressed harder and harder until my nails were digging into the skin. I imagined just tearing. Ripping the flaps of skin away. My hair. Pulling off my cheeks and lips. I realized it wouldn't help, would only make everything worse. The gleaming skull just beneath. The very last thing seventeen people saw just before they were killed.

Maybe not literally *my* face, of course. But they saw it all the same. One that looked identical to mine. Yeah, and no doubt about it. It was the same face in the mirror. HIS face.

I suddenly imagined the face with painted-on eyes. . . .

This is what a killer looks like.

I turned the hot water faucet all the way. It took another minute to steam the mirror completely. Faces, or maybe only the shapes of them, had already appeared in the emerging coating of vapor. But my own had now vanished completely.

Thank God.

CHAPTER FIFTEEN

*C*astillo was pissed.

    I'd finally gotten out of the shower, and he was standing at the front door, eye at the peephole, arms angrily crossed at chest.

Turns out the drunk tattooed jerk from before had a couple of buddies now. And they were all in the parking lot making noise, breaking bottles and stuff. Castillo was totally worried that cops were gonna show up, start asking a bunch of questions. Maybe ask for some ID from the motel's one or two witnesses.

I got the feeling Castillo had 0.0 intention of being a "witness," to have ANY record of him ever being here. To have to explain why a sixteen-year-old kid who clearly wasn't his son was in his room. He stepped outside and calmly tried to get the guys to chill out some. That didn't go so hot. Castillo told me to pack up. He said: It's time to get the hell out of here anyway.

I moved as fast as I could. There were half a dozen reasons to finally get as far away from that place as possible. From open doors to torturous boredom. But the biggest reason of all was I didn't want to piss off Castillo. He looked like he was spoiling for a fight for sure. To that end, he seemed pleased with how fast I got ready. He'd packed even faster. I couldn't even imagine the kinds of places he'd been to in his life. Places in other countries where he'd had to move light and fast. There was no doubt he'd done this a thousand times before.

They were banging on our door now. Shouting stuff. Bored and drunk and stupid. At least two of those three, if not all three.

Castillo's pissed look was more, I think, amused now.

He told me just to stay close and we headed out.

If Castillo was looking for a fight, he got it.

. . .

First they gave us crap right in the doorway, even tried blocking us.

Castillo just kept talking calmly, moving both of us forward to his car.

There were now a couple of cars across the way. The door to their room was open, loud music coming out. There was another girl now too. The guys were saying more crude stuff about me and Castillo. Castillo just kept moving forward. The tattooed guy had gotten into his pickup.

Just get in the car, Castillo told me.

The pickup was now behind us. Blocking us. Castillo tossed our bags into the car, told me to stay put. This was not a problem for me. I twisted around in my seat, watched as he asked them to move the pickup. This went about as well as MY earlier conversation with this same guy.

I was trying to think of something to do, *anything*. Felt like I should lend Castillo a hand. But there was nothing to do. There were four guys out there. All of them in their twenties at least. Maybe if I . . .

Before I could even imagine some fantastical heroism I might have pulled off, it was over. I'm not even sure if I saw most of it happen.

One second, there's four guys surrounding Castillo, giving him shit.

The second later, or maybe ten, there's four guys lying on the ground.

Holding bloody faces and crooked knees. One guy, my tattoo guy, was just out. I mean OUT. Lying in the parking lot like he was sound asleep. Peaceful almost. I swear to God, I thought the guy was dead. (He wasn't.)

Castillo retrieved something from the unconscious guy, the keys, and tossed them to one of the girls. Anna, it was. I could swear she was almost smiling. He told her to find other guys to hang around, and then he got into the car.

There was all this heat and energy coming off his body like the engine of a car that had just driven ten thousand miles. I'd done horseback riding at camp a couple of times (still not a big fan), and that's what it was like. I was sitting next to something extremely powerful.

Too powerful.

Anna moved the pickup. Castillo knew I was staring at him and told me to shut up, even though I hadn't been talking. So I looked away and just stared at the four guys lying on the ground as we slowly backed up.

And then drove away.

As the car exited the parking lot, my eyes moved up from the four broken men.

Up to the second floor just above.

I knew the room there.

She was standing in the window now. The curtain pulled back just enough.

Staring out into the night. Watching our escape.

Her monster cartoon eyes had seen everything.

I spun away from her stare.

Castillo made a sound of disgust and annoyance.

I didn't know if it was directed at those guys he'd beaten up or at me. I dared a final look, but the curtain had already shut again.

• • •

Yeah. I think I was going crazy.

• • •

We drove all that night, the other cars and roadside signs moving by in soft fluid blurs of light and color. It felt almost like moving back through time. I didn't know where we were going, but I don't think Castillo did either. This, surprisingly, helped some. I relaxed knowing that he was just maybe—just a touch, even—as lost and confused as I was. Ha!

I put the seat back some, tried sleeping again. My eyes were so heavy. I hadn't slept for real in a couple of days now. No wonder I was seeing strange women in black dresses. No wonder that delusional monsters from my father's journal (delusions he'd called the THING ON THE BED)—yes, I recognized her for what she was—had somehow become my very own delusions. My own waking nightmares.

Though my father hadn't ever specifically described the THING ON THE BED in the journal writings I'd yet seen, the likeness of her had still, obviously, taken root in my brain. I'd somehow, just like my dad, personified this imaginary woman.

We weren't even related by blood, apparently, and yet somehow my father had infected me anyway. Madness, apparently, was contagious enough without any need for REAL genetics.

The THING ON THE BED had become the THING AT THE WINDOW in a hurry.

There was no doubt that in my twisted mind she'd become the THING CHILLIN' IN THE BACKSEAT OF THE CAR if I didn't get some real sleep in a hurry.

I settled back into the seat, tried relaxing, wrestling away the terrifying chill that very last thought had given me, of that woman sitting directly behind me. Our eyes meeting in the rearview mirror. I shivered the image off. And, even if she had been REAL, some sort of ghost from my father's nightmares who'd found her way into the waking world, Castillo was here.

I'd just seen what he could do. Why should I be concerned, afraid, of some weird lady in a weird mask and black dress? Castillo was still probably the scariest thing I'd ever met.

This would change, of course.

And soon.

• • •

I slept, but it was not good sleep. Far, far from it. In the dream, she was standing in the park surrounded by little children. The Woman. Dozens of little boys and girls played in a circle, chasing and romping around her black dress. Clapping and giggling and saying words I couldn't quite understand. Dream words. In the distance behind them, dark shapes moved about the swing set and wooden fort. There were six dark shapes. One waved to me. I could see his terrible smile. *Hey, Jeffrey!* he said, and laughed. Behind them, still another shape. Taller. Darker. My father. I started moving toward him, but with every step, he seemed farther and farther away from me. I tried calling to him, but nothing. No words would come. In fact, silence had captured everything. There was no sound anywhere now. I looked at The Woman again. Her black dress had grown, was swelling and spreading out in every direction like a living thing. And the children were dropping down into it. *Vanishing.* The blackness enfolded them. Embraced. Enclosed. For they'd all stopped moving and playing. They just stood completely still as if paralyzed, all

GEOFFREY GIRARD

of their heads turned to me, like deer in headlights or a row of dolls on a shelf. First one child and then another and another and . . . Gone. Until all were absorbed into her total blackness. The dark continued to spread, noiselessly swilling over the seesaw and rope bridge. Toward me. I tried stepping backward but found I could not move either. The dark curled first around my toes. Cold. Cold and yet comforting. I knew that if I gave myself over to it, just let it enfold my body, everything would be fine again. I wouldn't know pain or fear or worry ever again. Still, I tried screaming again. *Dad!!!* Nothing. I tried looking back toward the swing set, but he and the others were gone. The blackness had moved to my legs. I looked directly at her now for the first time. I wanted to see that painted face as the darkness consumed me completely. But her face had changed. The big gaping doll eyes and red cheeks and lips were gone. Now the eyes were enormous blue triangles. And the mouth a huge jagged smile that covered the whole bottom half of her face in red. Sharp points up as if smiling, but just looked like thick bloody fangs. It was the face of a painted jack-o'-lantern. Or a monstrous clown. Freezing cold raced up my back and chest, wrapping tight around my throat like icy hands. Strangling me as I stood rooted in place. Its face widened, the blood-red mouth stretching open to reveal more blackness. The invisible hands in the darkness enfolding me squeezed tighter still, trapping my last breath like another soundless scream in my throat. . . .

• • •

I jerked awake. Pressed my arm against the car door to steady myself. My whole body still shaking. Still cold.

Castillo was driving, asked if I was all right. Hadn't even looked over. Yeah, I lied.

• • •

We ate at a Steak 'n Shake at, like, two in the morning. I think it was the best meal I've ever had in my whole life. I told Castillo just that.

Me too, he said.

But he said it sarcastic. He was just being mean.

• • •

Castillo got us a room at the Baymont Inn early that next morning. We both collapsed into our beds immediately, but I don't think either one of us slept very much. I knew when I woke, it'd be another day of watching TV with the sound off and trying to stay out of Castillo's way. Of trying to think of some way, *any* way, to help.

For the first time I thought about giving Castillo my father's phone number. The new one he'd told me to call if I needed anything. The number he hadn't answered that whole first night and the next day, too. Maybe he'd pick up if Castillo rang. Maybe he and Castillo could work this whole thing out together. Figure out what had really happened at DSTI and where these six guys were and even how to get my dad back home.

They both seemed like two guys who could handle something as simple as that.

This is the thought I carried as I finally slipped into glorious unconsciousness.

Hey. Jacobson . . .

It was Castillo. Already shaking me awake. It felt like only four seconds had passed, but, squinting at the room's little digital clock, I saw that it had been most of the morning. It was past noon.

I fought to wake. Sat up, reached around for my glasses.

We gotta go, he said. Told me to hurry up. He was staring at his smartphone.

Where? I asked groggily.

Harrisburg, he said.

We're going to a baseball game, he said.

It was not, you'll agree, the strangest thing I'd heard that week.

CHAPTER SIXTEEN

*T*he Harrisburg Senators were hosting the Erie SeaWolves. I'd never heard of either team and was only vaguely aware of the cities. The minor-league ballpark in Harrisburg was mostly packed, maybe five thousand people. After several days living in almost constant silence in my own house, the car, and a twenty-by-twenty motel room, you'd think I would have welcomed all their company. I didn't. I actually found their combined noise and bustle kinda distressing.

We were there for some guy called Ox.

He was some contact of Castillo's who might know something about what was going on. Specifically about what Shardhara was and what my father's notes on that might mean. Funny. With, like, several teenage serial killers running around in the world, Castillo was apparently still mostly interested in this one map and cryptic mentions of this Shardhara place. And I also could tell Castillo was a little nervous about the meeting. It wasn't like he'd just called this Ox guy on the phone and they'd agreed to get together. Apparently Castillo had had to use special foreign websites and routers with hard-core cryptogram stuff to reach this guy. And even then it had just been a long shot that this guy would ever write back. He moved around a lot, was hard to get ahold of. But he did write back, and so there we were. What concerned Castillo the most, I think, was the speed with which Ox had set up the meeting. Sure, it had taken him a couple of days to get Castillo's message, but once he had, it was: *Bam! Meet me in Harrisburg somewhere public.*

Castillo bought the tickets and led us to our seats somewhere past third and closer to the outfield. I don't even think he went to where our tickets were for. I stayed close behind him the whole way. He stopped briefly and paid ten bucks for the program and bought us two Cokes and four hot dogs when we sat down. Not because he thought I was hungry or anything. I knew it was all just part of the disguise. Camouflage. Making us look as normal as possible. I had to give him credit for trying.

I asked Castillo how long it would be before this Ox guy showed up. Castillo, of course, totally ignored my question. He was excellent at that. I'd grown up with adults hanging on my every word. Tutors, speech therapists, counselors, my dad . . . This guy gave me as much thought as the hot dog he'd just eaten. So I settled into my seat and kept quiet. I tried following the pregame stuff. There was a guy dressed as a giant tooth being chased around the bases by a little kid (still no clue what that was about), and then a race between two fans from the stands now dressed up as Mr. Ketchup and Mr. Mustard. I had never been to a baseball game before.

It was not the kind of place my father had ever taken me.

• • •

To that point, I know next to nothing about sports. I discovered this on one of my soccer teams when the other guys were talking excitedly about people I'd never heard of. So I studied sports the way I studied history or geometry. Spent a good half an hour every day. It wasn't too hard to look up on the Internet the names and teams I needed to know. This is also how I learned about important things like popular movies and music and popular Web stuff. Important if you don't want to look like the horribly clichéd, homeschooled, spelling bee geek. But being homeschooled had nothing to do with it, did it?

My "peers" were—unknown to me at the time—all eight years older than I was. And when they'd all been watching *Family Guy* for the hundredth time, I'd been—I now understood—just learning to talk.

• • •

The stadium announcer's deep steady voice echoed over the whole stadium like the voice of God, and the God voice was saying something about "Bark in the Park" (an upcoming event for dogs) and Applebee's Military Monday, when all veterans could attend the game for free. I imagined the same voice saying, *WHERE IS ABEL, THY BROTHER? WHAT HAST THOU DONE?*

When they did the National Anthem, I put my hand over my heart like Castillo and everyone else, but when everyone else cheered and clapped at the end, Castillo just sat down. So I did that also. The SeaWolves were up, and after the very first batter got on base, it was a pop-up to the catcher, and then the third batter hit into a double play to end the inning. The home crowd cheered. It was a good sound. I flipped absently through the program Castillo had bought. The first Senators player, a little guy named Hackman out of Ohio, took a high strike for the first pitch. The crowd booed the umpire. Castillo sat, still and patient, beside me. The next pitch, the guy knocked the heck out of it, and it went sailing up and out. Everyone but Castillo tensed for half a second and then settled back as the ball sailed foul right, deep into the stands directly across from us. The stadium's JumboTron in center field showed a couple of kids scrambling around their seats for the ball. Kinda funny. On the screen one of them finally lifted his hand up with the prize.

I looked back across the field to where, for real, the ball had just landed.

That's when I saw the face of Richard Guerrero.

At least fifty feet high and thirty across. A giant's face absorbing—or more like superimposed on, maybe—whole sections of the stadium.

• • •

Before I explain who Richard Guerrero is, I need to explain the faces.

Have only tried to do this three times in my whole life. This'll be the fourth and last.

First time was to a counselor at the Massey Institute. I was, I thought, maybe eleven or twelve at the time. She prodded me for as much detail as possible and then wrote down everything I said. She'd given me no thoughts at all on what this was or how to fix it. She'd, in retrospect, merely been gathering data for my father and his colleagues. They'd probably been thrilled. The second time had been with Amanda Klosterman, a girl I'd met at science camp. The third time would be Castillo. You're fourth.

For as long as I can remember (over however many years we're calling my life), I have seen faces in very odd places. In clouds, the wood grain of a table at some restaurant, within a shelf of books, a folded shower curtain, a dirty pile of clothing.

Or, as another example, in a paintball field, or even in dyed water running down a shower drain. . . . You get the idea.

Scientists call this phenomenon "pareidolia"—when people recognize shapes, patterns, and familiar objects in random stuff. One of the most popular forms of pareidolia is recognizing faces. A toaster or the back of a car or pancake or whatever looks kinda like a face. There's eye potential, a mouth, maybe a nose. Experts claim it's so important as a survival instinct for us to recognize and respond to the countless forms of the human face that we're looking for them constantly, unconsciously. So just about everyone recognizes something that looks like a face every now and then and in the most unexpected of places. Some people just do it more than others.

The faces I saw were more complicated than two circles for eyes and a straight-lined mouth. What I saw usually had hair, eyebrows, lips, ears. Shades of color. Eyes with pupils and everything. For years I wrote it off as coincidence. A funny trick of the light. My stupid imagination. But then I just kept seeing them. Not every day or even every month. But every couple of months for sure and sometimes for a couple of days in a row. (I was clearly in hyperdrive *this* week!) Eventually I realized there were patterns in what I was seeing. For instance, I could tell now that all the faces were the faces of men. Some of them had white faces, but most of the others were darker. At first I thought it was just the same face shown different ways.

But these were *distinct* and familiar faces. The same ten, maybe more, guys, over and over. I didn't know any of them then. I couldn't connect them to real people in my life. I figured they might be people I knew from "before the accident." Some half-formed memory. And, in a way, they were.

Online I found all sorts of information about other people who claimed to see faces. Mostly right when they were falling asleep. But most of what I found talked about weird stuff like astral projection and past lives and something called the Akashic Records, which is like a universal storeroom for all human knowledge that can be accessed during deep meditation. None of this was too helpful, so I basically just went around for years weirded out by it all.

The mystery was solved only when my father handed me that folder. Inside, remember, were pictures of all of Jeffrey Dahmer's known victims. Pictures with names.

I'd looked only at the top sheet. Hadn't known any of the names.

Their faces, however . . .

I'd recognized every one.

. . .

So now Richard Guerrero's face was in the stadium directly across from me.

One of the few names I'd recently learned, but a face I'd seen more than a dozen times in my life.

A cotton candy vendor here, a couple of empty blue seats there. Some white shirts, an aisle of concrete steps. A massive collage of colors and shapes forming into a single distinguishable *something*. Ordinarily I would just look away. Not allow the face to form any more than it already had. But this time I would not (or could not) look away. I saw everything.

The long thin face and extended chin, the big sad puppy-dog eyes, stuffed lips, the hint of a thin mustache even.

A memory of mine. A killing memory.

. . .

Richard Guerrero was murdered on March 24, 1988. That day, he was given a drink laced with sleeping pills and then strangled. His remains were removed in pieces in the garbage for the next several weeks. This all happened in the house of Catherine Dahmer. One of three murders there. Eventually Catherine Dahmer got tired of the chemical smells and the noises from her basement and she kicked her grandson, Jeffrey, out of her house.

• • •

Castillo asked where I was going. I'd lurched up from my chair. I was stammering back some sort of reply. Who knows what I said, but I finally claimed to need to go to the bathroom. Castillo eyed me suspiciously per usual. There was sweat on my forehead, trickling down my back. I think my whole body was shaking. But he nodded. Told me to hurry up.

There was no one sitting next to either one of us, so it was pretty easy to get up and out to the steps and down to the bathrooms. I didn't really need to go, of course, but I sure needed to change the scenery. I knew I hadn't killed Richard Guerrero. He'd been dead twenty years before I'd been born. And yet . . . I *had* killed Richard Guerrero.

The skin and bones and hair and heart I was walking around Harrisburg with were the exact same that had been in that Milwaukee room in 1988. Like one of those Russian nesting dolls that you keep opening up and finding another smaller one just like it within. That was me, a "smaller" Jeffrey Dahmer. I could not deny this, as much as I tried while shuffling, half-dazed, to the nearest bathroom.

I tried peeing just for something to do, but it took, like, five minutes for a couple of drops. I washed my hands and caught myself staring at the mirror again. I reset my glasses, studied my own face like I was looking at it for the very first time.

The last face Richard Guerrero had ever seen.

I guess it was only fair I had to look at *his* face now.

Marvelous night for baseball, a deep voice said beside me.

I turned. Fully expected to find Richard Guerrero standing there. His swollen neck bruised all purple and black. Or even a woman in a black dress. Why not? I was fully prepared to go downright insane at this point. Embrace it, you know?

Instead at the next sink was a black man who nodded hello to me. Not a hallucination. About my size, gold rounded glasses, a slender goatee, and a shaved head beneath a red Senators baseball cap. He wore a burgundy silk suit, a pair of large Chinese-style goldfish embroidered in crimson across his button-down shirt.

Sorry? I said.

A glorious night for a baseball game, he said again.

Yeah, I replied dreamily, I guess so.

Go, Senators, he said, and grinned hugely and turned back to his own sink and mirror.

I lumbered slowly from him and the bathrooms, the memory of Richard Guerrero's face waning at last. When I took my seat, Castillo didn't say anything at first. We just sat there in silence as usual and watched the next couple of batters. I'm not even sure I knew which team was which anymore. I made a point of trying to refocus on that. On something—*anything*—real.

I stole a quick look at where the face had been and saw only people.

Castillo asked me if everything was good.

I turned. Thought about it.

I didn't know the answer. I didn't know much of anything anymore. I for sure didn't know that I'd just met Ox.

CHAPTER SEVENTEEN

*H*e arrived an inning later. The black guy in silk. I was kinda shocked when he first entered our row, but then Castillo stood to greet him and I figured out who it was. Ox hugged Castillo warmly, then shook my hand. Marvelous night for baseball, he said, and winked at me.

Castillo sat down again, sarcastically thanked Ox for dressing so "covertly," and Ox grinned back, taking the empty seat next to Castillo. Covert enough, Ox said. (I loved that smile already. His was a smile that said, *No matter how shitty things had been or were or would be, things were really all right in the grand scheme of things.* It was a much-needed attitude during all of this.)

Right away Castillo asked about Shardhara.

No messing around here. He'd called Ox for one thing, and he'd waste no time getting to it.

If Ox knew what Shardhara really was, maybe some of my father's other notes and plans would start to fall into place. It was a puzzle piece that could maybe pull so much more of the picture together. At least enough for Castillo to find my father. Maybe the others. Maybe enough to end all of this.

Ox tilted his head, said: Never heard of it.

• • •

About Ox.

He was raised in Nashville.

His father was a minister with the Church of Christ Holiness USA who'd hosted a lecture by Martin Luther King the day before King was shot. His mother had died a couple of months after Ox was born. He'd been raised by his grandmother, who was the daughter of former slaves and had been a famed psychic and healer in Nashville until her death at age 105.

He'd done ROTC in college and learned computer programming and software development. He'd been in the military for almost twenty years and had lived in seven different countries. In the Army he'd been a cook, a demolition expert, or a lieutenant who'd trained Special Forces for Afghanistan. His story changed depending on who he was talking to. In all cases, the job he gave was a cover for his real role: working with the CIA to recruit and nurture relationships with dozens of tribal leaders and factions during the war.

It was in this time that he'd met and befriended Castillo.

He has no doubt that the Loch Ness Monster is real. Bigfoot, too. His favorite movies are *Escape from New York* and *The Magnificent Seven*. His favorite singers are named George Jones and Prince. (I don't much care, despite his best efforts, for either.)

He'd been in jail for six months in Kentucky on weapons charges. He has a very young wife and two young sons. He is bald by choice only, and every other year grows a thick Afro to "confound The Man."

He likes to play the card game Magic. He makes his own beer and ice cream. He says things like "The lion takes no counsel from the warthog" and "When you're roasting two potatoes, one of them is bound to get charred."

He believes that the government isn't worried about giving everyone false answers all the time because it has successfully gotten everyone to ask the wrong questions.

• • •

Castillo doubted that Ox had just driven nine hundred miles just to say he didn't know anything. Or to watch the SeaWolves play baseball.

Ox retorted he might have driven *eleven* hundred miles to see an old friend, and then raised his hand for the beer vendor. What'd you contact *me* for anyway? he asked.

You know something about everything, Castillo replied.

Ox's face had gone blank in thought. No emotion, no response as he focused only on the game below.

That bad? Castillo asked.

But before saying anything more, Ox first wanted to know more about what Castillo was involved in. They both spoke in hushed voices beneath the game's noise. I could hardly hear them myself.

Castillo had just apologized, said he couldn't get too specific. Ox's eyes had narrowed some, a trace of irritation. He requested a "taste," just to make sure he and Castillo were on the same page. Said he didn't want any "unspecified nastiness" coming upon him and his family.

So Castillo told him the basics: that a private company was doing shitty things for his and Ox's former bosses. Horrible shitty. Involved experiments. Kids. Civilian deaths. And someplace or someone named Shardhara. Their bosses had said they had no clue what that meant, but Castillo could tell when people were bullshitting him, which they

GEOFFREY GIRARD

were on this topic. He also noted how quickly Ox had gotten back in touch.

Ox kept looking only at me now.

You one of the kids? he asked.

I glanced nervously at Castillo, who nodded that it was OK to reply.

Yes, sir, I said.

For the first time, Ox stopped smiling.

• • •

Castillo noted that Ox didn't seem too surprised by any of this, and Ox replied that nothing had surprised him since he was four, and then he teased Castillo for still being puzzled by such things.

Castillo leaned back in his seat and admitted that he had been surprised by some of what he'd seen this week.

And that's why I love you. Ox's smile had returned, and he looked directly at me again. You working with a man who still believes in GOOD GUYS and BAD GUYS, he told me.

(My first thought: *Thank God.*)

Ox was trying to get a rise out of Castillo, and it had worked. Castillo argued he'd worked some "morally questionable" operations in his day. That he wasn't a "child." That he knew the US military had to "cross the line" sometimes.

Cross the line. Ox snickered at that phrase, then sipped his beer.

He asked: You know your history, boy? He'd asked me, technically, but had been totally looking at Castillo when he did. I figured he was using me to make some kind of point to Castillo. I was a prop. Then he asked me if I knew about the Nazis.

Sure, I replied. He must have thought I was four years old or something. (Which, I suppose, is technically closer to the truth than sixteen, but Ox did not know that then. He was just making his point. And so I looked at him like it was a stupid question, accordingly.)

Ox said: The Nazis were famous for killing millions and conducting lethal experiments on humans, right? Famous for being evil? And these United States of America got rid of the evil Nazis. Yes? Only problem is, at the exact same time, the USA was *also* conducting lethal experiments on humans.

I looked straight at Castillo, who was looking back at me. We were both thinking the same thing. Ox still had no clue how bad it'd gotten at DSTI. Castillo'd admitted to the experiments, but not the specifics yet. And as horrifying as those specifics were, I admit: It was nice sharing a secret with someone like Castillo. It was the only real connection we had, I guess.

The government *still* is, I said.

Ox winked.

Well, of course, he said.

• • •

He told us a story about this guy named Cornelius Rhoads, an American scientist who purposely put cancer cells into a bunch of people. They all died. The United States had recently invaded Puerto Rico, and this guy began using underprivileged Puerto Ricans for his tests, so no one really paid much attention to what was going on. A local politician named Campos got ahold of some letters where this American scientist was bragging about killing all these Puerto Rican people, and Campos went to the American newspapers with the letters. His reward? This Campos guy was arrested for being a "terrorist" and spent the next *twenty years* in a Puerto Rican jail, where he was declared insane and Dr. Rhoads used *him* as a subject for radiation experiments. Can you believe that? Dr. Rhoads was soon promoted to run the US Army Biological Warfare department.

Ox said: Research it yourself sometime online. Some days it's almost funny.

Ox then said: Before you can truly appreciate Shardhara, you gotta know your history.

• • •

Ox talked for, like, two hours. It was probably only ten minutes, but it was definitely a monologue and one he'd clearly given before. I tried to follow as much of it as I could. Castillo, I saw, was doing the same. Listening like a kid with a test the next day and really trying to learn the material.

Here's what I can remember:

1. The Department of Defense recently admitted, despite a dozen different treaties banning research and development of biological agents, that it *still* operated biological-agent research facilities in more than *one hundred* institutions and universities across the nation. One hundred illegal projects! And that's just what they'd been forced to admit.

2. When the Manhattan Project scientists finished the world's first atomic bomb, they started a second project: injecting plutonium directly into hundreds of American men, women, and children. Their mission was to study the effects of exposure to atomic weapons. Their very first test subject was a civilian who'd *simply had a car accident near the lab*. One of their last tests was giving irradiated milk to disabled orphans.

3. Ten years later, these same military scientists were dropping light-bulbs filled with *Bacillus subtilis* (a common flu) in the New York subway system, just to see how effective biological weapons would

work on a large population. Within four days, a million New Yorkers were infected. It was just for practice. (Ox said the military loves to practice.) Later the Senate confirmed that more than two hundred populated areas in America were deliberately contaminated with biological agents between 1949 and 1969. Places like San Francisco, DC, Key West, Minneapolis, St. Louis. The CIA had forty *different* universities and drug companies working on this.

4. Something called MK-ULTRA. A covert drug test secretly given to military personnel, mental patients, prostitutes, and the general public to study if psychotic drugs could be a potential weapon: LSD, heroin, morphine, pot, whatever. They kept people stoned 24/7 for weeks, just to "see what would happen."

That's when Ox asked me if they'd taught anything about Tuskegee in school. I told him I didn't go to *school*-school but that I still knew what the Tuskegee experiment was. My father might not have cared much about baseball, but we had talked about science and its history a lot. Between him and my various camps and science tutors, I knew my scientific facts pretty well.

Ox looked at me, curious. Told me to go for it. So I told him what I knew.

That American government scientists got a bunch of poor farmers, African-Americans, in the South and gave them fake treatments for some disease. They could have cured them but let more than a hundred die just to see how the disease progressed.

Ox nodded in approval and asked how I knew all that. I told him my dad was a scientist. There was still a touch of pride when I said it. I did not add that this same scientist had maybe engineered six killers and somehow helped them escape and had maybe been involved in the murder of a dozen people.

His dad's most definitely a scientist, Castillo said. HE, however, was not saying it like it was a good thing. It was clear that Castillo knew my dad as only one thing.

Ox thought about that a long while. I think he was still trying to figure out how I fit into all of this. What exactly my father DID as a scientist. He knew he wasn't here to discuss food dyes or plastics or the weather.

Ox told me it wasn't just any old scientists at Tuskegee. It was the US Public Health Service, and they infected hundreds in Guatemala also, which America had invaded in 1901. Mostly institutionalized mental patients, with diseases like gonorrhea and syphilis without the patients' knowledge or permission. The infected were even encouraged to pass the disease on to others as part of the study.

Again, just to SEE WHAT WOULD HAPPEN.

It was sounding all too familiar.

. . .

Ox then gave this huge list of secret tests the US military had conducted over the years. He'd put his beer down between his feet and was ticking them off on his fingers faster than I could even count: Project Artichoke. Project Paperclip. Third Chance. QK-Hilltop. Project Derby Hat. The names were almost hysterical. But when I looked them up later on Google, I learned how many people had maybe died and it didn't seem so silly anymore. Project Chatter. Camelot. Operation Whitecoat. Montauk. MK-SEARCH. MK-NAOMI. MK-OFTEN. Project 112. Project SHAD. DTC Test 69-12. H.R. 15090. Big Tom. Fearless Johnny. The Philadelphia Experiment. Program F. (Have fun brushing your teeth tonight, he added. He'd grinned at me with that last, and I had no idea what the heck he was talking about, but it was the first one I looked up later.)

And now he could add PROJECT CAIN to his list.

• • •

Ox warned that we wouldn't find out the real truth about any of these projects (not even Project Cain, it turns out) until years and years from now. When it was finally declassified. When people were too old to worry about being silenced or punished for talking. When there were worse things to think about. He said it wasn't until 1995 that Americans learned that four hundred people had been injected with plutonium fifty years earlier. With the admission decades after the fact, there was also an apology. Apparently the government *always* did it that way. The US apologized for the experimentations on Pedro Campos in 1994. Apologized for the LSD tests in 1995. Apologized for Tuskegee in 1997. Apologized for Guatemala in 2010.

Ox asked Castillo how long before the government apologized for what they'd done to the US soldiers in Iraq and Afghanistan. Vets like they are. He was referring to all sorts of dangerous chemicals American troops had been exposed to, chemicals almost entirely provided courtesy of the US military. Various injections and radiated bullets and toxins. I could tell from Castillo's face that there was enough truth to the claims Ox was making. It seemed to me that some of this was accepted and well known and some of it was still totally hush-hush.

Ox asked: When will the government admit to all of it in public? When will they officially apologize to *us*?

Or to us? I wondered out loud, the words just escaping.

I was thinking about ALL the kids at Massey. Those that'd been murdered, those still on the run. And, well, me too.

Ox looked at me. We'll all be dead first, he said.

And he wasn't just talking old age.

• • •

Ox told us more about the government's top secret MK-ULTRA/ LSD tests, and about Dr. Frank Olson.

Frank Olson was the scientist in charge of the whole MK-ULTRA project. During the project, he'd directed a covert test in 1951 done on a small French village called Pont-Saint-Esprit, where LSD-derived toxins were dispensed throughout the town by American scientists. Ten people died and thirty spent the rest of their lives in a mental institution.

Olson knew the experiment was WRONG and so he quit. Maybe he'd planned to go to the *New York Times* or *60 Minutes* or something with the whole story, right? No one ever found out. A few days later it was reported in all the papers that Olson had committed suicide by jumping out a thirteenth-story window. That there'd been LSD in his system.

His family didn't believe ANY of this and fought for the truth for the next forty years. And when Olson's body was finally exhumed in 1994, the medical examiner termed the death a "homicide" and pointed to cranial injuries that indicated Olson had been knocked unconscious *before* he'd exited the window.

The United States apologized for that too and then paid his family $750,000.

• • •

Ox said: You understand yet? What they're willing to do? These fucking people.

Ox said: You think a dozen, a hundred, kids matter to these guys?

They don't, Castillo agreed. So tell me about Shardhara.

...

Ox had gotten this story from a soldier he'd met through some doctor he'd known at a veterans hospital in Miami. Ox had gotten talking about secret government tests one day, and the doctor had kinda laughed it all off and mentioned this one guy who'd once hinted at some pretty wild claims. Ox got the guy's name, and when they met, he could tell this second guy had just been waiting/begging to tell someone, *anyone*, who just might believe.

To get it off his conscience. To finally let Shardhara out.

This guy was Sergeant First Class Hollyman.

In 2008 (as Hollyman had told it to Ox and Ox told it to us), Hollyman and five other soldiers escorted a couple of Defense Department agents on some secret mission into northern Afghanistan. They were always doing "secret" missions so it was no big deal at the time. Shardhara was a typical remote Afghanistan village. No electricity or running water. Depopulated. Overrun and controlled by the Taliban. Hollyman figured it was a standard operation: capture some weapons, maybe shoot a couple of Bad Guys, done. Then he was ordered to pull on an NBC (Nuclear, Biological, and Chemical) suit, like a hazmat suit for biological weapons like sarin or mustard gas. And a biological weapon is exactly what they found.

The village had been destroyed. Everyone dead. *Everyone*. The bodies apparently shredded by a hundred bullets, folk hacked to bits. Missing limbs. Ripped apart. Bitten. Men and women stripped naked and attacked. Hollyman and the other soldiers couldn't make sense of it. Some kind of Taliban reprisal, they thought, but the twenty Taliban soldiers there were just as dead as the villagers. They found kids dead with knives, what looked like self-inflicted wounds. They

GEOFFREY GIRARD

found only one survivor. An old crazy woman they located in one of the huts. Hollyman told Ox that she'd been eating the dead. Just sitting on the floor, eating the bodies that surrounded her.

Zombies, I said out loud. It's all I could imagine.

Wasn't *that* crazy, Ox said. The dead were dead. The old woman was just insane. Hollyman said he wanted to pull the trigger himself but the Defense Department agents wouldn't let him. They took the woman away, lifted her out by one of the copters, and then started collecting samples. Air samples. Dirt. Water. Tissue and blood from the dead. You name it. Apparently they spent half the day collecting what they needed, then burned it all. The bodies, fields, livestock, dogs, everything.

What did Hollyman think it was? Castillo asked.

What do *you* think it was? Ox challenged. He knew he'd just revealed a heck of a lot more about what was going on than Castillo had. Still, Ox continued. Hollyman knew only that the Defense Department had tested *something*. Something biological had been used on these people. He didn't know what it was, but he said he'd never seen nothing like it in his whole life. Said the crazy woman, the woman's eyes . . . Not even in his nightmares. Hollyman was his detachment's senior medical sergeant. He'd seen plenty to have nightmares about. Said he'd burned *things* that day. Not people. *Things*.

Castillo asked if he could get ahold of Hollyman, but then Ox said the guy killed himself with a shotgun two years ago.

Suicide? Castillo questioned suspiciously.

Ox agreed it was a shady death and then noted it'd been open season on scientists for years.

More than three hundred Iraqi scientists have been killed since the war began—in accidents, bombings, and suicides. More recently it's been the Iranians. Check and see yourself which Iranian scientist was mysteriously blown up, misplaced, or poisoned this month.

But that's our enemy, Castillo argued. If Hollyman's death was somehow faked, now you're talking about the United States government eliminating US civilians.

Civilians, Ox said, and laughed. Hollyman was ex-military, not a civilian. Then he asked: And, what's that word even mean to a country that's been at continual war for sixty years? You want dead Americans, dead "civilians," go to bioweapons. It'd been a decade of "DNA guys" dying mysteriously, and he found Castillo's naïveté on all this almost funny. Or perhaps he was only trying to hide how terrified he really was by making light of it.

Just like the LSD guy who'd died so peculiarly. Ox was talking about the government actively killing American scientists to cover its tracks. American scientists who specialized in bioweapons and DNA research. American scientists like my own father.

• • •

- DNA expert Dr. David Schwartz stabbed to death in Virginia.

- DNA expert Dr. Don Wiley, a Harvard teacher, shows up floating in the Mississippi.

- DNA expert Dr. David Kelly worked for the Navy—found dead after somehow slashing his wrists *and* throat and then dragging himself a mile away from his home.

- DNA expert Dr. Franco Cerrina found dead in his lab at Boston University. Cause of death still unknown.

- DNA expert Dr. John Clark, the guy who ran the lab that made Dolly the sheep, and spoke out against cloning afterward, was found hanging in a remote cottage.

- Bioweapons expert Dr. John Wheeler found dead in a Delaware landfill.
- Bioweapons expert Dr. Robert Schwartz found murdered in his home in Virginia.
- Bioweapons expert Bruce Edwards Ivins, of the United States Army Medical Research Institute of Infectious Diseases, found dead from an apparent overdose. Of *TYLENOL*! No autopsy was permitted.

• • •

Look these names up yourself. Until I did, I didn't believe it either. It's an American egghead bloodbath.

• • •

For the record, DNA expert Dr. Gregory Jacobson, my father, is officially listed as the victim of a workplace shooting rampage.

For the record, this is a total lie.

He died another way.

• • •

Castillo thanked Ox and apologized for not being able give him any more information in return yet but hoped to someday.

Ox seemed cool with that and told Castillo to check in anytime. Then he asked Castillo about someone named Kristin, and Castillo got all weird. You could tell right away he didn't like talking about her. Whoever she was. (I, of course, had not met her yet but soon would. Turns out she meant an awful lot to Castillo. To all of us, really.)

I was pretty damn curious about this girl now. This Kristin. I think at this point it was the only piece of personal information I had about Castillo. I'd just learned that he may or may not have once dated a girl named Kristin. Wow. The full extent of how close we now were.

Before I had time to learn anything more, Ox said something strange. Something about "GHOSTS." Some kind of "exercise" that Kristin had taught the two of them. I couldn't make any sense of it, and Castillo shut down the conversation pretty quick.

We'll leave first, Castillo said, and stood to go. I followed him.

Ox tipped his red Senators hat at the two of us. Wished us well.

Castillo nodded. I kept quiet. When we were down the steps and about to vanish into the tunnels that led out of the stadium, I turned for a last look at Ox.

He, of course, was already gone.

CHAPTER EIGHTEEN

*W*e sat in the car in the middle of the ballpark's parking lot. The sun had almost set, and the stadium lights were now on and shimmering like heaven or something above us. All the surrounding cars were empty because it was only, like, the fifth inning. Castillo hadn't spoken a word yet. Hadn't even put his key into the car. He just stared straight ahead, thinking, processing, hands on the wheel like we were actually driving somewhere. I sat perfectly still too, moronically looked ahead like I was enjoying the scenery.

Richard Guerrero's face was now just the dimmest of shapes ghosted on the windshield. I almost had to concentrate and fight to keep it there at all. I wanted to tell Castillo about what I'd seen but decided it had no bearing on what he was doing. Did it really matter that I and maybe the other clones had some kind of weird retro-physiological link to our original selves? That this Dahmer guy's victims had been burned forever genetically into my eyeballs somehow? Maybe. Maybe it mattered a whole lot and I was just too stupid to understand that yet. Regardless, Castillo already thought I was sickening enough, without adding any of this weirdness to the picture. So I kept quiet.

I thought about the last time I'd told anyone about seeing these faces. I mentioned her before: Amanda Klosterman. Met her at Summer Science, this two-week camp I went to once at McDaniel College in Maryland.

This camp was two weeks of experiments and lectures and games and group projects. Building robots or recording devices from scrap parts, erecting fish hatcheries, tests with lasers and solar power, etc. This was two years ago now. It was a pretty good camp. I was always a big fan of these things because I was off the radar again. At home, everyone (the students at Massey or my tutors) thought of me as the kid with the dead mom. The kid who'd been in a coma or something and talked a little funny. The boss's kid. But at these camps, I was just Jeff Jacobson. I could be anything I wanted. Every new camp was another opportunity to reinvent myself. I could become the goth kid or the arty hipster kid or maybe even the jock if I wanted. (I do NOT exactly suck at soccer, I'll have you know.) Of course, I never actually reinvented myself all that much. It was always a good idea the night before or on the drive to these places, but by the time I got there, I was still always just me. Too quiet, low-flying, and just sorta watching everyone else. The world already had enough legitimate goths and hipsters and skate rats and frat boys, etc., in the mix and didn't need a two-week imposter.

So I was being my typical quiet unimposing self on the second day when we were given the task of making a paper airplane. First we'd all gotten an hour-long lecture and demonstration of how airplanes and flight worked. We studied models and watched videos with birds, bats, bugs, and airplanes, from the Wright brothers' *Flyer* to modern stealth jets. We had a half hour to craft a plane that was "mostly made of

134

paper" and that flew the farthest using anything else we could find in the room. The only other rule was NO TEST FLIGHTS. Each plane could be flown only once, and that would be in front of everyone. It was pure chaos for the next thirty minutes as sixty kids fought for glue and balsa sticks and paper clips and string and just about anything else we could get our hands on.

There were some amazing planes built that day. Long dowel-enforced tails, or shaped like butterflies, double edged, double hulled, double winged, you name it. One kid made one about three feet long that looked exactly like an X-Wing Fighter ... in thirty minutes. When time was up, they brought us all out into a long courtyard, and we took turns flying our inventions. There was a lot of crash and burn that day, planes making it only a couple of feet before nose-diving straight into the ground, but most people took it pretty good. Lots of cheers no matter what the planes did, really. Several took off about forty-plus feet, and one kid's made it all the way to the end of the courtyard, like fifty *yards*. He looked as surprised as any of us. The rest of us were now fighting for second and third place.

My plane was this: I'd taken a couple of coins from my pocket and put them into the center of several pieces of paper, which I'd balled up and then taped with some masking tape. It was a ball of paper. When I stood up at the launch spot, I got some Ooohs and Ahhs from the crowd and one kid shook his head approvingly and smiled. "Nice." I backed up and ran up to the line and tossed it. The thing went *forty-two* yards! Now I got a couple of "unfairs" and "stupids" mixed in with the cheers. I was feeling pretty good in second as the other designers took their turns.

Amanda Klosterman went a couple of people after me. Amanda

Klosterman's plane was the size of a nickel. She hadn't even folded it or anything. It was just a normal little square piece of paper. A couple of kids were laughing. But others—me too—had crowded in for a better look. The instructors looked rather amused about the whole thing as Amanda Klosterman waited and waited. Waiting for wind. She hadn't been the first to do that, but when a breeze finally swept again into that courtyard, she *was* the first to just lift her hand up and do nothing.

Her "plane" rose from her hand like a magic trick, swirled in two circles just above her hand, and then sprang up and over all our heads. The whole courtyard watched as the paper then glided down the courtyard, snaking and rippling this way and that along unseen currents. Sometimes lifting twenty feet into the air before drifting back down into the courtyard and skimming just feet from the ground. It floated and wandered freely in the air for minutes that seemed like hours, and then, as we'd all hoped it would/could, her paper finally lifted up out of the courtyard entirely and disappeared forever. The whole camp went nuts. We all spent days making reference to the fact that Amanda Klosterman's plane was probably still flying around somewhere.

We got certificates for First, Second, and Third places and got special desserts at dinner that night that we could share with our smaller teams. Amanda was, like, the most popular girl in the whole camp now, so I was a bit shocked when she came up to me. She said she liked my design a lot and that we were both working on variations of the same idea: FREEDOM. She told me the only science she liked was the kind that proved we still didn't know all that much and had a long way to go before we did. She told me the best kind of science

GEOFFREY GIRARD

was the kind that proved there was no such thing as a universal rule. Things like Time and Distance and Molecules were just words we used to try to explain the unexplainable. She told me that we would never understand the Truths of the Universe but that the search was "so totally worth it."

We talked a lot that first night. I don't even remember most of what I said. We mostly shared stories of scientific history and the silly things we'd done at other camps. The whole rest of the week, Amanda Klosterman would sit by me every chance she got and was always hugging me and stuff. Called me "Jeffy Bear," which I absolutely hated, but I didn't mind the massive random hug attacks. And she usually did them in front of other people, so within a couple of days I was almost as popular as Amanda. We continued to talk every night. Again, I don't know about what. I didn't really care. I just liked that someone liked being with me. Someone noticed when I came into the room. And not because I was the kid with the dead mom. Or the kid whose dad was in charge.

The night before camp ended, I finally told her about my mom and the accident.

And eventually I told her about the faces.

She smiled so big. And then told me I was lucky. Said I'd probably never know who these faces or people are and that meant they could be ANYTHING.

It was a logic that'd helped for two years. Until my father handed me that folder.

I got a kiss on the cheek that night, but mostly more hugging. I'm not sure how I felt about the kiss, but I liked being hugged.

Honestly, I think it's the first time anyone had ever done it to me right.

. . .

Real hugs hadn't been prescribed to me by DSTI yet.

. . .

My thoughts had turned to my father and got dark. Too dark. It got to where I couldn't take another moment in that car's silence. I looked over at Castillo.

I said: So . . . (Not really sure what to say next.)

At first I thought I might get from him nothing but more mute staring for another hour. But he echoed me and said, So . . . , his mind still wrestling with the next words. Like he'd gone to a place that was too dark also.

I tried the next words for him. I said: So the Army tested some kinda biotoxin at Shardhara.

He said, YES.

And all those people there died?

He said, YES.

I pictured the map found in my father's secret office. The different-colored circles rippling out like someone had tossed a stone into the center of the village. A stone that had caused people to rip each other and themselves into pieces. How many white sheets had they needed, I wondered, in each of the colored circles?

I said: And DSTI made this stuff.

Maybe, he said. Probably.

Then maybe that's what happened at the Massey school that night, I said excitedly. Excited because it freed my father and the others of all guilt. Right? I mean, if some poison gas that caused people to kill one another had somehow been set off, how could the students and my father be blamed for what had happened? It was the poison. It would have happened to anyone. I continued:

Maybe some of this stuff got leaked and everyone went crazy, or . . .

He looked at me. Maybe, he said again.

You don't think so, I said, and he just shrugged. I argued that maybe my dad was collecting information on DSTI to expose what they were really up to. Like a whistle-blower thing.

You should have seen Castillo's face. I must have sounded so truly pathetic, clutching at straws and getting worse with every sentence I uttered. The guy actually looked like he felt sorry for me.

I don't know, he said sympathetically. *Maybe.*

It didn't matter. My whirling thoughts had already taken the next turn. One of the missing puzzle pieces I, then, only understood faintly.

Part of the WHY.

Why they made me.

. . .

They made this stuff from *us*, didn't they? I asked. This biotoxin? The gas at Shardhara.

Castillo nodded.

My father had told me the serial-killer clones had been created to craft weapons for the military. I'd never really thought much about what that meant until now.

DSTI had explained it to Castillo as if each of us—the clones, I mean—was a little factory making billions of dollars of DNA, DNA they could use to make new military products. This killer-gas stuff was just one of their new products. I tried imagining others.

Factories? I repeated.

He said that's the word one of the geneticists at DSTI had used.

I thought about that for a minute, and Castillo let the silence remain for me to do so.

We'd been made so that they could harvest the evil growing inside.

Modify it, intensify it.

To kill more people.

This was, apparently, my life's purpose.

. . .

Castillo concluded: None of this changes the main objective. To find those six guys and your dad.

But then he added: If Shardhara comes up again somewhere, at least now we know what we're dealing with.

And Shardhara, of course, would come up again.

Big-time.

And even then we still only had the tiniest idea of what we were dealing with.

CHAPTER NINETEEN

I'd taken my now customary spot in a new motel room and prepared to settle in for the night. Or the week. Who knew anymore?
I was starting to get the sense that the next five years of my life could
be spent entombed in dark smelly motel rooms with Castillo. Staring
at the TV or water-stained carpet. Never really falling asleep. He'd
already gotten his laptops up and laid the Murder Map out for an
update. I watched him work for a long time, my eyes heavy, but I'd
grown way too numb to sleep.

Castillo suggested I watch TV or something, and I told him I was
kinda sick of TV and was more of a book guy anyway. He grunted and
continued to work. So I lay back and gazed up at the ceiling. I imagined Amanda Klosterman's tiny white paper airplane fluttering against
the graying stucco ceiling. Trapped in the room like us.

Then I thought of something I *could* do. Maybe to answer some of
the questions bouncing around my little clone brain. Maybe, at the
very least, to help me kill some time.

I asked Castillo if I could use one of his laptops to look up stuff on
the Internet.

Castillo seemed quite suspicious. Look up what? he asked.

I told him I just wanted to check out some of the stuff Ox was talking about. The dead scientists. The experiments and all. And this was true, partially.

He stared at me awhile, deciding. He looked way tired also. And probably felt just as trapped as I did in his own way. He tossed me over one of his smartphones.

I couldn't really remember any of the names Ox had rattled off. Parts of names at best. So I just did a search on "DNA scientists killed" and "bioweapons scientists murdered," and, like, thirty million results popped up.

List of Dead Scientists

Dead and Missing Scientists

Mysterious Deaths of Top Scientists since 9/11

100 Dead Scientists We Should Never Forget

More names. So many names. Some I even now recognized because of Ox. Top scientists who'd died mysteriously over the last twenty years.

"Suspicious" didn't quite cover it.

Then one name jumped off the page like it had burst into flames and jumped up out of the smartphone's screen.

Dr. Cornelius Chatterjee.

I'd seen the name before. I even knew what the guy looked like.

His framed picture was up on the wall at DSTI.

He'd worked there. He'd worked for my father.

And then someone had killed him.

. . .

OK, MAYBE someone had killed him.

Two years ago, he'd hanged himself. According to a couple of websites, his family said there was no way he'd done such a thing. They complained to authorities about that, but apparently, in the end, they'd just left the country or something. Chatterjee's name was now on several lists. Just another guy good at genetics who'd "died prematurely."

I immediately told Castillo what I'd found.

He already knew about Chatterjee.

How? I asked. (And what else hadn't he told me? Everything, probably.)

What the hell do you think I'm doing all day? he asked, and tapped one of his laptops.

I admitted I had no clue. I was also trying to sound like a jerk, trying to imply that he wasn't doing *anything* all day. That things were exactly as they'd been before we'd first met. We might as well both be standing in my bedroom. I think Castillo got my implication.

Chatterjee, he said, paying attention to me for the first time in forever, is one of several employees who've died mysteriously while working at DSTI. But I don't see how that helps me find these six kids.

Why do you do this? I asked then.

What do you mean? he asked.

Why are you doing this? Why are you helping them?

DSTI? I don't care about DSTI. I'm doing this . . . He thought, then said: I was asked to help find these people. And finding people happens to be something I'm good at.

Asked by the *government*? I confirmed. (I was developing all sorts of new ideas this week about what the term "government" meant.)

Sure, he said. As good a word as any.

You were in the war with Ox? I asked.

Castillo replied that he and Ox were at times "in the same operations."

I asked how long he'd been in the Army.

You done with my phone? he asked.

I wasn't, and he knew it, but he'd successfully found a new way to tell me to shut up.

. . .

I then Googled my own father.

There were half a dozen images of him online. (More now that he is dead.) Pictures of him receiving awards or giving them or sitting at a table with other scientists. It was the first time I'd seen him since he'd left me.

I looked at him now as if I were looking at a total, utter, outright stranger. I could have been looking at anyone. All those years eating dinner, watching movies, going places, and I'd had no idea who this guy *really* was, what was *really* going on his mind. But that was the thing. How many kids ever really know what's going on in their parents' minds?

Some parent somewhere is always planning a divorce, sampling her kid's Ritalin pills, secretly mortgaging the house a third time to cover gambling debt, meeting some lover at some motel, sneaking drinks in the garage, stealing from the company, thinking about putting a shotgun in his mouth, collecting weird porn, and so on and so on and . . . And mostly, us kids just bop happily along, oblivious until it's really, really bad. Until the conclusion is in perfect sight and utterly unavoidable.

Like now.

I wondered if my father was on this dead scientist list now. Already gone. Another victim of some huge inexplicable government conspiracy. Would someone be reading about my own dad on some site in a few weeks? Maybe both of us? Listed as a car crash, a murder-suicide thing. Truth of the matter: I maybe wished he *were* dead. That way I'd know he was innocent.

I read a couple of news articles about him and DSTI. More break-throughs in genetic engineering. Funny. In not a single article did they mention cloning serial killers. Or the development of weapons for the United States military.

Ox had said that these things always take time. That in fifty years everyone will know that some small company outside Philly cloned serial killers as a part of some military testing. But in fifty years no one would care. There'd be other more horrible things to worry about then. Not a bunch of guys in their seventies claiming to have been part of some secret test when they were kids.

I then looked up Program F, the fluoride thing Ox had mentioned.

It was one of the few in his list I could recall at the time, honestly. (I've since heard the list a dozen times.) I mean, what could fluoride possibly have to do with clones or dead villagers in Afghanistan?

A lot, actually.

• • •

When the United States first started building atomic bombs in the 1940s, it discovered that one of the by-products of manufacturing so much uranium for nukes was a shitload of *fluoride*. Millions of tons. Even more was being created by the emerging industries of rocket fuel, plastics, and aluminum. Unfortunately, fluoride poisoning was proving even more deadly than radiation. It was totally toxic hazardous waste.

Local crops and livestock were dying. Plant workers and nearby citizens experienced crippling arthritis, uncontrollable vomiting and diarrhea, severe headaches, and even death.

Lawsuits started. But the United States government, and the companies building bombs and jet fuel and aluminum washing machines for the USA, didn't want lawsuits. They wanted more bombs and jet fuel and washing machines. So the scientists who'd worked on the Manhattan Project (the same who'd injected citizens with plutonium) were given a new mission: Figure out a way to make the public THINK fluoride is GOOD. That way the growing lawsuits wouldn't have a prayer in the court of public opinion and would then fade away forever.

The American scientists visited German scientists (ex-Nazis, all), who'd been using fluoride for years. All during World War II, when THEY'd been the ones making rocket fuel and aluminum weapons, the Nazis had put *their* fluoride waste into the drinking water at their death/work camps because it "made the prisoners docile" and "eventually led to sterilization." The plan was to eventually use the fluoride-laced water in ALL occupied territories. The whole world would become brainless sterile sleepwalkers under the waving red swastika banners.

While the ex-Nazis were explaining this to the Americans, they added a little "oh, yeah" sidebar to the conversation. When using the fluoride-laced water, the Nazis had noted that—along with the sterilization, the death, *and* the damage to the parts of the brain that managed creativity and determination—the prisoners had, well, whiter teeth.

The American scientists shouted "Eureka!" or something similar.

If they could prove to all Americans that fluoride was a GOOD THING, the lawsuits would go away and all those new factories and military projects could continue to spew out fluoride into the world. And white teeth could, surely, be seen only as a good thing.

First they went home and secretly put fluoride into the water of a city called Newburgh, New York. They told no one in Newburgh they were doing this. They then secretly collected blood and tissue samples from the people with the assistance of the New York State Health Department and local physicians. People thought they were getting routine blood tests or having a little mole removed. They, in fact, were being analyzed and itemized.

The United States government called this Program F.

Their studies proved that fluoride, even at low levels, was dangerous. Deadly. Poison. BAD.

While making teeth whiter, it actually created more cavities. Hollowed teeth. It also—scarier, and as the Nazis had discovered ten years before—affected the central nervous system. Lowered IQs. Increased immobility. Long-term use would lead to issues ranging from arthritis to Alzheimer's disease.

These reports were buried. As if they'd never happened. Locked away for forty years.

No further testing was ordered.

Next the men who owned these fluoride-producing factories spent hundreds of millions of dollars working with the government to convince Americans that fluoride was a GOOD THING and should be in our water. Doctors and scientists were enlisted (paid) to support the government's claims. Advertising and marketing experts were brought in to help with the PR. Scientists who disagreed were dismissed in the press and at their universities as fools. Most were fired. Ruined professionally and never heard from again. (Just a few years ago, a Harvard experiment confirmed lower IQs, increased fatigue, and recordable brain damage, with likely links to autism, ADHD, and Alzheimer's. The leader of the team was fired.)

Meanwhile, the companies making all this fluoride waste were now

SELLING it to the United States. One of the largest, I.G. Farben (owned and operated by American tycoons Ford and Rockefeller, *and* the Federal Reserve), also owned a small company called Colgate. Maybe you've heard of it. Maybe it's in your bathroom right now. I.G. Farben sold itself its own toxic waste and got Americans to pay for it at a 20,000% markup. They didn't know how to get rid of it before without getting sued, and were now being paid millions by states and cities to deliver it every day.

Within *three* years, with no further testing than that done at Newburgh, and the deadly results buried, more than half of the United States was putting fluoride in its water. Forty-two of the fifty largest cities. Most other countries absolutely refused to fall for this scam. But this is the country with the most to lose if the scam fails.

Today 70% of Americans drink fluoride-laced water.

• • •

If the United States is willing to knowingly poison two hundred million people, ignoring the truth in the name of money and continued military dominance, you really think they give one single shit about killing a village of poor farmers halfway across the world or, say, a couple of dozen clones?

• • •

I tried looking up Castillo on Google. But I didn't know his first name yet and couldn't find him. I would have given anything to have just one more thing about the guy.

Then I searched for Amanda Klosterman and Mandy Klosterman (guess a whole day of thinking about her, it was bound to happen) and finally found her. There was a link to her Facebook page and an article in a local paper about her being on her school's swim team. I read the swimming article, hoping there'd be a picture or something, but the picture was of some other girl. I was creeping bad. So I didn't click on her Facebook page. I didn't *like*-like her or anything. She was 1,000% just a friend.

But I'd realized—after all the years, however many it really was, I'd spent on this earth—she'd been the only person who'd ever truly given a damn about me. Even if only for a week.

. . .

I looked back over at Castillo. He'd finally fallen asleep in his chair. Chin down on his big tough-guy chest. I'd watched him do this once before. He'd pop awake again in twenty minutes, not much more. He slept even worse than I did. (I didn't yet know why—that as bad as some of the memories in my head were, memories that weren't even all mine technically, his were worse.)

I historied back to the search on my dad. Just kinda looked at his picture again.

I suddenly needed to talk to him, more than anything else in the whole world. I was getting so anxious, it felt like my skin was literally catching on fire. I had to get out of this room NOW and talk to my dad NOW. Right *NOW*!

And Castillo sleeping was a sign from above that that's exactly what I should be doing too. With such a persuasive sign, phone in hand, I decided to sneak outside. Make my call and be done before Castillo woke up. And even if he did, so what? What was he gonna do about it anyway?

Yeah, right. It took me, like, ten minutes just to quietly turn the door handle. I was absolutely terrified of Castillo waking up. But not, clearly, terrified enough to stop.

Finally outside, I called my dad using the special number he'd given me.

Worth a try, right?

He picked up on the first ring.

CHAPTER TWENTY

*D*ad?

Dad, hey, yeah . . . it's me.

Jeff.

I'm good. I'm . . . I want to go home.

I don't know. Pennsylvania somewhere. There's this—

No. There's this guy.

His name is Castillo.

I don't think so.

I think he's with, like, the Army or something.

DOD?

Yeah, Department of—

No.

He wouldn't do that.

No, he won't. He wouldn't—

I'm *not* a baby. Where are you?

No, it does matter. Where the fuck are you?

Yes, I am. I am "upset." I'm . . . I don't understand what's happening.

You didn't tell me anything.

You didn't tell me anything.

You're lying. You're always lying.

What happened?

At DSTI? Massey. What happened there? What did you do?

It does matter. It's everything. Did you ... Did you kill someone?

I don't understand what that means. I—

Yes. Yes, I'm listening to you.

No. No. I don't understand what any of that means.

No, I never will. Where are you?

Are the other guys with you? David? Ted—

Yes, that's who Castillo is looking for. And you ...

No, I don't think so. I'll ... No. It's just me. I wanted—

When are you coming home?

No, Haddonfield is home. That doesn't— When are you coming home?

Then come and get me. You—

Why not?

Come and get me.

Why? What ... What did I do wrong?

Then why did you take them and not me?

I don't believe that.

You hate me, don't you.

Another lie.

Well ... I hate you.

Dad?

CHAPTER TWENTY-ONE

*T*he woman in the black dress covered the whole world, her absolute darkness continuing for as far as I could see in any direction. I stared up at her, defeated, sitting with my back against the motel wall just to keep from crumpling to the ground. I was still outside. It was cold, the parking lot quiet and still. I don't know what time it was. Two moths fluttered just above my head by the outside light, slamming themselves against the bulb, killing themselves, just to get away from the woman's terrible shadow.

She'd somehow swallowed all the surrounding streets and buildings. Trees, mountains. Everyone. Above, the whole sky. Everything. The stars shimmered within. Small, lost. Futile. Trapped above forever in her unbroken grasp like teeny white sheets over lifeless lumps or like twinkling dots on a map. Her untold victims. Her brood. Thousands upon thousands scattered far and wide. Both the killers *and* the killed. Victims all. One star shined the brightest and largest of all but still so small in her immeasurable gloom.

I imagined that desolate single star as my father. Caught somehow in "Her" mysterious sway. She'd apparently first called to him when he was a boy, reaching out across eternity. An inherited memory from another age, he believed, from an ancestor who'd lived more than a hundred years before. And who was I to disbelieve him? Just as I saw the faces of Dahmer's victims, my father had seen her. Calling out to him, luring him, for decades until finally, I figured, he'd succumbed. Now, I feared, he was finally hers. Maybe always had been.

And when my dad had hung up, I'd looked up to the night sky and finally seen her for the first time. What I'd seen in that motel room, in my dream, had been only a hint. This was she in her full glory. Terrifying *and* beautiful. And then I surrendered. What else could I do? In nightmares I'd had, there'd always been a point when I knew to quit. The THING chasing me was simply too strong, too powerful to escape or defeat. It was better just to stop running. The fear of the thing catching you was surely far worse than the actual end. It was, in the dreams, always a comforting thought. Surrender. Of course, I always woke up just as the THING— whatever it was in the dream—got me. Not now, though. When *this* Evil was ready to fully claim me, as she had my father and so many years before, it would just happen. This time, there'd be no waking up.

• • •

I eventually somehow pulled myself back to my feet and then slowly got the door open again. Castillo was still asleep in the chair. I tiptoed into the room and the darkness from outside snuck right in after me. I could feel its fingers on my back and I would swear to this day that the room grew darker as I entered. I crawled into bed and carefully laid the phone on the desk between our beds. I'd already deleted the history of searches I'd made and my call to my dad. I don't know why. I didn't really care anymore what happened or what Castillo thought of me. In the morning, I would ask him to take me to DSTI. They, at least, knew what I was.

A factory, a source—of Evil.

And while I didn't really expect the black-dressed woman, that Evil, to sweep down and claim me in the flesh, surrendering to DSTI seemed the next best thing.

. . .

I lay awake, my thoughts finding solace only in the darkest corners of the room. Castillo startled awake. Scratched at his week-old beard. Looked around the room like he'd never been asleep. Started to work again. Finally I faded in and out of sleep myself.

There, images of my father came to mind. He was with a woman. A young woman. And she was smiling. No, screaming. I could hear her screaming.

Next I saw Spanelli. David Spanelli.

One of the six clones that Castillo was looking for.

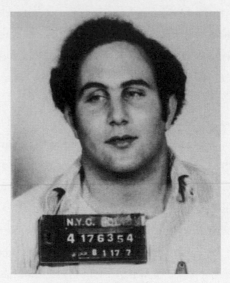

A clone of David Berkowitz. Also called the Son of Sam. This Berkowitz shot a bunch of strangers once, said his dog was possessed by the devil and told him to do it. (Clichés always start somewhere real, you know.) Anyhow, I didn't know anything about David Berkowitz at this point and certainly didn't think of David Spanelli in this way. David Spanelli'd always been cool and would never have had anything to do with any of this regardless.

And yet . . .

And yet, I now envisioned us all standing together and there was this car and something happening behind it. There were other people there. Two other teenagers. One had a rock in his hand.

He was swinging it down at something behind the car.

And the car's taillights were flashing, making everything red. Then a sudden flash of white light!

I shivered awake. The dream—what else could it be?—was already slipping away.

(Note: I had no idea what that dream meant at the time, and never really would. I know only that the six boys who escaped Massey, and some of the guys *they* then helped escape, ended up doing some really terrible things. And sometimes, somehow, I saw these things too.)

That woman in the dress. Evil. Murder. Cain XP11. I don't care what you call it. I know it was black. (Clichés always start somewhere real, right?)

And in that same blackness I found sleep again but also more thoughts and fears and fancies taking shape. More nightmares.

• • •

It was Ted again now. And he was in a doorway. Standing over me in the doorway so that all I could see was his silhouette in the small dark room. But I still knew it was him without a doubt. He looked a hundred feet tall like that. I turned. There was something in the bathtub. Something rocking slowly back and forth. Making strange sounds.

And Ted was laughing now. And I felt myself being pulled down some back street. Running. Moving faster than I'd ever run before in my life. The dark streets and buildings moved by so quickly. I was looking for something. . . . The faces merging now, the dreams swirling into one. My dad's face, spattered with blood. A knife in his hands. No, Ted's face. David's now.

Then something more skeletal emerging. Something even blacker than the woman's dress. Eyes glinting like the edge of a knife.

Jaws widening . . . becoming MY face now.

Jeffrey Dahmer's face.

Jaws widening . . . stretching too far. Bones cracking.

Because the blackness wasn't some evil trying to get IN.

It was something deep inside me trying to get OUT.

I felt it crawling up my throat. Choking.

I awoke again.

My body was covered in sweat. I lay still in bed in the total darkness. My heart thumping like a hummingbird's. *Good,* I thought. Let the nightmares come in battalions. I'd accepted my fate. The world wasn't just a "half-empty glass." The world's glass was smashed into a million jagged pieces, and its contents spilled over the table like warm blood.

You'd think this was a bad thing. But it wasn't.

I'd found great comfort in knowing it couldn't get any worse.

That's about when Castillo started screaming.

• • •

Castillo had three nightmares during these two weeks. I can't really say which was "the worst." For me, of course, it was hands down this one. The first. And to say he scared the shit out of me is crude hyperbole but not by much.

I'd never heard a sound quite like it. At the time, it was the most horrifying sound I'd ever heard. (Later I would hear worse. [I'd *make* worse myself.]) But in that pitch-black room, half-lost in sleep and nightmares myself, this was not a sound from the tomb but deep from behind the very gates of hell itself. It sounded like someone had just slit his throat. And for half a second I thought that's what had happened. A scream that went in, Castillo sucking in air in a high-pitched wail of terror that just kept getting higher and louder. It lasted, like, ten seconds, but I would have sworn then it was an hour.

I scrambled off my bed and put a hand on the door.

Across the room Castillo made several grunts, fumbled for the light switch.

I had vague memories at that point of a similar scream earlier. A scream from one of my dreams nights before. I thought I'd imagined it. Now I suspected it'd been Castillo and maybe this wasn't the first. I don't know. It doesn't really matter.

Castillo turned the light on. The room was totally empty.

We were alone. He was unhurt.

Castillo's whole body was shaking. His breath coming out a hundred miles an hour. I thought he was gonna have a heart attack. He mumbled: What the F was that? He mumbled: You good? And I told him I was, but could hardly get the words out myself because I was, I gotta admit, trying not to laugh.

This Army assassin was totally trembling. The UFC-built badass with the gun and tats, the amazing stare-down, and the nasty scars all over. *Trembling in fear.* Castillo even tried acting as if nothing out of the ordinary had just happened. Tried making it seem like I was the one who'd done something wrong. Gave me this annoyed

Why-the-hell-are-you-standing-by-the-door? look. OK, he told me. Get some sleep. Like I was the one who'd just had a total freak-out and woken everyone up. You gotta be kidding me.

He turned the light back off and turned to the other wall away from me. In the total darkness I could hear his breathing. It hadn't slowed at all. I'd swear I could hear his heart thumping too. And it went on like that for a good hour.

You'd think I wouldn't be able to get to sleep after something like that.

But I did. I actually slept more soundly than I had since before all this had started. Since my old life.

Because it was the very first time I thought of Castillo as "normal."

His world was just as terrible as everyone else's.

He was human after all.

My only question now: Was I?

In the morning I would convince Castillo to just take me back to DSTI. There they'd know what I really was. And there, when they were done with me, it probably wouldn't matter anymore.

. . .

While we were sleeping, the police finally found the bodies of Mr. and Mrs. Nolan in Delaware. Two days before, Mr. Nolan had been shot and Mrs. Nolan had been raped and strangled to death. And, across the street, another dead woman.

In just a few hours now, Castillo'd have all three up on his Murder Map.

The three red dots he was waiting for.

Radiant new stars.

Deaths that would change everything.

CHAPTER TWENTY-TWO

*G*OT YOU!

The sound of Castillo's voice boomed like shattering thunder in the small motel room. I jumped awake to an echo of: I got you, you son of a bitch!

I assumed he was talking to me. The magnificent *son of a test tube* that I am. Maybe he'd figured out I'd made a call on his phone or that I'd laughed my ass off as I fell asleep thinking about him freaking out like he had. Maybe he'd just decided that catching and killing the clone of Jeffrey Dahmer was a good start. But he was only talking to his laptop.

I sat up as Castillo pumped his fist at nothing (the laptop perhaps) and hurried across the room to the map. I asked WHO?, wanting to know who the "son of a bitch"—if not me—was.

Don't worry about it, he grunted. Just more dead people.

Oh, I said. His quick dismissal of me only served to remind me what I'd committed to the night before. It was time to talk about DSTI. To tell Castillo I just wanted to go "home." No matter how dangerous that home might prove to be. It was still clearly the only place in the whole world where I truly belonged.

Castillo stopped, sighed. Guess he felt bad. And before I could get a word out about DSTI, he told me that a couple of new names had just come in. Names somehow connected to all of this. Specifically three new homicides in Delaware. The police had found them only a couple of hours ago in two different homes. Goddamn, he added. I got you guys.

He'd grabbed his red pen and marked the map.

Husband and wife, he said. A Mr. and Mrs. Nolan.

These names meant nothing to me.

But another woman was murdered in the house just across the street, Castillo said. That was the important part. Castillo said: Want to guess her name?

I said no.

•   •   •

The other dead woman was named McCarty. Nancy McCarty.

McCarty

McCarty, Castillo continued. Nancy F-in' McCarty. Chicken girl.

Yes, chicken girl. I pictured one of my dad's most shameful notebook scribbles, and then said the name out loud. My mind focused more on the cartoon.

Bet your ass, Castillo said, and beamed. Want more?

I said no again. I didn't wanna hear a single other word. These three people had been killed because of my dad. I didn't know how exactly, but there was something. This dead woman's name *had* been in his notebook.

But I was so tired of thinking about all this. My whole brain hurt. My heart hurt too.

I didn't want to think anymore about anything. Least of all about

GEOFFREY GIRARD

my dad or murder or . . . well, any of it. *DSTI*, I thought, looked for the words to shout it out, *JUST TAKE ME TO DSTI!* Then, whatever happened, even if they *killed* me, I wouldn't have to think so much anymore.

But I kept quiet. *Something* about that chicken, bird . . .

Castillo found the TV remote. Her teenage son was missing too, he said. *And* the prime suspect. Then he cursed some more, and said we were "cookin'." He asked if I wanted to guess HIS name? The missing kid? He'd put the television on. Found the news channels.

What is it? I asked. He seemed so excited, it felt rude not to. I wondered if it were that simple? The picture, I mean. My dad's clue.

Castillo said: Al. Albert McCarty. Age fifteen. Albert Fish, maybe. Or Albert DeSalvo. Both names are in your dad's notes.

Of course they were in my dad's notes.

Fish and DeSalvo were famously violent serial killers.

• • •

What we learned later.

Thirteen years before Nancy McCarty's death, she'd agreed to adopt a baby boy.

For this she was paid two thousand dollars in cash every single month.

Every few months a doctor from the institution she'd adopted the baby from would stop by to check in on things. His name was Dr. Jacobson.

The baby's name was Albert.

The baby was a clone of Albert DeSalvo.

A man better known by history as the Boston Strangler.

Albert DeSalvo sexually assaulted and then murdered at least a dozen women in the Boston area in a two-year period back in the 1960s. He was murdered himself in prison in 1973. His clone, one of them, was born more than thirty years later.

The original (DeSalvo) had been raised by an alcoholic father who'd often beat his wife and forced his sons to watch him have sex with prostitutes he brought home.

The copy (McCarty) was raised by an alcoholic mother who used a good slap across the face as the best form of punishment and often had sex right in the living room with guys she'd picked up. Guys who'd often taken a punch or two at young Al.

You'd think this was absurd coincidence. But it wasn't.

It was business. It was an experiment.

Because Albert was, as noted before, on the list Castillo had found in my father's notes.

That's what two thousand dollars a month was for.

Light beatings and a little sexual irresponsibility now and again.

Just imagine what the "parents" getting *five* thousand were doing.

• • •

GEOFFREY GIRARD

Castillo was already back on his phone, flipping through the digital pics. Hoping to find anything he could in my father's notes about a clone named Albert and/or the McCartys. He told me to pack up. Said we we're leaving for Delaware "five minutes ago," which I assumed meant now.

M. Carty, Castillo kept saying. McCarty. So . . . So, then what's with this damn chicken?

He thought it was a stand-in for the letter *C* maybe.

I now knew that it wasn't.

I said: It's not a chicken.

I said: It's a hen.

Chicken, hen, he scoffed and asked what the difference was.

I retreated to my book bag and kept packing.

Forget that shit. Castillo waved his hand. He was all like: You got something to say, Jacobson, say it.

So I dropped my bag and confirmed that those three people had gotten killed in Delaware.

So? Castillo asked.

I said: They're the Blue Hens. (He didn't have a clue.)

Blue Hens, I repeated.

And then I told him: The University of Delaware sports teams are called the Blue Hens.

He still didn't get it.

It's the state bird, I told him.

He cursed, stammered some. It was fun to see. Castillo then stared at his phone.

Is that all this is? he gasped. McCarty in Delaware. *That's* the big secret code?

I just shrugged.

I thought about telling him of my time at the University of Delaware. One of my science tutors had driven me down once a month for the whole year as part of some national science club. My dad would always ask what I'd learned when we got back.

But Castillo didn't seem so interested in any of that. So what're these, then? he asked, all angry. These other birds? This circle? The squiggle? Castillo waved me over and pulled up the next images, staring at the screen.

I slid off the bed slowly. I took the phone and thumbed through the pictures too. Nothing made any more sense than it had the first time. I thumbed back through—

And then one did.

For the first time in days, something actually maybe made sense.

Al Baum

Something about it. I'd stopped on the image and now just stared. A memory on the tip of my mind. I knew this one. I . . .

OK, so what the hell is *that*? Castillo barked next to me.

Could be . . .

What? *Could be* what, goddamn it?

I glanced briefly at the Murder Map taped to the wall.

What? Go ahead . . . Castillo turned and nudged me toward the map.

I studied it. Moved toward the map now slowly, crossing the room like I was sleepwalking again or something. Ran my finger across all those red dots and half-formed lines.

GEOFFREY GIRARD

I'd pointed to a small cluster of blue dots. What's this? I asked.

Castillo explained it was missing persons. Now he was up and standing beside him.

A mother and her two children last seen at a playground in Ohio. Little park just outside McArthur. Maybe a custody thing with the husband, Castillo said. Maybe something else. Why? he asked.

I turned and looked him in the eye for the first time ever.

I told him I thought I knew what the squiggle was.

It was a snake.

He wasn't buying it. Thought it could be anything.

But now we know it's places, I explained. The Blue Hens, the doodles represent *places*.

Maybe, he replied. He didn't seem so sure.

Then *maybe* it's a snake, I said, and then told him it looked kinda like Serpent Mound.

Castillo asked: What the hell is Serpent Mound?

• • •

I remember walking over hundreds of dead people. And the bees.

My dad was a guest speaker at a symposium on genetics being hosted at Xavier University in Cincinnati. Geneticists from all over the world were attending. Most times (and there were plenty) he'd have someone watch me for a couple of days. But every so often he'd bring me along. I've been to New York and Boston and Baltimore and Annapolis. I even went to Montreal in a private jet once.

From Cincinnati we drove an hour east one afternoon and ended up at someplace called Serpent Mound. Three feet high, a thousand feet long, a thousand years old. Curving back and forth over acres of land in the shape of a giant snake. At its head the snake's mouth is open and eating something round. An egg? The whole world? No one knows. The Indian tribe who built the enormous figure has been gone for centuries. Many of that tribe are buried beneath and within the colossal grass-skinned reptile.

My dad and I walked together along its twisting shape, following the enormous spine framed with woods and a small stream. Beneath our feet human ancestors from more than a millennium ago.

There is no escape, my father said. *We are the sum of our ancestors' measures.*

I had no clue what he was talking about. (I do now.)

I remember climbing a metal ladder and some scaffolding that over-looked the head of the giant snake and most of its half-coiled body. My dad did not climb up with me. He waited below. As I climbed, several bees buzzed around me, and the higher I climbed, the more bees there were. A dozen. As if blocking my ascent. I turned, decided to turn back down.

Below, however, my dad just looked up at me.

He seemed even bigger to me than the snake.

So I kept climbing.

• • •

I told Castillo only that it was some old Indian burial site built in the shape of a giant snake. Something my dad took me to once. I told him it was on the list I'd made for him.

Where? Castillo's eyes were wide.

I dropped my finger on a spot in southern Ohio.

Castillo put his own finger over the missing family in McArthur, Ohio.

A third person, if one had been there with us, might have drawn a straight line between our two fingers. A straight line and less than a two-hour drive.

It's not Al Baum, I said. It was Albaum. Just like McCarty. And the picture was just a hint to the location.

Castillo agreed, then cursed happily. He grabbed his laptop, typed.

There are only two hundred Albaum families in America, he reported aloud, clicking.

Better than twenty thousand Baums, huh?

Hell, yeah, Castillo said. He nodded, impressed. I'd just given him back the exact same number he'd quoted days ago. I gotta admit, I'm no dummy.

So how many Albaum families in Ohio? I asked.

Castillo turned, smiled.

There was one.

CHAPTER TWENTY-THREE

*T*he Boston Strangler" (the man from whom Albert McCarty had gotten his DNA) is one of the more famous nicknames for serial killers. You're not, it seems, officially part of the club until you get a nickname. I haven't, actually, found a single serial killer yet without one. It comes gratis with the dead bodies. (I assume it helps sell newspapers.)

These names seem to come in four main categories and, whenever possible, favor alliteration.

1. Location (the most popular): The Bavarian Ripper, The Rostov Ripper, The Pied Piper of Phoenix, The Vampire of Sacramento, The Werewolf of Wisteria, The Monster of Rillington Place, The Cincinnati Strangler, The Sydney Mutilator, The Buttermilk Bluebeard, The Demon of the Belfry, The Skid Row Slasher, The Berlin Butcher, The Butcher of Hannover, The Mass Murderer of Munstberg.

2. Technique: The Sunday Morning Slasher, The Granny Killer, The Happy Face Killer, The Doorbell Killer, The Machete Murderer, The BTK (Bind, Torture, Kill) Strangler, The

Cannibal, The Singing Strangler, The Mad Biter, The Torture Doctor, The Night Stalker, Charlie ChopOff, The Vampire Rapist. Oh, and Jack the Ripper.

3. Appearance: Metal Fang, Candy Man, Green Man, The Fat Man, The Alligator Man, The Red Spider, Killer Clown, Bloody Face, Rattlesnake Lissemba, The Red Demon.

4. Generic Death: The Angel of Death, The Mad Beast, The Terminator, The Boogeyman, The Death Maker, Citizen X, The Sex Beast, The Monster.

• • •

The "Milwaukee Monster" is what the press called Jeffrey Dahmer for a while, but it never really stuck. "DAHMER" was enough. You don't need a nickname to make it any worse than it already is. Folk just say his name and everyone knows exactly what you mean. The MONSTER part is implied.

• • •

Castillo dumped me in another motel room while he went off to check out the Albaum family. If I was right, if my dad's notes made sense and that squiggle really was supposed to be Serpent Mound, the Albaums would have an adopted son. A clone my father had given to them to raise as their own.

Now, what Castillo would do if I was right ... That was another story.

• • •

He'd been gone for hours.

I stared at several sheets from the dozens Castillo had gotten printed before he'd left.

Rich Ardson Size More H Owell Gil Ronan

The last names, if we were right about "Albaum," were easy enough: Richardson, Sizemore, Howell, and Gilronan. But the stupid pictures were nothing but a big bunch of MAYBEs.

I scanned Castillo's Murder Map again, searching for any town that made sense.

But there were thousands. Tens of thousands of little towns all across the country.

Castillo had told me to focus mostly along Route 50. Still, there were hundreds of possibilities. And hundreds is better than thousands, Castillo had said when he'd left.

I eyed the room's small digital clock again. Castillo'd said he'd probably be gone a while, but it'd been five hours. Had he found the Albaum boy? The clone? Had something bad happened?

I tried refocusing on the printouts. Made my own lists and notes next to each name and symbol. My blocky lettering right next to my father's scribbles. Beside "Richardson" (was it a heart or a bow and arrow?), I'd written down everything from Bowmansville, Pennsylvania, to Points, West Virginia. Then there was Hunter, Ohio. Or Sherwood Forest? Or Center Point? Or maybe even Loveland? It was maddening.

The bird could easily be Birdsville, MD, or the Baltimore Ravens or Birdseye, Indiana. Maybe Odon, Indiana, because the Norse god king Odin had two ravens as messengers. But "Odon" was spelled wrong, so I crossed it out. The other two symbols—something with a moon and a bug with a hat.

No clue. None.

And besides, even if I *could* figure it out, then what? More of the clones would be found, sure. But for the first time I stopped to think: What happens to them?

And me?

If this Albaum kid existed at all, he wasn't a killer like the six who'd ripped through Massey. He was just a kid. Probably didn't even know he was a clone. Let alone the clone of some terrible serial killer. He was just a normal kid. (Or "normal" like Albert McCarty in Delaware, right?)

And thanks to me, Castillo was coming for him. Just like DSTI had come for me a week ago. Would Castillo tell this kid who he really was? Would they take this kid from his family now? Bring him to DSTI? That had become synonymous with *something bad* to me. Something unspeakable.

I brushed the printouts aside onto the floor and eyed Castillo's other files. He'd just left them in a pile on the chair on his side of the room. Almost like he wanted me to take a look.

I stood over the chair. Fingers ran over the same folder again.

JD658726h56-54 it read up top. I'd already peeked inside. Jeffrey Dahmer/54.

The Dahmer clone Castillo was after. Jeffrey Williford. One of the six.

I'd already flipped the folder open twice before. Just enough to see the name.

To see pictures of the guy I would soon become. Or already was.

Whatever else was within, I didn't yet know.

Didn't want to. And, at the same time, wanted to.

My eyes moved instead to Castillo's book. Castillo kept it in his duffel bag, and I'd seen him reading it late at night when he thought I was sleeping. I picked it up and riffed through its pages. It was a copy of *The Odyssey* by Homer. I knew it had something to do with Greek mythology but hadn't read it yet. Castillo had made little notes throughout in the margins. Had underlined and bracketed stuff too. A lot of the pages were dog-eared.

I read one of the underscored passages:

I am a man of much grief, but it is not fit that I should sit in another's house mourning and wailing. It is wrong to grieve forever without ceasing.

Then flipped to another, one Castillo had put a little star next to:

*Since it is not possible to elude the will of Jove or make it vain,
let this man go alone over the barren sea.*

I wasn't sure what it meant, but inspected some of the other marked passages.

To me, O stranger, thou appearest now a different man from what thou wast before, thou hast other garments, and thy complexion is no longer the same. Thou art certainly one of the gods who possess the whole of heaven.

I closed Castillo's book, moved my eyes and hand to the folder again. Jeffrey Dahmer/54.

I propped the folder open some. The first page was just numbers and a picture. The numbers made no sense. The picture was . . . The picture was what I would look like if I were . . . what? Cool, maybe. Jeff Williford looked exactly like me but not. He looked way older. Tougher. Like he wasn't afraid of anything. (I, however, was a guy who looked like he was afraid of *everything*.)

I cleared space on the small desk and opened up the folder all the way.

There were a lot more numbers. The next page. More numbers. Asymmetry scores, MMPI fmab, MAOA, karyotype levels. And so on. It meant nothing. This folder had, at first glance, even less meaningful info than the folder my dad had given me back at the house.

My heart weighed a thousand pounds. Hand shaking.

What would the next page reveal?

I'd expected everything to be spelled out. Black and white.

THIS IS WHAT WE HAVE LEARNED ABOUT "JEFF."

THIS IS HOW MUCH OF A KILLER "JEFF" REALLY IS.

THIS IS WHAT "JEFF" SAID ABOUT WANTING TO MURDER.

There was none of that.

Just more numbers. A human being reverted to nothing more than a bunch of charts and graphs. No more than a summer science lab trying to figure out the pH levels of Ivory soap or the density of some random liquid. No more than Mendel and his stupid peas. I turned the pages over one after another. Nothing.

Until the second to last page. There, I saw a few notes someone had typed. My father? Another one of the smiling shrinks at DSTI? Maybe it had been Mrs. Jamieson. She was one of the smiliest shrinks they had up there. (And one of those murdered, btw.)

```
need for stimulation, prone to boredom, lack
of realistic long-term goals

propensities to risk-taking behavior,
promiscuous sexual behavior? deprecating
attitude toward the opposite sex-likely
homosexual, lack of interest in bonding

conning/manipulative, inclinations of
excessive boasting

Ritualistic behavior/OCD? how much alcohol
introduced? killed cat with bb gun. buried?
```

That was all. Then another page of numbers. I turned back to the notes and looked for anything that was the same. Anything that was *different* between Jeffrey Dahmer/54 and me. It did not say if the other Jeffrey had musical talent. But I only played bass and not particularly well. Maybe it meant nothing. *Or everything*.

"Lack of realistic long-term goals?" What the hell did that even mean? I'd never thought much beyond what was for dinner or what I needed to do that same week for schoolwork. I wanted to be a teacher maybe or, I don't know, work for NASA or something. It wasn't really something I spent hours sitting around thinking about. If I ever thought about the future, it was daydreams about playing bass professionally or getting paid to invent new video games. These were not, I think, "realistic long-term goals."

"Promiscuous sexual behavior?" Stupid. I hadn't even kissed a girl yet.

GEOFFREY GIRARD

Or any guy, either, for God's sake! So I wasn't *likely* anything. If anything, I was kinda asexual, and the whole notion of hooking up and falling in love and stuff like that quite honestly terrified the shit out of me.

Was tapping my knee all the time "OCD"? Or making sure my books were lined up in certain ways on the shelf? Or the fact that I would never, ever use the last bit of milk left in the jug, but would pour it out into the sink? *Did that count?*

I'd never killed an animal like this guy had. Unless the thing with the bird . . . which had been a total accident. *Did that count?*

Me and this Williford kid in this folder were genetically, physically, the exact same person.

And genetically, physically, the exact same person as the original killer.

But beyond the blue eyes and blond hair, how much else was the exact same? Judging by the details in the folder, not much.

In that empty room, I cursed my father. Closed the folder, stuffed the whole thing down to the bottom of Castillo's pile.

I crossed the room and retrieved the scattered notes from the floor and end of the bed. The last clue had led us straight to Serpent Mound and, probably, a clone in Ohio. I'd seen it almost immediately once I'd really thought about it.

Of all the little pictures to draw, why that? Had my dad known his adopted son would recognize it? Did you? I asked the empty room. Serpent Mound was on purpose. For me to figure out. Right? Maybe they all were. But the big remaining question: WHY?

Something to ask my dad later, if I ever got the chance.

I collapsed onto the bed, my mind racing a thousand different places with questions as I stared up at the ceiling. Another hour went by, maybe more. My eyes grew heavier, my thoughts darker. Eventually sleep came for me again. I didn't mind. It would be a break from thinking.

I closed my eyes. Slept.

And then I murdered someone.

. . .

You hear his blood. From a hundred miles away, you hear it. Like . . . like the sounds of traffic moving by whizzing past through veins or rumbling like eighteen wheels his pounding heart shunting out even more blood in the whoosh whoosh whoosh sound. You hear his blood because its sounds echo in your own veins. His heart whooshing perfectly with yours now one shared heart shared blood like a car engine starting firing alive. And it's calling out to you. Many miles pass by, you drift easily over them in the dark, always in the dark. You started at his house, moved past the dead woman in the living room followed across the street. Your own heart thumping at what he'd done there and then you just listened. For more blood. He is close now. Your prey. Your brother. You smile, the blades in your hands are sharp and brand-new they are nine inches long they were made to cut and slice meat. You see him now across the parking lot. Move slowly behind him, wait in the darkness. Hold the knives out in the glow of the building lights. He moves, you move. When he goes in, you don't want to be seen, and wait just a little more. The sound of his blood roars like goliath machinery in your ears. Pounding, pounding. Your hands on the door, black fingers. There is a voice but it's lost beneath the pounding, pounding. Knuckles pushing painfully at the door. The knives leave long scratches. Now you are moving, gliding over the wall as if flying behind him over him floating. The tune of his blood is boundless like God. He sees you now your dark skeletal face mirrored in his widening eyes and he is scream-ing but you can no longer hear his screams over the lyrical blood. You start stabbing and new sounds fill your ears, hands driving downward slicing meat. Sputtering sounds. Hissing sounds. Like . . . like air from hydraulic brakes or maybe even a slashed-open tire . . .

. . .

I was outside. *Huh?* Behind the motel. *Wait!*

Reality returning as softly as it'd first snuck away.

Crouched behind a huge dumpster. *No.* . . .

Both my hands remained clenched into fists like I was holding something. I thought of sharp steel.

How I got there, I still haven't a clue.

There was no one else around.

I'd killed no one. (I told myself this anyway . . . not really knowing if it was true or not. I mean, there was no blood on me. I had no weapon. There was no body.)

Worse thought, maybe, I'd only *imagined* the whole thing. Dreamed it.

Spellbound. Sleepwalking.

Lunatic.

I stood up straight and got my bearings. The empty parking lot. The darkened motel. Just past the motel was the freeway, the sounds of passing cars whooshing by all too familiar.

Obviously (or so I told myself) the reality of the nearby freeway had bled into my dream, as sounds sometimes do. What else *could* it have been?

I moved slowly back to the room. The door had been left open. First I thought Castillo might be back, but then I realized I'd just left it that way. But how? Why?

I hadn't killed anyone, that part was still true. But that didn't mean there wasn't a dead guy *somewhere*. As much as I wanted to write it all off as some nightmare, I felt in the pit of my mind/body/soul that there was something else going on here. There was, in fact, great suspicion in my mind/body/soul that someone else *had* just killed. *Something* else.

Because, as I crept back into the room, I could still hear all that blood.

And I could tell that Someone Else, whoever/whatever it had been, wanted to hear more.

I could tell this killer was just getting started.

GEOFFREY GIRARD

CHAPTER TWENTY-FOUR

*T*he Albaum kid *was* a clone.

His parents, against my father's instructions, called their new son Bryce, a middle name they'd added in honor of his adoptive mom's grandfather.

But his legal name, his REAL name, was Edward.

Edward Bryce Albaum.

The clone of Ed Gein.

. . .

This was another name I did not know. Castillo says he hadn't heard of him either but the boy had a folder completely filled with information about Gein. (You know, charts, pictures, biographical data. That old story.) Ed Gein only murdered a couple of people. Small-time killing compared to the other guys DSTI had collected. But he is still a deity in the pantheon of serial killers. His nicknames were: "The Plainfield Ghoul" and "The Mad Butcher." Mostly, he just dug up graves and did stuff with the bodies. Really disgusting stuff. Again, I won't go into details here. That's up to you. But here's a hint:

Ed Gein was the specific inspiration for Norman Bates (the killer in *Psycho* who dresses like his dead mother and keeps her corpse in the house).

Ed Gein was the specific inspiration for Buffalo Bill (the killer in *Silence of the Lambs* who abducts overweight women and then uses their skin to make a "woman suit" for himself).

Ed Gein is the specific inspiration for Leatherface (the killer in *The Texas Chainsaw Massacre* who eats people and keeps bodies hanging on huge hooks in his house, just like dead cows).

That's three of the most famous serial killer movies EVER made. All from this same guy.

It's kinda amazing.

The police could simply not believe what they'd found in Gein's Wisconsin house. In fact, the local sheriff in charge was so traumatized by what he saw that he died of a heart attack less than one month after testifying in court against Gein. This sheriff was just forty-three years old.

Neighbors burned down Gein's house.

In the early 1980s representatives from DSTI visited Ed Gein at the Mendota Mental Health Institute and took blood and tissue samples with his permission. They told him he'd "live forever." And though he died a couple of years after, DSTI hadn't completely lied. There was still a whole lot left of Edward Gein in the world.

Skin, hair, eyes, cells, muscle, brain tissue.

Only now, everyone was calling all that stuff Edward Bryce Albaum.

A rose by any other name . . .

This other-name's whole family had been murdered.

• • •

Castillo found the boy alone in his house. The kid was only eleven.

His family—mom, dad, and an older brother—were dead. Castillo said the kid had covered their heads with some opened notebooks so he wouldn't have to see their faces.

The Albaum kid had NOT killed his family.

Some other kids—the kids we were looking for—had done that for him.

. . .

They'd come to his house two days before. Four or five teens. Pulled up in two cars and came into his house like it was their own. They bashed his father in the face with a golf club. They did worse to the others. But they left him completely alone.

Because he was ONE OF THEM.

These kids told Edward Bryce Albaum he was a clone. They told him he was the clone of a famous serial killer. Then they gave him a folder. Then they left. Only thing missing here was my dad and a thousand dollars in cash. (They handed him only a handful of twenties.)

The kid'd been too terrified to call the police or leave the house for two days.

Castillo sat with him for hours waiting for Help to arrive. Castillo asked him questions. The boy mostly stared at the television. He'd been in deep shock, Castillo told me later.

The Help that showed up midday were some people DSTI and the United States government sent. The Help then took the boy away.

. . .

When Castillo first came back to the motel, I was practically bouncing off the walls. Because (a) he was back, which I admit always relaxed me a great deal because I didn't want to spend another minute alone in that motel room not knowing if I would fall asleep again or where my mind might take me, and (b) I'd done good. I mean, shit! I'd officially solved the puzzle, you know. I'd officially figured out what that squiggle was and had led Castillo straight to an actual clone. I was a hero or something. I'd really proved my worth to Castillo and, honestly, to myself.

That all lasted about thirty seconds.

Castillo was in a foul mood as usual. Worse even. When he and I checked out of the motel and grabbed some food at a diner an hour down the road, he didn't want to talk at all.

He'd stayed up with the Albaum kid all night, and I think he was finally starting to ponder over the same thing I was: WHAT THE HELL WAS GONNA HAPPEN TO THIS KID NOW? What would the government and DSTI do to Edward Bryce Albaum when both thought of him only as the clone of Ed Gein? This kid, if the truth of what had happened were to ever get out, would be a media nightmare. He was proof of terrible experiments. Secret experiments. An embarrassment. A threat to national security. How would the government handle his existence, what he'd been told? How would they handle the three dead bodies in his house? People murdered by teenagers claiming to be clones.

I hardly said one word while we packed, drove, and ate. Now the uneasy silence between us was amplified by the bustling diner. Castillo wasn't even eating. I asked him if I could have some of his bacon, and he was cool with that. I was starved, so it was, like, the best meal I'd ever had. Castillo kept looking at me all strange, but I figured, why let good food go to waste?

Castillo mostly studied the road map beside his plate. He dropped two fingers onto the map. Eventually he said: Unity, Ohio, and Lovett, Indiana. He said two girls had been found murdered in Unity. One found hacked to bits, apparently. A third girl, Emily Collins, was missing. A suspect. Her mother was also missing. Emily Collins's sister was

GEOFFREY GIRARD

one of the dead girls. He said: In Lovett, Indiana, a couple of teens had been found hanging from a tree. Both bodies had been badly burned.

They're heading west, Castillo said while running his fingers in a subtle swiggle across the map.

I didn't want to look. I was tired of his Murder Map. I was tired of not talking about what we should be talking about: the Albaum kid.

Actually I had one more question . . . really *two* more.

Route 50, Castillo was mumbling to himself. From what the Albaum kid had told him, it looked like the original group had picked up some kid named John a couple of weeks before they came for him. And apparently this John kid had been dressed like a clown.

WTF? One of the teens who'd killed the Albaum family had been dressed like a . . .

I was so completely done with all of this. I might have even envied the Albaum kid some. I mean, it *was* completely done for him now, right? He'd vanish back into DSTI and—if my father was right—probably never be seen again.

Then Castillo told me about John Wayne Gacy. Another famous serial killer. This guy tortured and murdered thirty-plus men and kept most of the bodies buried in his crawl space. Mostly he was known for dressing up like a clown sometimes at neighborhood parties and community events and stuff. A clown named Pogo.

This distantly evoked a dream I'd recently had. The one I'd had about the park.

I told Castillo I didn't want to know any more.

• • •

Castillo asked me if I'd ever met a boy named John, a question I completely ignored, so he tried again. Ever in my life? I just kept staring at my plate. This was NOT the talk I wanted to have. Probably, I told him. This kid on my soccer team two years ago was named John Vincent. Did that count? But if he meant a John connected to DSTI, the clown kid? The *clone* kind of John, then no.

Castillo glanced around the diner. Told me to keep it down and got all pissed and serious about it. Asshole.

My bad, I replied, looked up. Then I whispered: No, I don't think I ever met a John at the place-that-won't-be-mentioned, which I often visited with the man-who-won't-be-mentioned. I already gave you all the names I could remember.

Castillo said the Albaum boy thought the clown was definitely named John but that a guy named Ted had done most of the talking. But the Albaum boy couldn't really remember any of the other names. He thought he remembered "Al" and "Henry" but wasn't sure. He was pretty positive he never once heard a "*D* name."

Castillo said: Maybe David and Dennis aren't with these other guys anymore.

I told him again that David wouldn't be. Castillo didn't seem impressed.

Finally I'd had enough.

Time for QUESTION #1. *Was my dad there?*

Castillo said NO. While I thought about this, I absently used the fork to play with the food on my plate. Couldn't decide which answer would have been worse: (a) that my father *had* been there, had been part of the group that had murdered the Albaum family, OR (b) that my father was still missing, vanished into the world somewhere.

I then asked QUESTION #2: What about Jeff? Did this Albaum kid meet a Jeff?

GEOFFREY GIRARD

Castillo looked straight at me. His face looked pained. He greatly preferred the first question, I think. I asked if we were just supposed to pretend Castillo *wasn't* also looking for a Jeffrey Dahmer clone. Castillo admitted he was. He also said the Albaum kid wasn't sure if he'd heard that name or not. He'd questioned the kid specifically about each of the six, and the kid hadn't remembered a tall blond guy.

QUESTION #3. What happens to him now?

Albaum? he said. He's halfway to Pennsylvania by now. Back to DSTI.

Yeah, I pushed, so what happens to him now?

Castillo said he didn't know.

They're just gonna kill him, I said.

Castillo cursed at me. Man, he was angry. He asked: Why the hell would you even say that?

I reminded him that my dad had said they'd kill me if they ever caught me.

Well, Daddy ain't thinking too clearly these days, is he? he replied. Castillo so wanted to punch me in the face. Instead he added: I'm sure the kid'll be fine.

Are you? I asked. Didn't care if he wanted to punch me in the face. Castillo drank his stupid coffee.

I asked: How long before you turn ME over? I was getting kinda angry too. Castillo had just turned this Albaum kid over to the government. Like he would turn in the others. And eventually me.

Worse, I'd helped him do it. (I was, I think, mostly angry at myself.) Castillo said: They don't even know you're with me.

But they knew I existed. Castillo would need to turn me in eventually.

You're helping me do my job, he said.

And when I couldn't, anymore? Or wouldn't?

Don't know, he said. Guess I'll decide then.

I nodded. And just like that, it was over. The questions had been answered—or not answered—but they didn't matter anymore. Castillo's matter-of-factness had taken the steam out of my tantrum. There was nothing left to say, really.

Castillo changed the topic. He said: Here's what I know now. Based on what the Albaum kid says, I think a couple of guys split off, together or alone. Guys like your David, maybe. I think Jacobson . . . I think your father might have been with these guys at the very start but has also gone on alone.

I told him I thought that too.

· It was the group heading west that Castillo was most worried about. He ran his finger along Route 50. He said: There are murders and disappearances all over the country, but if I wanted to draw a straight line down Route 50 today, I finally could. *This*, he tapped the map. This is the fresh game trail. The blood trail. You ever gone hunting?

Isn't that what we're doing now? I asked.

Castillo made a noise that sounded like a laugh but wasn't.

He asked of I'd figured out any more of my dad's notes.

I had.

· · ·

But I stalled. Had to. Yes, I HAD figured some stuff out. After my nightmare, my hallucination, my trance, whatever the heck you want to call it, I'd locked myself back into that motel room and had gone through my dad's notes again. Terrified to ever sleep again. Fearful of where I might wake up or what I might see when I did. And so I'd looked at the list I'd made at Subway, cross-referencing with the atlas Castillo had left me. And I'd found some stuff, but . . .

But giving this info to Castillo meant possibly finding more clones.

More little Edward Albaums out there.

Or Richardsons or Sizemores or Whatevers.

More kids to find and lead straight back to the slaughterhouse.

• • •

Castillo asked me again if I'd figured out anything more.

I admitted, Maybe. (And just *maybe*, I thought, some good could come out of this.)

The guys who'd escaped from DSTI hadn't stopped at this kid's house randomly. They'd been SENT there. I knew this as clearly as Castillo did. It was the big elephant in the diner.

The very first night, Castillo had read it in my father's journals: *My dad wanted the clones free.* All of them (all of us). And he'd probably SENT those kids to find Edward Albaum. Just as he'd first sent them to find Albert McCarty and *his* dead family.

Had my dad told these guys to kill the families? Had he told them to kill the clone kids who wouldn't play their game properly? Or had he simply left that decision up to the six boys?

How many other families were going to be visited this week?

Had the things I'd seen in my nightmares been only in a nightmare, or some kind of premonition of what was to come? Or a memory? And if so . . . could I still stop these guys? Were these killers just working from the same list of names I had?

I told Castillo I thought maybe the black bird might be Hitchcock, Indiana.

The Birds is this famous Alfred Hitchcock movie. It's way too slow, like most old movies, but there are still one or two cool scenes. My father and I watched it together one night. He said it was a classic I should probably know. He even made popcorn.

Castillo found Hitchcock, Indiana, on the map. It was right on Route 50. It was right on his growing "trail of blood." He told me to go on, so I told him about the monkey.

The monkey and Salem, Illinois.

What monkey? He'd pulled out his phone to thumb through the images.

Gilronan, I explained. The monkey with the graduation cap.

Gill Ronan

Castillo thought it would make more sense if a Salem reference featured a witch's hat instead of what-I-thought-was a graduation cap. Because, you know, the Salem witch trials. But that would not in ANY WAY have explained the monkey. I decided it best not to tell Castillo he was being stupid.

Instead I just explained that Salem, *New Hampshire*, was a small town where John Scopes went to high school. Now, Scopes was NOT a serial killer. Not at all. He was a high school science teacher who got famous when he was arrested for teaching evolution to his class. This was against the law in Tennessee in 1925. (A law which remained in Tennessee until 1967, currently one of only two states where it's legal, thanks to a *new* law in 2012, for teachers to present the Garden of Eden as a truth, and evolution as a disputed guess, if they want to.)

The trial was called "The Scopes Monkey Trial." And the guy who eventually prosecuted Scopes in court for teaching about evolution just happened to be a guest speaker at Scopes's own high school graduation when Scopes was a teen. This was, like, ten years before the trial. Total coincidence. This man's name was William Jennings Bryan. He'd been the presidential candidate for the Democrats three different times and had lost each time. He thought Charles Darwin's evolution theory was nonsense and that people really came from the Garden of Eden.

He believed in Cain.

At the famous Scopes Monkey Trial—famous because the whole country was watching to see if Science or Religion would win— William Jennings Bryan claimed he actually remembered Scopes in the Salem audience that graduation night ten years before and that the younger Scopes had been laughing and basically being an ass.

Castillo seemed impressed that I knew this. Or disturbed, maybe. I tried explaining that my dad was a scientist and that this was the kind of stuff we'd talk about. I'd remembered Scopes and the Bryan guy, but I'd needed Castillo's phone to look up where Scopes went to high school and confirm: Salem, New Hampshire.

Salem, *Illinois*—however—right near Route 50, and right on Castillo's growing "blood trail."

Castillo asked if I thought the pics might be clues just for me. I shrugged and Castillo mirrored the move perfectly as I did it. Kinda funny. (Castillo wasn't so bad.)

He asked about the other cartoons, and I admitted I hadn't a clue on the rest yet and that I needed more time.

Castillo decided we'd maybe head first to Hitchcock. Said he'd need to get on his laptops to check if any Sizemores lived nearby. Worst case, he said, we're totally wrong and we can cross off one more town.

On the way he wanted to stop at that park outside McArthur, Ohio. It just happened to be where that mom and her two kids had vanished. Castillo said: Maybe we'll find something. Killers sometimes return to the sites of their crimes.

Then he said: Nice job, man.

I figured I'd cash in my "nice job" coupon right away and maybe ask just one more question.

More like REQUEST #1, I suppose.

Screw Hitchcock. That's what I wanted to say. *I don't give a rat's ass about this Sizemore kid or the other clones either. Let's just keep looking for my dad instead.* But I didn't have the balls to say it. Instead, needing to say *something*, I just asked if I could order some more food.

Castillo said: Yeah.

I'd done good. I thought he was maybe even starting to like me.

Didn't yet realize he was absolutely terrified of me.

• • •

For the record, the jury found Scopes guilty. It took them all of eight minutes. Scopes quit teaching and went to work for some big oil company. Back then, Religion won over Science. Now, it seems, Science just does whatever the hell it wants. Maybe Tennessee wasn't/ isn't so backward after all. Maybe they just saw where the world was headed.

CHAPTER TWENTY-FIVE

*T*hen we're at the park. Goebel Park in Ohio. Just a little community woodlands and playground. It was night. Early morning. Two days before, a mother and her two children had maybe vanished here. Their minivan had been found a few miles up the road, nose-down in some creek.

I wandered around while Castillo walked the playground and picnic area. He was tense. Worried the cops and news vans would swarm back anytime. Apparently the whole place had recently been crawling with reporters and volunteers and ROTC guys from Ohio University, all looking for this family.

Ashley Nelson. And her young kids, Michael and Cassie.

I could almost picture them at the park. Maybe a blanket on the picnic table and some cheese sandwiches or something. A couple of toys spread out. A Frisbee or something maybe tossed around together while killing some time on a warm afternoon.

And then maybe THEY show up. A carload of kids. One of them maybe dressed as a clown. Then things get bad, and "killing time" takes on a whole new meaning.

It was easy to imagine. Too easy.

It was, I realized, basically the same park from my dream. The park where the "Woman in the Black Dress" (sic "THE THING ON THE BED") was swallowing up all the children with her evil. The same long plastic slides and planked bridges and turrets and swings. The same chunky mulch and narrow trees, and benches and shelters. The same dark shadows of night spreading in every direction. I expected to look up and see her at any moment. To feel the cold tender touch of her blackness first coiling around my feet, legs.

But I saw nothing.

It was just another park, of course. Any park. Every park.

How could I possibly recognize it? It would be like recognizing the faces of dead people you'd never really met, right? *Ha!* Maybe I *had* been here before. Thirty years before, even. Parts of me. Maybe. I shook off the terrible thought, the thought that my whole body was just some organism carrying the memory of another. I moved deeper into the park.

Castillo warned me not to get too far, told me we were leaving soon. I waved him off, kept walking. Needed to get away from the growing night shadows ever winding around the equipment and trees.

Found myself moving toward a small skateboard pit just beyond the playground. There were no lights. But something was there. Something warm and bright cutting through the vast gloom. I found painted asphalt, a concrete half-pipe, and a couple of bars. Graffiti, chipped and old, where someone had written band names and "POSERS" and someone had written "WAX MAN" and drawn a weird picture.

But the biggest graffiti, the source of the unnatural luminance, ran along one whole side of the half-pipe. It was a big carroty fluorescent paint that glowed in the dark like a living thing.

It blazed: *EXTREME FOR LIFE.*

EXTREME FOR LIFE. I stood staring at those words awhile, thinking about what it meant. EXTREME LIFE would have been simple enough for any skate park. Extreme sports and lifestyle and all that stuff. It meant "to stay radical and colorful and dangerous and loud and outrageous." And I'm sure that's how most of the skaters here took it. But the "FOR," I think, added something else entirely. Something that whoever'd spray painted this message however many weeks, months, or years before had meant for the whole world to see. Or maybe just for himself or herself. It meant, I think, to fight FOR life. To be radical and colorful and dangerous and loud and outrageous FOR life. Not taking it for granted. Call it carpe diem or YOLO or whatever. This person embraced life, was mad for it. It meant don't take one minute of life for granted. It meant DON'T EVER BE AFRAID OF THE DARK. A challenge. And a promise, too.

. . .

I stared at those simple words a long time. Memorized every line and curve of each letter. Until, by the time I walked back toward Castillo again, I could feel its power still burning within me.

I even moved in deliberate, slow steps through the swings and stopped to shove the swing bridge that connected the two halves of the huge castle swing set. Watched it sway back and forth in the darkness. Darkness I no longer feared. I was almost daring it, HER, to even try coming for me.

My father might have spent his life living in such fears. But I refused to.

I heard night bugs chittering. And frogs maybe. Or an owl.

Or the ghosts of a mother and her two children screaming.

Castillo had said the woman's husband had been brought in for questioning. The simple answer, probably not the right answer.

Castillo had also said a boy had been found murdered in nearby Vincent, Ohio. That the boy had been sixteen. He'd played varsity volleyball and caddied at Pinehill golf club. His name was Howell. Rick Howell. Students from his school were crying and stuff on TV, saying what a supernice kid he was. And no one understood why someone would beat a person like that to death.

But none of them knew that Richard Howell was the DSTI-manufactured clone of some guy named Richard Ramirez. A killer called "The Night Stalker." A guy who broke into houses when everyone was asleep and then murdered and raped, like, a dozen families. I wondered if his classmates would still be crying and carrying on if they knew THE TRUTH. Would his classmates still be crying if they'd seen my father's notes?

GEOFFREY GIRARD

The Starry Night. Van Gogh's most famous painting crudely mimicked.

My dad had taken me to see it at this exhibition at the Museum of Modern Art in New York. Something from our shared life together.

VINCENT van Gogh. Vincent, Ohio. Right near Route 50 again.

Another clue seemingly just for me. One I hadn't gotten until AFTER this kid had been killed.

Was I supposed to find these notes, these kids? Did my dad expect me to free them? Or to stop the others from doing what they'd done. Or . . . was this something my dad and I were supposed to be doing together? If I ditched Castillo and figured out enough of these clues, would I eventually catch up with my father? Was he just testing me? (I still wouldn't let that idea go.)

Then why'd he leave you, you dumb dick? Why won't he see you now?

The negative thoughts rushed back in with all the questions.

EXTREME FOR LIFE, I hollered triumphantly in my head. Tried chasing the bad thoughts away with this ridiculous new mantra. Some of the questions too, maybe. Questions I didn't yet want answers to.

• • •

Castillo spent maybe thirty minutes in the park before we were back on the road again.

In the car I asked him if he thought it'd been THEM. The bad kids.

Don't really know, he replied.

I said: Yeah, you do.

The car moved away from the rising sun toward Hitchcock.

If I was wrong about Hitchcock, we'd have wasted hours. If I was right, God only knew what we'd find. I think we were both hoping I was wrong.

I closed my eyes and tried unsuccessfully to sleep.

The orange letters in my memory already fading with each mile.

• • •

Oh, and as to why this particular clone had been murdered but others were allowed to live, your guess is as good as mine. And Castillo had no idea either. I mean, how did these guys decide which clones to kill that very first night at Massey? Were they following orders? My dad's orders? Or was there just something they hadn't liked about Rick Howell?

Something in his eyes that said *NOT ONE OF US*.

• • •

And if so, what would they see if they looked into my eyes.

• • •

The rest of the morning moved by in a blur of fields, one-church towns, and Dairy Queens. Ohio and Indiana were kinda boring.

Or not.

Just down the road there'd been a holdup a few days before. Couple of teens, a boy and a girl, tortured and killed behind some store. The town sheriff said it was related to drug gangs.

Castillo wasn't so sure.

And also the two women found murdered in Unity. They'd just found the mom and another male victim in the apartment across the hall. Still looking for the older daughter.

Castillo wasn't so sure.

We mostly drove in silence still. I held my hand outside the window

GEOFFREY GIRARD

and rode waves on the wind. Tried to vanish. Castillo talked to someone on the phone. He mostly just grunted short answers, and I couldn't figure out what they were talking about. At some point I knew they were talking about the missing girl.

He thought maybe this one girl had joined up with the other guys. That she was even helping them. Turned out he was right.

• • •

The girl's name was Emily Collins, and, the authorities suspect, she met one of the guys on Facebook and agreed to "party." Guy had funny instant messages about blowing up malls and raping soccer moms and wild Snapchat pics. She thought he was a riot. Next thing you know, her roommate and sister and mom were dead. And also some guy who lived in the next apartment. And also, a couple of days later, her. (They found her body in an Indiana dumpster.)

There are, it turns out, some girls who actually find serial killers hot. Like musician or sports groupies. It's called "hybristophilia." It's not the norm, obviously. But it's more common than you would ever think.

The original Ted Bundy confessed to killing thirty women and still received *hundreds* of letters every single month from girls all across the country. He was visited by dozens of them and even married one while in jail.

Henry Lee Lucas killed two hundred people. He only had one eye. He also had hundreds of female admirers and also got married in prison.

John Wayne Gacy, the clown guy, was overweight and gay, and even he got fan mail from GIRLS every day and married a woman while in prison.

The Night Stalker, Richard Ramirez (the genetic source of the boy murdered in Vincent, Ohio, two days ago), raped and murdered twenty women, and there were lines of suitors outside the courthouse every day to see him. Lines. During the trial, one woman sent him a cupcake on Valentine's Day with the message "I LOVE YOU." That woman *was on the jury.* Later, he married an editor from *Teen Beat* magazine, who has sworn to kill herself when he is finally executed.

I apologized for all guys earlier.

Someone else can apologize for this.

• • •

Castillo wouldn't tell me who he'd been talking to, but I kept giving him crap, and eventually he admitted it was a friend of some kind. Some type of shrink who was helping him with this case. I suspected it was this Kristin girl who Ox had mentioned at the ballpark, and the fact that he'd even admitted he was talking to a friend who was a shrink was surprising enough, really. I kinda think he *wanted* to talk about her, you know? He wanted to make her more real while we were driving in that car. But when I tried to find out any more, Castillo had no interest in pursuing that line further.

So I tried instead asking him what his nightmare was about. The one from the other night when he'd woken up screaming. Again he acted like nothing had happened. But he was totally flustered. He knew I knew. He was embarrassed, too.

I figured it was as good a time as any to maybe tell him some of the things I'd been seeing. Not all of it. But just that I understood, I guess. Maybe I was just hoping he'd tell me the same thing. It was time to get some of my nightmares out into the sun. It was time to maybe get "Extreme for Life."

So I was thinking about first telling Castillo about the dreams with Ted. The Woman in the Black Dress. The murder I'd seen/imagined. The face at the ballpark. Maybe even all of it.

To start, I admitted out loud that I "saw stuff."

Generic enough so I could see how Castillo would react. Good thing.

Castillo replied: What kinda stuff? You tell me "I see dead people," I'm gonna kick your ass right out of the car.

He was making a joke but I didn't know that. Because I didn't know how he knew. (I didn't yet know he was making a reference to some movie I'd never seen.) But he clearly didn't want me to bring night thoughts into the daylight and I retreated quickly. Dropped the whole conversation.

I let the silence hang for another couple of minutes and then asked Castillo about his scars. If he didn't want to talk about imaginary things, the least he could do was tell me something about something real. I pointed at the scar that ran the length of Castillo's arm.

Fishing, he replied.

I tried again and he told me to take a nap.

I tried again.

War, Castillo said, and shifted to maybe hide the scar better.

He said: Someone cut me.

What about the others? I asked.

Yeah, he said. Those, too.

• • •

He'd tried to hide them. But we'd been together a good week now. Even trying NOT to look, I'd caught enough glimpses. More than enough. Pale scars almost completely covered his stomach and chest. The marks crisscrossed the defined muscles in continuous disfigurement and design, wrapped over his shoulders and arms. Weird symbols. (I learned later they were Persian letters.) Others were something else, foul characters no one has yet determined. There were snakes with too many heads, and bugs with human hands, and trees split open and filled with fangs. And eyes. Staring eyes. Etched in flesh.

. . .

I asked if he'd ever gotten the guy who did it. The guy who'd cut him, I mean. I was thinking I'd sure want to if someone had done that to me. (I was wrong, I found out later.) Castillo adjusted the rearview mirror a fraction. He said he didn't remember too much. It was certainly reasonable if he'd blocked *that* out. But still, I couldn't tell if he was lying.

I asked him about WAR and he just blew me off. Told me it was loud.

So I asked him if he'd ever killed anyone.

He cursed at me and told me to shut up. (Talking to Castillo was a real treat those days.)

So I shut up. For a while. Until I saw a couple of kids playing in the front yard up ahead and got my nutty brain thinking again.

I asked what he supposed DSTI was doing with Ed right now. I was referring to Edward Bryce Albaum again. The kid we'd found together, the kid I'd likely sent to his doom.

No clue, Castillo said. Told you last night: He's not my job anymore. He's DSTI's job now.

Those little kids waved at us as we passed. I couldn't help but wonder if recently they'd waved at anyone else interesting on this same road. Maybe a carload of travelers, teens, also headed toward Hitchcock. The kind of travelers/teens you shouldn't ever wave to.

GEOFFREY GIRARD

I waved back.

Perfect, I said to Castillo. Then I'm sure he's doing just great.

Castillo didn't reply, turned up the radio. He'd discovered a whole new way to blow me off.

We drove without speaking another twenty miles. It felt like a hundred.

. . .

The Sizemore family lived on 7422 OldeGate Lane.

I waited in the car while Castillo went to check if they were dead.

Or if, best case, their son was the clone of a vicious killer.

Another experiment cooked up in some lab. The clone of Gary Ridgway. The "Green River Killer." A guy who killed almost a hundred women in the Northwest during the '80s and '90s.

So maybe Hitchcock, Indiana, *looked* just like anywhere/everywhere else. The same houses and fences and trees and dogs and families. But it wasn't. Not, if I was right, according to my dad's notes.

Maybe this family'd been paid to molest this kid. Or encourage him to drink. Maybe this family'd been paid to just leave him alone. Or maybe one family had no idea where this kid had really come from. Or maybe, rather probably, the black bird in my dad's batshit-crazy notes had nothing to do with Alfred Hitchcock at all.

And just maybe, rather probably, my dad hadn't wanted his freak son to ever help solve ANYTHING.

It'd been a whole week. I could hardly wrap my head around it. But sitting alone in that car, it was sure becoming clearer and clearer that I was alone. *Alone*-alone. And there wasn't another single person on Earth who wondered where I'd gotten to. Not a single one. My name wasn't in any papers. No one was searching for me. Some woman and her kids vanished, and half the state was looking for them. My own dad didn't even care where I was.

What kind of life was this?

And I was totally conning myself into thinking that Castillo gave a damn about me or my situation. To him, I was just another dirty piece of the grand experiment. Another clone freak. Something to hunt and capture. Something to turn over to DSTI when it was time. No different from any of the other kids from the facility. *No different at all.*

In the name of science. For the betterment of man. Et cetera. Et cetera. To understand what caused aggression, violence, evil. Isolate it. Cure it. Control it. Then to one day unleash it again.

The Cain Gene.

Was it really only a matter of the chromosomes floating around in our blood?

If so, I wasn't stupid. I'd read enough Warhammer paperbacks and watched enough Syfy channel to get the big picture. And if fiction ain't your thing, I'd heard what they'd found at Shardhara. I could EASILY imagine biological weapons that would infect the enemy with a murderous hate so bad they'd turn and kill one another. Or provisional injections of rage to boost aggression and strength in battle-fatigued troops.

No wonder the Department of Defense was running the show.

Castillo appeared around the corner, moved casually toward the car.

He got in and started the car to pull away. Looked kinda mad again and didn't say a word.

I assumed Hitchcock had been a total bust. So I apologized.

For what? Castillo frowned. You just found another clone.

• • •

The kid's family was still alive and everything.

CHAPTER TWENTY-SIX

*C*astillo recognized the boy from his picture.
The picture of Gary Ridgway, I mean.

The original Ridgway had fifty CONFIRMED kills in Washington state and was suspected of another forty. Mostly preyed on runaways and prostitutes and kept their bodies hidden in various woods so he could "visit" them again later. When he was sixteen, he'd stabbed a little kid because he'd "wondered what it was like to kill someone." He was in jail in his seventies now.

His clone was a hundred yards away.

Like father and son, Castillo said. A "spitting image."

Castillo'd been trained to look at a photo once and know the person by sight immediately. Seriously. Our government trains people to do stuff like this. Castillo said he'd found terrorist guys who had gotten nose jobs and face-lifts and totally changed their hair and beards. One guy, he said, had been disguised as a *woman* for two years, and Castillo claimed he'd slapped the guy in his nuts when they'd found him. Castillo was messed up.

OK, the idea, the plan, the strategy, was to wait THEM out. Whether or not THEM was three guys now or seven, Castillo didn't know. But he knew they'd killed the Albaums and probably some others along their way west.

And—thanks to me—we'd gotten to Sizemore first.

IF they were working from the same "list," IF they knew Sizemore was a clone, they'd eventually show up. Or maybe even my father. Eventually . . .

Castillo said: The problem with TV shows is that they make it seem like stakeouts involve parking the car outside a house and staring at it until something happens. But neighbors eventually notice strange cars sitting on their street and dial 911. So we had to be somewhere else when/if the "shit went down."

There were two empty houses to choose from. Both for sale. One was directly across the street from the Sizemore house. The other was down the street on an adjacent cul-de-sac. (FOR SALE! REDUCED PRICE!

MOVE-IN READY!) Castillo said: I love this housing market.

He explained that sometimes overseas the soldiers would have to commandeer a house.

Castillo said: I am half prepared to do that here, too. I think he was tired of all of it too.

Instead we waited until it was two in the morning, and he broke into the cul-de-sac house. The house was empty, furniture removed, the last owners long since having moved on. As Castillo had surmised, the top right back bedroom window looked out perfectly over OldeGate Lane.

He set down the recently purchased foldout chair and a bag of groceries. He'd left the car three blocks away, with plans to move it to a new street each day.

I told Castillo we were gonna get busted but he just shook his head and tossed me something.

It was a paperback. *The Pillars of the Earth*. Something about building a Gothic cathedral in England. What's this for? I wondered out loud.

Castillo said: You said you were a reader. He positioned his new lawn chair at the back window. Unless you wanted a romantic thriller, he said. That's all the store had.

I flipped through the book. It was, like, eighty thousand pages long and weighed fourteen pounds. I had the feeling Castillo had bought it only because it was the biggest one they'd had. Guess he thought we were gonna be in an empty house awhile.

Castillo watched me, looked like he wanted to say something, and then turned to look out the window again.

So here we are, he said. I walked over to behind the chair and asked NOW WHAT?

Castillo said something corny about us being lions hunting and all. I kinda thought he might even be warming up to me.

. . .

We were in that stupid horrible house a couple of days. The first day was the worst, as we just sat and watched another house. Castillo never talked. We ate peanut butter sandwiches and cold hot dogs quietly together. Every so often I took watch for a couple of hours so Castillo could get some sleep. I'd just stare out the window at a house where nothing ever really happened.

Once, the big thrill of the day, I saw the kid's mom drive out to do some food shopping. I didn't really get a good look at her. The thing I most noticed was that she had those stupid little family decals on the back of her prerequisite SUV. The cartoon dad with his little golf club, cartoon mom with her little shopping bags, big brother holding a basketball, and then little cartoon Gary. The youngest son. Smaller figure than the first but another basketball.

As she pulled away, I got this funny idea of another figure next to Gary's sticker. Another figure just like Gary's small one. And another. And another. And another. And another. And another.

Fifty, a hundred, cartoon stickers of Gary Sizemore running up over the first family and filling the whole back of the windshield. All perfectly identical. Not a single difference between them.

My dad and DSTI could have done that. Easily.

The next day I actually saw the real boy, little Gary Sizemore, play basketball in the driveway for a bit. Not an imaginary sticker but another flesh-and-blood freak my father had made.

. . .

GEOFFREY GIRARD

Note: DSTI could—and did—produce clones of various ages. Any age they wanted, really. If they wanted a normal baby (which is what this Gary Sizemore had been), they could make one of those. This was the easiest way to make a clone. Implant the egg into one of their, say, Ukrainian girls (not that a girl from any other country wouldn't do just as well) and wait nine months in the—relatively speaking—traditional method. Now, if they instead wanted to, for whatever reason, make one *older* (which is what I was), they had two options: (1) *start* the embryo in a biological host (i.e., a Ukrainian woman) and then extract the embryo to incubate in a special vat of liquid for almost as long as they wanted, or (2) speed up gestation through artificial means while in the vat and make the clone come out at—by physical size and appearance and physiological development—four years. Or fourteen. Or (in some very rare and expensive and horrific cases) thirty.

• • •

Castillo told me that half of all adoptions in the United States occur through private arrangements. Seventy thousand babies a year trading hands that no one really knows anything about. Kids just like ME. How easily it might have been ME we were now watching. Adopted out to some unsuspecting family. Maybe even a family that was paid to abuse me. Jeffrey *Sizemore* of Hitchcock, Indiana. How easily Gary could have ended up as Gary Jacobson from Jersey. All us little clone babies. Nothing more than a dozen cosmic coin flips.

• • •

So when I wasn't looking out the window at "what-might-have-been," I mostly read the book Castillo'd picked up for me. (A gesture I appreciated.) It was actually a pretty good book because it had stuff about the Hundred Years' War and witches and the plague. But it was also, like, a thousand pages, and made me sleepy. I slept on the floor in the upstairs room behind Castillo and his chair.

Other times, I just wandered the empty house. Tried imagining what the family who'd lived here had been like. What furniture had been in each of the now-empty rooms? How old were the kids? If there'd been any. Did they have a dog? Were they a NORMAL family with a mom and dad and kids? Or one more like mine? An imaginary mom. A mad scientist. A test tube. Some cells from the world's most loathed serial killer.

I explored each room a dozen times, running my fingers across bare walls where once there'd hung pictures and knickknacks, their ghost-like outlines now imprisoned in muted stains. What had the pictures shown? My own house back in Jersey had been turned just as empty and ghostlike.

Eventually I found the house wasn't so empty after all.

Eventually I found that THE WORST was still coming.

• • •

While most of these two days proved a blur of reading and sleeping that felt like a month, here are some moments that stand out. Some are good and some bad. Honestly it's getting harder and harder to tell the difference anymore.

• • •

On the second night, I talked with Castillo.

I told him what I knew about Dolly the cloned sheep. That the scientists made her from a cell that'd been taken from another sheep's mammary (a fancy word for tit), and that there was this singer once named Dolly Parton who was famous for having really big tits. So the

GEOFFREY GIRARD

scientists called the sheep Dolly. He got my point. The most signifi-
cant experiment of the last hundred years, the scientific advancement
that brought man closer to God than any other before or since . . . was
a tit joke.

I wondered from what Dahmer cell they'd made me. I did not wonder this out loud. And I tried really, really hard not to wonder very long.

To change the subject, I voiced to Castillo that I thought we were
totally wasting our time. That the guys were never going to come to
the Sizemore house. Castillo just told me "never" was a long time
and to be patient. He reminded me that he'd hunted that terrorist
guy two years.

So then I told Castillo about Mendel and his experiments with
hawkweed. Castillo made some joke about Mendel having big tits.
But I continued. My father might have been a crazy bastard, but he'd
definitely spent good money and time teaching me all sorts of science
stuff. I figured it was the least I could do to help Castillo understand
what a waste this was.

I told him that after his famous pea experiments, Mendel had also
worked on another plant, called hawkweed. Why hawkweed? Well, a
famous biologist in Germany read Mendel's paper on peas and wrote
to him, said he's gotta give this hawkweed stuff a try. The guy was, like,
the only real biologist who ever wrote to Mendel. Said he'd experi-
mented with hawkweed before and even sent Mendel some seeds to
help get him started. Nice.

The hawkweed didn't work, however. The plant had/has a very
weird "reproductive pattern." Random. Even makes clones of itself
sometimes, instead of true offspring, just to keep things interesting.
Mendel's notes and ideas on heredity suddenly made 0.00 sense. He

wrote a paper and admitted to the whole world he couldn't repeat his pea experiments with the new plant. He admitted he could be wrong about everything.

My dad said this German guy set Mendel up. The guy wanted Mendel to fail. Wanted him to understand you can't predict shit.

Castillo got my point again but told me to give him a break.

Then he said: You done good, man. Getting us this far. Really.

Hawkweed, I replied.

My implication was that you can't predict shit. I probably hadn't gotten us any farther than we'd been a week before.

Castillo just turned back to the window. Maybe, he agreed.

• • •

That was the same night I saw Konerak Sinthasomphone.

• • •

I did not yet know who Konerak Sinthasomphone was.

Like Richard Guerrero's, his was a name I'd have to learn later. (Soon, actually.) That night, he was only a face I recognized. Completely. One I'd seen a dozen times before in various forms. In the treetops and skyline of some new city. In the wallpaper pattern of some hotel lobby. A face that, this night, had slowly once again filled the whole world.

Castillo was upstairs staring at the Sizemore house as usual. Still waiting. And I was a couple of rooms away, stretched out in a small upstairs loft that overlooked the dark family room below. Castillo said he wouldn't need me again until morning. I hoped to sleep again. Couldn't. The paperback was open and across my face. (I'd already read the whole thing twice.) I breathed in the scent of its pages. Tried to clear my mind of all its concerns and questions and

GEOFFREY GIRARD

doubts. Every fifteen minutes or so a car'd go by and its headlights would briefly sneak around the book and my closed eyes.

Eventually, hours later, maybe, I gave up.

He took shape then.

I opened my eyes, and between the railing posts the boy's face emerged in the darkness beneath me. The shadows playing off and up the family room walls and corners, the shallow ruts and lines in the carpet; streaks of black where furniture had once been. Muted light from a neighbor's porch light bleeding through the back windowpanes, casting curious streaks and shapes across the whole room. All trickling slowly together in the blackness and combining into more-distinguishable things. A mouth. Eyes. Jawline. An ear. A smile.

Soon a complete face. An Asian kid.

Sometimes I can force myself to look away. Like in the motel shower. But not this time.

It was as if I'd been caught in a magical trance, or I was a deer in headlights. Once the face started to take shape, I felt I had to let it finish. I was unable to look away, and he now filled the whole room below.

· · ·

Later I would learn that Konerak'd been only fourteen when killed by Dahmer. That he and his family had come to Milwaukee from Laos to escape the Communists. That, after Konerak's death, his family had removed all of his pictures from his house because they could not bear the pain of seeing his face.

· · ·

Those same giant black eyes gazed up at me now as I struggled to break away.

The lines of the mouth bending, opening as if to speak. To scream.

I closed my own eyes, unwilling to look, to maybe eventually hear. When I opened them again, the face had already all but faded.

An illusion. Imagination. No more . . . Yet another shape had already taken his place.

A darkness moving into the room below from the unseen kitchen. A terrible blackness spreading steadily across the carpet, consuming whatever faint memory was left of the boy's face.

The Woman in the Black Dress. The Thing on the Bed.

Standing perfectly still just within the opening of the kitchen, just out of sight. A glimpse only. (Thank God.) The boy's face continued to dissolve away from her widening reach. Her shadow consuming the whole room as it had the park, working up the wall toward me. The neighbor's porch light muted, vanishing also. Her despair filling the whole world.

I looked up from the spreading blackness to where her face should be. Again, only a glimpse. Horrendous white. So artificially bright, it looked wrong. Sick. Perverted. And an enormous unblinking eye. I could only see the one. Gaping straight back at me.

Then long black fingers trailing up her mask. Monstrously elongated. Deformed. Fingers a foot long. Tapered at the ends in sharp nails like needles. Peeling the mask back.

I thought that I would scream bloody murder or that my chest would explode from my beating heart, but it was calm. I was lost. Peaceful. As if time were standing completely still. Waiting to see the monster within.

The taloned fingers skinned back the white mask. The enormous unblinking doll eye lifting to the ceiling. Beneath the mask, the glimpse of the real face beneath.

My father's face.

Spattered in blood.

I rolled over, away from all the monsters below. Shivering. Queasy. Lost. Gone.

• • •

I pulled myself together later. Hours later, I'd say.

And then went to Castillo. What I would say to him exactly, I had no clue.

He didn't want to hear about the things I'd seen any more than I did. They couldn't help him in any way. And they would only make me more of a monster in his eyes.

Yet . . .

I still stood in the doorway to the bedroom, half in the hall. Afraid to commit to the conversation I really, really wanted to have. I ended up trying pointless small talk. He told me to go read my book. I figured I'd get more specific, try to get us to where I needed to be, and asked about Ox. Castillo started to blow me off again but I just kept pushing. I had to. I wasn't going back out into that dark house again until I'd found out more.

I asked where he and Ox had met, and he admitted in Afghanistan ten years before.

Then I finally asked about the ghosts. About talking to ghosts.

• • •

"Talking to ghosts" was the last thing Castillo and Ox had talked about at the baseball game. I hadn't forgotten that little exchange. Far from it. Both of them kinda joking about it but, at the same time, seeming to me they were, just beneath the surface and all, both dead serious about whatever this thing was. Something they did with ghosts, something this mysterious Kristin woman had taught them about. And since "ghost" meant a hundred different things to everyone, I was real curious here. You can't deny I was a bit of a ghost expert myself.

• • •

At first Castillo acted like he didn't know what I was talking about. But I stepped fully into the room now, kept pushing. Castillo searched the ceiling for an answer. He finally admitted it was "something" that "someone" taught "some of us." You couldn't get more vague if you tried, but it was still the most Castillo had EVER told me about anything personal. All I had to do was sort out the pronouns. I assumed by "someone" he meant Kristin, and said so. He seemed surprised I knew her name, and I explained I'd picked it up when he'd spoken with Ox at the ballpark. He admitted she was the "someone."

It was a start. So, naturally, I kept going.

I asked if she (Kristin) was the girl he spoke to on the phone sometimes. The person feeding him information about serial killers and whatnot as we traveled across the country together. (I'd kind of already put this together at this point but wanted confirmation all the same.)

No, he lied then. (He didn't want to involve her yet. And I didn't/ don't blame him.)

He would only admit to what Ox had already given up anyway. That Kristin was a psychiatrist who worked with soldiers who'd come back from the wars in Iraq and Afghanistan with a lot of bad memories and feelings. Guys now fighting depression, alcoholism, nightmares, rage, detachment from society, and thoughts of suicide. (These are all symptoms of post-traumatic stress disorder, PTSD, a condition those who've been in war often develop.) It was her job to help soldiers get rid of, or at least manage, all those feelings.

GEOFFREY GIRARD

And then Castillo admitted to me he was one of those guys. One who'd come home angry, always looking for a fight that never came. Filled with regrets. People he'd let down somehow. He'd learned from Kristin that talking to some of these people was the best thing to do. Often, however, he couldn't talk to them. One way or another, a lot of 'em just weren't around anymore.

So this Kristin woman taught this exercise where vets would try to face specific regrets, these "ghosts." Instead of letting them haunt you, you just kinda meet 'em head-on. Talk it through.

He held up his hands to indicate the explanation was over, that it was so simple and silly, it hadn't even been worth talking about.

But we both knew that was another lie.

• • •

30% of the soldiers returning from Iraq and Afghanistan have been diagnosed with PTSD.

That's more than 250,000 people.

It is believed that susceptibility to PTSD is genetic.

• • •

I then asked Castillo who Shaya was. Shaya was a name he'd mumbled in his sleep more than once. It totally freaked him out. I don't think he had any idea. He told me only that Shaya was a boy he knew in Afghanistan during the war. Not something I talk about, he said. And he seemed sad. An emotion I honestly didn't think he was capable of.

War's stupid, I offered.

He agreed it was but then told me a cool story about fighting the Taliban when he was younger. Like a hundred guys with tanks and stuff on both sides. Bullets flying, guys yelling charges and orders and prayers in a dozen languages over the gunfire. And the US troops had ridden horses. American Special Forces guys working with a powerful Afghani warlord against the Taliban. They'd had to cross this huge field, hundreds of guys, and the best way had been in waves of horses. Castillo's whole face lit up when he told the story, and I asked Castillo if he liked being over there. If he liked war. I remember he said he "liked being good at something."

Killing people, I verified.

He said: That's not all we did. . . .

But you did, I said.

He agreed finally with a yup and added it was never something he *wanted* to do. Then I saw something in Castillo's look that suggested it was time to drop the topic. So I did.

Instead I asked if he thought the guys were still coming here (he did) and then again what he would do with me when this was all over (he still didn't know). It was honest but not very comforting. I suggested I could run away. Wondered if he'd still let me. Before, he HAD given me money to run away. Now, not so much. Instead he brought up about my being only sixteen and all, but I reminded him that kids did it all the time.

He agreed but seemed sad again. An emotion, perhaps, he carried more than I'd ever thought, now that I knew what to look for.

Then he handed me a book. *His* book. *The Odyssey.* The one he was always reading right before the few hours of sleep he got each night. The thing looked like it was fifty years old, it was so used and abused. Dozens of dog-eared pages and a spine broken in twenty different places. He told me to read a chapter called "A Gathering of Shades."

Said it was about how to talk to ghosts.

• • •

That next day, I probably read that chapter a dozen times. The hero of the story, Ulysses, travels to the Underworld to get information and ends up talking to a bunch of dead people. To do this, he has to sacrifice a couple of sheep because it's their blood that lures the shades/ghosts. As the ghosts gather around the fresh blood, he ends up talking to guys who died beside him at Troy, his own mother, a bunch of dead princes, and even a guy who killed himself because of Ulysses. He ends up learning a lot about where they've been and what's been going on in the world while he's been traveling. One of the ghosts, a famous oracle, even reveals Ulysses's future. A future of eventual victory. And, of course, more blood.

Ghosts always want more blood.

• • •

That night, I ran away.

CHAPTER TWENTY-SEVEN

*D*on't blame *The Odyssey.* I was probably most likely headed that way anyway.

I just couldn't take it anymore. Any of it. All of it. Sitting in that house like some kind of caged lab rat. I might as well have been back at DSTI again in some tank. I was sick of the faces of "my" victims appearing. Sick of the black dress lady. Sick of worrying about what my dad was up to. Or IF the other guys would actually show up. Or IF Castillo was starting to maybe like me or not or was gonna dump me in some ditch. Or IF I was really just some horrible monster.

My whole life had become a huge pile of IFs, and I felt like I was gonna explode if I sat there thinking about it for one second longer. Ulysses had his path. A path home. He'd been warned by the ghosts that everyone he was with would die but him and that things would get worse before it was over. And he'd taken the challenge.

I had no such promises and warnings. I had no mission. There was no HOME for me to go to. And no one was telling me things would get worse before it was over. All I was getting was MAYBEs and I DON'T KNOWs and WE'LL SEEs.

OK, maybe you *can* blame the book a little.

Castillo'd given me some money when it got dark and told me how to get to a convenience store a mile or so down the street. This was not because he hoped I'd run away. Quite the opposite. It was something to help make me STAY. Something to do. A chance to get out of the house. I think he recognized I was getting a little nutty wandering around that house.

By the time I reached the store, I'd decided just to keep walking. I had the $40 Castillo'd given me. Figured that was enough to do something. *Anything.* Get on a bus or something. Or walk to the next town and figure out what to do then. To do something ACTIVE. Not just sit around waiting for something to happen to me.

So I just walked straight past that gas station for another few miles.

• • •

This was not anything like the first time I ran away. I mean it was, I guess, if you were a total bystander watching me from afar go buy food but really meaning to leave Castillo forever. But the first time, Castillo had given me $100 with the clear hint that I wasn't supposed to come back. He'd wanted me to take off. And I'd come back to prove to him (and maybe myself too) that I wasn't some piece of shit to be discarded like that. THIS time, however, I really think Castillo trusted me and totally expected to see me back again. And any delusions that I wasn't some piece of shit were, at least by my personal estimation, long, long gone.

• • •

It had probably been an hour. I don't know. Cars kept passing. Black things filled with black shapes I couldn't see. A hundred people going God knows where. Just pairs of headlights racing past on their own life journeys. It was cold. I thought of getting back East somehow, to find my dad. Because he had more explaining to do. A hell of a lot more. A whole lot more about WHEN and WHO and WHERE. But mostly a whole lot more about WHY.

I didn't need talking ghosts for that. I needed my goddamn dad.

HE held the answers to EVERYTHING. My past AND my future, too.

It was another mile before I figured out I hadn't a single clue on how to find him.

The only thing I knew how to do was tune my bass, use the oven, and hook up the PlayStation. It was a pretty depressing realization. I think I cried a little.

I was a total loser. I couldn't do it myself.

I only knew one way to find my dad. Only one person who could help.

As much as I hated to admit it, I needed Castillo.

So I turned back.

• • •

There was a phone outside the convenience store. My last chance. I got five dollars in quarters inside and tried the special number my dad had given me that first night.

He did not answer.

I stood there for twenty minutes. Kept dialing. Used all five dollars' worth of quarters. The rest I just dropped to the ground.

My big real "run away" had been six miles and less than two hours.

When I came back to the house, Castillo was all Where-the-hell-were-you? about it.

I may have told him to F off.

• • •

Things kinda went back to normal. Our normal.

Castillo perched in his lawn chair like a hawk or a wolf or a lion or whatever the heck he was calling himself. Me in the hallway alone with the shadows. This time, however, I asked Castillo to lend me one of his phones to do research on. I told him I was trying to figure out more of my dad's notes. Same lie I'd used before.

Strange hours passed then. Hours I will never, ever forget.

My first real hours with Jeffrey Dahmer.

. . .

I read everything I could about him.

The murders. Trials. His childhood. Interviews with doctors. Stupid jokes.

I learned the names of his victims. All seventeen of them.

I've already told you I'm not going into details here.

I will share only a couple of things I found specifically interesting. The discoveries that both answered questions and created whole new ones for me to wrestle with. The discoveries that gave me both hope and fear.

. . .

No one had ever called him "Jeffrey" until he was arrested.

Family, friends, coworkers, had known him only as "Jeff" for thirty years.

Jeff Dahmer was his real-person name.

Jeffrey Dahmer was his monster name.

. . .

I made a list of REASONS. *Possible* reasons.

Why had some middle-class kid raised in the suburban Midwest become such a monster? He hadn't been molested or physically abused. A "normal" kid by all standards well into high school. *So what the hell happened?* Here's what I got:

1. Jeff Dahmer's mother got prescribed lots of medications during her pregnancy. Barbiturates and stuff to calm down her various anxiety issues. Sometimes she took a dozen pills a day. Had these changed Jeff's chemical makeup while he was cooking in her womb?

2. He'd broken his foot during delivery and had a cast on his leg for the first few weeks of life. His first minutes of life on Earth were filled with PAIN.

3. His mother had violent seizures and mood swings throughout his childhood. He was too embarrassed to bring other kids around the house.

4. His parents fought all the time. Screamed at each other and finally got a messy divorce when Dahmer was in high school. What emotional trauma had that caused?

5. He was kinda bullied at school and had no real friends.

6. He started drinking at fifteen.

7. He recognized around this same time that he was probably gay and lived in a place and time that would condemn and likely attack this lifestyle.

All these possibilities on what had led to the killings.

Chemical. Physical. Social. Emotional.

None of which I'd had any relation to.

No broken leg. No drinking. Etc. Had I been picked on once or twice? Sure. Had it sucked growing up without a mom? Yes. Did I feel like a total goof being homeschooled? Some. But, come on. That wasn't the same thing. Right?

Regardless, I couldn't deny this simple fact: I'd been crafted from the genes of a thirty-three-year-old Dahmer. Had all that he'd gone through until that point been carried in his genetic makeup? Had it already modified his physical makeup? How many of those life hardships had transformed into real physiological changes in his brain development, chromosomal makeup, protein sequences?

How much of his life was still swirling around inside of me?

Was I really just the sum total of his thirty-three shitty years?

What had MY eight years on earth added? Hadn't MY own experiences had some effect on my physiological and emotional development?

So maybe my Nature guaranteed I could never write music like Mozart. But did it also guarantee I would HAVE to kill like Dahmer?

Anymore, was I really still technically HIM?

. . .

In prison Dahmer got interested in Intelligent Design, a theory that God, whatever that means, was purposefully and personally still managing things like evolution and the universe. We weren't just, to quote Dahmer, "things that'd crawled out of the slime." There was a purpose and a Creator. And the Creator was still with us.

Dahmer, whose father was a chemist, had grown up with the modern scientific world view. Humanist. Atheist. The spiritual notions of God replaced by Darwin and Edison. (That's how I'd grown up too. The only Faith I knew was that taught as mythology or history.) But Dahmer concluded in prison that without a God to answer to, people would do whatever they wanted. People would do BAD things like he had. So, later than he should have, he went searching for that God.

An anonymous donor had contributed some money to his prison account, and Dahmer used every penny of it to buy books on Intelligent Design and the ongoing fight between evolutionists and creationists.

The same fight Scopes had fought in Tennessee forty years before Dahmer was born. Intelligent Design offered a sort of compromise. A chance for God to be found again IN the Science. The wonders of DNA and split atoms and carbon dating didn't disprove the need or existence of God. Rather, it showed God's guiding hand in a scientific way that we could measure and understand.

Dahmer claimed to have realized a new moral center.

He claimed to have finally realized God's presence in our modern world.

• • •

God had a funny way of making himself known in Jeff Dahmer's life.

• • •

When Jeff Dahmer's parents first separated, he once got left alone in the family house for, like, three weeks. Now, for years he'd had a specific fantasy of picking up a hitchhiker. (He'd wanted control of something. *Anything.* Even if that meant a dead guy. Even if it meant MURDER. Damnation. He'd have control.) And during these precise three weeks, one appeared. A hitchhiker. A teen named Stephen Hicks on his way home from some local concert. As if placed down deus ex machina by some unseen author for *The Story of Jeffrey Dahmer.* His very first victim.

DAYS LATER Dahmer drove to the city dump at two in the morning with the teen's body in three different trash bags. And got stopped by the police. They made Dahmer get out of the car and everything and asked why he was out so late. They even asked what the stinky bags in the back of his car were. Dahmer told them he'd simply forgotten to set the garbage out and was taking them to the dump because he couldn't sleep. They said "be careful" and let him drive away.

MONTHS LATER his father found a locked box in Dahmer's

224   GEOFFREY GIRARD

closet and demanded to be shown what was inside. Dahmer lied, claimed it was pornography, threw a fit about his privacy, and promised to get rid of the magazines first thing. It was not magazines. If his dad had only opened that box . . .

YEARS LATER one of Dahmer's victims escaped. His name was Konerak Sinthasomphone. (Yes, him.) He'd been drugged, and Dahmer had already done "experiments" on him. Konerak was naked and bleeding in the street. When the cops showed up, Dahmer convinced them the boy was nineteen and drunk and that they were just two gay lovers having an argument. The cops led Konerak straight back to Dahmer's apartment. They thought the place smelled funny but had seen enough and went back to command, making jokes about having to "delouse" after spending time with two gays. Witnesses of the event followed up with police but were told "everything was fine." When the witnesses, who knew Konerak, explained that the boy was just fourteen and had looked to be in shock, the cops got mad and told the witnesses "enough." (You can find these actual recordings online, and I'm sure the fact that these witnesses were poor blacks had nothing to do with the police blowing them off.) Dahmer killed Konerak that same night. And then he killed five more men in the next three months.

• • •

My point: How many different times and ways might he have been stopped but wasn't?

It was almost as if he were destined to commit these crimes.

Protected by some higher power. By Fate or God or Chance.

Just like Cain.

Marked.

• • •

Once he was finally arrested for his crimes, Dahmer could have pled guilty and been sentenced to a psychiatric ward for life as opposed to the much harder prison. But he wanted the full trial. He wanted the months of exams and private interviews and experts from every side and discipline. At the end of the trial, he was sentenced to the thousand years in prison. He thanked the judge and then admitted he'd "only wanted to find out just what it was that caused me to be so bad and evil."

. . .

"I don't know why it started. I don't have any definite answers on that myself. When I was a little kid I was just like anybody else. If I knew the true, real reasons why all this started, before it ever did, I wouldn't probably have done any of it."-Jeff Dahmer

. . .

So much for the trial.

Jeff Dahmer bled out on some prison floor still not knowing WHY.

He died not knowing how he'd become *Jeffrey* Dahmer.

I did not have this same problem.

I knew exactly how I'd come about.

How I'd become Dahmer.

CHAPTER TWENTY-EIGHT

You hear their blood. From a hundred miles away you hear it. Like . . . like the ocean. Wet. Rhythmic. Sloshing in a cavernous devouring sound. Swilling through veins breaking against their muscles. Skin. The lights are too bright. Too many people. You wait. In the dark, always in the dark. So many places to hide. There are three of them. Moving among the others on the boardwalk. Through them. Never part of them, though. Three who are different. Like you. Selecting following talking to the girls they might take. So many here to choose from. Their prey. One willingly follows the three into the darkness. You're waiting there also. In the dark, unseen seagulls scream for fresh meat over the breaking surf. Your hand black fingers too long stretches wide over the door. Pushes. Their prey is stripped and bound. Ignore her. You've come for the three. It's THEIR blood, their mark, that cries out to you. One face you know more than the others as the name forms on your lips. David. The sound jagged like wet sand and broken shells. The three boys move. You move faster. Blades shriek and whistle like hungry gulls, and the blood sprays in crimson mist as surf exploding against the shore, and—

. . .

Castillo shook me awake.

Jacobson! Jeff!

I fought to regain reality. To shake away/awake from the nightmare. The echo of shrieking gulls and surf still pounding in my ears as Castillo all but dragged me to the window. Guess he didn't notice I was having a major seizure or something. Sleepwalking again. Forces unseen somehow pushing me this way and that.

I steadied myself with arms spread out against either side of the window. Focused on the view outside. Expected to see apartments, sand, boardwalks. Like before in the motel room, I couldn't tell if I'd just seen repressed cosmic memories of some kind (more of Dahmer's life somehow caught in my skin and bone and blood) OR something else. Something *new* happening right now that I'd somehow been given a real-time glimpse of.

My whole body was shaking, clammy, feverish.

I tried focusing on what was in front of me. The window. Backyard. Outside.

And outside a blue car was parked across the street. One I'd never seen before.

Castillo said something. Sounded muffled. I refocused on his voice, and he told me it (the car) had been there for five minutes. No one had gotten out yet.

And we waited another ten minutes.

The memories of the dream fading too slowly. My body still trembling inside in ways Castillo apparently couldn't even see. Or just didn't care about because he was so focused on the potential prize outside.

Eventually the car door opened. A man climbed out.

A teenager.

GEOFFREY GIRARD

Jacobson? Castillo murmured my name, calling me closer. Away from the darkness.

Below, I got a perfect look at the driver.

I recognized the kid completely. One of the original six from Massey. It was Henry.

．．．

Castillo told me to get the car. I totally froze. The car, he said again.

He handed me the keys. His voice hadn't changed at all. If anything, he sounded even calmer than usual. I would have preferred if he were cursing and yelling at me. THIS Castillo was somehow scarier. This was the same Castillo who'd calmly beaten the shit out of four guys. He told me where he'd last parked the car. I didn't know if I could even make it out of the room, I was so far out of it. That memory, the screaming gulls, the blood, it all . . .

I blathered some kind of response, not sure if he really wanted me to—

Castillo stopped me.

He said: Albaum's family was killed in minutes.

He said: I'm not letting that happen here.

He said: *We're* not.

He said: Go!

We're not.

I liked that. Needed, really. I *needed* that.

I'd never run so fast in my life.

．．．

I was gasping for air by the time I reached the car. Felt like acid was pumping through my whole body and I could hardly even get the key in the door. Took, like, a hundred times.

Finally I got inside. Sat down. Got my hands on the wheel. SHIT!

Finally remembered I'd never driven before. My temps and lessons planned for the summer had been swept aside by a more "distracted" father. (By a man losing his mind . . .)

I tried to chill. Told myself driving wasn't anything. Put the key in the ignition. Car started right up. So far, so good. Fumbled with the gear shift, found DRIVE. Foot on gas. The car pulled forward and everything. Coasted about two miles an hour down the street and eventually somehow made the necessary turn to the corner of Ashbridge and OldeGate. Totally ran onto someone's lawn as I stomped on the brake and the car shuddered to a stop.

I couldn't see anything down the street. The Sizemore house, Henry's blue car, and half the block lost beneath a low dip in the road. Thought about getting out of the car to see. Did Castillo want me to just wait in the car or what? My eyes darted about the car's various mirrors, a hundred angles showing more of nothing.

Looked down to study the gearshift, finally found PARK.

By the time I looked up, a car was passing. A dark blue car.

And Henry was driving.

I froze. I'd met Henry a dozen times at DSTI. But in less than a month, he already looked like a different kid. Older. *Darker*. Maybe it wasn't even him (wishful thinking). Because if Henry turned right then and saw me . . .

But the car totally passed. Kept going.

I'd already collapsed against the steering wheel.

The car door flew open. I cursed, scared.

It was Castillo yelling at me to get out of the way. So I scooted over, and Castillo hopped in and tossed the car into reverse and pulled a quick K-turn that would have made stuntmen applaud. Castillo told me Henry had just knocked at the door, talked to the Sizemore dad for a minute, and then taken off again.

Castillo thought he was just casing the place and would probably come back later with the other guys.

To free Gary Sizemore. And to kill again.

• • •

We followed Henry's car. Just like in the movies. Always a couple of cars back.

I could easily imagine Castillo doing the same in some car over in the Middle East. Slowly weaving through some crowded Baghdad street. Guy looked like he was having fun. His specific prey right in front of him now for the first time in years, I figured.

He called his Department of Defense boss and told him he was pursuing Henry in Hitchcock, Indiana.

For the first time it really hit me that *I'd* done this. I'm the one who'd figured out the town and the family that had a clone. I'M the one who'd captured Henry and probably the others. And I'd figured out more of the clues too. Working with Castillo, I really could fix this whole thing. Get everything back to normal.

Or whatever the new normal was going to be. But something NOT this.

At the VERY least we'd found one of the original six.

A murderer. A guy who'd killed teachers and classmates.

At the VERY least, we'd found Henry.

• • •

About Henry.

He was seventeen. His adopted name was Henry Roberts.

His Clone Name was Henry/61. One of SEVENTY Henrys made

in DSTI's laboratories. Sixty alone had died in various Ukrainian girls' wombs. (Quite normal for clones. The miscarriages, I mean.)

His Parent Gene (his original DNA) was that of Henry Lee Lucas.

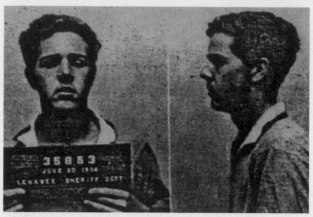

Henry Lee Lucas murdered about a hundred people.

Lucas's first victim was his own mother. He was twenty-four. He'd used a knife.

Of course, when Lucas was a boy, she beat him and his brother so badly, they often went into comas that lasted days. One beating, Henry Lee lost an eye. She would have sex with men in front of her children. She'd dress her son up in girl's clothing and encourage the men to touch him. One day, the teachers at school gave him a teddy bear, and when he got home, his mother beat him for "accepting charity." (And I'm not saying it's right that he killed her. Only, I suppose, that it maybe shouldn't have been a surprise for either of them.)

After his mom, Henry drifted along between the southern highways and towns from Florida to Texas. Killing and killing until he was caught in 1983. Lucas was supposed to be executed, but the governor of Texas at the time (that'd be one George W. Bush), changed his

GEOFFREY GIRARD

death penalty sentence to life in jail. Lucas was the only Texas inmate on death row ever to get this pardon. All the rest were executed.

Why? Because my father made a phone call. That's why.

See, when George W. Bush was the governor of Texas, *his* father was president and an ex-director of the CIA. Word trickled up, and then down again, that a little company outside Philadelphia doing work for the Department of Defense wanted Henry Lee Lucas to stick around a little longer. Done.

The next batch of Henrys showed up just two years later.

I always thought Henry, Henry Roberts, was a dick. He'd do stupid things like fart on you or run his thumb between your ass cheeks as you walked past. He'd call you over to look at something on the Internet, and it'd always be something gross and sexual. I hated when he was at Massey. I hated being around him.

But I didn't know everything about him then. I do now.

Or enough.

I know that Henry Roberts was "adopted" out to a woman DSTI found somehow.

I know she was paid to beat him. Paid to dress him up as a girl.

I know she was paid to have sex in front of him with men. And sometimes the men would do stuff to Henry, too.

I know that somewhere in the tristate area, *another* "Henry" was adopted out to *another* family who never did a thing to him. They were paid to raise him as tenderly as possible. To dote on him. Spoil him. With love. (Guess money CAN buy you love after all).

DSTI, my father, did this to determine if there'd be a difference in the end.

Nature/Nurture.

Did the NATURE of our genetic makeup determine who individuals eventually became? OR was it the NURTURE of our environment and upbringing? Or, likely, if it was some combination of the two, was one the more dominant influence?

One of the world's oldest and deepest questions still being sorted out, it seemed.

Would BOTH Henrys end up with knives in the their hands in the end?

Would the violence inside grow if nurtured properly?

This is what the Department of Defense was doing with its money.

• • •

I didn't want to know any of this.

I didn't want to know anything about what was really going on.

I didn't want to know how the world really worked.

I wanted to be clueless like everybody else.

• • •

We followed him for maybe half an hour. Castillo hadn't made a single sound, and I followed his lead. Henry did a Burger King drive-through and then finally turned into something called the Paddy Creek Park. Castillo drove past and doubled back after a few minutes.

Henry had parked and already vanished. The rest of the parking lot was empty. The summer sun had dipped behind the heavy trees that surrounded the park.

Castillo parked far away from Henry's car and got out. Told me to stay put.

He handed me his cell with a number already punched in. Told me to call it if he wasn't back in ten minutes. To tell them Paddy Creek.

I assumed "them" was the Department of Defense. Or DSTI.

Technically different players in all of this, but still on the same team as far as I was concerned.

Castillo said: You don't have to be here when they arrive.

It occurred to me finally that Castillo could be coming up on four, five, six ruthless killers. Bred for their violence. Already killed before. Sure, I'd seen Castillo handle those dirtballs at the motel, but this . . . this was something else entirely.

I wished I could help him. Get out of the car and go into that park with him. But there was nothing I could do now. I'd done enough. Or, if not enough, maybe I'd done all I really could.

I just said: Be careful.

Castillo nodded and started off into the park.

He'd been gone about a minute. Alone, phone.

I figured it was a good time to call my dad.

· · ·

Hello? Is there—

Dad? Dad!

It's Jeff. Yeah, I . . . I'm in Hitchcock.

Yeah. Yeah. I figured out *The Birds* and—

Yes, I saw him.

I figured out some of the other clues too. I—

Oh. I figured you wanted me to—

OK. Then OK. Fine. Henry is here too.

Yes. I don't know.

Where are YOU?

Fine. I guess it doesn't matter anyway.

Hey, I want . . . I need to ask you a question.

Why me?

Why ME? Why Dahmer? You could have chosen any of them.

It matters to me.

OK.

Well, that's not what—

No. I haven't.

No. I won't.

You're wrong.

Why can't I? How much worse?

But, Dad—

Yeah. Bye.

CHAPTER TWENTY-NINE

I'd gotten out of the car and made off in the same general direction that Castillo'd gone. Couldn't stay in that car one minute longer by myself. I followed along the upper road, with the park down below. I passed Henry's blue car and wandered deeper into the park. There were picnic tables and then some restrooms and a playground to my right. And trails vanishing deeper into the woods. To my left, a gravel drive down to a wide open space of some kind. The thought of going into the woods didn't appeal, so I went left. Good choice.

The path overlooked a small outdoor amphitheater. The seats were long descending rows of grass marked off with sunken wood planks. Below, a concrete stage four feet off the ground, covered with a simple wood roof. Perfect for a small concert or something.

Tonight's show was something altogether different.

There was Henry right up on the stage. Something at his feet.

A body.

Wrapped in an old blue tarp.

Castillo was at the far right side of the stage. He was talking to Henry. The specific words lost in the distance between them and me. Talking, yes, but Castillo also had his gun out.

I crept behind a tree and watched.

Watched them talk more. Watched Henry pull out a knife.

Watched Henry crouch down to grab hold of the body.

A woman, I saw clearly now.

Castillo getting closer.

Henry shouting. Lifting the knife.

Castillo shooting. Henry folding over sideways like he had no bones.

Castillo rushing to Henry's body. Trying to stop the bleeding. Trying CPR. Cursing.

Henry dying anyway.

I approached slowly. Castillo saw me, tried waving me back away, but I just kept moving closer. I had to see.

Death had been hovering just out of sight for weeks now.

It was time we officially met.

• • •

My relationship with Death prior to all of this, prior to watching Henry bleed out on that stage:

1. I had been brought to a grave and told my mother was buried there. For a long time, I thought that was Death. Just not being HERE. Being somewhere else. In the ground. In Heaven. Whatever.

2. At a summer camp once, a boy named Collin kept picking up caterpillars and pulling them apart. The big fuzzy ones. He'd just hold them between his two hands and pull. Kept laughing the whole time too, like it was the greatest thing ever. I told him to stop. He wouldn't. I got crying pretty good and the counselors eventually got involved. Collin acted like he didn't know it was wrong, apologized, and was off playing again in ten seconds like

nothing had ever happened. The counselors talked to me for, like, half an hour, like I was the one who was the freak. A small pile of dead caterpillars at our feet. For a long time, I thought that was Death. Something that was done TO you.

3. About four years ago, we were living in Bryn Mawr and this older kid from the neighborhood was on drugs and stuff and spent the night out in the woods stoned in the middle of winter and got hypothermia. My dad and I were there when they pulled his half-frozen body out of the woods. There were all these police and stuff, and everyone was there. The police lights flashing against the newly fallen snow. His body was covered. My dad said he was in a coma. The next day, my dad said they had to cut off his feet and hands to try to save him. Couple of days later, my dad said the kid was dead. This was Death now too. Something that just happened.

OK, one more Death Story. The incident with the bird.

I'd never given the whole thing much thought after the day it happened. But these Project Cain days, I was thinking about it all the time.

It'd gotten into our house when I was younger. Flapping all over the place, confused, scared, trying to get back out, and my dad was trying to chase it out with a blanket. I was just a little kid. I thought it was funny. Exciting. I kept running around the house. Making too much noise. Jumping around in my pajamas kinda thing. Being a little kid, you know. Well, as I was running around, this bird, it, like, swoops down for the opened door. I mean, it's a foot away from freedom.

And then I stepped on it.

Not on purpose. I will go to my grave swearing that. But it happened. One in a million, right? Chance. Or Fate. Or an "On Purpose" I will never, ever, ever recognize. But I somehow stepped, *stomped*, right on it. Felt it squish beneath my bare toes. Warm and soft. Blood and guts burst onto the carpet. Tiny drops. I'd never screamed so loud in my life. (I have since.)

I remember looking up and my dad just staring at me. His face. Horror. Shock. Fascination. I don't know. Now, of course, I get why he was staring at me like that. I'd just ruined everything, maybe. Ruined the "perfect" nurtured environment he'd created for me. Or maybe this was just the opportunity he'd always been waiting for. To see the true MONSTER hidden inside his clone. *Would I pick up the bird? Play with its exposed intestines? Would I run outside and immediately stomp another bird?*

No. THIS monster ran to his room and cried himself to sleep.

. . .

Henry was dead. There was blood everywhere.

I mean EVERYWHERE.

It was like he'd exploded.

And there was weird black stuff all over Henry's stomach that wasn't blood.

I didn't know what it was.

Castillo was on his phone. Talking to his people. He put the phone away and bitched about me being out of the car.

I'd stopped moving toward the stage but I could see the woman now.

Now that Death and I had met more formally, he was everywhere.

She looked bad. Dirty. Her skin was odd colors. Bad colors. I think she'd been dead for a while. I asked: Is that . . .

Castillo told me it was one of the missing nurses from Massey. One of the two that had vanished the first night with my father and the six boys. He confirmed that she and Henry were both dead.

I asked Castillo why he'd shot him.

Castillo explained that Henry had a knife, that he'd thought the nurse might still be alive and Henry was gonna kill her. He explained that he'd only and purposefully hit him in the shoulder and didn't expect it to be such a damaging shot. Then he cursed at me.

I just stared at the two bodies. Perfectly level with my view of the raised stage.

Castillo said: Look, Jacobson, I ain't gonna apologize for this shit.

Castillo said: Henry gave me no choice here. I just did what I was trained to do.

I looked up from the two bodies to Castillo.

I said: So did Henry.

CHAPTER THIRTY

*W*e crashed in some motel in east Missouri. It was afternoon. Castillo lay on his back in his bed, fully dressed, staring up at the ceiling. I was in my own bed kinda freezing my ass off. Maybe from the room's AC, which was clearly broken, the unit frequently humming and rattling like a living creature nested across the room. Mostly I thought I had a cold or something. Felt just awful, really.

I'd spent most of that whole day hiding at the end of the street, waiting for Castillo to finish up with the people he worked with. They'd eventually come to the park. Cleaned up everything. Henry and Nurse Stacy, too. Just as if none of it had ever happened.

Here we were, just a few hours later. Castillo looked upset. I was used to seeing him mad, but this was different. He looked kinda sad. I asked him what was wrong. I expected him to say something about killing Henry. That he was upset about that, which I honestly think he was.

Instead he sat up, passed over his smartphone to me. On it was a picture I hadn't seen before.

A picture of a notecard.

Words written in my father's handwriting.

A notecard and words smeared with blood.

ShARDhARA

ZODIaC BaBYSITTeR PhaNTOM

Independence Day

I also gave birth to the 21st century

Castillo's government contacts had just sent this to him.

Pictures from some crime scene.

They'd already confirmed it was my father's handwriting.

• • •

The AC started shuddering so bad, for a minute it felt like the whole room was shaking.

Shardhara?

I asked Castillo where they'd found the card.

Just outside of Indianapolis.

He'd wanted me to see just the picture of the notecard, but I thumbed back to the previous picture. I couldn't tell what I was looking at.

Something spread all over a bed. Black stains everywhere. Mostly red, however. I think it was a woman I was looking at. I saw hair. Wet with blood.

I cursed, slammed the phone against the wall. Castillo lunged up to take the phone back from me. Too late, I said, and gave the phone back. I asked: Who is she?

Just some woman, he said and added that the card was next to her when they found her.

Had my father done this? Had he just written the note? Had he really killed this woman? No, not just killed her. Butchered her...

For so long now I'd clung to the possibility that my dad had really nothing to do with this. That he'd just been another victim in all of this.

But not a killer himself. Not . . .

It was getting harder and harder to make excuses for him. To pretend like I didn't know what Castillo knew. That my father was behind (in front of?) all of this.

He was the one calling the shots.

And people were getting killed.

Castillo asked: You OK?

Yeah, I lied again.

• • •

Castillo tried to move on from the woman and focus on the card my dad had written. Turns out all three names on the card were serial killers from specific cities. Three serial killers who'd never been caught. NOT clones, because no one ever figured out who these guys were.

The Zodiac Killer. The Babysitter. The Phantom.

Three more marvelous names to add to our marvelous serial-killer names list.

The Zodiac killed as many as thirty in San Francisco.

The Babysitter (who bathed each of his child victims after murdering them) had claimed a dozen in Detroit.

The Phantom strangled half a dozen girls in Washington, DC.

All three men had written letters to the authorities—teasing them for not being able to solve the case. Promising more death.

Castillo's bosses figured my father was warning something big was going to happen in San Francisco and Detroit and Washington on July 4. Something *awful*.

Something having to do with SHARDHARA.

• • •

Turns out, just before he'd died, Henry'd bragged to Castillo that the other guys were heading west already. San Francisco, maybe. It made sense (if the Zodiac thing was a genuine lead of some kind). And when Castillo asked his bosses about Shardhara, they told him it was outside his "need-to-know" status but that he should keep an eye out for any references to the word moving forward. They weren't all that excited, apparently, about Castillo's having found Henry.

Or about the leads (my leads! But Castillo didn't tell them *that*) on Salem and Sherwood Forest. They didn't care. And from what I could tell, they weren't even asking about me yet either. Still didn't know I was with Castillo, or simply didn't care.

It was apparently now all about the guys heading west.

Castillo's bosses wouldn't tell him anything beyond that. They just told him the situation was "grave."

Then they told him to keep an eye out for a canister of some kind.

You know, the kind of thing you might transport a deadly biotoxin in.

Why had my father put "Shardhara" on the card? Was he implying that whatever had happened in that Afghanistan village was somehow gonna happen here? All that death?

I said something like, Wow.

Castillo said something like, Uh-huh.

• • •

I asked Castillo what was up with: "I also gave birth to the 21st century."

He said nothing, but I wasn't buying it, and eventually he admitted it had "something to do with Jack the Ripper." My dad sure had a thing for Jack the Ripper.

So what was THIS message? What did it mean?

• • •

There's this famous quote attributed to Jack the Ripper:

"One day men will look back and say I gave birth to the twentieth century."

It's made up. It's not in any of the letters he wrote to the police. It's just one of those quotes that gets attributed to someone famous on the Internet, and off you go. The whole "If he didn't say it, he should have."

The quote captures the idea that Jack the Ripper was a sign of things to come—the recreational violence, the media exploitation, the replacement of God with Self.

My father's variation, "I also gave birth to the 21st century," was both a nod to Jack and also a reference to things to come—the rise of psychopaths, the government's deception, the replacement of God with a gene splicer.

• • •

Castillo yawned, a long groan that turned into a half-formed thought.

He said: Gotta nail these little monsters. . . .

Little monsters?

I could tell he regretted the words right away. He even apologized. Not the Sizemore kid, he said quickly. Not *you*. I meant the other guys.

Sure, I said. I told him not to worry about it, but then he got all pissed. Guess I'd made him feel bad or something. He was all: Sorry if it "offends" you, but it is what it is. He told me how he'd tracked down some major Bad Guys over the years. Guys who'd killed for religious fanaticism or Greed or Power or even Duty. And that he *understood* those guys. Their motivations. But not these guys. Not the Henrys or Teds of the world. Not guys who dressed up like clowns. Or kids who dragged around nurses who'd been dead for days. Either the original versions or new. Guys who killed for FUN. He said THESE guys made no sense. These guys had become only monsters to him.

You've killed people, I said. Are *you* a monster?

War's different, he replied.

I asked if he thought I was a monster. Some clone. Evil incarnate.

Then I shared with him something my father had told me the night he'd left. That he and DSTI had taken one of Dahmer's cells and retrained it to become, like, an egg cell. Then they'd fertilized that egg with another one of Dahmer's cells. Never been done before. Other clones, the egg cell comes from an outside donor and affects the DNA by as much as 2%.

But I was 100% Jeffrey Dahmer.

In genes only, Castillo agreed. I guess that's how it works.

Then he said: So what? So, you'll be tall and blond and probably need LASIK. And? Good for you. I wish I was tall and blond. So you're maybe genetically prone to being an alcoholic, so what? Go to AA meetings and keep away from alcohol. So you're genetically prone to, what, being gay? Good. You're not being raised in the sixties. Fall in love with whoever you want and live happily ever after.

I asked: And the murder? The death? The corpses?

Castillo couldn't even look at me. I never said . . . , he tried. I'm not saying you're like Henry.

I told him I didn't want to, you know, hurt people. I didn't ever even

THINK about hurting people. I didn't care whose blood was running in my veins. (I'm not sure I really believed that last part. I think maybe I just wanted to hear what it sounded like. Like maybe saying it out loud would make it true.)

I told him I now understood why my father had done all this.

First with all the other boys and then, as the years went on, more directly.

With me. His own "son."

He'd wanted to explain the terrible thoughts in his own head.

He'd wanted to prove that the bad thoughts (THE THING ON THE BED, etc.) were all in his blood, that he *didn't have a choice*. So he took the most terrible person ever and raised him like a normal boy to see what would happen. To prove that the genes, the blood, that Nature would win.

I told Castillo I wasn't some disgusting monster.

He said: I know.

Do you? I asked. Do you really?

Castillo didn't reply.

Well, don't feel too bad, I said. To tell the truth, I'm not totally sure either.

• • •

We both lay in the silence for a long time. I was full-blown shivering now. Pulled the quilt out and wrapped it around me. The AC had stopped grumbling but now there was this constant drip drip drip sound somewhere deep inside the unit. Hypnotic. Maddening.

Through clenched teeth I told Castillo I wanted to find my dad. Right now! I was maybe trying out a two-second tantrum at the same time. But Castillo wasn't buying any of it. At all. And told me that unless my dad was in San Francisco (which is where everyone thought some of the clones were going with a vial of that supertoxin), I was basically shit out of luck.

Then he told me I could look for him alone if I wanted.

As in, I could leave now if I wanted to.

My first thought was a thought of rejection. But he wasn't saying this as a jerk, I quickly realized. I could see it in his face. He seemed genuinely on my side all of a sudden. Like whatever I needed, he was OK with right now. Regardless of his mission or how I might still be able to help. Maybe he wasn't proving such a robot after all. But . . .

Alone? I needed his help. And he knew that too.

We'll look *after* San Francisco, he promised.

And again, like most every time Castillo says stuff, I believed him.

I told him I wanted to, at least, START now. To do more research. Like he was always talking about. Do my homework and understand my prey and all of that. I needed to, God help me, understand my dad even more than I already did.

I told Castillo I needed some books on Jack the Ripper.

He nodded.

Maybe I'd "find" my dad—figuratively, I mean—in 1880s London.

This is the prospect I held on to as I closed my eyes again and listened for the next series of drips.

• • •

You hear his blood. From fifty miles away, you hear it. Like . . . like some steam-driven contraption of rusted machinery forgotten yet still humming and rattling. Now moving over the chain-link fence, the night's chill roiling across your whole body, you'd been following the other one. But the sound of his blood is gone now this is another drip

drip droplets like trickling rubies. So many out there you realize and here is one more churning chunking away just inside this door. Kill the Other first, the man. Then your brother, blades drawn, slams your body against the door—

. . .

The motel room, like, exploded.

I swear to God, I thought the whole world had just blown up.

I flung up out of bed in the dead of night. Watched the motel room door bouncing off the wall. Pieces of the doorframe splintering out in a hundred directions.

There was something standing at the end of my bed.

Enormous. Black. Misshapen. Something glinted in its hands.

The first thought I had was, The Black Dress Lady. The Thing on the Bed. She'd found me. Followed me. And she was totally what I saw for half a second. The big huge cartoon eyes. Vacant. Dead. The face the color of a shining skull in the yellow light from outside.

Then I realized it was a man. Dark not just from the room's shadows. It was as if he were not really there at all but still half in the dark from which he'd sprung.

The dark man was just standing there. Staring at me.

My father came to mind.

Then Castillo started shooting.

CHAPTER THIRTY-ONE

I cringed against the wall, curled away from the gunshots.

And from the man standing there.

Then, just like that, both were gone. The doorway now empty.

Castillo had somehow rolled from his own bed across the floor and was now behind mine. Gun pointed at the door. He asked if I was OK and then told me to keep quiet. He'd slid over the foot of the bed toward the doorway. Kept low to the window, clinging to the same darkness the other guy had just retreated to. He told me to get behind the bed, while looking out into the parking lot outside.

Then he cursed and ran out the door. Yelled back for me to stay put.

Forget that.

I immediately found my glasses and then started crawling around in the dark, getting my shit together. When Castillo got back, we'd go. That was that. There was no way I was gonna stay another minute in that motel.

The guy, whoever it had been, was Evil. Pure and simple. I could feel it surging through my entire body. Icy. Trembling like thousands of worms in a dark grave. We HAD to go. Besides, I knew Castillo couldn't stay here. Not after gunshots. He'd been worried about the cops since Day One. He sure as heck didn't want to talk with them tonight.

I was right. Castillo returned, tried shutting the broken door, which bounced back freely on its newly busted hinges. He seemed quite pleased I was already good to go. Asked if I was OK.

What *was* that? I asked.

Who, Castillo corrected me.

. . .

This particular who/what question continues even to today. Though it largely goes unspoken, because arguing too much on if this "dark man" was technically a man or a "thing" is directly related to whether or not Jeff Jacobson, technically, is a thing or a man. Which, out of common courtesy to me, folk around here generally avoid debating.

. . .

I can tell you only what we now know.

Who/what came to our room that night was constructed in a DSTI lab just like me.

Constructed as a special type of weapon for the United States military.

A biological weapon. A life-form weapon. And 100% human. (Technically.)

I'm now gonna oversimplify a process that took a team of men almost twenty years and a hundred million dollars to accomplish. Like Frankenstein's monster, but instead of body parts stitched together from a dozen different corpses, the geneticists at DSTI had cobbled together the DNA from a dozen different serial killers. 10% Bundy + 8% Gacy + 15% Fish + 10% Dahmer, etc. Until 100% of a "full" person.

We've been breeding dogs and horses this way for thousands of years. Crafting this special hybrid of human wasn't, in the simplest explanation, that different. And once the government had these specimens blended together, the scientists even "tweaked" them a bit more. Not much different than someone on steroids or ADD meds or birth control. The specimens were gestated in special incubator tanks to whatever age and size the company wished. Raised and trained, but kept in the vats to reduce decomposition. During this state, DSTI also amplified the aberration of their XP11 strand—the one that controls violence. (The gene already way off the genetic charts even for us "one-source" clones!) DSTI also modified their genetic codes for hearing, strength, metabolism (to control the body temperature), skin pigment, etc.

The original idea was to send these special killers into unique zones of conflict. Deep into enemy territory. Underground bunkers and tunnels miles beneath the earth. During testing DSTI discovered that these men had a unique—and rather fortunate—ability. They could *sense* one another. The way twins sometimes know when their "double" has been hurt or is experiencing a particularly strong emotion.

And not just one another. They could, it was soon realized, somehow sense *other killers*. Including men who had absolutely *nothing* to do with Project Cain. But somehow (I describe it as a sound) they could find these men who'd killed, wanted to kill, etc. And then eliminate them. Field tests were run. These specimens were first assessed in Afghanistan and Iraq. The Philippines and Colombia. Then in Iran and Pakistan. Then the United States.

Later I learned that when Castillo had been captured and tortured somewhere in Iran (thus the scars), it had been one of these men who'd freed him. (Castillo did not yet really remember this, but it would soon explain his nightmares.)

And as far as what *really* happened when Osama bin Laden was killed, why there is no real evidence of his body, or what happened to the crashed American helicopter or the half dozen Special Forces operatives who died that same week on "other missions" . . . that is a story best told by Ox.

• • •

Two more things about these special men made by DSTI.

1. They were not crafted from the DNA of the original serial killers. They were crafted from the DNA of us clones. DNA that, in some cases, had been modified to create more violent specimens.
2. There was more than one.

• • •

But the night that the dark man attacked our room, Castillo didn't know any of this. And it was not yet a memory he was willing to take on. So he ignored the guy completely and told me he'd have to deal with the cops now and for me to go to the Waffle House down the street. I did like I was told and got the heck out of there.

But I never even got to the Waffle House.

I'd almost reached it when Castillo pulled up with the car.

Get in, he said. I think we're screwed.

• • •

"Screwed" was not exactly the word he used, but you get the idea.

Also, he was totally right.

CHAPTER THIRTY-TWO

*D*STI had put tracking chips into their clones.

Standard operating procedure. Inserted just beneath the skin in the feet. Little metal pellets the size of a fat grain of rice. Protecting specimens worth more than a million dollars apiece. Castillo figured the dark guy had been sent to find me and had probably tracked me with one of those.

The solution?

We broke into this vet's office.

• • •

I hid in the shadows, terrified, while Castillo busted the alarm, opened the back door. There were just four dogs caged inside, barking as one, and loud enough to wake half the state. Castillo made me find them treats while he looked around some.

Five minutes later, the dogs were totally chowing and Castillo was testing something called a DR 3500 Digital Navigator Plus. The vet's X-ray machine.

Then I was up on the table.

The alternative involves cutting, Castillo said.

He knew this from experience. Apparently the six boys who'd first escaped had cut theirs out at Massey. Placed them in the shape of a smiley face (two eyes, nose, three for the mouth) with the head drawn in blood on the Activity Center's pool table. There'd been a dead counselor next to the face.

My father, Castillo figured, had told them the chips were there.

He didn't tell me, I said.

· · ·

My father hadn't told me because I didn't *have* a chip implanted.

Neither did any of the dozen clones my father had personally adopted out into the world.

He didn't want DSTI to know where they were.

He wanted us all completely free.

Almost.

· · ·

Castillo X-rayed my feet first. Nothing. Took another two dozen close digital shots of different body parts. Hands. Legs. Neck. More whole lot of *nothing*. I wondered out loud if he were giving me cancer. If they find you, Castillo said, that won't matter. Then he took another dozen X-rays, I figure. I stayed quiet. He couldn't find anything. No tracking devices. At least nothing metal. I asked Castillo how it had found me, then. (I tried not to think about the dreams I'd been having. The visions. The blood sounds.) *He*, Castillo corrected again. And also, he had no idea who this guy was either.

· · ·

We slumped across from each other on the office floor. Castillo with his back against the desk and his legs out. Me all cross-legged. Each of us had a dog resting at our side. Piles of treats on the floor between us.

The mystery of how or why this guy had found us wasn't even the biggest issue.

Castillo's boss now was.

Castillo'd spoken to him back at the motel, and apparently this guy now for the first time suspected I was with Castillo. Didn't out and out say it but had, according to Castillo, hinted pretty strongly and had given Castillo an opportunity to come clean. Castillo hadn't.

And then things evidently had gotten weird.

Castillo said his boss wanted him to come in and "talk about things" in person. Which was, according to Castillo, Defense Department–speak for "You're done." Castillo figured his days were numbered. Like his bosses were getting ready to sell him out. He'd somehow become a LIABILITY just like I was. Probably knew too much or something. Or maybe he'd just shot at the wrong guy.

I felt terrible. I sat there wondering if Castillo was in trouble for not admitting to them about me. How simple for him to have just said, *Oh, yeah. Jacobson's private Dahmer clone, got him right here. Not a prob, Mr. Boss! Come and get him.*

But, for whatever reason, he hadn't.

Now he just sat there in the dark, pondering. Staring into space, chewing his lower lip.

Eventually I asked what now. If he was just gonna quit the whole mission now that his bosses seemed mad at him. (What I really wanted to say was something like. *WHY DON'T YOU JUST TURN ME IN?* or maybe even *HOW LONG UNTIL YOU DO?)*

Castillo answered my out loud question: If they tell me to.

But I noticed he hadn't answered his phones in hours. It would be tough for his bosses to tell him much of anything.

Remember the Albaums? he asked in the dark.

Edward Albaum. The first kid we'd found at Serpent Mound in Ohio. The kid whose whole family had been murdered by the kids from DSTI.

I nodded.

Castillo told me that a news story about the Albaums had just appeared online. The story reported that they'd died that morning when their house had burned down. Fire started in the garage. Old paint cans. Community in grief. Et cetera, et cetera.

This morning?! It made no sense. They'd been dead for three days! The Albaums' neighbors and coworkers and friends, the whole world, were being fed a total lie.

I asked if DSTI burned their house down.

Someone did, Castillo said. And he bet me that DSTI would be getting rid of other adoptive families and would be missing some more employees at their next company Christmas party.

God, I wondered out loud, can these people just do whatever they want?

Yes, Castillo replied.

• • •

What did that mean for us?

According to Castillo, it meant my dad was right. I was a liability.

A lot of people were now. Castillo, too, it seemed.

He talked a lot that night. Castillo did. More than usual. Like ten whole words!

He talked about maybe ditching me, about us going our separate ways. I appreciated his honesty. I really did. It was rare these days, and he seemed to be the only guy who gave me any. But he decided that

GEOFFREY GIRARD

wouldn't work out for either one of us. He predicted I'd be dead in a couple of days. That he might get a couple of weeks. (More honesty.)

No. The big plan now was that we still had time to work together and Save the Day.

If we could just find the other guys. Find this canister of the biotoxin stuff they probably had.

I said: My dad gave it to them, didn't he? This *stuff.*

Castillo didn't care. He just knew that if we didn't find it by July 4, lots of people in three cities were gonna die. Die bad.

He said: We need to find all of them. Your dad, too.

He said: It's the only way you and me get out of this safely.

It sounded funny for Castillo to say it out loud. He and I had to basically save the world now just to save ourselves. Crazy talk. More crazy, he had no idea how to get started. No clue where the other guys had gotten to. Just "west." My father was maybe, unlikely, still in Indianapolis.

Castillo said we'd sleep a bit, try to think. Think less crazy maybe. Get moving again in a few hours, in any case.

I handed him back his worn copy of *The Odyssey.*

You're done with it? he asked.

Sure, I said. Plus, you like to read before you sleep.

Castillo reached for the book, smiled wearily. He said: I try to tell myself it relaxes me.

I asked if it did.

He said mostly, but obviously not always. He was referring to his night terrors. He'd tucked the book away. Not even gonna try tonight, he said.

I asked him if Kristin was the one who'd given him the book.

He closed his eyes. Yes, he said.

I asked if they use to, like, date and stuff, and he told me to go to sleep.

Turns out they had a pretty complicated relationship. I figured it best to drop it.

I slumped down, exhausted, reached out to pet the closest dog.

I said: Good night, Castillo.

Hey, Castillo said, and opened his eyes again.

He asked: Where would you go to meet girls?

I reminded him I was probably gay. How would I know?

Castillo smiled back. It was honestly pretty damn cool to see him smile.

He said: Dude . . . seriously, where?

Then he told me that Kristin had said some of the guys would be looking for girls. Specifically Ted would. Cops had just found the body of Emily Collins in that dumpster. Cops were saying she and some unidentified boyfriend had butchered her whole family.

Castillo asked again: Where would they go to pick up girls?

I stared around the empty vet's office, thinking. I was tired, but it was a pretty easy think. Just kept coming back to the same answer. Unless science camp was an answer, I sure know the only place I'd ever really talked to a girl. A place pretty much all the guys visited all day, every day.

I told him to toss over his phone.

Castillo looked real curious. Asked WHY.

I was like, 'Cause I know a way to meet girls.

He got up from the floor.

Facebook, he said.

Not bad for an old guy.

. . .

I hadn't been on either website in more than six months. I mean, I was homeschooled. What was the point? Every science camp, I'd collect a dozen new contacts. This time around I had just four new friend requests. Twelve new messages about nothing. Had a total of forty-two friends on Facebook and only twenty followers on Twitter.

One of them was named David. One was named Al.

We clicked onto Al's page and read the various threads and messages there.

Clicked on to the pages of some of the girls Al was friends with.

Henry was friends with Emily Collins.

Jumping from site to site to site, reading *their* messages.

These weren't the fake sites these kids gave their parents to look at.

These were the real sites. And everyone's privacy setting was for shit.

Then we hit a chain of messages on Twitter. Big party.

Some girl named Laura Schriml bragging about the new guys she'd met. They were coming to the party. "Ready to party." "Totally wild." "YOLO." Blah. Blah.

Where is Orchard City? I asked.

. . .

Orchard City was in Colorado. Fifteen hours away.

Castillo drove as fast as he could, and we arrived just before dark.

He tried the parents first. The Laura girl's parents, and then a close friend of Laura's. Trying to figure out whose kid was having the big party. Castillo told the parents he was with the FBI or something and that some kids were planning to sell bad LSD at a local party. Just one more lie for the masses.

Didn't matter. These people had no clue where their kids were. Any more than us kids really know where our parents are sometimes, I suppose.

But Orchard City isn't that big, so we just started driving around town a bit, cruising down streets. Hoping to get lucky. Did this for about an hour.

That's when we heard the sirens.

Castillo and I looked at each other right away.

Knew exactly where those cars were going.

We'd been close. But late.

The killing had already started.

CHAPTER THIRTY-THREE

We just followed the flashing lights.

Red, blue, and yellow lights spinning and blinking at eighty miles an hour.

All heading one direction.

When we got there, the house with all the dead kids looked like every other house. Looked a lot like my house back in Jersey, actually. Wooded lot. Tucked back a ways. Big suburban we got money house.

Castillo parked us just outside the flashing emergency vehicles. There were already lots of people wandering around. And not just the cops and stuff. The gawkers of Orchard City were showing up in full force. Even some parents looking for their kids. Teens still standing around, or just now showing up, waiting for their pals to come out. Their neighborhood now twinkled and flashed like a giant pinball machine.

Castillo got out of the car. I was like, What the Hell?

He said he had to check it out and for me to stay put. He'd be back. Same old Castillo.

Castillo vanished into the crowd in half a second.

I got out of the car.

Same Jeff, too, I guess.

● ● ●

It was so damn loud. All the different sheriff cars and state troopers and fire trucks and ambulances showing up. Each one had its own annoying sound. Chirping and beeping and farting up a storm like some circus out of hell. Flares along the driveway cast the whole house in matching red flames.

I was shivering cold even though it was still warm outside. People probably thought I was in shock or something. I worked my way easily through the growing crowd. No one knew what the heck was going on. The police were still arriving themselves, trying to organize, trying to block people off.

I got pushed a dozen different directions. Someone even grabbed me. Some lady. She asked if I'd been in the house. I said no and she just looked at me like I was a piece of dog crap or something. Walked away without another word.

Whatever. I kept moving deeper into the crowd. Drawn to the house. Like everyone else, I guess, I wanted to see what had happened in there. I wanted to know what these guys had done here. *I deserved to know, didn't I?*

Cops were yelling now. I saw this one kid get arrested. He was shouting at the cop about his brother. He didn't know where his little brother was. Just kept yelling, My, brother, man. Gotta find my brother! while the cop was pulling him away.

I moved back a bit with the crowd. Saw why the cops were yelling. Two stretchers being rushed down the driveway. With a dozen people around each one. Both completely covered with white sheets. The shapes beneath tiny. So very still.

I naturally thought of DSTI and the pictures I'd seen.

How many white lumps would THIS night bring?

How many full-page portraits in the next Orchard City High year-book?

I pressed closer. Wanted to see more than a white sheet. Not because I was twisted and stuff. I just . . . I don't know. I just did.

KID, COME HERE. I heard this voice over the total commotion of the crowd.

I think it was one of the cops. Figured he was talking to me. But didn't wait around to find out. Dipped out of there in a hurry. Castillo was probably already back at the car, for all I knew. Getting ready to kick my ass in front of everyone for taking off on him.

I started back. Worked my way through the crowd again, snuck between two ambulances. One of the guys in the back was complaining about how he couldn't find his gas mask. He said the whole house reeked of "ammonia." The guy he was with said he'd heard the bomb squad from Denver was flying in.

Then the first guy looked over at me, said, What the hell do YOU want?

I kept moving. So damn cold. I'd swear you could see my breath.

I was about half a block from our car when I saw it.

Him.

Standing just outside the flashing lights within the night's shadows among a clump of trees. Just a silhouette. Like the wooden cutout of a man.

Standing there. Staring right back at me.

I knew right away it was the same man from the motel.

I knew it even before I saw his knives.

• • •

You hear their blood. From a hundred miles away, you hear it. Like music. Pulsating through veins like a bass drum, swilling like notes because its sounds echo in your own veins. Shared heart. Shared blood. And it's calling out to you. The melody of his blood is infinite. Like a god. He sees you now, your dark skeletal face mirrored in his familiar painted clown's eyes. And he is screaming, but you cannot hear his screams over the lyrical blood as you start stabbing and new sounds fill your ears. Hands driving downward. Slicing, splashing sounds, spraying sounds, blood has so many wonderful songs . . .

• • •

My whole head suddenly so heavy. Dizzy. Overstuffed all of a sudden with memories, echoes of something just passed. Then older remembrances blending with the new and the sounds of loud music, throbbing blood, screaming.

I remembered walking down a long dark hallway. And the room filled with tall containers. Tanks filled with yellow water. Something floating within. Someone. Dozens of someones.

The swelling hum of blood blotted out the next image/thought, and I stumbled in the street like I was drunk.

The man with the knives moved toward me.

• • •

Then there was a bright light, blasting down from above.

A helicopter—news or the cops—sweeping the scene. Its glowing beam cutting a path of light across the street and along the line of trees.

Broken free from whatever spell I'd fallen under, I told myself I'd just imagined the dark shape. No different from the black-dress lady or nightmares or any of it. Except . . .

I chased the thoughts from my mind, dashed the rest of the way to the car.

Got inside in the backseat and warmed my arms with my hands. Seconds passing like minutes.

Castillo finally emerged from the crowd. He looked pissed. Walked slowly, head down.

I asked if it was them.

Yeah, he said, and then handed me his cell phone.

I was like: What's this?

Castillo'd started the car and was pulling slowly away down the street.

He said: I need you to make a call.

I said OK and asked who I was calling.

Castillo stared me down in the rearview mirror.

Your goddamn father, he said.

. . .

I'd been busted.

Turns out one of the dead kids at the house was John Burton— John was the one who'd dressed like a clown because that's what his DNA source had done—and he'd been gutted in the basement in his clown suit during this wild party. (There were, Castillo said, also, like, seven other dead kids lying around John. None of them was a clone, he thought, just regular kids who'd gotten in the way. Gotten in the way of some guy with knives.)

And when Castillo had checked John's body, he'd found a cell phone.

And on that cell phone John had made several calls to a specific number.

And so then Castillo got curious, checked his own phone records online.

And that was that.

Same number was on HIS phone records too.

The three calls I'd made to my dad.

Guess my dad had given out his new secret number to ALL his sons.

. . .

Hey. Hey, Dad.

It's me.

Jeff. Jeff!

No. Jeff Jacobson.

Yeah. I'm . . . I'm OK. I know you told me not—

Where are you? I need . . . I need to see you.

No. It's just . . . Yes. I guess. Is that OK?

Winter Quarter? Quarters. No. Utah? Yeah, I can look it up. Thanks. I . . .

Midnight. Yes.

Are you OK? You . . .

Dad?

When will you—

Yeah. OK. . . . I—

Yes.

Yeah.

I love you too.

. . .

My dad had finally agreed to meet me.

The next night at midnight. Someplace called Winter Quarters in Utah.

Castillo asked if I'd ever been there, and I told him no.

I told Castillo: Sorry.

He ignored that and just kept driving west.

I didn't care if he was furious or disappointed with me or not. I was totally excited.

We were finally gonna see my dad!

Or at least that was what I thought.

CHAPTER THIRTY-FOUR

*I*t was another whole day until it was midnight again, the time when we were supposed to meet up with my dad. But Winter Quarters was only five hours away. So we slept some outside a McDonald's right near Grand Junction, and then later in the morning Castillo found a Barnes & Noble and picked up a bunch of the books I'd asked for.

Books on Jack the Ripper.

These I read quietly while we drove for another three hours.

• • •

Castillo found somewhere to park at the Green River State Park. An hour north of Winter Quarters. Waiting for midnight. Castillo tried sleeping again. Couldn't. He seemed anxious. Ready to get the day started for real. I kept reading, dozed off a little bit too. Neither one of us was much for talking. I assumed he was still pissed about me secretly calling my dad and not telling him about it. Probably assumed there was all sorts of things I was keeping from him.

I was too embarrassed to talk. I HAD betrayed Castillo a bit.

Figure he'd saved my neck a couple of times already. I probably should have said something earlier about the calls. But I didn't even know what to say about them now. So I just kept my mouth shut.

Lunch was Pop-Tarts and warm bologna. Dinner too.

Waiting.

Around seven I about jumped up through the roof of the parked car.

What? Castillo even reached for his gun.

I'd finally found something in the book.

One of the biggest puzzle pieces yet.

This puzzle piece, like so many of the others, was blood colored.

• • •

Tumblety! I almost shouted.

Castillo wasn't impressed.

The dead guy in your dad's secret room? he asked.

True. But he was also one of the prime Ripper suspects, mentioned in all three of the books Castillo'd bought for me. And so I explained to Castillo what I'd just read.

After the Ripper murders, Tumblety escaped to America. The New York City police were always watching him and stuff. Apparently he was a bit of a character. Eventually settled in Rochester and got married twice. First time to Margaret Zilch and the second to . . .

I checked to see if Castillo was paying attention. He was.

I said, ALICE JACOBSON.

Castillo nodded and said: And there it is.

There was a son. William. William later used his mother's name because Tumblety was a Jack the Ripper suspect AND had also been arrested for being involved in the Lincoln assassination. "Tumblety" was not a name you wanted to walk around with.

Castillo asked: So, William is your . . . what? Grandfather?

Great-grandfather, I replied. Maybe. And not mine. I wasn't a Jacobson.

Then your adoptive father's grandfather? Castillo said.

Maybe, I agreed again, and suggested we could double check.

Now I had Castillo's attention. He asked if this Tumblety guy was *really* Jack the Ripper.

I reached for the other book Castillo had picked up and explained to him that most evidence now points to an artist named Walter Sickert. They've done DNA analysis and everything. Pretty much case closed.

Wouldn't your father know that? Castillo asked.

I said: Maybe he didn't really want to know it.

I mean, if my dad was running around for years thinking he was some kind of descendent of THE Jack the Ripper and that somehow gave him a genetic excuse/reason to have all those violent fantasies and to turn into some kind of killer himself, why ruin that with something such as, say, the Truth?

So, Castillo said, if he still thinks he's a direct descendent, some kind of rebirth of Jack the Ripper . . .

It's totally in his sick head. I finished Castillo's thought.

Yeah, Castillo said.

Yeah, I echoed. And if he's wrong about that the whole Tumblety thing . . .

Castillo now finished mine: Then he's wrong about a lot of things.

We both let that sink in for a while.

• • •

Why This Possibility (That My Father Was Wrong) Was Important to Me

By now I'd figured out I'd been raised only as a science experiment. My father had constructed and raised me only to further prove his hypothesis that Nature overwhelms Nurture and that the chromosomal makeup

272

that'd led Jeffrey Dahmer to kill all those people would, despite anything I tried to do to the contrary, eventually lead me to do the same. That the Evil coursing inside me would eventually reveal itself.

Why This Same Possibility Was Important to Castillo

My father had run a pretty good game up to this point. He'd sort of gotten out ahead of DSTI—and Castillo. The original Massey clones were free; new secretly adopted clones were free. There were vials of some terrible biotoxin out in the world. And it looked like my father was now murdering people and teasing the authorities about it. I think Castillo was maybe looking for proof that my father wasn't perfect. That he could mess up. That he was, despite all his planning and brilliance, rather insane.

• • •

Castillo suddenly said his own dad had taken off when he was nine.

Yeah? I prompted.

Yeah, Castillo said. I hated the son of a bitch for close to twenty years. And the more I tried hating him, the more I became just like him. The way he moved, talked. Things he said. Christ . . . I don't know. In a couple of years I'll probably *be* him.

A strange silence fell between us again.

I knew what he was thinking, because I was thinking the same thing.

But I wasn't worried about becoming my father someday.

I was worried about becoming Jeffrey Dahmer.

Becoming, well, ME.

Guess Castillo was worried about me becoming that also.

It's time, Castillo said. Let's go.

CHAPTER THIRTY-FIVE

*W*inter Quarters is a "ghost town" in Utah. Past Colton and down Route 96 to Scofield. Deserted canyon with dusty dirt roads, rotted railroad ties, and the gutted shells of a couple of ancient brick buildings. The biggest structure has only two sides left. Whole place looks like a little kid just randomly plopped some gray LEGOs into the ground.

A hundred years ago it was a prosperous coal mining town. Then the mine exploded. Every available casket in Utah was shipped to Winter Quarters. It was not enough. Two hundred men died in one day. Burned, buried alive, poisoned by coal dust. The entire town was completely empty ten years later. I looked it up on the Internet. Said the place was seriously haunted: strange lights in the mines, the desperate wails of the dying men and their mourning wives. All that stuff.

I sat in the car alone as usual while Castillo went down into the canyon to retrieve my father. He'd left just maybe fifteen minutes before. Castillo's intention was to get down there before my dad even showed up. He'd parked on a dark service road. I was freezing again. My whole body shaking with fever chills even though I had no fever. I dealt with it, just stared out the window. Giant slender trees running along both sides of the road and into the surrounding hills. The sky above was pitch-black, a zillion stars blinking overhead.

I tried not to think of them as dead people this time.

Didn't care much about dead people or ghosts tonight. Any kind.

Tonight was not about them. Only about finding my dad. Getting ANSWERS.

Soon Castillo would bring him to the car. (Even though Castillo hated me now for lying about the phone calls. But that didn't matter either. Castillo would do what he said he would. Make things right. He'd find my dad. Even *help* him.) Then we would all talk. Figure it all out. Make things better. Maybe even somehow get back to the rest of our lives.

The cursed dead could wail all they wanted. Tonight was only about the damned souls who were still living. Me and my dad.

In the dark I saw someone up ahead of the car walking on the dirt road toward me.

Castillo was already coming back.

• • •

I did not yet know that Castillo was still a mile away.

• • •

I got out of the car to see what the story was.

But by the time I got out of the car, "Castillo" was gone. No one there.

Like I said, I was in no mood for ghost stories this night. No black dresses or dark men with knives either. So I marched right down that gravel road toward where I'd seen something. If it wasn't Castillo, it was *someone*.

Figured I would go check things out. Maybe it was my dad. Maybe *I'd* be the one who found him, talked him into giving himself up and whatnot. I'd be all: *Hey, Castillo. It's cool, dude. I got my dad right here and everything's gonna be just fine.* Sure.

I kept walking, and the canyon below finally revealed itself. All the brick ruins and overgrown cart paths and concrete foundations. Half a dozen hills and ravines framing ancient mine openings into the more ancient earth deep below. Most of them blocked with decrepit wood structures and signs of danger. Still the gaping black spaces just behind were even darker than the night. A darkness from hell.

A darkness formed almost like a curious eye, a mouth forming its first word . . .

Then, despite my best intentions, all my earlier tough-guy declarations, it became a night of ghosts and dead people after all. Safe to say they were officially running things now.

• • •

This "ghost" I saw—the face forming in the landscape below—was Ernie Miller.

(Dahmer's eighth victim.)

This was NOT the Castillo figure I'd seen earlier. I still didn't realize who that'd been.

No, this was something else.

And at first I didn't know it was Ernie. I thought it might be Oliver or Errol.

While researching Dahmer, I'd studied and memorized ALL their names.

His victims.

This face filled up almost the entire canyon. Broad nose, full lips.

GEOFFREY GIRARD

Definitely a black guy. Then I recognized the unmistakable line of a mustache above his smile. Most of Dahmer's victims happened to be black, and I'd narrowed this face down to three guys. And please don't think I'm racist or something for not being able to tell these three men apart, because it was an enormous dark face made of boulders and rotted wood beams and shadows and bushes and piles of hundred-year-old brick. Not exactly the world's clearest image.

My first instinct was to simply turn away. What I always did. OK, sure, maybe this genetic memory had snuck into my conscience, but I didn't have to keep it there. All I had to do was look away, think about something else for a while, and the image would slowly burn off in my memory. I'd tell myself later it was nothing.

But now I had names to go with these faces. Real names. Real people. This wasn't some hallucination. This was a human being who'd been broken by my genetic father in every way a human can be broken. How the memory of his face had crossed over with Dahmer's DNA into mine was a riddle for the scientists. Or maybe a priest.

In any case, however I was seeing this man, I WAS seeing him. He WAS part of my history. He deserved better than my just turning away.

And I'd read Castillo's *Odyssey* book. I knew how to handle ghosts, right? You don't run from them. Don't hide. Or scream. Or attack them.

You talk to them.

So I talked . . .

• • •

Spoke the words out loud and everything.

And felt like a total idiot.

The first time I tried, my voice was so quiet, I barely heard myself. I tried again louder. First thing I asked was WHO ARE YOU? It

seemed the polite thing to do. (It's what Odysseus would have done.)
I tried again and asked: What is your name?

I swear the name ERNIE came into my head. Not spoken. No
ghostly whisper on the summer wind or any crap like that. Just a word,
a sound, in my head.

ERNIE.

My heart was pounding now. The "summer wind" was icy, super-
cold. I wanted a jacket or something, curled my arms around myself.
I'd read that Ernie Miller had moved from inner-city Chicago
to Milwaukee to escape the bad crime rate in Chicago. He'd met
Dahmer outside a bookstore a few months later.

What do you want? I asked.

Nothing.

What do you want to tell me? Again, spoken out loud. Talking
to an entire canyon. Castillo and my father were probably below,
listening to my muted echoes. Laughing their asses off or shaking
their heads in embarrassment for me. Right then I got this feeling of
hyper-embarrassment. But not my own. This was way more. This was
something else entirely. A feeling bordering on anger. Disgust.

Shame.

I got the sense that being a victim was no fun. No good.

All Ernie Miller was was another victim. Number 8.

I had no clue about his family, talents, plans, occupation, hopes . . . etc.

Only a few family members and friends got to know this stuff.

To the rest of the world, he'd become only number 8. September
1990. 1 of 17.

Let's just say it was a feeling I could relate to.

• • •

GEOFFREY GIRARD

I wasn't sure if this was me talking to myself or if I'd really tapped into some other spirit/memory/soul. Even as I thought this, images formed in my mind . . . images of people. His family, I assumed. And then . . . And then NOTHING.

Because right at that moment SHE showed up.

Yeah, her.

The lady in the black dress. THE THING ON THE BED.

That bitch.

. . .

Where once I'd seen Ernie's face—getting clearer, and closer, and smaller each passing moment—now was this terrible darkness. Like the sky had just collapsed in exhaustion onto the desolate ground below. Or maybe the mines had barfed out all the blackness they had. Up from the ground or down from the night sky, I didn't know. I just know that that whole canyon had turned pitch-dark in about two seconds. All the rubble and unkempt trails. The mines.

Gone. Replaced now by a small gleaming white face in the center surrounded by an outspread black dress. Its ridges and folds from the shadows and ravines. Her dark spreading out, running up the hill toward me.

But she wasn't there for me, I told myself.

She'd come for my father.

So, this was not *my* ghost to talk to.

And I turned and ran.

. . .

Back at the car I rested up against the side hood. Catching my breath. Still freezing cold. Kept murmuring my new mantra of: "Extreme for Life, Extreme for Life." Trying it out to see if it might really stick.

Which apparently worked just fine for evil visions because she did NOT follow me up that hill.

It had little effect, however, as I was about to find out, on real people.

• • •

I'd climbed back into the car. Trying to somehow get warm even though it was, like, eighty degrees outside. Trying to enfold myself. Separate myself from the rest of the world for a little while. Closed my eyes.

Then the side-door window exploded.

• • •

Glass went flying everywhere. All over me.

I jumped up in my seat. Looked around frantically.

The back window now splintered. Something slamming against it out of the darkness.

I lunged for the car's horn. I think I managed to press on it twice before someone grabbed me.

Hands reaching through the shattered window beside me.

Pulling me back away from the horn. Yanking me up and out through the side window.

Shards of glass digging into me as I passed. Ripping into my skin.

Someone was laughing.

• • •

There were three of them.

I swear I gave a decent fight, considering.

• • •

I recognized Ted immediately. He smiled. Hi, Jeff.

Where was Castillo?

The second boy was smaller than me, darker, older. He just kept throwing rocks at the car.

Where was Castillo?

The third and final kid had kept quiet throughout. Hadn't laid a hand on me yet.

He walked up slowly.

We were just about the same height, but he leaned forward to get right in my face.

It was like looking at a dark foggy mirror.

He placed his cold hand on my cheek.

Hi, he said.

I'm Jeff, he said.

• • •

Then he kinda beat the shit out of me.

• • •

You hear his blood. From a mile away, you hear it. Like sobbing. Wet gasps. Panting. Gulps of air. The one who gave you life, the FATHER who must be killed for the SON to assume his proper throne. The others are here too. His other sons. You sense three—no . . . four of them. You are to kill them all also. But not tonight. Tonight is for the Father. Those are the orders. The Father is with the other one, though. The Warrior, the one who shot you two nights ago. You know he has killed before also, but he is different, he does not yet kill for . . . for fun. A minor complication. He will just need to die first. You draw the blade again. You feel the blade slicing across his back. Now the good doctor, the Father, Jacobson. One hand around his throat, lifting him off the ground. The other, the hand with the knife, stabs forward. . . .

CHAPTER THIRTY-SIX

*T*he night my father left, he'd told me I was part of the special 5%. That when living conditions become too crowded in any environment, 5% of the population will resort to violence to achieve its goals.

They've done studies with rats. Perfectly calm and nonviolent animals until they're introduced into an environment with limited resources. Limited food, mates, and space. Then 5% of the previously nonviolent rats get medieval. They murder other rats. Rape other rats. Eat other rats. Even though they'd never done any of these things when in small groups or appropriate space. It was just part of their nature to adapt. To survive and thrive in a more challenging environment.

These are the dominant ones, my father said. The ones meant to rule their world.

That's, I guess, who I was with now.

• • •

We were in a house. That's all I knew. But I didn't even know what state I was in anymore. The last ten hours had been a blur of slaps and punches and being locked in the trunk of some car and simply collapsing in exhaustion. I figure I was in the trunk at least six hours. Maybe more.

Back at Winter Quarters they'd wrapped duct tape around my ankles and wrists and locked me in the trunk of their car. I could hardly breathe in there. I wanted to puke so bad. I couldn't believe the smell. (Later I would learn they'd kept and transported the nurse, Stacy Kelsoe, in the trunk for more than a week.) I passed out from the reek, I think. Every so often I came back to consciousness. I remember hearing them come back to the car, could hear their ragged breaths and cursing through the backseat. They were excited. *Something* had happened. Strange memories and visions trickled into my brain again. Then the car peeled out to muffled laughter, and we were off.

And I kept wondering what had happened to Castillo. What had happened to my dad?

Such strange images still in my head. Faded but ... The rest was only a blur. A nightmare.

They'd stopped about a mile down from Winter Quarters. To cut my feet. They were looking for my tracking chip. I told them I didn't have one. They just kept cutting anyway.

How they found the house hours later, I don't know. I guess Castillo wasn't the only one willing to bust into a deserted home. This one was a raging mess, however. It'd probably been condemned. Wires were hanging everywhere. In a lot of the rooms the walls had been half-busted. Torn drywall and exposed moldy studs. *Like exposed bone,* I thought.

They dragged me into what had once been a family room, I guess.

It was the middle of the day, I think. I still don't know these things entirely.

Every step I took, I left a fresh crimson print.

The kid named Albert, Albert Young, was told to watch me for a while. He tried tying me up to this old wood chair in the room but failed completely. Kept muttering to himself the whole time. Guy was weird. I mean really F-in' weird. He moved weird. Spoke in a weird high voice. His sentences broken into small bites. Robotic almost. Like he was less used to talking than I was. For all I knew, this was true. Maybe the guy was only really four years old. I think the other two guys hated him also.

Albert had been made entirely from the DNA of Albert Fish, who'd been killed in an electric chair way back in 1936. His genetic source had raped, murdered, and then *eaten* as many as a hundred children. He even sent letters to his victims' parents, describing every detail. *How she did kick, bite, and scratch*, one letter reported to the grieving family. *It took me nine days to eat her entire body*. With a hundred confirmed kills, he'd acquired several nicknames, including, "The Werewolf of Wysteria," "The Brooklyn Vampire," and "The Boogeyman."

GEOFFREY GIRARD

His whole life Albert Fish had this habit/fascination with jamming sewing needles up into his gooch, that weird little area between your ass and balls. He got off on the pain somehow. Prison doctors found two dozen needles wedged up there when they did an X-ray looking for contraband.

How weird was this Albert Young kid? He'd picked up the same habit. Read about it in some serial killer book and thought it was worth a shot. A proper nod, perhaps, to his former self. Maybe something else. Some memory of pain/pleasure that still resided deep in his genes somewhere. . . . I don't think he was up to dozens of needles yet, but I know it was more than one. And that was enough as far as I was concerned.

Mostly he kept to himself. Kinda wandered around the house. Breaking shit. Talking quietly to himself. Looking around nervously like a little rat.

It was Ted and Jeff who were most interested in me.

Mostly Jeff.

*   *   *

Ted asked me a lot of questions about Castillo, and I told him exactly who Castillo was. Figured there was no point in being all coy about it.

I even told them that Henry was dead. (Ted laughed at that.)

In return for all this info, he told *me* about killing families in Maryland, Ohio, and Indiana. Described the house in Maryland, then the Albaum kid. He described a park. All so familiar. From dreams I'd had, from strange thoughts, from snippets of conversation with Castillo. All blending together. I didn't feel well. He described a house in Indiana. A wooden swing set there. How they'd taken a rope and hung the mother and her kids from it when they'd left.

I threw up.

Ted stood over me.

He said: If you'd been at Massey that night, we'd totally have killed you.

He told me: And your daddy would have applauded us.

. . .

Ted showed me a canister. It looked kinda like a soda can.

And then he asked if I knew what it was.

I didn't. My guess was it had something to do with July 4.

I was right.

. . .

Ted explained that on July 4 he and the others were supposed to go to an Independence Day celebration at some park, any park, in San Francisco and open the canister. Simple enough.

He said the stuff inside had been developed by DSTI using special chromosomes taken from the clones. He said something about an XP11 gene. In short the clones at DSTI had been utilized to cultivate very specific gene structures and calculated mutations. And then the clones had been harvested. For their DNA. Which clones specifically had been used, no one could say. They'd taken so much blood from each of us, it could have been any or all.

In any case, when the DSTI scientists were done, they had their weapon: a new neurological biotoxin.

Ted said it would infect all the people there. Drive them mad with RAGE. He said they'd tear themselves to pieces. He said five thousand people would die.

I whispered the word: Shardhara.

He didn't know at all what I was talking about. When he asked what

I'd said, I told him not to worry about it. He punched me in the face. My lip split open. There was blood on the floor. My blood.

Ted asked what I knew about the "dark man."

I told him honestly I didn't know anything. I said only that he'd tried to kill me too.

Ted considered that for a while.

Then he said my dad could go to hell and they weren't gonna open a canister on the 4th and make HIM famous. They weren't just gonna be little puppets in his big plan.

I said OK.

Ted asked me if I wanted to open the canister right now. Forget five thousand nobodies. Just open it up in this house and see what comes out. What happens.

I said OK.

• • •

We didn't open the canister.

He just patted me on the shoulder.

He said: Maybe you're OK after all, Jacobson.

Then he told me my father was dead.

I said OK.

• • •

Jeff Williford was three years older than me.

There'd been pictures of him in Castillo's files, which I now knew well. He was different from his pictures now. In those, he'd looked more like an older, sadder version of me. He'd looked like the real Jeffrey Dahmer had while in prison. Sedated, unhappy, ashamed.

THIS Jeffrey was something/someone else. This one was vibrant, alive. Filled with abundant energy and excitement. This was the

Dahmer who joyfully struck. Strangled. Killed.

The evil within sparkled like a black star. A perfect shadow of "Extreme for Life."

He looked, I think, "Extreme for Death."

Where I'd imagined life's colors as *bold* and *radiant*, now the color was crimson, dark. His look said "YODO." You only *DIE* once. EMBRACE THE DARK.

A challenge. And a promise, too.

He smiled. Jeffrey Jacobson, he said.

Jeff Williford told me a story then. He started it like this:

Once, there were ten baby boys.

Ten little piggies.

Each one exactly same. 100%.

This little piggy died during gestation.

This one did also. And another.

This little piggy was born without working lungs and died.

This little piggy was born with cancer and died.

This little piggy lived but was set aside for lab work.

This little piggy, I have no idea.

This little piggy was given to a pedophile, a DSTI employee, and eventually committed suicide at the age of twelve. This caused much disappointment and several harshly worded memos.

This little piggy was raised as an alcoholic by a DSTI employee. They broke his foot the day he was born to induce early trauma. His fake mother had fake seizures and yelled at him for stupid things. His fake father mostly ignored him for fifteen years and started fights with the fake mother. By the age of twelve he'd been encouraged to drink alcohol by older students at the Massey Institute, where he went to school. He'd been shown violent gay porn websites. He'd been exposed to dead animals. One kid, paid fifty dollars by a man named Jacobson, showed him how "cool the insides were."

Now, the last little piggy . . .

The last little piggy got taken home by a man who proved to be a kind and supportive father. Got sent to science camps and was given piano lessons and private tutors. And one night, out of the blue, the father finally tells the piggy what he really is.

• • •

Jeff Williford thought this was all pretty interesting.

The chance of it all. The randomness.

I couldn't agree more. But didn't say so.

It could have been you, he said.

YOU could have been the one throwing up before class, he said.

YOU could have been the one crying yourself to sleep, he said.

I couldn't agree more. But didn't say so.

He said: And I could have been you.

Yes, I said.

He laughed. Touched my hair.

It's OK, he said. I'd rather be this.

Then it got bad.

• • •

After, the dead came to see me.

From the fringes of my vision and thoughts. Dahmer's victims. Not as enormous vague faces this time. But as shadows. Shades. Human shapes crouched in the darkness just beyond my reality.

I'd been stuffed into some kind of crawl space.

The room was dark and smelled like dirt and mold and spiders.

My feet felt on fire. My wrists and ankles taped again. I did not have all my clothes anymore.

I did not want to see them yet. These ghosts. I was too ashamed.

I was a victim now. Like them.

• • •

Still, my chance to escape came that night.

CHAPTER THIRTY-SEVEN

*T*here was a hole in the floor filled with water. An old rusted sump pump. The rainwater inside rank and oily. Old cobwebs running all up the top of the well liner.

I dunked my hands into the dark water. Kept moving the palms back and forth against each other.

The duct tape loosened.

I did this for what seemed liked weeks. (It was maybe an hour.)

My wrists moved more freely every time in the water.

Eventually I got my thumb, its nail, beneath the tape.

Back and forth times forever.

The duct tape loosened.

Two fingers and the other thumb now. The duct tape was now ripping. Enough.

I turned my one wrist and pulled. It totally came out.

Five minutes later I was completely free.

The only light came from the wide cracks in the doorframe to the next room. I thought it might have been morning.

I moved quietly around the crawl space, up on my fingers and toes. Moving as slowly and silently as possible. Every step was agony because the sides of my feet had been cut up so bad.

I had no idea where the guys were. When they'd be back.

I found a small pile of bricks. Remnants of construction done forty years before.

I choose one.

It felt good having a weapon in my hand.

• • •

The door opened easily enough. They hadn't blocked it or locked it or anything. They probably hadn't given me a second thought. I crawled out into the next room. Water-stained carpet. Seventies wallpaper. A rusted metal table in the center of the room and steps leading up. Up and out. My breathing was all messed up. A freaky combo of rattling gasps or long inhales followed by nothing for far too long. I was terrified. I moved up the steps, where each little creak sounded like the whole house caving in.

Halfway up I saw him.

Al.

He was sound asleep at the top of the steps. His legs on the second step, knees bent, leaning back through the doorway to the next floor. Guess he'd been given "watch duty" and had fallen asleep some time ago. I got closer.

Past the doorway I spotted hints of a kitchen, windows. But no clear sign of a door to run to. Didn't know where the other two were. Ted or Jeff Williford. Or where the closest door was to escape through.

I looked up at Al. I was about his age, but a lot bigger than he was. Probably stronger too, I figured. But I wasn't Castillo. Not by a long shot. I'd never been in a fight in my life. I figured I could at least get by him. Maybe even get in a couple of good punches. The kid was out cold. But ultimately he'd wake. Scream for help. The others would know what was going on immediately. Escape ruined.

The other option was simple and obvious enough.

Kill him.

· · ·

I squeezed the brick tightly.

Fingers trembling with rage. Fear. Knuckles white.

I moved up to the second step, carefully straddling his legs.

I had a clear shot at his head. All I had to do was slam down once right in the center of his forehead. It'd make a noise, sure. But just for a second. Not him yelling for help.

It was simple enough.

As simple as pulling apart a caterpillar.

Or stepping on a bird.

· · ·

I'm not gonna make a big production about what happened. My decision. The short version is, I didn't use the brick. I made a run for it instead. Jumped over/on Al and ran for where I thought the door would be. The door was there, but it was too late. Al woke up and started yelling, just like I thought he would. I think Ted grabbed hold of me first.

To this day I still don't know why I didn't just kill Al. Why I *couldn't*.

I guess the same way that Jeff Dahmer didn't know why he *could*.

· · ·

Ted wanted to kill me, but Jeff Williford wouldn't let him.

He said we still had a lot to talk about.

More bad stuff happened.

. . .

One day, I don't remember which, Jeff Williford put this small pile of bones on the table. Animal bones. Small animals. Mice and birds, mostly. A squirrel he'd found. And a cat from the house in Maryland where they'd collected John. Tiny vertebrae, ribs, tibiae, and skulls that he'd pulled together over the last few weeks. He carried them in an emptied box of Frosted Flakes reinforced with the same silver duct tape they'd used on me.

Williford told me that when he was five, someone had made sure he'd found similar bones behind the Massey facility one morning, with the hope that he'd find them amusing and play with them. And they hoped this because that's exactly what Jeffrey Dahmer, the real one, had done when *he* was a kid. The scientists at DSTI must have been quite pleased with the results.

It's the sound, Williford told me. When they rub together. Or when the pile collapses and they roll off each other. That *click, click, click*. He leaned in close as he spoke and he picked up some of the pile to let the tiny bones trickle back off his fingers onto the table. *Click, click, click.* Do you hear it? Williford asked me. He picked up and dropped another handful. *Click, click, click.*

I didn't. I said nothing.

He got mad and made me drink more beer. There was already a half-empty case of Budweiser on the table, and Williford angrily reached for another can. Called me a faggot and shoved my head back so he could pour the beer down my throat. I spurted and choked as the beer ran down my chin and chest. Thrashed against the weight of Williford's hand. He was too strong. He was me two years older, a hundred years meaner.

　　　GEOFFREY GIRARD

Ted was in the room watching the whole thing like he was just watching reality television.

Williford tossed the empty can across the room.

He said: You'll get used to it. Even start to like it, I bet.

I coughed up more beer. Tried to stop choking. I thought: *Extreme for—*

He stopped me. He told me that they'd had him drinking by the time he was ten. That they'd wanted a genuine alcoholic just like THE ORIGINAL. He moved behind me again, but kept his hand on my face. He said: Of course, you're just really a baby, aren't you? Still wet behind the ears with formaldehyde and whatnot. New and improved insta-clone.

His fingers moved slowly over my chin, forced their way into my mouth. He gave me crap for being only, like, eight years old technically. (My father, I assume, had told them about that. What else had he confided to these killers?) Jeff Williford said this made me even less of a real person than he was, since *he'd* lived a legit eighteen years.

I agreed with him completely but still couldn't hear any more. He was preaching to the choir, and the choir just wanted to die. I begged him to stop talking.

He told me to relax. It didn't matter when I was technically born.

He said: You're still one of us. Right here and right now, you and I are exactly the same.

He said: We are one.

I'm . . . I tried talking.

He said: You're what, Jeff?

I'm *nothing* like you, I said.

He grabbed my face in both hands.

He said: All evidence to the contrary.

Then it got bad again.

Real bad.

. . .

I know part of this is an exercise in putting into words what happened to me.

By writing it down, making it more real, it becomes something else.

Something I can eventually even understand and accept. Move on from.

But I'm still not ready to do that yet. Someday, maybe.

I don't know.

. . .

I lay curled on the concrete floor again. Everything hurt. The cold damp floor against my face was the only feeling that wasn't burning, piercing.

They sat with me now, the other boys from someone else's life.

The ghosts born in my head for too many years.

James and Matt and Ernest. (*Now the souls gathered . . .*)

Curtis, Tony, and both Stevens. (*From every side they came . . .*)

I'm sorry, I said.

I'm sorry. I'm sorry.

They'd never spoken to me before.

Now they did.

They'd told me apologies were unnecessary.

They called me brother. Whispered to me for hours.

Konerak even stroked my hair in the darkness.

Be brave, he said.

There was a hole drilled into the back of his head. I could see it.

Long ago someone had injected hydrochloric acid into the frontal lobes of his brain while he was still alive. Someone had wanted to make Konerak a "zombie."

Be brave, he said. *Castillo is going to find you.*

Be brave. Castillo is going to find you.

I heard the door open.

Konerak and the others were gone. Returned to the underworld . . .

(*My heart longed, after this, to see the dead again.*)

Who you talking to? a familiar voice asked.

It wasn't Castillo.

• • •

You hear their blood. From down—

• • •

—a long hallway. My father is working in his office, and I am left alone to explore. Find somewhere new, a doorway, a hallway never noticed before, like the hidden door of a secret room. Come with me down that long dark hall. Bright color glowing at the end like gold almost. Come with me to the door, hold our hands up to the security panel and watch the door open. Inside are the tanks ten feet high— five, ten, two dozen—in four neat rows across the whole room and each one glowing like gold, the liquid inside shining. There is something in each tank, something floating. Walk up slowly to inspect the closest tank. There's a man inside and he is naked. His skin is dark gray almost. Place our tiny hands against the warm thick glass of the tank. Inside the tank, eyes open. Gray hands move against the glass to mirror my hands.

We meet for the first time.

The dark man and I.

This is only a memory.

But I somehow knew he was close again.

. . .

The dark man found the house on the third day.

I saw none of it. I don't remember much of that time.

I'm told he killed Al and Ted and Jeff Williford.

I can almost picture him doing this, but these are images I chase away quickly.

I can tell you that when he was done killing them, he came for me.

. . .

I think I'd been tied or taped again or something to a chair. It's all . . . I don't know.

I remember the sounds of screaming.

I could almost hear his thoughts again. The REAL killer.

The dark man.

Pictured him chopping into Albert, ripping away that muscle and weird fatty stuff inside. Almost as if I were doing it myself. I imagined David and heard gulls screaming. I imagined my father being torn in half. I welcomed the enclosing darkness.

Soon, I prayed, I would see nothing else.

I remember feeling the thing/man standing right behind me. Breath hot and wet against my shoulder blades. The warmth off his body. Several jagged nails moving slowly under my chin.

Stuck in the chair, this killer behind me.

It seemed sort of silly now. All of it. I'd been wrong.

There was no real Jeff Jacobson. Or Jeff Williford.

Or Jeff Dahmer for that matter either.

There was only Cain.

Death manufactured in laboratories, mined from physical evil.

I waited to die.

Then, what I thought was warm water splashed over my back and soaked the top of my head. It wasn't water.

Because the table beneath me turned red. Like a magic trick. Like a sorcerer's spell. And the red on the table was blood, I realized, and my silhouette—my own head and shoulders—instantly appeared on the table between the spatter.

All sound vanished. Then something like thunder filled the room, pierced my ears.

THIS is Death, I thought. Not squished birds or frozen boys or graveyards.

I felt great weight fall against his body and then slide away again.

I heard more thunder.

Gunshots.

Something touched my face, lifted my head.

The light above burned my eyes, and I crept back into the darkness again. The burn from the ropes slackened suddenly. Then nothing.

I felt myself being lifted from the chair.

Like flying.

I forced one eye open.

It was Castillo.

. . .

castillo (noun)

Spanish word for "castle"

  (1)a fortified stronghold; (2) a place of security
      or refuge

CHAPTER THIRTY-EIGHT

I woke. For all I knew I was back in my own house in Haddonfield. Or maybe, at worst, it was still the night my dad left. The night Castillo had arrived. And all the rest, all of it, the most terrible of it, had been a nightmare. I had imagined the whole thing.

But my entire body ached a thousand different ways. And a man stood at the end of the bed. Fading like another ghost. It was not Castillo or my father. Maybe the world was nothing anymore but half-formed ghosts. Maybe that's all I was now too.

Coming into focus again, a small black man. A face I knew. A *real* face.

You're safe.

It was Ox I was looking at. But Ox hadn't spoken.

The voice had been Castillo's and I tried turning to it.

Take it easy, his voice said.

I slowly took in the rest of the room. Sparse. Bare walls, a cot, rusted metal desk.

You're safe, Castillo said again and then tried to get me to focus. I tried concentrating on his face. He looked totally exhausted, sorrowful. I didn't need a mirror to see what Castillo was looking at. As well as Castillo was trying to hide it, I could see in his eyes.

I was broken. I'd been messed up pretty bad.

Castillo told me we were at Ox's place. Somewhere we'd be safe for a little while.

Castillo confirmed that my father was dead, and I didn't let him know I somehow already knew that. That I'd seen/felt it happen in my own mind/body. It still hadn't sunk in yet, and I stayed quiet as Castillo recounted what had happened.

How he'd found my dad at Winter Quarters and was bringing him out when the same man from the motel showed up. The dark man. He's the one who killed my father. Who stabbed Castillo, too. (All of this familiar in the back of my mind as some sort of half-formed dream-memory.)

When he finally returned to his own car and found it all busted up and me gone, Castillo called his bosses finally. Told them Dr. Jacobson was dead and that he'd found one of the canisters.

Then he told them to let out more of these supersoldier things. These men who could somehow find the boys so easily. He understood this now too, I think. The link between us all. Something in our blood. Synthetic or whatever. Told them *he'd* now "vanish forever" if they'd find the boys and tell him where. Otherwise he was going to the press with everything.

His bosses accepted, and when the dark men found Al and Ted and two Jeffs, they called Castillo as promised and he was ready. Castillo was too late to save three of the boys. (By choice or not, I still don't know. Don't want to.) But he killed his second dark man.

Castillo told me there was now just one more thing to take care of, and then it'd all be over.

I knew then he was going back to DSTI.

· · ·

I said: They'll just kill you, too.

Castillo figured they were going to try soon anyway. This way maybe it was on his own timetable. His terms. He thought it'd help.

I told him I wanted to go too, but he wanted none of that. He told me I needed time in a real hospital with real people who could help start putting me back together again.

But it was more than just the cuts and punches and other stuff. More than whatever psychological damage I had to carry now. Castillo let me know it was something else.

His eyes led down to a bandage on my arm. The bandage was not for cuts or anything.

It was, it turned out, for the black stuff on my arm.

The same stuff Henry had been covered in.

The same stuff Ted and Jeff had too, according to Castillo.

Turns out my "allergy medications" were not for allergies.

They were for something else.

• • •

Dolly, the famous cloned sheep. Remember her? Her lab name was 6LL3. She died at only six years old. Most sheep live to twelve. But there were giant black tumors growing inside 6LL3's chest. And her legs already had arthritis. She couldn't stop coughing blood.

So they euthanized her.

In the biopsy they found surprisingly shortened telomeres, the parts of the cell connected to age. The scientists figured these midget telomeres had been passed on from the "parent," who'd been six years old when the DNA was taken.

So, genetically, Dolly was already six years old the day she was born. Weird, huh?

• • •

To officially get all the numbers straight.

I developed in a vat at DSTI for close to two years.

I have the physical appearance and development of a sixteen-year-old.

The chromosomes I was made from were thirty-three years old. (The age Dahmer was when they took tissue samples from his brain and made me and Jeff Williford and others.)

I was born eight years ago.

So, best I can figure I'm forty-one years old. (In clone years, I mean.) Whatever.

I try not to think about any of this.

I will avoid celebrating future birthdays.

• • •

The original plan was that Castillo was going back to DSTI to get rid of DSTI's scientists and his own bosses once and for all. Also, to get me the medications I needed.

I asked about the other kids, those who might still be at Massey or DSTI, and Castillo told me they weren't my problem but promised if there were any kids left, he'd get as many as he could.

I didn't think that was a good enough answer. I wasn't the only one who needed to be saved and protected from these people. I was, however, the only one who could really help do something about it. So I told Castillo I could help.

Castillo said I'd already done more than anyone else (I suppose I was getting credit for helping to find most of the missing clones), and even Ox piped in about how he and Castillo could handle things now. I was supposed to just hide out with Ox until Castillo got everything taken care of.

I lifted my hand. It was shaking. The nails worn to nubs. But I got it up there all the same. I said: It'll be easier to handle it with this.

What's that? Castillo asked. He leaned back, curious. Half smiling, even.

I wiggled my fingers. Five keys, I said.

DSTI's security system.

Ox looked at Castillo with excited eyes.

Castillo said no. Said I was done. No more.

He said: Those monsters will never harm you again.

I needed to let Castillo know I was ready. That I wasn't a victim. I wasn't afraid of monsters anymore. I was "Extreme for Life." I didn't think he'd get that skate park mantra the way I'd hoped. I'm not sure how well it was really working for me, either.

So instead I quoted a line from *The Odyssey*. Something Odysseus's son says to him right before that huge battle at the end.

In short, the quote meant I could handle it.

Castillo obviously knew the line. Took it pretty hard, in fact. He, like, cried and stuff.

I told him I wasn't gonna hide anymore from the monsters.

No, Castillo agreed, looking up. We're not.

I asked about the dark man, but I called him a "thing."

I killed him, Castillo said. But . . .

But there's more, I said, and pictured rows of liquid-filled tanks.

He admitted this was true and asked how I knew.

I explained I just did and that I kinda thought they were looking for me even now.

I said: And I think they're getting close.

GEOFFREY GIRARD

CHAPTER THIRTY-NINE

*C*astillo's plan-number-one of taking care of things himself and leaving me safely behind was done. There was no more "safely behind." DSTI and the government knew where I was and they were coming for me. They knew because the "dark men" knew, and I could literally feel them looking for me.

So plan-number-two became to not get caught in the open but maybe fight it out there at Ox's place.

The "Good Guys"

Castillo and Ox and a handful of Ox's pals. Who were all pretty hard-core rogue prepper/survivalist types. Hated the federal government. Most of them were vets like Ox and Castillo. One was just a guy who was angry about some "New World Order." He told me I was just a pawn in all of that now. There were four of them. McLaughlin. Wilke. Rosfeld. Some other guy. Added up, they had more guns than God.

The "Bad Guys"

Castillo predicted his government boss, Colonel Stanforth, would send a couple of Special Forces–trained mercenaries (like Castillo) and a group of agents from the Bureau of Alcohol, Tobacco, Firearms and Explosives. And probably a bunch of local cops. Small-town sheriffs and such. Castillo figured the locals would be brought in to make a mess of things and make the cover-up even easier. Afterward, Castillo said, the press would simply report that the ATF had conducted a raid on terrorists or right-wing extremists. No one would ever know what really had happened.

Also. The dark men. Castillo agreed with me that there'd been several.

DSTI didn't make just ONE of *anything*.

So they'd be coming also.

For me.

. . .

There were, like, a hundred acres at Ox's place. Wooded. Uninhabited. Middle of nowhere up on some mountain somewhere in South Dakota. There were half a dozen different trailers and sheds spread among the trees. Solar panels, generators. Kitchens, storage. Paddocks for livestock, chicken coops, a small dog kennel. Barns for a couple of horses. Underground bunkers for when the bombs or sun flares ever started falling someday. Ox and his pals had spent all sorts of money and time on this stuff.

And they were pretty damn serious about two things: (1) bad days were coming, and (2) they were gonna survive.

Everyone now knew Part 1 was true.

They spent all day planning what would happen when the Bad Guys found us again.

Still, I got the feeling not even Castillo was so sure about Part 2.

. . .

All that whole day, Castillo and Ox and the other guys prepared.

A lot of it involved explosives. Mines and stuff.

Consequently I was asked to stay in my room.

A room surrounded by concrete that was a hundred feet below the ground.

They took turns guarding my door.

I tried to sleep. To heal.

All that whole day, I could feel the dark men in my head.

Listening for me. For my blood.

All that whole day, I could feel them getting ever closer.

I closed my eyes.

Come and get me, I said to the dark.

CHAPTER FORTY

*C*astillo had been in the military since he was eighteen years old.

He told me that the key to every successful operation was the same and quite simple: Everyone just had to do the job they'd been given.

I didn't have to think about the traps and tricks and escapes and whatnot.

I only had one job: stay near Castillo.

And IF something happened to Castillo, stay near Ox.

And IF something happened to Ox, it wouldn't matter.

. . .

Ox had these special suits we wore that would help conceal our body temperature. Standard US Army stuff he'd bought from some German company. Apparently this was a good thing because all the guns that'd be aimed at us would have thermal imaging. We also had gas masks.

Castillo told me to expect smoke grenades or worse. And again to just stay close.

I wasn't walking so good yet. One of Ox's guys had stitched up my feet in a couple of places from when Ted cut them looking for the nonexistent transmitter. They were still pretty swollen and sore. And I was still sore. Everywhere. Muscles and tendons I didn't even know about a week before. I still felt half-dead.

But even half-dead I was ready to end all of this as much as Castillo was. My father was *all*-dead, killed by something he'd made at DSTI years before. (Ironic, yes. And sad too.)

And now those same things, this same organization, was coming for us.

It WAS gonna end soon one way or the other.

The gas mask felt funny on my face. I could hardly see a thing through the bug-eyed lenses. It didn't help any that my glasses had been smashed back at Winter Quarters.

We were stuck in this long ditch that ran along the front of one of the concrete buildings.

I could hardly stand, but I was doing my job—Castillo was next to me. The other guys were in their spots. On roofs, in the woods. In the next trench.

We waited like that for hours.

I started to get really cold around eleven at night. And understood exactly what that meant. They were close. I told Castillo, and each passing hour, the cold got deeper and deeper inside me.

I could feel other thoughts poking around my own. Like tiny fingers moving and scratching under my skin. Bubbling though my blood.

I sat down at Castillo's feet. Tired. So very tired.

I could picture them clearly moving through the woods. The trees and bushes blurring by as shadows. Unnatural speed. Drifting . . .

It was probably two in the morning.

I sprang awake. Like an electric shock, a blast of cold had detonated up and down my spine. I thought my eyes were gonna burst out.

I thought I was gonna die.

Castillo, I said. They're here.

About ten seconds later guns started shooting.

Let me tell you, it was loud as shit.

Just like Castillo had said war was.

- - -

So all these guns shooting. I don't even know from where.

People shouting directions at each other over these walkie-talkie things. Smoke bombs flying. I honestly had/have no idea what was happening. The whole thing was a total blur of noise and smoke and getting dragged around and people shouting.

Castillo kept lifting me and pulling me this way and that, then shoving me down again. I just kept trying to do my one job. It wasn't easy. My thoughts were just as confused as all the crap going on around me.

I could swear I saw something jumping past us from the smoke, scaling the wall of the building behind us.

I mean a man. A dark man. And I literally just watched him shinny up.

I reached for Castillo, but he was shooting his rifle and yelling at Ox about something.

One of Ox's guys was above us with a sniper rifle or something.

I stumbled back against the trench to support myself. My head was suddenly so light. Could hardly stand.

I suddenly imagined slitting a man's throat. It was terrible. But all the same and all of a sudden I could see that knife going in and the blood and everything. My head filled with such terrible thoughts.

I grabbed out for Castillo. Tried to warn him . . .

Of what, I had no idea. I just . . . I don't know. I could see it like it was happening.

Then it started raining. Felt it hit my shoulders and back.

I looked up.

My goggles splattered with huge drops.

Of red rain.

• • •

I could visualize two men above me. One dying. The other, a shadow.

I held my hands in front of my face. They were now speckled with blood. I reached out again for Castillo, tried telling him what was going on above us. But the words came out jumbled, confused. It was like trying to talk in a nightmare.

Castillo stared in confusion.

The drops of blood just kept raining down on us. The next drops hit him.

He finally looked up, and I found the courage to look with him.

Above us the wall was dripping blood. An arm dangled off the rooftop. Braced by the elbow, the wrist and fingers sagging and lifeless.

The blood dribbled steadily from the dangling hand.

Then the arm slid backward. Something slowly dragging the body back from the edge.

Castillo gave some kind of signal and everything kinda exploded.

• • •

I mean the woods and ground were shaking and everything. The boom, a long series of quick and succeeding detonations, lit the woods like it was noon. A hundred detonations, I figure, each following hard on the last.

All through this total chaos Castillo acted like nothing was going on. Like he was walking into the kitchen to get something to drink. He just dragged me back into the underground bunker. My feet hardly touched the ground.

We followed this long narrow hallway down into the ground where some of the living quarters and storage rooms were. Ox and one other guy came with us.

I didn't know Castillo's true intentions yet.

I didn't know that he wanted the dark man to follow us.

That I was bait.

• • •

We were all at the end of the hall. Me and Castillo on one side and Ox and this guy McLaughlin on the other. McLaughlin had a flame-thrower. I mean, these guys!

All three of them had special night-vision sights and stuff.

I, however, couldn't see a thing.

I could *feel* it, though. That cold. Just when I thought I was used to it, it'd grabbed hold again. I let it sink in a bit. Tried to focus. Listened. If it could hear blood . . . If this thing could hear MY blood, maybe I could hear its.

I had this image of it moving down the hall toward us, and I told Castillo. He checked. Said it was "nothing," trying to assure me (and himself also, I think).

Getting closer. Crouched in the dark, listening for the blood pumping though my veins. Blood they'd partly used to give this thing life. My whole body was shaking again. I was practically having a seizure there in the dark. I wasn't even looking down the hall, but I saw it just the same. Feet away from us.

I tried calling out again to Castillo for, like, the third time. To warn him.

He just told me there was nothing there again. To hush, to wait—

I wouldn't quit. I told him: *It's right there.*

There must have been something in the way I said it. Something that suggested these were my last words, maybe.

Because next thing I know, the whole hallway burst into flame.

The guy with the flamethrower just torched everything in front of us.

I heard screaming now. I heard blood boiling.

• • •

The thing was on fire, screaming in agony as it slammed into the concrete wall and then crumpled to the ground, twitching and flailing. The fire burning it lit up the whole hall.

Its mind somehow in mine, its thoughts my thoughts. Thoughts of rage and hatred and fire. *Get out of my head!* I screamed, but not out loud. *Killing. Pain. Death.*

Even through the gas mask I could smell the man's, the dark man's, burning flesh, couldn't avoid looking at it, the man, as we stepped around—and it *was* a man now, not a thing anymore. A man with open, staring eyes and a gaping, terrified mouth.

A man that could have been me, as we were made, more or less, from the same stuff.

Made by my father.

• • •

Castillo dragged me away and outside again. Sporadic gunfire filled the woods. The more-human troops moving in for the kill now.

Castillo said something, but I couldn't hear. My ears were still ringing, my head crowded still with too many strange thoughts and feelings. I could feel this guy still burning at my very core.

Next thing I know, all this smoke detonated from a dozen different places, filled the whole trench. I couldn't see six inches in front of me. Then someone shouting about grenades and Castillo was throwing me into the trench.

A tremendous boom filled the whole world. I slammed against the bottom of the trench almost as a relief, the feel of the ground the only thing that kept me pinned to the earth. Arms flailing, hugging the ground and praying that the wet cold earth would stop spinning beneath me.

Where was Castillo?

Around me were curses, orders, and the sound of more guns firing and bodies moving, but my own blood was pounding so loud in my ears that everything seemed like just an echo of the initial boom. I scrambled farther along the trench, seeking cover, seeking safety. I had to find Castillo. Or Ox. My one job was simple.

I lifted my head to find him. Pointless. There was still smoke absolutely everywhere, bodies rushing around like ghosts.

No Castillo. No Ox.

I spun back around. Called out for Castillo, but in the rain of gunfire my voice was completely lost. I whirled around again, scrambling down the trench back toward where I thought Castillo was, had been, should be, must be. Bullets zinged over my head, and shouts, voices I didn't recognize, rang through the air.

Up ahead the smoke cleared just enough.

I saw Castillo.

Crouched ahead, not twenty feet away.

I waved at him—his face obscured by his gas mask and his body tight and coiled, as if he were ready to spring.

I shouted Castillo's name and pushed myself forward, relief washing through me for the first time in what seemed like hours.

Castillo looked up as I approached and smiled at me.

Except you can't smile through a mask.

I stumbled to a complete stop.

It wasn't Castillo.

And the face I'd seen wasn't really a face at all anymore.

Just an open gaping maw, dripping, leering at me with glee.

I'd seen that same non-face look a hundred times before. The same that had reigned over my nightmares and stared out of dark shadows for as long as I could remember. It wasn't really a face anymore because it was *every* face.

Another dark man.

With the face of the man I'd seen in the tank so many years before.

The face of the man with knives at the foot of my bed.

The face of the man who'd murdered my father.

And it was Ted's and Henry's. And Al's and David's, too. All of them.

Even the one painted like a clown.

Each and every copy of them too.

All the killers DSTI and my father had brought together blended into one.

And so it was my face too.

• • •

I ran.

Away from the second dark man. Away from the trench, the bunker. From my whole life.

Where was Castillo? I had to find Castillo!

But Castillo could be anywhere—probably was fighting for his life too. And I had no idea where Ox was either. I'd failed in my one task.

I spun around, eyes skimming buildings, forest, men. Flashing bursts of gunfire. The smoke had cleared enough that I could see the line of trees not thirty feet away. I'd never make it to Castillo or Ox. I just needed to get away and hide. Just had to make it into the woods.

I could hear the dark man behind me. Its sounds. Following.

My lungs burned as I reached the deep black trees, as I stumbled over roots and fallen branches, my breathing coming so fast and hard that it steamed up the inside of my mask until it was dripping with condensation and my vision was entirely blurred again. It was like running in every nightmare I'd ever run in. I ripped the gas mask off, dropped it, and picked up my pace, the sudden rush of oxygen all I needed to keep going. But I couldn't just keep running. Soon it would catch me.

I broke free so quickly from the trees that I stumbled. Three buildings in this clearing, and barns beyond. I hid in the second building.

It was a storeroom. Mostly filled with food.

My hope was to hide. *Hide. Survive.* Wait for Castillo.

Behind me, the door opened at the front of the building.

I felt the breath die in my throat. The footsteps that came into the room were a man's footsteps, but it wasn't Castillo. Slow. Measured. And coming my way.

I tried to make my next breath more quiet.

The steps came just close enough, and I knew completely now.

The dark man.

GEOFFREY GIRARD

Thoughts flooded through me again, incoherent but eerily familiar. Rage again, and death. Extreme focused purpose. Hunting, always hunting. For something that seemed never to be found. It was him again. *It.* The thing. Just another copy.

And coming ever closer.

• • •

Past the strongboxes of canned food and the MREs. Past the stockpiled oats and bags of flour and rice. I could almost feel it in my bones as it passed the first row of water drums. Knew it was there just like the other one had been.

I thought, *I'm dead.* A thought so clear and simple. It was going to get me. Castillo wouldn't come. Castillo *shouldn't* come.

This man was just me, who I would eventually be, who I was destined to be.

I deserve this.

This terrible thought came swift and hard, and I gasped for air. I'd been invented in a lab just like this thing had been. They'd maybe used me to make the toxins, these things, all of it. I'd also been created from some terrible killer.

The dark man walked down the aisle toward me. Knew exactly where I was hiding. Almost as if it knew the truth I was only now coming to see.

I *was* the monster here as much as it was. I *deserved* to die too.

It stopped not five feet away. Stopped, and waited.

Waited for me.

To be a man? To accept my deserved fate?

The same fate of the real Jeffrey Dahmer.

I deserve to die. I deserve to burn in hell forever.

He was right. My father was right about me.

I crawled free from my hiding place and stood in front of myself.

The monster I would become. The monster I already was.

I looked up at it.

And the monster looked right back.

CHAPTER FORTY-ONE

A man made partially from my own blood.

A brother. A cousin? A *son* even, maybe. I don't know.

I knew only that he had a long knife.

And I had the realization that—whether I "deserved" to or not—I didn't *want* to die.

And also that I was going to anyway.

• • •

I was shoved to the ground. Thought my head had been knocked clear off. Slammed against the concrete floor.

Castillo was there. For real this time. He'd sprung from the darkness like one of the room's shadows had come to life.

He and the other man fought directly above me as I writhed on the ground in agony. I honestly couldn't tell them apart. The whole room was growing dark at the edges. My head burning.

I struggled to pull myself away. Rolled to my hands and knees. Blood dripped onto the floor in front of my face. I touched the side of my head, felt the wet hot gash there. But kept moving.

I could hear them struggling behind me. And I could hear the dark man's thoughts.

How much he *wanted* to kill. To kill Castillo.

I kept moving away. Looked back.

Castillo's gun was on the floor, but I would have to get past the two men to reach it. There was no way. I dragged myself up to my feet, looked around for a weapon of some kind. Anything at all. To somehow help Castillo.

I could hear the other man's thoughts more clearly. He was torturing Castillo. Punishing.

And I could feel the man's fingers and nails digging into Castillo's throat.

I could feel the man enjoying it. Watching Castillo die, I mean. Knowing that when he was done with Castillo, he'd then find and kill me, too. Knowing that Castillo understood this also. Castillo's helplessness like a drug rushing through the dark man's whole body.

Looking around, all I found was a warehouse of food. Crates, boxes. Rows of giant cans.

I grabbed hold of one of the cans.

I stepped free from an aisle of shelves and could see them again. The man was choking Castillo, Castillo's feet kicking off the ground, his hand up under the man's jaw, tearing. Struggling to free the two dark hands from his throat.

There was blood all over the floor at their feet.

I could hear the man's blood pumping wildly, hotly. Filled with life.

And I could hear Castillo's blood fading.

I swung that tin can as hard as I could.

Again and again and again.

• • •

The man was on the floor. His head split open pretty good.

He wasn't dead.

Castillo had collapsed also. Was gasping for air. Fighting to get back to his feet. Leaving a smear of blood on the floor every time he moved.

I picked up Castillo's gun.

Moved back across the room to where the dark man was.

I could barely stand. Or walk.

But I could aim.

. . .

Castillo stopped me. Told me NO.

I told him I could do it. That I even *wanted* to do it.

He just took the gun from me.

He said: No, you don't.

He said: And you never will.

Then Castillo shot three times.

And then he collapsed back onto the ground.

. . .

In all the different ways Castillo ever saved me, this was, I think, the one that mattered most.

. . .

Castillo had been cut pretty bad. He used special glue to fill in the wound for a bit, but even I knew it wasn't anything that'd last. I kept expecting him to pass out for good.

He got on his walkie-talkie and checked in with Ox. The whole compound was overrun with cops and ATF guys now, fighting for the Bad Guys. Castillo and Ox argued some over what to do next.

Castillo and I were too far away from the others for the original plan. (Something about sneaking down the back of the mountain with special parachutes.) Castillo told Ox to proceed anyway. Which he did.

They wished each other luck and then signed off.

It was now every man for himself.

I hoped it was not every *boy* for himself. It wasn't.

Castillo pulled me close. His shirt was wet with blood.

The whole world started shaking again. An even bigger explosion than before. A huge distraction of explosives that'd confuse the advancing cops and soldiers just enough. Long enough for Ox and the others to get down the back of the property as planned.

As for me and Castillo . . .

Castillo could hardly stand. I wasn't much better. I followed him to the door, the current plan to sneak through the woods and back down the hill. Past a dozen or more armed men.

Even if Castillo had been in perfect shape, it would have been a terrible plan.

At the door I had a better one. Not much, but better.

I'd noticed the stables across the way. Three horses.

I reminded Castillo of that time in Afghanistan. When he and the other soldiers had ridden across the open field on horses. Kinda suggested it'd be cool to do again.

Castillo agreed.

· · ·

And the next thing I know, we were in the stables. The horses were all freaked out. "Spooked," I guess, is the word. It took a couple of minutes for Castillo to get one of them calmed down enough. But he did. Tossed on the bit and bridle. But didn't even put on a saddle or anything else as he led it to the open door. Just kinda jumped on. No time, he said. He held out a hand. He pulled me up onto the horse behind him. The animal jerked and shuddered beneath us.

GEOFFREY GIRARD

Castillo turned to me, told me the *real* key to every successful operation was the same and quite simple: When the first plan goes to shit, which it almost always does, quickly invent another.

• • •

Hang on, he said. So I grabbed on to his waist. The shirt sticky in my fingers. In the near distance, the glow of raging fires lit the whole woods. The horse charged forward away from the fire into the darkness. Racing through the night between unseen trees, as if it could see perfectly. Castillo urged it to go faster with soft forceful words. The horse went faster.

Gunfire racked from the left. I pressed close against Castillo's hunched back, my arms around his waist now. I don't know how fast that horse was going, and don't want to.

Lights ahead. Castillo banked left, more gunfire followed. Castillo's pistol cracked back in response. Tree branches whipped past, tearing into my arms and back. Above, a helicopter with a searchlight swept over the forest. The beam of light cutting through the darkness behind us, to the left. Castillo always twenty yards out of reach of the spotlight.

And every gallop, every turn, felt like it would be the last. Like I would just bounce off the back of the horse. But I didn't. The helicopter pulled away, moved back up the hill again, away from us. The horse continued straight down the hill. Breathing fiercely as if it wanted to get as far away from the place as it could. Probably did.

We hit a stream and Castillo turned against it, heading north of the hill. He'd slowed some. The helicopter was a faint echo in the distance now. He looked back. You OK, he asked.

Told him I was. I wasn't sure how much longer he had, though.

His face was pale. His lips trembling when he spoke to me.

Now what? I asked.

He said he needed real stitches. And fast. After that, he said, he'd find Ox again and it was back to the original plan.

I nodded. Smiled even.

I was finally going back to DSTI and its monster labs.

I was going home.

CHAPTER FORTY-TWO

A memory.

On some Sunday morning. Early. We'd stopped at this little deli on the way and bought hoagies for lunch and some jelly doughnuts for the drive. The car smelled like coffee and fresh aftershave. The office was empty, and I'd wandered the rec room while my dad took care of some work in his office. Played Xbox on the big TV. Tried playing myself in foosball. Motionless and quiet for miles in every direction, like the whole world was still asleep, or had disappeared, except for the two of us. What's this? I asked. Security system, my dad replied. How's it work? My dad smiled, checked his watch. I'll show you, he'd said. He put my hand on a special scanner and took images of my hand. Said I could go anywhere now. Anywhere at all.

This memory was one of the few real ones.

• • •

It was like the spare key to his secret room back at our house. For whatever reason, he'd *wanted* me to discover what was really going on.

• • •

When I think of my father, or of his death, these are the kinds of memories I think of. Watching movies together or taking a hike. Eating a pizza while he talked about history and science and stuff. So maybe he wanted me for all the wrong reasons. And maybe I was just another specimen to him. Another lab rat. Maybe he was a terrible, terrible monster. A murderer. But he was also my dad.

. . .

I'd been gone for only two weeks. But now DSTI already seemed like a faded memory from some *other* guy's past. Like something I'd only imagined. But it was real, and I was back.

I held my hand to a security touch pad. The back gate opened.

Ox's van rolled slowly down the tree-lined pathway.

Castillo drove. Everyone else, including me, hid in the back.

We'd all spent the night at some remote farm somewhere in West Virginia. The original rendezvous spot. Ox had already been there with four guys when we'd arrived. Two from the night before. Castillo and I had gotten there in a stolen car. I'd driven. Castillo had bled, had tried not to die. Somehow, we'd both made it to West Virginia. Some woman named Yvette, a friend of Ox's, had made us all food and stitched up Castillo. I'd stayed at his bedside the whole rest of the day. Watched his feverish nightmares. Watched Yvette's medicines eventually do their thing. I was there when he called his boss—Colonel Stanforth. Told him it was time to "settle accounts." End things once and for all.

Now here we were.

In the distance loomed the Massey Institute, the school menacing and dark. Watching the slowly approaching van. Closed post-tragedy for the summer but still filled with the ghosts of foul secrets and unknowable grief and pain. I imagined a woman in a long black dress walking its empty halls. Awaiting the return of students that would, now, hopefully never come again.

We stepped free from the van. Ox and the others all had guns again.

I held my hand to another touch pad. Another door opened.

Castillo joined me in the doorway. Ox and two of the other men waited behind.

Castillo told me to stay with Ox this time. To use my security-thumping hand to free as many of the kids as we could. If there were any still alive.

I told Castillo we were gonna try to find ALL of the kids. The "Good" ones and the "Bad."

He nodded in agreement. Then started to go.

I grabbed his arm. Asked where he was going.

He told me he was taking the front door and that they were expecting him. He'd put his hand on my shoulder. Stopped whatever next words I might have gotten out.

He told me everything was OK now, everything was "good" again.

I didn't understand what he meant.

He grabbed me. Gave me this awkward bear hug.

My whole body was shaking.

With fear. And regret.

And love.

I tried to say his name . . . to say *anything*. It all came out funny.

He pulled back, held me at arm's length. His eyes were glassy with tears also.

He told me to just focus on the job, focus on the others.

He meant the rest of the guys from my father's list. Those adopted out by DSTI or the ones my father had snuck out himself. The other names and squiggles. Guys we hadn't found yet. Guys who might still be out there. Guys maybe still being tortured in the name of an experiment that'd been canceled. Or guys and families who had no idea what they were and who'd eventually be targeted by the government looking to erase the whole thing.

Castillo told me a friend of his had all the files now. Everything. And that I'd get it all soon. I knew right away he meant Kristin.

And I also knew now that he was planning never to see me again.

Any of us.

He'd come here to die.

. . .

I couldn't breathe.

This guy who'd terrified me for weeks. Hated me. Feared me.

Saved me. Cared for me.

The thought of never seeing him again . . .

I swear I couldn't breathe.

I said: We'll find them together.

Castillo just smiled.

He said: I hope so.

He said: I'm not sure what happens next and don't really understand everything we've been through. But I know one thing, and I don't need these scientist assholes or any of their damned tests to prove it either.

He said: There *are* Good Guys and Bad Guys.

His next words wouldn't come out. He squeezed my shoulder instead.

I tried to say something too. Couldn't either.

Go, he said, and then he left me.

. . .

I watched him disappear around the corner.

My whole body was trembling.

Jeff? I heard Ox behind me. I turned slowly.

He smiled. As genuine and open as if we were sitting at a baseball game.

He said: Let's do this thing, little man.

I looked to where Castillo had just been. The image of his exit already fading in my mind.

Then I turned to Ox and said: OK.

• • •

Inside, I held my hand to another touch pad. And another door opened.

Ox stepped through first, tugged me along. The two other men followed.

We'd been inside the building for maybe ten minutes. Small lights were flashing different colors in each of the halls. But the place looked pretty abandoned. Hallways totally dark and empty. Didn't look like anyone even worked there anymore.

My father's office was just down the next hall. I thought of leading Ox and the other two there. Why? I don't know. I guess I just wanted to see it again. To fully remember being there with him. To maybe touch something of his. Take something. Remember how things were just two weeks before. When everything was "normal." When everything was a wonderful lie.

But I didn't. This wasn't about him anymore. Or me either, I guess.

I suppose that's what Castillo had decided also.

I led them away from his office to another section of the building. One I remembered being in only once before.

The hallway that led to the room filled with tanks.

The room filled with monsters.

. . .

We found the room. I remembered the long hallway as clearly as if I'd walked it just the day before. As if I'd walked it a hundred times. Inside the room the tanks looked exactly as I remembered. Two rows of a dozen each. Except now the cylindrical tanks were completely empty. No men floating inside. No liquid even. DSTI was cleaning up their mess.

Still, I could feel that familiar chill surging through my blood. The sound of pulsing hearts and rushing blood. One of them—one of the beings from one of these tanks—was close.

But it wasn't interested in me. Wasn't looking for me. Not here.

Come on, I said.

. . .

My handprint opened the next room just like all the others, but inside THIS room were five boys lying on cots. IVs dripping into their arms. They were all half-awake and all looked totally drugged out of their minds.

Ox and another man moved to free and wake them.

I tried waking the fifth boy, noticed the tag on his wrist.

It said only EDWARD.

I leaned into the boy's face. His eyes totally empty. Lost.

I don't think he even knew I was there.

Albaum? I asked. Bryce Albaum?

The kid's eyes fluttered. Drool bubbled over his lower lip.

I told Ox this was one of the kids Castillo and I had found. (I didn't know this 100%, but I *felt* it completely.) I said I think they've "done something" to him. (DSTI had, we would learn later, given several of the boys chemical lobotomies.)

Ox shook his head. Sighed deeply.

This is bad, he said.

Ox should have waited to say that.

The next room was more bad.

• • •

My hand wouldn't work. I kept trying the security panel, but the door wouldn't open.

So Ox smashed the screen with his gun and then did something with the tiny wires inside.

It took a couple of minutes, but it worked.

Inside there were three boys propped up in chairs.

Metal held their arms and heads in place.

Tubes fed them. Wires connected computers directly to their heads. Each skull opened at the top with a section the size of a credit card so that the dozen or so wires coupled to devices implanted into their exposed brains.

These boys were awake, cognizant.

One of them looked exactly like me.

• • •

It's OK, I told them all.

You're safe now.

• • •

The kids from the first room shambled like dead things down the hall around us.

I had a hand on the arm of the boy named (per his tag) Albert, and another hand on the boy called Theodore, who was only maybe ten years old.

The ones from the second room, those from the chairs, couldn't walk at all. So Ox carried one on his shoulder. Another man carried the other two.

As we all moved down the hallways back toward the van, I kept an eye on the man just in front of me. He carried the boy from the chair who looked just like me.

His tag read JEFF.

(This "little piggy was set aside for lab work," according to our "brother" Jeff Williford.)

He hung over the man's shoulder. Head tilted, his eyes never leaving mine either.

He knew too.

That he and I were, well, "related."

Gunfire popped several hallways away.

Screams.

I turned to look back at Ox, who shook his head.

Just go, he said.

• • •

I waited with Ox outside the van.

There were ten kids in the van with us. We'd found two more, boys no older than ten, sleeping in another room at the end of the hall. All of them now sprawled out in the back like bodies in a crypt.

Also, one of Ox's men had filled two duffel bags with medications. Bottles he'd found by the hundreds in one of the rooms. Thousands of blue unmarked pills. Pills that looked exactly like my "allergy medication."

Ox and the other guy now stood outside the van, an automatic rifle aimed at DSTI as if they would shoot down the whole building. A third man was still inside the building, downloading what files he could off the DSTI computers.

And I was still waiting for Castillo. Frantically wondering what was going on inside that building. Who he was meeting with and what they were doing. Why he'd had that strange look in his eyes when we'd parted.

A couple of minutes later the man who'd been downloading files came bursting out the back door.

Still no Castillo.

Ox checked his watch. Five minutes, he told me.

I got him to wait ten.

• • •

That's not to say we just left then.

I mean, I suppose that was Ox's intention. Or Castillo's plan or whatnot.

But it wasn't mine.

And this is exactly when all the alarms went off.

The whole building lit up. Flashing lights and piercing electric sirens.

I jumped out the van door and dashed back into DSTI.

I was not going to leave Castillo.

Ox jumped out of the van too and made to stop me, but I was already scanning my hand and in the door before he'd gotten halfway to me.

Behind me he shouted for me to stop. I let the door shut in his face.

He could do his smash-wire thing if he wanted, but I knew it'd take a while.

I was alone in DSTI now. And I needed to find Castillo.

• • •

Inside, the hallways flashed. Emergency lights blinking in every corner.

The walls blushed red like they were covered in blood.

A detached electronic voice neither male nor female came over the building loudspeakers.

"WARNING. EMERGENCY. LEVEL THREE. EMERGENCY. PLEASE REPORT TO SAFETY STATIONS IMMEDIATELY. WARNING. EMERGENCY. LEVEL THREE ..."

And so on.

As if all of DSTI were under some giant microscope and were being watched by some other person as part of a cosmic experiment. Like we were ALL part of the experiment.

An experiment of Good and Evil.

If so, I wonder what they'd have concluded.

• • •

I dashed through the dark flickering hallways.

I already knew where he wasn't and so tried the other part of the building.

I found Castillo in the Command Center.

It was the building's largest room. Oversaw half a dozen different laboratories and housed a hundred large monitors and a table large enough for fifty people.

The whole room was encased in special floor-to-ceiling glass.

Soundproof. Bulletproof.

Secret-proof.

And the entire room was also filled with billowing puffs of purple smoke.

Through the glass I saw the thick vapors curling and rolling in every direction. I couldn't even see fully into the room. Just these shapes moving within the smoke. Maybe half a dozen bodies. WHO, I yet had no idea. Those people who'd agreed to meet

Castillo, I supposed. People from the Army, from DSTI.

My hand couldn't open the door. Its scanner light wasn't even working. (I found out later that Castillo had shot it from the inside, locking everyone in.)

I raced the perimeter of the whole room, turned the corners. Hit another hallway. There was no other way in. I moved along the side of the thick Plexiglas again. Ran my hand along it. Trying to figure out what was going on inside.

Castillo appeared then. Stepping from out of the mist to stand against the glass.

He looked strange. Lost.

He collapsed. Put one hand against the translucent wall.

In the other hand he held a canister. No bigger than a soda can.

One I recognized. One that another Jeff had shown me.

Castillo let it roll out onto the floor and into the room.

His eyes were red and something else.

Something horribly wrong.

Something Evil.

I pictured the people in Shardhara ripping one another and themselves into pieces.

And I was glad I could not really see the dark shapes moving in the mist behind Castillo.

I crouched down next to the glass to be closer to him. Put my hand up against his. The glass was cold to the touch.

He turned, his back against the glass, his fingers still up against mine.

Then that purple smoke covered him completely and his hand slowly pulled away.

I couldn't see at all anymore what was happening within all that smoke. I thought about just sitting there, waiting for the police or government or whoever to show up and arrest me. But it wasn't just about me anymore.

There were ten kids waiting just outside who needed to get as far away from police and government and whoever as quickly and completely as possible.

Castillo had sacrificed himself for us.

Buying time, I guess. Or maybe just taking out all the major "Bad Guys" at once with, ironically, a weapon of their own creation.

The least I could do was get up.

I pulled myself to my feet.

And walked out of DSTI forever.

· · ·

As to WHY Castillo opened up that canister in the room, you'd have to ask him.

That's his story to tell.

I know the stuff he released is called IRAX11 and that it was developed at DSTI by my father and his colleagues.

I know the people in that room included Castillo's boss, a couple of mercenaries, and several scientists who'd worked at DSTI. I know that most of them had been involved with Project Cain from the beginning and that it was not the most innocent group of people in the world.

I know that Castillo probably found the irony of their end fitting.

Testing their own experiment on them and all, I mean.

I know that, partially, Castillo wanted to find out what HE was *really* made of.

Like we all do.

GEOFFREY GIRARD

CHAPTER FORTY-THREE

*O*x is convinced the world is going to collapse on itself pretty soon and that we'll go back to the Stone Age or something. Part of me kinda hopes he's right. He and some other folk live on a hundred acres. Somewhere secret. Another property tucked away for special needs and even more remote than the first. They had more than enough room and supplies for a dozen kids, including me. And whenever we find another kid, they'll have room for him, too.

It's good here. Not a single scientist for a hundred miles in any direction.

• • •

For a week all the news channels reported how Captain Shawn Castillo, a decorated vet suffering from severe post traumatic stress disorder, had taken his paranoia and delusions out in a killing spree at a small research facility in Pennsylvania.

The dead list was all scientists and "consultants."

Castillo hadn't really killed any of them.

They'd done that all themselves. To each other.

Thanks to the IRAX11 poison.

Still, Captain Kristin Romano, the doctor who'd once treated Castillo, was interviewed by several stations. "Terrible delusions," she told them. "A tragic reminder for this country to remain committed to advancing the clinical care and social welfare of its veterans."

Yes, she was lying.

Castillo is alive. He lives here too.

All the news stories about *his* death were a total falsehood, of course. These same stories claimed my father had died *at* DSTI that same day and that Castillo had shot him and some others in this work-rampage shooting thing.

Just part of the story invented by the government to cover up all of it.

A story that allowed us to vanish forever.

• • •

Just not *completely* vanish.

Castillo has all my father's notes still, and together we've even managed to find a couple more clones these last months. Clones my father had adopted out to parents who—well, to people who'd done bad things for money. Those kids are safe now also.

They're here too.

And if anything bad ever happens to any of us, about a hundred newspapers and serious bloggers are gonna get a shitload of data and photos and facts—info about serial-killer clones and dead employees and abused children and bioweapons tested on civilians in Afghanistan.

Not all of it.

No one would believe all of it.

But enough of what happened that the right people might.

• • •

GEOFFREY GIRARD

Kristin supported and nurtured the lie to protect Castillo and me and all the others.

Because she knew it was a lie that might help keep us all safe. A "deal" the government could maybe live with.

Mostly. Maybe.

Kristin visits here whenever she can. She talks to us. Helps us.

She's always afraid of being followed. And she should be.

It's been six months, but you never know.

Maybe someday they will come for us all.

. . .

There are two missing pieces to the puzzle of this story that I will try to explain as best I can, but don't expect too much. To me these pieces are also still missing.

1.   The Dark Man. Monster. Supersoldier. Bio-drone. Son of Cain. So many names I've heard used these last six months. But call them whatever you will, it doesn't really matter. There is still this question of how I was hearing/seeing their thoughts and actions. Hearing the blood of the other clones through these dark men somehow. Some kind of psychic/mental/chromosomal/spiritual link between all of us, I cannot deny. That was real. How it worked—I don't think even the scientists at DSTI or my father understood that. I learned that David Spanelli (one of the original six clones we'd been looking for) had been murdered by the Dark Man somewhere along the Jersey Shore and that what I'd imagined during my vision of his murder, when I'd dreamed of the beach, had not been that far off from what really happened. I know that part of me had been standing outside our motel room that night for just a second when we'd been attacked.

How, again, I just can't explain. But it had happened.

2.   Why did my dad leave clues in his journals that only I could solve? Did he want me to help him free the clones or stop him or . . . I've long since stopped worrying about this. I think the clues in his book made sense to me only because he and I shared a life for a while. For eight years, I figure. Eight years he'd included me in his world, and that had happened to include certain places and movies and pieces of art, and that's that. Many of the doodles I still don't understand at all. And I never will. Because the images probably weren't for me. They were for him. And I knew my father only enough to figure out a few.

· · ·

One thing I've learned from all of this is that there aren't answers for everything.

Science and logic and facts can't cover all of it.

Sometimes stuff just can't be explained.

· · ·

I am sorry my dad is dead.

And, more than I should perhaps, I still both love and miss him.

· · ·

Kristin is the one who suggested I try writing all this down.

Another step in a long process. To both remember and forget.

To come to terms with MY ghosts now.

To understand more about WHAT I survived. WHO I am. WHY I am.

The "Clone who Lived." Piggy #10. The boy behind tank number two?

My name is Jeff.

For now, that should be enough, really.

Because that's the thing at the end of all of this. At the beginning too, I suppose.

I'm me. You're you.

And I'm not gonna let someone else tell me who I "really am."

Not the counselors or newspapers or geneticists. Not my father.

I'm not even gonna let ME tell me that.

We are like little pieces of paper floating in the wind.

Extreme for Life.

But not powerless or accidental. Not something tossed carelessly into the air, not something that may fall or may fly depending on the whims of pure chance. Nor something hurled with purpose by another's intrusive commanding hand either, our destinies somehow preset only by the stars above or some blood within.

Once airborne, WE choose the paths to follow. The currents to chase, elude.

Because WE'RE ALL CAIN.

And we're all Abel, too.

No, it won't be from some blood test that I figure out who I really am.

I'll figure that out by the choices I make. I'll figure it out later myself.

We all will.

You too.

ACKNOWLEDGMENTS

*A*uthor Don DeLillo once described a book in progress as a hideously damaged infant that follows the writer around, dragging itself across the floor, noseless and flipper-armed, drooling, etc., wanting love until fully formed by the writer. The writer, however, is not the only one made to endure this insistent child care. And raising two books (*Project Cain* and brother *Cain's Blood*) at the same time, all those extra hands/eyes/minds/hearts are much appreciated.

Special thanks to: Jason Sizemore and *Apex Magazine*, who first carried my Cain fetus; Foundry Literary & Media's Peter McGuigan and Stephen Barbara for suggesting twins and becoming steadfast godfathers, and Katie Hamblin and Matt Wise, the lads' favorite/coolest babysitters; the devoted fostering of Megan Reid and Stacy Creamer, and Kristin Ostby (who discovered this peculiar child in a blanket on her doorstep and still cared for it as her own). To family and friends who've supported the process throughout (one son finally asking: "Will you *please* stop talking about Jeffrey Dahmer?"), in particular Mary for encouraging, and accommodating, my own lengthy and selfish parenting of the Cains.

And now, an excerpt from Geoffrey Girard's *Cain's Blood*,
an adult thriller that tells the story of *Project Cain*
from the perspective of Sean Castillo.

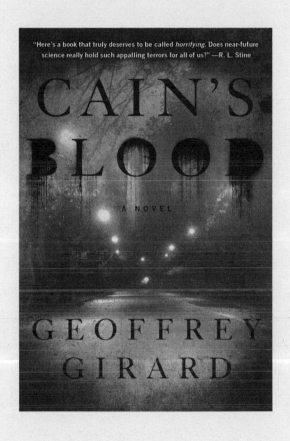

W hen Ashley saw the clown, she knew for sure.

Before that, it had only been a suspicion, prompted by that inimitable nervous tickle in her stomach that hinted that she might now be in a threatening situation, that something bad could happen. Could. But not fear. Not yet. Not nearly enough to make you grab your two children and run screaming for the car. That'd be too embarrassing.

The two cars pulled in beside each other on the gravel parking lot. Both filled with kids, teenagers. Mostly all boys. *Why come to a playground?* A girl among them. Older. Dirty hair hung over her eyes. Moving strangely.

Ashley turned back to find her daughter still winding through the top of the park's small wooden castle. She absently handed little Michael another pretzel stick and looked back toward where two other mothers had been having a picnic lunch with their own children. Was overly relieved when she saw they were still there, chatting away.

"Pox," Michael burbled beside her. "Pox." Pox, Tik, Mop. The ever-evolving official language of young Michael Steins, fifteen months. Made-up words she collected in a small diary to share with him someday.

"Pox," she smiled. "Pretzels."

Michael giggled.

Two of the boys had already taken seats at the swings and were using their feet to twist themselves up in the chains. Another pair was wrestling atop the seesaw. *Fine,* Ashley thought. Only trying to recapture some half-remembered joy of childhood. First weeks of summer vacation. Very Holden Caulfield. They'll be bored in five minutes. The girl was probably just high.

Ashley fumbled for her cellphone, half remembered she'd left it in the car. She started packing their things. "Honey," she called out to Cassie. "Honey?" Wanting to get her attention without using her name. Why, she wondered, was that suddenly so important? Her daughter moving away from her deeper into the castle. Ashley stood and trailed after her. Clapped her hands. "Honey, come on now. Time to go."

Her daughter turned. "Whyyyyy?" she whined from the top parapet, her dark pigtails hanging over a yellow dress.

"Come down, honey. Hurry up."

The four-year-old scrunched her face in displeasure.

Closer, several of them looked older than teenagers. Young men.

"Come on." Ashley waved her down. Can't get up there quick enough. "We'll get ice creams on the way home."

"Mikey, too!"

Don't say his name, baby. Don't say his damned name.

"Yes, yes. Let's go now, honey."

A horrible sound. Van doors shutting.

Ashley spun around. The other table suddenly empty. The other mothers VANISHED. The other children already somehow collected, small bags of books, toys, McCalls and Pringles already packed. Their SUV somehow at this very moment backing slowly out of the long gravel parking lot. Leaving her alone.

With *them*.

She turned back to her daughter and almost collapsed to the ground as the whole park seemed to tilt. She was gone. Her daughter. Where once there'd been a little girl, there was now nothing. *What do I . . . dear God, this is really happening.*

Ashley approached the castle like a half-formed ghost.

She's gone. She's really gone. What have these monsters done to my—

"Shit!"

Her daughter appeared with a squeal at the bottom of the green tube, sliding to the end until her feet dangled above the mulched ground.

"Cassie . . . God damn it!"

"What, Mommy?" She climbed off the slide.

"Nothing." Ashley fought the urge to collapse again. "I'm sorry, baby. Come on, let's go." Yanking her back toward the picnic table.

She saw the clown then. Standing perfectly still by the cars. A demonic scarecrow.

Watching her. And her children. *My children.*

A red suit with white frills and buttons and a matching red hat. Huge blue triangular eyes like a jack-o'-lantern. Its mouth bloodred and covering the entire bottom half of the face. In the shape of an enormous smile.

Now, she knew.

Scooping up the rest of their things and slinging the bag over her shoulder. Dragging little Michael in one arm, pulling her daughter with the other.

"Pox," Michael said. "Pox!"

"In the car, baby. Hush now."

She looked up at the swing set, clearly saw the girl there for the first time. A woman. Her "boyfriend" slowly and mechanically pushing her swing from behind. The woman's face masked behind grimy hair, head drooped to the side. What Ashley had thought was a shirt was not. The woman was nude from the waist up. What she'd figured was a shirt's pattern was dried blood.

"What's wrong, Mommy?"

Ashley staggered forward to her car. Michael started crying.

"Mommy, what's wrong?"

"Shut up," she hissed, wrenching her daughter closer. "Please, baby, just . . ."

One of the boys laughed.

She'd reached the car.

"Pox," Michael yelped again. "Pox!"

"Pox," Ashley replied in a half laugh that shuddered through her whole body. "Pretzels. That's right, baby."

She had the door half open when they finally stopped her.

The first boy squatted down to playfully wave a finger at her daughter. The girl's eyes were wide, her grip on Ashley's hand like a vise.

Another boy reached out and touched Ashley's mouth.

"Please . . . ," she stammered over his probing fingers.

Around the back of the car, a third shape moving toward them.

A horrible thing made of white and blue and red. One she'd somehow been waiting for.

"Pox." The clown smiled at them in a bloody grin that now filled the whole world. "Pox?"

Michael giggled.

DNA n.

short for deoxyribonucleic acid

(1) A nucleic acid capable of self-replication and synthesis which carries genetic information in every cell; (2) Two long chains of nucleotides twisted into a double helix and joined by hydrogen bonds between the complementary bases adenine and thymine or cytosine and guanine; (3) Sequence which determines and transmits individual hereditary characteristics from parents to offspring: see also genetic code; (4) DNA: see also Do Not Alter; (5) DNA: see also Do Not Ask

> While Odysseus pondered thus in mind and heart,
> Poseidon, the earth-shaker, rose up a great wave,
> dread and grievous, arching over from above,
> and drove down it upon him.
> And the wave scattered the long timbers of his raft
> but Odysseus bestrode one plank.
>
> THE ODYSSEY

DSTI was founded by Dr. William Asbury and incorporated in 1977. Its chief executive officer was Dr. Thomas Rolich, M.D., Ph.D. Its director of research was Dr. Gregory Jacobson, recipient of the Zonta Science Award and The Genetics Society of America's prestigious Novitski Prize for "exhibiting an extraordinary level of creativity and intellectual ingenuity in genetic scholarship and application." Castillo lifted this from DSTI's corporate website.

The rest came from Brody. Pete Brody had worked on half a dozen missions with Castillo as the chief analyst from the DI, the CIA's Directorate of Intelligence, and was now working in the private sector, something to do with Wall Street. His choice, but he'd still seemed genuinely interested when Castillo had called earlier. "I'll see what I can find," he'd said.

Ten hours later, and Castillo had info DSTI had not quite included on its website. "They were acquired as a subsidiary by BioStar in 1990 to obtain several of DSTI's cloning patents," Pete reported. "BioStar is a subsidiary of Goodwin Bio-Med, formed by the Nerney Institute in '87. Nerney's a sister company of Terngo Engineering, who designs and builds vehicles and industrial machinery for the U.S. Defense Department."

"Go on," Castillo said. He'd stopped taking notes.

The boy, Jeffrey, still lay asleep in a bed across the room. At least he looked asleep. Castillo wasn't sure. The kid had dozed off a couple times in the car, but for no more than a couple minutes. Probably needed to sleep for a *week*. It had been a long day crisscrossing Pennsylvania to search the local malls, convenience stores, and high schools. They'd even checked out several local paintball fields. Shown pictures of the six escapees and Dr. Jacobson to fifty-plus kids. Questioned various store managers. Nothing.

He'd gotten maybe an hour of sleep himself. *Maybe*. He wasn't sure. Like that, his chronic insomnia had reverted from being a disorder worth fighting back to an occupational advantage.

He'd pulled into the motel around 1900. Dyed and cut the Jacobson kid's hair. Wasn't sure if DSTI or anyone else would be looking for him, but the kid's father had convinced him he was dead meat—a "liability," the kid had quoted—if he was caught. Maybe the boy took some comfort in the fact that Castillo hadn't killed him yet. Castillo doubted it. Since Erdman hadn't been particularly forthcoming with the knowledge of Jeff Jacobson's *existence*, Castillo felt no real compunction to share with Erdman what, or *who*, he'd found. For now, he'd get what he could out of the kid and turn him back over to DSTI when the idea wasn't so repugnant.

If he could get anything at all, that is. The malls and paintball fields had been a bust, and the kid'd looked catatonic throughout, in full-blown, understandable shock. After the haircut and dye job, Castillo had had him look at some more of his father's journals, see if anything made any sense, and that hadn't gone much better than the first time. The boy barely read them, had mostly looked like he'd wanted to throw up. *Who could blame him?* Castillo felt the same way and had never even met Gregory Jacobson. While this lunatic was this fucking kid's father and the guy—

"Terngo's prime shareholder," Pete was saying, "is Plainview Inc. I've no doubt you know them."

"Intimately." Castillo had lived within their version of reality for ten years. Everything from lodging and meals to laundry, Internet access and gym equipment. They were Halliburton's little brother, but with a forty-thousand-person staff, including foreign mercenaries, not by much.

"Annual revenue of one hundred billion dollars," Brody said, "including an additional ten billion a year from the U.S. Department of Defense."

"That's a lot of money to trickle down."

"'Tis. DSTI is also partially and directly funded by Johns Hopkins University, which receives another two billion annually for federally funded research and development. Mostly, again, from the DOD."

"Incredible."

"Remember, Castillo, it's simply a giant global shell game meant to hide one thing from all of us: The money."

"And the monsters," Castillo said. "Anything else?"

"There've been some deaths."

"Go on."

"There was a plane crash ten years ago. Three DSTI geneticists and a marketing VP. Twin-engine Beechcraft King Air over Kentucky heading to a conference in Nashville. The NTSB concluded likely cause was the flight crew's failure to maintain adequate airspeed, which led to an aerodynamic stall. None of the other typical causes of a small-plane accident—engine failure, icing, pilot error—appeared to have been involved. The company plane was not required to have a cockpit voice recorder."

"Convenient."

"And a couple of suicides."

Castillo nodded against the phone, focusing his thoughts. A "couple" didn't sound too bad, not when each year more vets killed themselves than died in actual combat. "How many?" he said.

"Three. Over the last twelve years. Above average for a company that size, statistically."

"Suspicious otherwise?"

"Aren't they always?"

"No." Castilllo had heard enough. "That it?"

"Most recent suicide was a Dr. Chatterjee, Sanjay Chatterjee. Hung himself two years ago. Family started a fuss, wouldn't believe he'd do such a thing, but then they vanished back into India. Need more?"

"Might later. Is that cool?"

"'Tis. You want the names of the other dead employees?"

"Email 'em to me. Thanks, Pete." Castillo ended the call.

He watched Jeff again. The teen looked remarkably peaceful. Castillo couldn't remember ever being that young.

He checked his phone for the time. Kristin had sent a text message midday that she would call him back directly before ten. An hour from now.

No response yet from Ox. Probably never would be. It'd been a long shot anyway.

Ox was another war pal he'd first met in the field almost fifteen years ago. If Erdman and Stanforth didn't know who or what SharDhara was, Ox was an *hombre* who just might. He was a notorious enthusiast and purveyor of government cover-ups and conspiracies and one of those individuals who always knew a guy who knew another guy who knew . . . and so on. Always good for the latest bit of military gossip, even as paranoid as some of his musing often got. The real trouble with Ox was getting hold of him. When he'd retired, he'd more or less vanished with a bunch of other survivalist whackballs into the hills of Tennessee, or West Virginia, or someplace. Castillo hadn't seen him in years, and they'd only spoken on the phone once since his own return to the States. He did still have specific directions on how to contact the man using a special nym server with an untraceable email address, PGP key pairs, and some anonymous remailer based in Norway. *Insane.* His email to Ox had probably gone straight to Santa's workshop in the North Pole. As he'd hit Send in the Dunkin' Donuts parking lot, only one thing had been for sure: If he did somehow actually get hold of the guy, only he and Ox would ever know it. Anything less, and the man would never contact him back. Part of his charm, Castillo supposed.

He checked the FBI feed again for any new crimes, made some unproductive notes, and then rummaged back through the images of Jacobson's journals for another hour before his phone rang as promised. He rushed for the door.

"Hey," Castillo said, stepping outside quietly. It was surprisingly warm, the day's heat still lurking on the night's breeze. He surveyed the mostly vacant lot. His perusal widened to the traffic on the bordering streets, no direction seeming any more promising than another beneath the reddened moon. "Thanks for getting back so—"

"I've looked at the files you sent," she said. Paused.

"Thanks, I . . ." Too many thoughts folded in on him again, and nothing he could say to her. He cast his eyes back to the ground. "What can you tell me?"

There was another pause. Enough that he knew she was still deciding if she should lecture him, hang up, or just give him the info he'd asked for and continue on with her life. "How much of the situation *can* you share?" she asked, choosing Option Three. "Any?"

"Just know I gotta find these guys."

"OK, look: All six are classic loners, with documented sociopathic tendencies ranging from just-above common all the way to full-blown psychopathic monster. Three are lacking almost every benchmark of ordinary human social development. And some of these numbers, to be honest, don't even make sense to me. How well do you understand the terms?"

"*Sociopath? Psycho?* Assumed they were the same thing."

"They're similar but different disorders, especially in the way they manifest. Which could help you know what to look for. Even though they're always lumped together, you should probably understand the two beyond some vague *Webster's* definition before you go much further."

"It's why I called you." He'd found the outside stairs leading to the motel's second and top floor. He took them unhurriedly, stretching his legs, relishing the feeling of warm air against his skin. Yet somehow still cramped, chilled. Nervous.

"All right. About one half of one percent of Americans could be diagnosed as sociopaths or psychopaths. So says the National Institute of Mental Health."

"Two million psycho killers?"

She laughed softly, the sound tender and familiar. "Not at all. There are degrees to everything. Ninety-eight percent of that two million are only sociopaths, and most sociopaths are little more than flaming assholes."

"Skip the technical jargon, please."

"Guys with no regard for the feelings and rights of others. Care only about Number One, steal for the hell of it, moody guys who screw over coworkers, start bar fights out of boredom, won't talk to their kids . . . that kind of thing. True psychopaths are much, much rarer. The difference is important, and also horrible."

"Go on."

"First how they're the same. They both manipulate to get what they desire with no true sense of right or wrong. See people as targets, opportunities, and believe the cliché that the end always justifies the means. And so lie with almost every breath. And steal. And sometimes even rape or kill. Both are unable to empathize with their victims' pain, and even hold *contempt* for their victims' distress. Oblivious to the devastation they cause, lacking remorse, shame. Both usually surface by age fifteen; often cruel to animals, have an inflated sense of self, no awareness of personal boundaries. Feel entitled, spoiled. Shallow emotions, incapacity for love. Need stimulation and enjoy living on the edge, and believe they are all-powerful, all-knowing, and warranted in every wish. Both carry a deep rage."

"Copy. How different?"

"Sociopaths have a life history of behavioral and academic difficulties.

They're less organized; they struggle in school and work. They'll often appear nervous and easily agitated. They act spontaneously in inappropriate ways without thinking through the consequences. So, they typically live on the fringes of society, without solid or consistent economic support. They have problems making friends, keeping jobs, tend to move around a lot. Since they disregard most rules and social mores, their crimes are typically spontaneous because they don't give one damn *and* don't care if you know it. The prisons are filled with these guys. Most of us would not be comfortable with a sociopath in the room. You would totally know he was there."

"But not so Mr. Psychopath."

"You got it. Mr. Psychopath, as you say, is extremely organized, secretive, and manipulative. While he also has no regard for society's rules, he *understands* them. He's studied them for years like it's a job, and he can mimic the right behaviors to make himself *appear* normal, even charismatic and charming. He's often well educated, can maintain a family and steady work. He's learned The Game, and he's playing it to win using our own rules against us. You would be comfortable with a psychopath in the room because you would never know he was even there."

A Q&A with *Project Cain* author Geoffrey Girard

Where did you get the idea for *Project Cain*?

I teach high school English and one day my students somehow got on the topic of serial killers. Next thing I knew, we were looking up various facts online and having an interesting discussion about who, and how, and why. Since it was a topic I already knew a bit about, it was extra interesting both to see how fascinated they were and also to discover what they didn't yet know on the subject. (Not that I knew much about serial killers at sixteen myself.) It made me want to write a sort of "intro to serial killers" novel, one that would pull together all the essential facts, lore, and real-life infamous characters, something my own students could read. I went home that same day and dusted off an old story I'd written about cloned serial killers and started rewriting it as a full novel for young adult readers.

As to the inspiration for that original story, I'd been trying to get something published in a particular magazine that specializes in horror science fiction. Not just horror, and not just science fiction. It had to be *both*. I figured clones of famous serial killers matched that criterion perfectly and could be much scarier than clones of dinosaurs. The Cain universe started there, with Jeff Jacobson as a more minor character.

What kind of research did you do for *Project Cain*?

Research is my favorite part of writing. I'll typically research for six months to a whole year before I write a single word of the story. The main topics I studied for *Project Cain* were serial killers (of course!), cloning, military science, post-traumatic stress syndrome (which Castillo suffers from), and the genetics of violence. All added up, my research came from fifty-plus books, articles, taped interviews with serial killers, biographies (focusing mostly on the killers' childhoods), the latest psychiatric and genetic research I could find, and a slight bit of surveillance on teenagers in general (studying my students and my own teen sons): how they talk, move, think.

Project Cain is partly nonfiction. I wanted to get in as many facts and strange findings as I could, trying to recapture some of that fun my students and I had that first day in class discussing serial killers and randomly popping around the Internet together. I personally read mostly "to learn," so if someone learns something/anything from the material that made its way into *Project Cain*, all the better. There are a few reviews where the reader disliked the book but still confessed to having great fun looking up stuff found *in the book* on Google during the read. That makes me very happy too.

The trick was, and always is, not to get lost in all that research. While *Project Cain* is meant as an "intro to serial killers" for readers new to these men, the novel is mostly a story about people. And any research achieved needed to go toward that. How does *this* information help shape a specific character? How does *that* new technical paper affect a character's knowledge or reaction/ attitude? For Jeff Jacobson to become "real," I had to fill my head with facts and slowly let the boy within all those facts start to take shape. Add in a dash of studying several real-life teens and poof! It was like Pinocchio springing to life. There was no stopping him.

What surprised you most about the research you did?

What surprised, and disturbed, me most was the military science information. *Project Cain* was supposed to be about cloning and serial killers. Period. All the government conspiracy stuff and criticism of military science only came *after* I started the research. I had no idea the United States government had done so many terrible things in the name of national defense and weapons research. I knew we spent a lot on weapons, but I didn't know it was this much. I knew we'd done some questionable experiments in the past; I didn't know how much damage we'd done *and* how far the government had gone to cover it up.

I'd started down that rabbit hole and soon came to just appalling things America has done to explore various types of weapons: The trillions spent, most in black budgets none of us can ever know about. The apologies for secret testing done for fifty years on everyone from mental patients and prisoners to children and entire U.S. cities. Murders that have been committed, and admitted to, in our name. One night, very late, and deep into some really conspiratorial documents, I fully expected my front door to be kicked open by the infamous men in black glaring "He knows."

I don't even feel the need to be unbiased here. The U.S.

government itself has publicly apologized and made huge payments to express regret for crimes against humanity committed decades ago. There is no reason to suspect that similar discoveries and apologies won't be made decades from now. The fun for an author is imagining what those discoveries may be. The fear for a citizen is that some of these imaginings may prove true.

Project Cain was published the same day as Cain's Blood. How are these books the same/different?

Cain's Blood and *Project Cain* are two different novels written about the same fictional event: cloned serial killers escape. The idea was to publish one book for adult readers and another for *young* adult readers. Admittedly, the terms "adult" and "young adult" are mostly for marketing and to help booksellers know where to best display the books. *Cain's Blood* is definitely much darker and very "R-rated," but that's the kind of book I read as a teen. And *Project Cain* may be more "PG-13" and meant for readers new to serial killers, but I get letters all the time from *adults* saying how much they loved the book. It's mostly a question of which style of writing you prefer and how dark you want your story.

Cain's Blood uses the form/devices of a traditional thriller. It follows the story from a dozen viewpoints; it's mostly from Castillo's narrative point of view, but there are also chapters/scenes from the points of view of various killers, military schemers, evil scientists, and victims. All capture the big picture as the full story unfolds. *Project Cain* is told from the POV of only one character: Jeff Jacobson. It's a much more personal story/journey told with the voice and reflections of a smart, lost, and thoughtful teen. A thriller specifically written as an intro to serial killers.

These are stand-alone novels; you can read the one and never bother looking at the other and have a complete story. Reading both just gives a more complete story. It was very important to me that readers curious enough to read both Cain books would be well rewarded.

The voice and POV of Jeff Jacobson is very unique. Why did you do this?

Cain's Blood was finished and ready to be sold as a thriller to adults, but my agents and I were still trying to figure out how to do a version for younger readers (my original goal and submission to them). We thought a book entirely from Jeff's point of view would work, but we all agreed I would only do that if Jeff's voice was special and worth writing from. It was a great chance to try something really different with this second book, and that was exciting as a writer. Fortunately, Simon & Schuster was feeling equally creative.

Jeff Jacobson is *not* me or any form of me, so it first took some time to get into his head for the telling. I spent a lot of time re-researching Jeffrey Dahmer to imagine and feel what Dahmer might have been like in a different environment/time. I spent months listening to actual Dahmer interviews and reading what others said about how he acted and spoke. (I've since met several people who knew Dahmer personally and have confirmed my take on his "voice.") I wanted the Jeff in *Project Cain* to sound like that, as he has the physiological mind of a sociopath. He reacts to and sees the world differently than most of us.

The result: there are readers who absolutely love the voice and Jeff, and there are readers who hate it and me. But it's Jeff's true voice, so that's a chance I was willing to take.

Also, Jeff's sociopathic mind—and the distinct way such a mind interacts with the world—fit perfectly with some peculiar writing devices I wanted to try, devices I hoped teen readers (specifically those infamous "reluctant boy readers") might find appealing: a lot of nonfiction, lists, photos, terse writing, a more clinical and detached narrator. As to the no-quotation-marks thing: It's rare in popular fiction and takes some getting used to (it's not a device I've used before). But *Project Cain* is meant as a journal written by Jeff Jacobson a couple of months after the incidents of the story, and I simply don't believe he'd use quotation marks in such a journal. It was his book to write, not mine. My book is *Cain's Blood*.

Voice is wonderful to play with. The original young adult book (which was totally rewritten to become *Cain's Blood*) was told from the point of view of a Jeffrey Dahmer clone who isn't even in the story—an omniscient narrator speaking *mostly* in the third person but sometimes the first. A guy who's met Jeff Jacobson but is another Jeff altogether, and not even the bad one Jeff encounters in *Project Cain*. It was a little out there, but I'd just finished a degree in creative writing and was feeling extra emboldened (a little *too* emboldened, perhaps) to experiment with and push the many ways to tell a story: who is telling it, and when, and why. There are so many different voices that can tell the same story, and it changes everything, so it's fun to try them all and see which works best for the specific story you want to tell.

The theme of nature vs. nurture runs through the book. Which do you think is more important?

That *is* the big question of the book, isn't it? Mozart was clearly born a genius. Would he have become a *musical* genius if his composer/musician father hadn't doggedly pushed composition on his son from birth? What if Mozart'd been born to a farmer or a banker? John Wayne Gacy was clearly born with antisocial personality disorder, as *millions* are, but most people suffering from ASPD never develop into homicidal sociopaths. Would Gacy have become a *killer* if his alcoholic, abusive father hadn't beaten him or he'd received the genuine support needed when first molested by a family friend? Most people suffering from antisocial personality disorder never kill *anyone*. What if Gacy'd just been born to a more loving and supportive family? That was always the simple question at the heart of both books.

I could have chosen any one of several notorious serial killers for the main teen character of *Project Cain* but wanted Dahmer because his case has the least to do with nurture. His family life growing up wasn't *that* terrible. Were there circumstances that could have played out differently had he been with another family? Yes, I think so. But to the question of *why* he became a killer: even Dahmer himself was struggling with that until his last day. He specifically refused various plea bargains in court, not because he believed he was innocent but to force a lengthier discussion by experts as to *why* he did these things. Because he, himself, had no clue.

Science claims to have found genetic DNA-level indicators for everything from predisposition to violence to musical talent.

On the other side of the argument, playing violent video games for half an hour temporally changes any brain's physical makeup, and being in a war zone for more than six months *permanently* changes any brain's physical makeup. I think the two (nature and nurture) are so intertwined and so fluid, we may never settle on a true "winner." Each provides us with both weaknesses and strengths. Ultimately, Jeff and Castillo realize, the choices we make can and should supersede both foundations.

Spoiler: The final scene of *Cain's Blood* features a very young boy who is a killer neither by nature *nor* nurture. He just wants to kill. Reason unknown. That happens too, I think.

Any advice for young writers?

Read. And then read some more. If nature gave you some writing talent, the nurture part comes from simply filling your head with words. Experience all the many different ways they can be used by discovering and thinking about what others have tried before. Books you love, books you hate; you'll learn from both. And don't just read one genre. You can have your favorites, but always make time for some new author/genre or an old classic you haven't gotten around to yet. If you can, take honors English in high school or even become an English major in college. Imagine years of deliberately and skillfully studying language and story, and spending all that extra time with our very best writers. Paraphrasing the poet T. S. Eliot, good writers borrow, great writers steal. Not a plagiarism endorsement, but a reminder to expose yourself to as many words and styles as possible to help find the ones that best fit you as a storyteller.

Did you love this book?

Want to get access to
the hottest books for free?

Log on to simonandschuster.com/pulseit
to find out how to join,

get access to cool sweepstakes,

and hear about your favorite authors!

Become part of Pulse IT and tell us what you think!

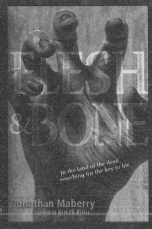

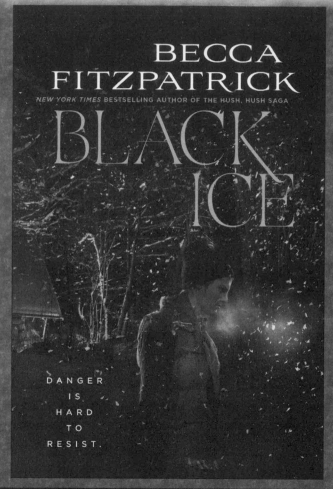

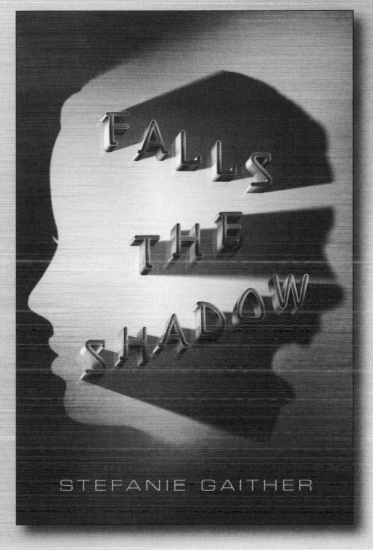